Praise for *100 D*

"Funny, moving . . . I defy anyone to finish this story without tears in his eyes."

—Graeme Simsion, bestselling author of *The Rosie Project*

"Why we're reading: We could all use a reminder to enjoy every moment."   —Esquire.com

"Brizzi encourages readers to analyze their lives, tackling tough questions about the realities of life, love, and reconciliation."

—Associated Press

"While there are times of grief and sadness, Brizzi also manages to fill the days with a humor and lightheartedness that you may not expect."   —InStyle.com

"Immensely readable and infectious. [A] warm and insightful novel . . . Brizzi's enchanting and often humorous story encourages readers to start now on their to-do lists."

—*Publishers Weekly*

"Depressing? No. Uplifting? Yes. Funny? Often. Although it's a countdown to death, this story is a celebration of life. Grab a doughnut and treat yourself to a good read."

—*Hudson Valley News*

"*100 Days of Happiness* is a celebration of everyday life masquerading as a countdown to death. To read it is to realize that the child within us is still alive and well, ready to laugh, play, love unguardedly, and eat hot doughnuts."

—Martha Woodroof, author of *Small Blessings*

PENGUIN BOOKS

100 DAYS OF HAPPINESS

Fausto Brizzi is an Italian director, screenwriter, and film producer. *The Night Before Exams*, his debut directorial work, won numerous awards, including the David di Donatello. *100 Days of Happiness* is his first novel, which was a bestseller in Italy and has been sold in more than twenty countries.

100

DAYS OF HAPPINESS

FAUSTO BRIZZI

ENGLISH TRANSLATION BY ANTONY SHUGAAR

PENGUIN BOOKS

PENGUIN BOOKS

An imprint of Penguin Random House LLC

375 Hudson Street

New York, New York 10014

penguin.com

Originally published in Italian as *Cento giorni di felicita*
by Giulio Einaudi editore s.p.a., Turin, 2013
First published in the United States of America by Viking Penguin,
an imprint of Penguin Random House LLC, 2015
Published in Penguin Books 2016

A Pamela Dorman / Penguin Book

Excerpt from *Parliamo tanto di me* by Cesare Zavattini. © 1931 / 2015 Bompiani – RCS Libri S.p.A.
Used by permission of the publisher.

ISBN 9780525427377 (hc.)
ISBN 9780143108504 (pbk.)

Printed in the United States of America
3   5   7   9   10   8   6   4

Set in Warnock Pro
Designed by Alissa Rose Theodor

FOR CLAUDIA, MY EVERYTHING

If I were a rich man, I'd spend most of my day lying comfortably in an overstuffed armchair thinking about death. But I'm poor, so I can only think about it in my spare moments, or when no one's looking.

—*Cesare Zavattini*

ACKNOWLEDGMENTS

Thanks to Grandpa Michele and Grandma Concetta for having always been there, even if they're no longer with us.

To Mamma and Papà because when I had to write a classroom essay on what I wanted to be when I grew up, and mine was "I want to be a writer," they didn't put me up for adoption.

To my sister, Sonia, an endless source of comic inspiration.

To Marco Martani, an eternal comrade in writing.

To my agent, Kylee Doust, who by now has become my invaluable life coach.

To Anna Chiatto, who first read my idea for this book and forced me to write it. If you don't like it, then by all means complain to her.

To Paolo Repetti and the staff at Einaudi, who immediately believed in this story.

To Severino Cesari, who encouraged me when this book was still in diapers.

To Francesco Colombo and Laura Ceccacci for their precious advice.

To Flavio Insinna, who is Lucio the way I imagine him. If you imagined Brad Pitt, start the book over from the beginning, thinking of Flavio.

To Neri Parenti, who taught me the art of making others smile.

To Giorgio Faletti, the most talented man I know.

To Chiara Della Longa for the idea of *The Little Prince*.

To Elena Bucaccio, who told me about how she pretends to be a cat when she wants to stop fighting.

To Mauro Uzzeo and Michele Astori for their fundamental suggestions.

To Robert Louis Stevenson and Carlo Collodi for their imaginations.

And to everyone who put up with me over all these months of writing. I'm so sorry.

100 DAYS OF HAPPINESS

Allow me to tell you about the three most important days of my life. I wouldn't want any of the three to think I'm playing favorites, so I'll list them in strict chronological order.

The first was Friday, October 13, 1972. Friday, the thirteenth.

On that date, as a Fokker turboprop crash-landed in the Andes with forty-five passengers who would ultimately devour each other to survive, Antonio and Carla, that is to say, my mom and dad, eighteen at the time, conceived me in the backseat of an unprepossessing off-white Citroën Dyane. The two teens had parked their vintage junker in a large empty square on the outskirts of Rome, included in the zoning plan by far-seeing city administrators as a handy refuge for lovebirds. It was a bleak setting, filled by the occasional abandoned refrigerator and stacks of battered cars.

A perfect backdrop for a tender love story.

Antonio and Carla had met that afternoon at a birthday party for Manrico, a sweaty overweight loser from Frascati who'd been pining after Mamma ever since middle school. She'd just turned down his offer to join him in a slow dance to the languid notes of a young Elton John. And that's when she saw Papà staring at her from a distance and almost choked on her tuna, mayo, and tomato panino. And, truth be told, Papà was the kind of guy who regularly made girls choke on their panini. He was tall, skinny, and too cool for school; he played the electric guitar and regularly wrote rock music cribbed shamelessly from lesser-known songs by the Rolling Stones. He resembled Sean Connery's better-looking brother, but with a scar on one cheek that gave him a mysterious smolder that 007 could only dream of. He could hold a roomful of people rapt for hours with stories about how he'd got that scar. Depending on the audience, either he'd received it in a bloody brawl in an open-air market in Mexico City, or else he'd been stabbed by a hulking rugby player from the mountains of Bergamo, brooding over a two-timing wife and a welter of painfully justifiable suspicions. Or else it had been that time that Frank Sinatra broke a bottle over his head because he couldn't stand what a good singer Antonio was.

Papà was a professional bullshit artist so outstanding in his lying skills that if he'd set his mind to it, he could easily have become prime minister of Italy. But I, and I alone, knew the truth, whispered to me by a dangerous double agent from the south, namely, my aunt Pina: Papà had taken a tumble with his tricycle when he was three and had landed face-first on the sidewalk. Be that as it may, Antonio the lady-killer liked to retire each night to the backseat of his Citroën Dyane with a different blushing passenger. That night it was Mamma's turn, and she was indeed seduced but not, however, abandoned because at the very instant of supreme pleasure, a red Fiat 500 smashed into the rear fender of my parents' car. At the wheel and riding shotgun were two half-drunk twenty-year-olds from Frosinone, completely unaware of the role they'd played in tearing a condom at a crucial moment, thereby directly contributing to my advent on life's grand stage. So let me say it now, guys, wherever you may be: my sincere thanks.

That fateful Friday, the thirteenth, I'd been set down on planet Earth as an uninvited guest, but that never kept Antonio and Carla from showering me with a fair-to-moderate amount of parental love, at least for as long as they were married. That's another story, though, and an infinitely sad one. If I'm up for it, I'll tell you about it later.

The second most important day of my life was September 11, 2001. While everyone in the world was staring at their TV sets as special news broadcasts played and replayed footage of two Boeing 767s slamming into New York's Twin Towers, giving the rest of the world a new enigma to puzzle over and the American people a new enemy, I was in a restaurant at the beach with all of my closest friends, and Paola, the love of my life. It was a classic end-of-summer dinner, and it had been planned for weeks, but in truth this was no ordinary grilled-seafood banquet: it was the night I was going to ask Paola to marry me, the furthest thing imaginable from her mind—and my friends' minds.

An elderly waiter had agreed to be my accomplice. For a twenty-euro tip he'd douse the lights, play our song (which, for the record, was and remains "Always on My Mind," in Elvis's immortal rendition), and triumphantly wheel in a gigantic mimosa cake with the engagement ring perched on top, concealed inside a bar of extra-dark chocolate.

It was a meticulously planned event: a night sky so bright with stars that it looked like a Christmas manger scene, a group of friends so warm and sincere that it could have been a TV commercial for an Italian after-dinner drink, and a gentle sea breeze so agreeable that it could have been God's ceiling fan set on low. Every detail was perfect. Or almost.

I'd failed to reckon with my best friend, Umberto, who is a veterinarian.

When the cake made its entrance, he leaped from his chair and prankishly swiped the chocolate bar, exclaiming: "Guys, this chocolate bar's all mine!"

Crunch.

Next thing you know, the gold engagement ring had shattered a molar.

Emergency run to the dentist's office. So long, magical and unforgettable romantic interlude.

Despite the pathetic outcome of the evening's main event, Paola said yes.

We were married early the following year in a charming little Gothic church on the outskirts of Milan, and it's one of the few things I've never regretted.

Paola is the star of my life. And as far as I'm concerned, she deserves at the very least an Oscar for her performance in the role of my wife. The story of her starring role in my life comes later.

The third day I'll never forget was a Sunday, July 14, 2013, exactly one week after my fortieth birthday. I should have guessed it was a special day because there were no shocking aviation disasters to steal my thunder.

It was a useless, tropical summer Sunday, and nothing noteworthy at all took place. Except for the fact that at about 1:27 p.m., I took my last breath and died.

I know, I know, now I've spoiled the ending and you're not going to want to read the rest of the book. Well, because you can't unread a spoiler and I've ruined the plot, but you've already bought the book and just stopping at page 4 is no fun either, I'll go ahead and tell you the name of the killer. That's right, even though this is no Agatha Christie murder mystery, there is a killer. In fact, I think we can say a *serial* killer because the villain in question has killed not just me, but millions of people, the kind of career achievement that could give Hitler or Hannibal Lecter an inferiority complex. Every year, roughly a third of all deaths can be attributed to this killer. Statistics tell us that we're talking about the leading cause of death in the Western world. In short, I'm in very good company.

This killer has just a short, simple first name, astrological and deeply unfunny: Cancer. Some call it tumor, which is Latin for "swelling" (so it turns out that studying Latin was useful after all), but physicians call it neoplasia, which means "new formation" in ancient Greek (so it turns out studying ancient Greek was useful too). But I've always called it *l'amico Fritz*, in Italian, just like the name of the opera by Leoncavallo. My buddy Fritz.

This is the story of how I lived the last hundred days of my existence here on planet Earth, in the company of my buddy Fritz.

And how, in spite of all expectations to the contrary, those were the happiest days of my life.

PREVIOUSLY, ON THIS SAME SHOW

At this point, I'll need to take a step back and give you a brief summary of my life up to the past few months; otherwise you'll have a hard time following the plot, sort of like watching the sixth season of *Lost*.

My first name is Lucio, which in the all-time hit parade of bad first names comes in seventh, after Pino, Rocco, Furio, Ruggero, Gino, and the unparalleled and unbeatable Gennaro. My mother was a fan of good old Lucio Battisti, whose voice back then was pouring out of every jukebox in Italy with songs like "La canzone del sole," and so there you have it, my John Hancock for the rest of my life: Lucio Battistini. Get it? The most popular singer in the country is Lucio Battisti, and I'm *little* Lucio Battisti because my father's last name was Battistini! Do you see now why my whole life has been an uphill climb? Just think of a kid in the seventies: Fatso, Pizza Face, glasses with Coke-bottle lenses, and stuck with almost the same name as Italy's most famous singer. Admit it, you'd have made fun of me too.

I'll confess, I was neurotic, miserable, and self-sabotaging. Today I'd go by a different, shorter, almost affectionate term: *nerd*. I had every defect needed to drive the girls away like an escapee from a leper colony, including an unhealthy obsession with comic books, splatter flicks, and songs by suicidal crooners. I had only two paths open to me in life: either I could become a computer genius, design an operating system in a garage somewhere and make billions, or else I could walk into a supermarket with a submachine gun and become a mass murderer. When my face made the evening news, all my neighbors, relatives, and friends would comment, without getting too worked up about it: "Odd? Yes, he *was* odd!"

Instead, I identified a third way, and, from ugly duckling that I was, I turned into a swan. Not a fabulous super swan, but a perfectly respectable swan, fully deserving a passing grade, a gentleman's C. When I was fourteen, I lost forty-five pounds, chiefly because of a raging hormonal hurricane, and got contact lenses. Three years later, still a minor, I became Italy's youngest water polo champion ever, Series A, Italy's major league, and no laughing matter. Truth be told, I was just a stand-in goalie, and I spent almost all my time warming the bench in a terrycloth robe, but I did play short stretches of two games that year, and once I even blocked a penalty shot, so the title still holds.

Swimming has always been my favorite sport, and my specialty was the butterfly, which kids all call the dolphin kick out of an innate sense of logic, because butterflies can't swim. I never became a real contender because of a basic conflict of interest with the other fully requited love of my life: bread, butter, and jam. Easy to calculate: 110 calories in a slice of bread plus 75 calories of butter plus 80 calories of jam, total 265 calories. Unfair odds.

I laboriously managed to maintain my washboard abs for ten years; then, when I hit age twenty-six, I gave up competitive sports after a Vespa crash that devastated the ligaments in my knee and resulted in the inexorable expansion of my waistline. According to my own disagreeable reckoning, I gained back the 45 pounds I'd lost as a teenager and possibly a few more on top of them. Think of a Chewbacca, standing six feet three inches and topping out at 240 pounds. Got it?

*   *   *

So: I finish high school with a focus on the humanities, I play water polo, I get a certificate at the Institute of Higher Studies in physical education, and at age twenty-eight I get a job in a gym. Not a gleaming picture-perfect gym like you'd see in a John Travolta movie, no, just a local gym in an outlying neighborhood, tucked away in the basement of a discouraging complex of fifties-style apartment buildings. There's even an undersized swimming pool with faded blue ceramic tiles that secretly dream of being reborn as part of a Club Med infinity pool somewhere in the Caribbean. I am the—cue drumroll and trumpet fanfare, thank you—swimming instructor, aerobics coach, LAB expert (make that L.A.B., for "legs, abs, butt") and, most important of all, aquagym point person. In my off hours, I also work as a personal trainer, on request, usually for plus-sized desperate housewives who are stubbornly holding out against the inevitability of liposuction. In short, I make ends meet, working with my hands—which emit a perennial odor of chlorine. By the way, did you know that the smell of chlorine—which we all know well as far back as we can remember—is actually generated by the chemical interaction of chlorine itself with swimmers' urine? The stronger the smell of chlorine the *less* advisable it is to get in the pool. Now don't say I didn't warn you.

In other words, after growing up on dreams of Olympic gold medals draped on my chest as the captain of the Italian national water polo team, the Settebello, with the national anthem blaring out over the crowd and goosebumps running up and down my arms, I found myself forced to settle for the job that life had saddled me with. That is, six hours a day spent in a calisthenic subbasement where the scent of sweat blended magically with the odors from the Vietnamese restaurant next door. But in my spare time, I did manage to achieve a little dream of mine: coaching a boys' water polo team. All of them between fourteen and fifteen, the worst of all ages. I recruited them at the school where my wife teaches, and I coach them at a city pool a couple of evenings a week, with results that I have to admit have been pretty disappointing. Last year, after lots of hard work and lots of goals put through at our expense, our ranking in the boys' water polo league championship for our province was a brilliant second from bottom. And luckily, we couldn't be kicked down to the minor leagues because we were already as minor league as it gets. This year, though, we're bobbing along in the middle of the league: could be better, could be worse. I can't complain: teaching kids to love sports is the most wonderful thing there is.

So that's my life in professional terms, and then there's the more important aspect, which I've already mentioned in passing: my family. I met Paola when I was twenty, at a pub; she was the girlfriend of a girlfriend of a girl in my class. Usually the girlfriends of the girlfriends of the girls in my class were uninteresting unlovely skinny runts. But when Paola walked into the place, it was like she was radiating with the phosphorescent glow of a yellow highlighter that called her out over all the other women there that night. A bright yellow aura gleamed around her entire silhouette, identifying her as the one thing I wanted to be sure *not* to forget. Like a phrase you need to commit to memory, learn by heart. Ten minutes later I'd already extended a pickup artist's smarmy invitation to come watch my water polo team compete (and I'd already made a mental note to go down on my knees and beg the coach to let me play at least two minutes in that match). At the time, I was still a professional player and she worked in her parents' little pastry shop, which, over time, played a fundamental role in the loss of my fighting trim and my abs. The house specialty was *ciambella fritta con lo zucchero*—sugar doughnuts. Fragrant, yielding—the taste of childhood. There's a tradition that dates back at least thirty years: at two in the morning, Paola's father, Oscar, rolls up the metal shopfront shutter to half-mast, so that the good-for-nothings and roving vampires from all over Trastevere can sink their fangs into sugar doughnuts that are still hot and greasy. Now that Oscar's wife is dead, there's no one running the pastry shop but him and a Sri Lankan assistant who laughs constantly. Paola ended up getting her degree in literature and philosophy, and, after substitute teaching for a while, she now has a tenured position at a good high school with a liberal arts focus.

After a couple of months together (everybody knows the first two months of any love story are always the best), I successfully got myself dumped by Paola in the way only men seem to know how—for flirting with a certain Monica, a good-looking girl from the Marche who studied psychology and sneered at the idea of shaving her armpits.

I lost sight of Paola for nearly ten years. Love is simply a matter of timing and we hadn't been properly synchronized at first: she already wanted a family, while what I wanted was more along the lines of bedding every fertile woman on earth, with or without shaved armpits. It was a challenge to reconcile the two objectives.

Then one day, fate chose to bring us together in a supermarket checkout line. Actually, on account of her transformation from long blond hair to brunette pageboy, I hadn't really recognized her at first, and for the first ten minutes I was convinced I was talking to the granddaughter of one of my grandmother's friends. But I never told her that.

I immediately invited her to dinner and unleashed my consummate tarot-card technique on her. Let me explain.

There's an aged and venerable tarot card reader known as Zia Lorenza who works in Piazza Navona. She has a tattered deck of cards, white hair tied back in a bun, and a glib line of patter. Obviously, she doesn't know anything about the future, but she can still hoodwink anyone, especially when she plays dirty. I regularly used her to impress girls. The tactic was as follows (by all means, feel free to use it; it's not patented): a romantic stroll arm in arm through the most beautiful piazza in Rome, a pleasant talk, a pleasant walk, and as we pass by the old fortune-teller's stand, I secretly toss Zia Lorenza a crumpled ball of paper with all the biographical details—her tastes and whatever information I've already managed to cull—about the girl in question. On our next circuit of the piazza, I've already adroitly brought up the subject of the "paranormal"—taking a skeptical approach if she's a believer, and a more accepting stance if she's a skeptic. That's when phase two of the plan comes into play: I invite her to have her cards read—just for a laugh, my treat. No woman on earth is going to say no. And sure enough, Zia Lorenza puts on her show, reconstructing with stunning accuracy the present and past, and of course creating a future life where, she states, "The name of the man of your dreams starts with an L." "L," as in Lucio. I take advantage of her bewildered emotional state: witnessing a paranormal event together can only unite our spirits and, in most cases, our bodies as well. I will say that no one can predict the future.No one but me when I'm squiring a young lady around Piazza Navona. In that case, I know exactly how the evening will end. And Paola was no exception. But I swear to you, that's the last time I used the trick. That night, caressed by a gentle westerly wind, we kissed for our second first time. We became officially engaged then and there, and in less than three months, we were living together in a studio apartment overlooking Tiber Island. A classic rekindling of the flame. But this time, we were finally fully synchronized and in love.

As I've already mentioned, we were married outside Milan, in the little church of Saint Rocco Flagellated Martyr—a considerable inconvenience to all our guests from Rome. But there was a romantic motivation behind that choice of church. Roughly fifty years earlier, my grandparents (on my mother's side), the glorious apartment building concierges Alfonsina and Michele, were married in that same church. After I lost my parents (more about them later), my grandparents were all the family I had.

I believe that on the seventh day God didn't rest: He dreamed up my grandparents, and realizing that this was the best thing He'd come up with yet, decided to take the rest of the day off to hang out with them.

I lived with them for almost fifteen years, and the dinners the three of us had, with chicken-fried turkey and mashed potatoes with gooey mozzarella, remain an indelible memory. In fact, even now, if I close my eyes I can smell the aroma of frying from the kitchen and the distant voice of my grandmother calling, "Dinner's ready and it's getting cold!" Whenever I go by the concierge's cage where the two of them worked and practically lived, I expect to see them still there, Grandpa with his glasses on, sorting through the mail, and Grandma lovingly watering her geraniums.

Alfonsina and Michele stood by me as my witnesses when I married Paola, and I have to say I believe it was the best day of their lives. I've never seen a couple of octogenarians cry for joy like that. At a certain point, the priest, Don Walter, skinny as a beanpole with a strong Calabrian accent, even interrupted the ceremony to scold the two of them, while everyone laughed.

A few years ago my grandparents passed away, a couple of weeks apart. They died in their sleep, undramatically.

They just couldn't stand to be apart. They'd only just met my son and daughter: Lorenzo and Eva.

It's not fair.

Grandparents are like superheroes. They should never die.

A few months later I finally cleared out the two-room flat next to their concierge's cage, and at the back of a high shelf I found an old-fashioned cardboard suitcase, the kind the traditional Italian emigrant carried. In it were pictures, lots and lots of photographs. Not the classic assortment of snapshots from vacations on the beach, strangers' birthday parties, and so forth. No. Grandpa had taken a photo of Grandma every day for the past sixty years. Every single day.

He never missed one; on the back of every picture was a different date, first black-and-white and then, in time, full color, Polaroids, and the last ones printed from digital files. The pictures were taken in all sorts of different places, in their concierge's cage, on the street, at the beach, at the bakery, at the supermarket, in front of the Teatro Sistina, on Piazza del Popolo, on the old Ferris wheel at the Luneur amusement park, at Saint Peter's, wherever fate took them over their long lifetime. I couldn't stop looking at them. First Grandma as a young woman, then gradually the first wrinkles and expression lines, the graying hair, the extra pounds, but the smile never changed. But what impressed me most wasn't the aging, it was the backgrounds. Behind Grandma was Italy being transformed. Behind her was History. You could glimpse blurry symbols and personalities of every era: the old Fiat 1100 and the Citroën "shark"; long-haired hippies, Timberland-wearing bomber-jacket-clad *paninari,* and punks; concert posters for Paul Anka, Charles Aznavour, and Robbie Williams; Lambrettas, Vespas, and other scooters; Big Jim dolls and Graziella folding bikes, Rubik's Cubes; SIP phone booths, yellow taxis, shops with hand-painted signs. By the way, the first photographer—though almost no one seems to know this—was a Frenchman named Joseph Nicéphore Niépce, one of the absolute geniuses of the nineteenth century. But once again, the earliest experiments were done by good old Leonardo da Vinci. There are even those who claim that the Holy Shroud of Turin was a rudimentary experimental "photographic plate" contrived by the hyperactive Tuscan inventor. A fascinating theory.

Forgive me, I'm losing the thread.

So, I was saying: the characters . . .

MY FAMILY

Five of the leading characters in my life have already shyly tiptoed on stage, namely: my wife, Paola; my father-in-law, Oscar: my son and daughter, Lorenzo and Eva: and my friend Umberto, the veterinarian who's always hungry and is missing a molar. To that list I should add Corrado, my other best friend, an Alitalia airlines pilot, divorced multiple times and very predictable (you know the type, a dark and handsome airline captain who's constantly seducing flight attendants).

But first and foremost, Paola. Paola. Paola.
My Paola.

Paola is beautiful. To me, she's beautiful. To others, she's likable. She's that girl in the third row from the front with hazel eyes, braids, and nice round hips who falls in love with you while you're stupidly chasing after the giggly little blonde who sits in the front row.

Paola is an Italian-style Bridget Jones. She's sunny, self-deprecating, affectionate, and with a self-supporting thirty-six-inch bust. A woman as rare as snow on the Maldives. She's an impassioned reader—she devours novels one after another with ravenous curiosity. Her favorite book is *The Little Prince,* and she has editions in every format and language.

As I mentioned, she's a teacher at a good high school. And not just any teacher: she's the Maradona of high school teachers. She teaches Italian, Latin, history, and geography, but with a genius and brilliance that—this time I have to admit it—not even Leonardo da Vinci could ever have equaled.

And I'm not saying this just because she's my wife. She's really a special teacher.

Let me explain.

The most important job on earth is teaching, and it's also the most monotonous one. Every year, a history teacher tells her students for what feels like the hundredth time who the Phoenicians were and why the Second World War broke out, a math teacher explains integrals and derivatives, a Latin teacher drills students in declensions and conjugations and teaches his students how to translate the poetry of Horace, and so on with all the various subjects. Sooner or later, teachers get bored and tired. And that makes them less effective and empathetic, and in short, worse teachers. Paola, who is well aware of this pitfall, has come up with an original method for combating boredom and repetitiveness: each school year she "plays" a different teacher, coming up with a set of characteristics for every course she teaches, a way of dressing and talking, and she never breaks character until the final report cards have gone out. One year she put on the show of a waspy, mean old-maid teacher, another year she became an athletic unassuming one, a different year she did a hyperactive teacher with radical mood swings, and then once she was a ditzy capricious one. Her students would watch her transform herself from one year to the next and they enjoyed it enormously. They absolutely idolize the "actress" schoolteacher, even when she gives them a demoralizing D after an oral exam. The principal, on the other hand, envies her popularity and has a dim view of her. Paola has been carrying on her one-woman teaching show for fifteen years now. I just laugh when I see her come home dressed as the sexy schoolteacher from a seventies movie, or else as Fräulein Rottenmeier, from *Heidi*. She has a passion for teaching that she and I share, even though what I actually teach my boys is lofting shots and counterattacks.

She's a very special woman, but that didn't stop me from cheating on her a couple of months ago. I know, I know, you were just starting to like me and I've already proved to be a disappointment. What can I say in my own defense? Perhaps I could show you a snapshot of the specimen of womanhood who dragged me into temptation? No, I'm afraid that would only strengthen the case against me. To make a long story short, people, there's no point beating around the bush—after eleven years of marriage, I fell into the pathetic booby trap of infidelity. I'm sorry, but I'm going to beg you to trust me, there were some extenuating circumstances. Let's take things in order. First of all, characters: Lorenzo and Eva. My children.

Shaggy-haired Lorenzo is in third grade and he's the last in his class. His teacher doesn't know what else to try with him, and unfailingly, she repeats the classic of all classic lines: "He's intelligent but he just needs to apply himself." And as if that weren't enough, my firstborn child is a discipline problem. Paola says that it's my fault because I'm never home, because I spend all my time at the gym or playing water polo, and I never really say no to him. The truth is that young Lorenzo has other interests. He doesn't give a hoot about how the ancient Egyptians fertilized the desert with the silt of the flooding Nile or whatever became of the Assyrians and Babylonians; he just wants to spend time pursuing his hobbies. The two principal ones being playing the piano and dismantling expensive electronic devices.

The upright piano belonged to my concierge grandparents, and no one ever knew how to play it, not even them. One day I heard some practically harmonic chords coming from the end of the hall in the three-bedroom apartment we live in. It was Lorenzo, hard at work on his preliminary efforts to become a self-taught concert pianist. Now he's capable of playing by ear any pop song he hears on the radio. I'm not saying that I have Wolfgang Amadeus Mozart in my living room, but my budding young musician is very promising.

The second hobby is a little more unsettling. For as long as he's been able to coordinate his little fingers, Lorenzo has been vivisecting with the deft precision of a medical examiner everything that comes within reach. But the autopsies are performed on objects that are still perfectly serviceable. From the television set, the dishwasher, and the engine of my station wagon to the snack vending machine at school, the blender, and the traffic light on the corner. He has a full-fledged passion for mechanical engineering and electronics. And as far as that goes, this pastime might be amusing and even instructive. But the problem is that he never puts anything back together again and leaves a swath of destruction worthy of Attila the Hun wherever he passes, transforming anything and everything into a still-to-be-assembled piece of furniture from Ikea, only without an instruction sheet. And so, evidently, there really isn't much time left in his day for studying. My wife, good and conscientious schoolteacher that she is, is quite worried. I'm not. What most worries me (actually, let's say, what most hurts my feelings) is that Lorenzo still hasn't learned to swim; in fact, he actually seems to be afraid of the water. He has the same flotation line as the RMS *Titanic* has currently. The minute he's put in the water, he goes straight to the bottom. It's really too bad.

Freckle-faced Eva, on the other hand, is in first grade and is the pet of every teacher in her elementary school. And she's a budding militant environmentalist. She strong-armed us into adopting animals and now we share the apartment with a cross-eyed limping German shepherd (which for simplicity's sake we named Shepherd), a white hamster (Alice) with urinary incontinence, and no fewer than three lazy stray cats that we named after the Aristocats: Berlioz, Toulouse, and Marie.

At home, Eva is a hurricane of words. She talks and talks and talks. Before getting around to the point, her conversation is interspersed with a series of whys and wherefores and detailed descriptions and circumstances so tangled that not even Perry Mason mounting a difficult defense could manage to produce so much smoke and mirrors and confusing details. I feel sure that when she grows up, she'll be either a television news anchor or a politician, which, more or less, amounts to the same thing. She applies her passion for environmentalism to everything. She demands that the family undertake a differentiated waste collection that turns recycling into a high-level form of connoisseurship and collecting—classified by shape, material, odor, and color. She's cute as a bug, but she doesn't take advantage of the fact. She only uses her smile and her big baby-blue eyes the color of the mid-August sky to persuade her fellow humans to go along with her exaggerated sense of civic responsibility. When she greets people, she says *miao* instead of *ciao* because she claims that she was a cat in a previous life.

Every so often she remembers that she's just six and a half years old, and she comes and snuggles in my lap on the sofa and watches cartoons. When that happens, time slows down and stands perfectly still. They say that the love we feel toward our children is the most genuine kind of love, the kind that lets you scale mountains and write songs. And it's absolutely true. When Eva runs to greet me or when it thunders with lightning in the middle of the night and she climbs into our big warm bed, I get a smile in my heart, my wrinkles stretch out, and my muscles regain the spring and power of when I was twenty.

The best possible medicine.

Eva is also the darling of yet another star of this story. My father-in-law, Oscar.

*   *   *

Oscar isn't hard to picture: he looks exactly like the Italian actor Aldo Fabrizi, with the same balloonish physique, the same gait and stride, and he even mutters and mumbles just like him. His life is divided into two parts: before the accident and after the accident. Ten years ago or so his wife, Vittoria, the kindest, quietest woman who ever lived, was killed by a hit-and-run driver while she was out with their binge-eating Labrador retriever, Gianluca.

I can't seem to keep from arguing with him, though as soon as he starts coming out with his theories on the meaning of life, he makes me laugh so hard that I'd gladly hire him as my own personal guru. One day they'll talk about him in textbooks, and students will hate him just as much as they detest his colleagues, Socrates and Plato. I'm sure of it.

His favorite theme is life in the afterlife. His theory is that those who were good in a previous life are born into this world hale and healthy, the children of wealthy industrialists, intelligent and good-looking. Those who were bad are born ugly, crippled, stupid, and poor, or else die young or live on as invalids. A theory that, to hear him tell it, would justify all the injustices of this world. To Oscar, luck and unluck are deserved. In which case, I ask him, "you're saying it's not worth doing anything? Fate has already written all our actions?"

Oscar shakes his head and goes on making doughnuts. He doesn't know the answer. He raises doubts and offers questions but not solutions, like all philosophers, come to think of it.

"When all is said and done, Lucio, my lad, the true meaning of life is nothing more than taking a bite out of a hot doughnut."

I smile and bite into one. As always, he's right.

SOMETHING THAT HAS NOTHING TO
DO WITH ANYTHING

You will soon find out that I'm obsessed with inventors, so we can't really go on until I've unveiled for you the solution to one of the most important mysteries in the history of mankind, namely, who invented the doughnut?

An Italian? Could it be the ubiquitous Leonardo da Vinci? No, my friends, it could not.

Leonardo did, in fact, invent a doughnut of sorts, but it was really a doughnut pool float, just a lifesaver for beginning swimmers, but, unfortunately, he had failed to invent inflatable plastic.

On the other hand, the doughnut has an origin that remains the subject of some controversy. It came to New York (which was still called New Amsterdam back then) from Holland, with the unappealing name of *olykoek*, which means literally "oily cake." It described a dough kneaded with apples, plums, or raisins. According to doughnut lore, one day a cow happened to kick a pan of hot oil onto a bowl of uncooked samples of the Dutch pastry, which resulted in what we Italians call the *bomba fritta*. There ought to be a monument to that remarkably creative bovine.

So far, so good . . . but how did that hole come to be?

In the year 1847 a woman named Elizabeth Gregory, the mother of Hanson Gregory, a young New England ship captain, tweaked the recipe for oily cake by adding nutmeg, cinnamon, and lemon rind, as well as inserting walnuts and hazelnuts in the center, which was the part that was always the last to cook through. The cake thus prepared became so delicious and irresistible that when her son set off for a long sea voyage, he always asked his mother to make a large batch of her oil cakes for the whole crew. The story has it that the New England captain disliked the walnuts and hazelnuts that his mother used to stuff the center of the cake, and he always cut them out before eating his, leaving a hole in the middle of the pastry. At the captain's orders, the ship's cook made all pastries from then on in the shape of a ring, removing the middle with a round tin pepper mill.

This was an invention that certainly didn't pass unnoticed. In Clam Cove, Maine, in fact, there's a plaque honoring Captain Hanson Gregory, "who first invented the hole in the donut," and in 1934 the Chicago World's Fair declared that the doughnut was "the food hit of the century of progress." The fact remains that the hole in the center marked the beginning of the spectacular international success of doughnuts.

Of course, we Italians, and my father-in-law, Oscar, in particular, find this story or legend—whichever it is—completely unacceptable. What? we say, doughnuts, or *ciambelle*, or better yet, *graffe*, as they call them in Naples—those aren't an Italian invention? Impossible.

Whatever the truth, the one thing I know for sure is that you're hungry now, and therefore, before you stop reading to get a snack, let me go back to where we were first interrupted. Characters.

MY FRIENDS

My passion for doughnuts is one I share with my best friends: Umberto and Corrado. We've all known one another since middle school and we've been friends our whole lives, even though Umberto was held back after flunking his freshman year of high school. We've always done everything together, spent our holidays, and even gone on camping trips when we were Scouts together. The three musketeers of North Rome. I was the oversized Porthos, Umberto was the pragmatic Athos, and Corrado was Aramis—the lady-killer. All for one and one for all. I really know everything about them—all of their secrets. We've beaten each other up, laughed together, fought over girls, lent each other money, and held lasting grudges. In other words, we've done everything that best friends do. And twenty years after, just like the three legendary musketeers of France, we're still here.

Umberto, aside from swallowing engagement rings, is, as I described to you earlier, a veterinarian. He's single, and none of the relationships he's been in has ever lasted longer than a year. Which is mysterious, given that Umberto is the living prototype of the ideal husband. He's never in a bad mood, he's self-deprecating, he's not handsome but he's healthy, maybe just a little untutored and impulsive when it comes to his manners. His one shortcoming, if you leave aside his heavy Roman accent, is his punctuality. Which is an unforgivable defect in Italy's capital. Do you know the kind of maniac who, if you arrange to meet in a restaurant at one o'clock actually shows up at five minutes to one? Or the kind of guy who's already waiting outside the movie theater when you get there, and has bought tickets for everyone? Or even worse, if you invite him over to dinner, when he shows up on time he catches you still in slippers and bathrobe, wandering around the apartment?

Umberto can be an inconvenient presence because most of the population of Rome lives about half an hour behind the rest of the world in time. I'm habitually late, and Umberto has always made a point of complaining about it. He claims that he's spent a total of one year of his life waiting for me. His life is just a series of wasted time periods spent waiting for other people, and so he's gotten organized and decided to find a way to fill in these stretches of dead time. He opted for the age-old but immortal lifesaver: reading books. He always carries a pocket graphic novel with him, and he calculates that the time it takes to read it perfectly matches my average delay.

Umberto often spends evenings with us. My wife and my daughter have a special relationship with him. Paola considers him sort of like the brother she never had; she confides in him and coddles him, serving him pans of eggplant Parmesan and lethally rich dishes of tiramisu. Little Eva calls him uncle and chats eagerly with him about their shared love of nature. It goes without saying that he is the trusted veterinarian of our little domestic farm. Sometimes, like so many latter-day Cupids, we set him up on blind dates with schoolteachers who work with Paola, but without ever seeing any dazzling showers of sparks.

Corrado, as I mentioned before, is an Alitalia pilot. In fact, he's a caricature of a pilot, a perfect archetype: tall, handsome, with a neat goatee, a gentleman, with a full mouth of straight gleaming teeth, and muscular without overdoing it. In short, any stewardess's dream. He's been divorced several times, he has no children, and he has a tendency to set the hearts of all the women he meets afire, only to abandon them, leaving them heartbroken and depressed. To hear him tell it, he hates women because of his two stormy divorces, which have left him with nothing except the obligation to write alimony checks to his two ex-wives, whom he refers to as "the parasites."

His main hobby is just having fun. His chief passion is statistics, and has been ever since our high school days together. We sat at adjoining desks: I had a C minus minus average, he had an A minus/A average. It was just a matter of statistics, he used to say. He never studied a bit, but he managed to foretell, with the accuracy of a Nostradamus, the day he would be given an oral exam and even the likelihood that he'd be asked this or that question. He remembered everything and he'd compute it all and draw the necessary conclusions: he invariably nailed it exactly. He applied this same method to everything, especially to women, who, as you must already have guessed, were and remain his weakness. Corrado has always gotten more girls than the Fonz. On account of statistics. This is his personal technique for hooking up: as soon as he gets to a party, he will always start chatting up all the girls there, in decreasing order of attractiveness. He'll go over to the prettiest girl there and ask her, with an overabundance of sheer nerve: "Do you want to have sex with me tonight?"

Courtship whittled down to the minimum, he gets straight to the point.

The answer is almost unfailingly: "Have you lost your mind?"

But as he checks off girls and works his way down the ranking, by the time he gets to the tenth or fifteenth entry in the improvised "Belle of the Ball" contest, he'll eventually wind up with a "Sure, why not?"

In my single days, I'd watch as he'd take her off to the nearest bed or dark corner, under my wide, sad eyes. Chalk it up to statistics. He'd calculated that out of a hundred girls, at least thirty would be willing to go to bed with him. To find those thirty, he just had to start optimistically with the prettiest one and then settle for the first one to fall into his net, never the homeliest girl at the party, and always one who was at least cute. All this while I was furiously courting the prettiest one there and coming up empty-handed after two hours of pointless conversation in a fruitless attempt to seem interesting and sexy.

When all is said and done, Corrado is the most thrilling and amusing man in the world to spend time with as a buddy. But, and now I'm addressing my female readers, if you ever meet him, avoid him like the plague. You'll recognize him immediately: he looks like Aramis.

WE'RE ALMOST THERE

Now you have nearly all the ingredients necessary to enjoy this story without a happy ending and witness the imminent arrival of my buddy Fritz. Just a few more essential details and we're done.

Until a few months ago, I'd leave our apartment in San Lorenzo around quarter to eight every morning, and first I'd drop off Paola at her school, then the kids, and then finally I'd park on the banks of the Tiber about a ten-minute walk from the gym because of the much-detested ZTL, the *zona a traffico limitato*—Rome's restricted traffic zone. That short walk served me perfectly as a second morning espresso. Nearly every day, as I made my way through Trastevere, I'd make a stop at Oscar's pastry shop, which was conveniently close. A pleasant chat about the weather and politics, then my favorite father-in-law would hand me a hot, sweet-smelling doughnut, without my ever asking.

I'd sit down at the badly painted wooden café table set up on the sidewalk out front, which looked as if someone had left it there at the end of World War Two. Those were the five best minutes of my day. The confectioners' sugar that puffed out over my lips, begging to be licked off; the crunchy spring of the golden crust that lasts just a fraction of a second before collapsing and allowing itself to be bitten into; the hurrying strangers there to be watched as if they were actors in a play. I was never alone. Wait a few seconds and there was always an extroverted sparrow gliding down onto the table to harvest my crumbs. It was always the same bird; I knew him by sight—not exactly friends, but close to it. I'd break off a few bits of doughnut and toss them to the bird, and on a couple of occasions the sparrow actually fearlessly came to eat from my hands. When the sparrow flew away, it was like an alarm clock going off: it marked the beginning of my day.

My "doughnut time" was a secret that remained between me, my father-in-law, and the sparrow. I never said a word to Paola, who urged me on a daily basis to go on a more balanced, healthier diet. She'd never forgive me.

Paola and I, during the past ten years, have had our ups and downs, and a few months ago we scraped absolute bottom thanks to a completely banal event, to which I've already made reference and which can be summarized in a single, nondescript word: infidelity. I had a little affair with a new customer at the gym, Signora Moroni. It was, in fact, a little affair. A very little one. We went to bed maybe two or three times total. In any case, no more than five. At the very most, ten or so. All right, a dozen. But it was just sex, never anything more than sex. For us men, that's a significant difference. And, I hope, a mitigating circumstance.

If my female readers have not already slammed this book shut and tossed it into the fire, then let me do my best to explain the situation to their satisfaction.

Signora Moroni.

Thirty-six years old, four years younger than me. Measurements worthy of a pin-up queen from the fifties: 36-24-35 (I read them on her file at the gym and promptly memorized them).

The face of a Raphael Madonna with surgically reconstructed lips.

Fair complexion with a sprinkling of freckles.

Funny as can be.

She had been married for years, to a man who traveled frequently for business.

When she chose me as her personal trainer, I immediately had one thought: "ouch!"

Seductive married women with husbands who travel for business shouldn't be allowed to go around on the loose, spending all the time they want in gymnasiums staffed by unfortunate trainers who have sex twice a month at most with their beloved wives of ten years plus. There ought to be a law against it. Buy an exercise bike and set it up in your living room, *per favore*!

At first I remained on a strictly professional basis with Signora Moroni. Or maybe we should say a reasonably professional basis. For the first few lessons I limited myself at the very most to the occasional chance brush of the knuckles against her thigh, or a grab and a squeeze here and there to test the muscle tone: I know what you're thinking, just like the classic dirty old man. Then one evening we stayed on after regular hours, alone, in the gym. I told the reception-ist that I'd lock up after finishing a series of training exercises with Signora Moroni. And in point of fact, according to the Italian dictio-nary, an exercise is: "an act or series of acts performed or practiced in order to keep oneself physically and mentally fit and to develop, im-prove, or display a specific capability or skill."

Well, that night we developed and improved greatly the world's oldest capability or skill.

And we went on training and exercising for a number of weeks. Weeks of lies, stress, and the fear of leaving telltale evidence. Usually, we did our exercising at her house, while her husband the musician was on tour with some evergreen singer or other, but a couple of times we did a series of follow-up refresher exercises in the gym. Never at home. I couldn't have done that. I know—that doesn't let me off the hook.

The serious thing is that Paola found out about it. Her investigation got started one night in February. I left my iPhone on the table during dinner. I know, it's the act of an absolute beginner, an amateur at cheating. But when it comes right down to it, I really was an absolute beginner. While we were enjoying an excellent dish of chicken curry, my phone rang. Large as life on the display: Dr. Moroni. An absolute beginner but not completely stupid.

"Aren't you going to answer that?" Paola asks.

"No, it's . . . it's Moroni, the doctor at the gym," I say, inventing freely with some embarrassment. "A tremendously tiresome guy; no doubt he just wants to talk my ear off."

"If you want, I can answer and tell him you're out . . ."

"No, it doesn't matter—*grazie*, my love. I'll call him back in the morning. This curry really is delicious."

Had she fallen for it?

Was I sufficiently believable?

Did she suspect?

Just forty-eight hours later I would discover that the correct answers were, in order, no, no, and yes. And that right there and then my wife had been transformed into Columbo turning even a shred of doubt into a hunt that ends only when his prey's been nailed for his crimes.

The evening, however, passes without incident, which calms my worries. I watch *Beauty and the Beast* with the kids, and more important, I put my phone into airplane mode. So no more annoying phone calls. But that night I don't sleep a wink, and in the bathroom, I delete all the compromising messages from the imaginary Dr. Moroni.

The next morning I call Signora Moroni and I discover the reason for the inconvenient phone call: she was hoping I could meet her after dinner because her husband had been called out of town for an unexpected gig. I tell her once again that I'm married, and perhaps more happily married than she is, and that I've decided to put an end to this kamikaze affair. That night, a few minutes before closing time, the lovely cheater shows up in the gym wearing a skintight tracksuit and we wind up having sex repeatedly in the shower stalls of the instructors' locker room. I'm a man of healthy instincts. But above all, as you may have figured out for yourself, I am a complete moron.

The next day Isabella Moroni writes me an odd text message in which she seems to have forgotten about last night entirely.

"When can I see you? I miss you so much! I don't know how to live without you."

I distractedly reply, without really giving any thought to the odd aspects of the text, thus walking straight into a gigantic booby trap. We go on texting flirtatiously back and forth all day long. Exciting, fun, and—especially—explicit text messages. That night, when I get home, there is Paola waiting for me, standing in the middle of the living room like a three-headed Cerberus ready to sink his fangs into anyone who tries to enter. The minute I see her, I understand. As if there were a subtitle clearly stamped across the screen: YOU ARE A COMPLETE IDIOT.

I'll admit it, I'd underestimated my wife's intelligence. After the suspicious midevening phone call from the mysterious Dr. Moroni, Paola had put in a call of her own to the gym and had learned, from the conscientious and razor-sharp receptionist, that there was no Dr. Moroni, but there was a certain Isabella Moroni, who—well, well, well, how do you like that—had none other than me as her personal trainer. A quick search on Facebook revealed that this Isabella is not only attractive but arguably hot. I know, I know, I could have and should have put a different name in my cell phone directory, but it's too late now, and even with the minimal precautions I'd taken I thought I was pretty damned smart. So now what did the Machiavellian high school teacher I married proceed to do? She went into my phone book and replaced Dr. Moroni's phone number with her own, deleting Isabella's phone number entirely. Every time I got a text message from my wife it was marked as coming from Dr. Moroni and I texted back accordingly, sinking deeper and deeper into the raging ocean of lies into which I'd dived headfirst. As she explains the various steps of the investigation, I desperately try to come up with a justification for all the text messages I'd sent that day. I decide to improvise and do my best to prop up the following creaky defense theory: "Isabella Moroni is a good customer at the gym and she's fallen in love with me. I'm trying to let her down gently, but firmly. I just didn't want to worry you about something of no real importance, *amore mio.*"

This pathetic appeal to the court's better nature withered and died after no more than ten seconds, and so, in an impetus of dimwitted heroism—at this point completely thwarted by the strength of the overwhelming evidence of an extramarital affair—I decide to make a complete confession and throw myself on the mercy of the court.

Huge mistake.

The court is so angry it could spit.

In short, a full-blown tragedy with all the trimmings. Family and friends are dragged into the shipwreck of our marriage, especially Umberto and Corrado, under suspicion of having backed my play for months. The truth is that Corrado was completely aware of everything, down to the tiniest sexual details, while with Umberto, who was a close friend of Paola's as well, I'd been rather discreet. I'd limited myself to the version that I'd found myself locked in a kiss with one of my clients at the gym, but I'd promptly nipped it in the bud. The most violent reaction is from my father-in-law, who, in Paola's presence, reads me the riot act in nineteenth-century style, lecturing me on my violation of family values and betrayal of his daughter's honor. He refuses to let me get a word in edgewise and watches impassively, standing like a majestic stag, as his daughter orders me out my own home.

That night I sleep at Corrado's place, bunking on his pullout couch. His chaotic studio apartment is littered with objects, trash, scraps of food, and dirty laundry. It looks like the field at Woodstock after the concert.

The next morning I walk past the pastry shop, tempted to venture inside and try to put in a word on my own behalf, but I chicken out and turn to go. Oscar's imperious voice stops me cold.

His first four words are explicit:

"You are a loser!"

I turn around. He's standing in front of me in all his Romanness.

"It was a mistake . . . I know that—" I try to defend myself but he immediately cuts me off.

"I told my daughter that you were a loser."

By now, the concept has become pretty clear.

"Yes, I have to admit—"

"Because no one but a pathetic loser would go ahead and confess!" he spits out, much to my astonishment. "Never, never confess. This is rule number one of all marriages; nothing else really matters. You can have three lovers simultaneously, forget birthdays, wedding anniversaries—all that's fixable. But never confess. The priest ought to include it in the wedding ceremony."

I was expecting yet another brutal tongue-lashing, and instead I'm presented with an unexpected display of male solidarity.

"Lucio, my lad, the truth is that sooner or later every man in the world has been forced to sleep on a cot in the office or in a basement bedroom."

"Even you?" I ask.

"Even me. But don't ask me the details. It's a private matter I'd rather forget," but then he can't help himself. "She was a Ukrainian apprentice pastry chef. Twenty-four years old, I was forty-five. She couldn't speak so much as a word of Italian, but she had a rack on her that had to be seen to be believed. Worthless in terms of making puff pastries or sugar icings, but she was good at everything else."

I smile at the thought of Oscar struggling to woo a Ukrainian girl in broken English between a profiterole and a tray of beignets. Meanwhile, he goes on with his dissertation on the dos and don'ts of unfaithfulness: "Cheating in marriage isn't a crime; it's a genetic transcription error; it's been a typo in male DNA since time out of mind. There's nothing you can do about it. You're a flesh-based computer and you're programmed to cheat. The only difference is that some men have fewer opportunities, less personal charm, less time on their hands, and not as much disposable income. So now, because of a defect in your DNA, you're sleeping on a cot in some friend's apartment! Possibly for the rest of your life."

I deeply appreciate the camaraderie of his confession, but I explain to him that in spite of all the emotional chaos and the fact that I've been kicked out of my home, Paola hasn't said a word about divorce. At least not yet. But she then mentions it about two hours later, asking me to take all my possessions and get out of her life once and for all. I have no real counterargument. It's only fair, and after all, I brought it on myself.

I have only one question: "What about the children?"

"We'll decide about the children later; for now I'll tell them that you've been working late and sleeping at the gym."

That strikes me as reasonable. Confident that this is just a passing tantrum, and considering that I'm not exactly a wealthy man, I decide to stay in Umberto's studio apartment, given the impracticability of Corrado's place. But I soon discover that my veterinarian friend likes to bring his work home, specifically a dozen cats and dogs that often clutter his 450 square feet of space. All I can do now is open my computer and start looking for a little one-star pensione not too far from the gym.

Then help comes in the form of an unexpected offer. From someone who by all rights ought to be on the opposite side of the barricades: my father-in-law.

Oscar offers me a place to stay in the back room of his pastry shop, at least until his daughter makes up her mind to forgive me, which by the way, just for the record, is not something she seems to have any intention of doing. Obviously, he's giving me a place to stay without telling Paola, who's convinced I'm staying in an imaginary and very affordable bed-and-breakfast in Trastevere.

So there I am, with a duffel bag shoved into the corner, doing my best to get some sleep while the Sinhalese assistant pastry chef bakes croissants, fills beignets, and decorates cakes. In the morning, I wake up wrinkled and oily. Every day I promise myself I'm going to find a new and more fitting place to live, but then, partly because of how close it is to the gym where I work and also because of Oscar's kindness—he really does treat me like a son—I remain there, sleeping between a tray of flake pastries and a bag of superfine baking flour. I'm only allowed to see Lorenzo and Eva a couple of evenings a week and on Saturday afternoon, but I'm hopeful the situation will stabilize soon.

So, this was the perfect time to find out that I now had a new buddy by the name of Fritz.

MY BUDDY FRITZ

Actually, warning signs had started cropping up nearly a year before my affair with Isabella Moroni but they'd been roundly discounted and ignored. I remember very distinctly the first time Fritz rang my doorbell loud and clear. That afternoon, I was in the pool with my boys running some plays. Water polo is a demanding and manly pursuit, and my job as a coach is pretty thankless—just take a look sometime at a picture of the skinny weaklings who make up my team. We bob along, as I was telling you, midway down the rankings. My goalie Alessio, better known by his nickname Soap-on-a-Rope, never seems able to stop a shot, even by accident, while the center defender Martino, our team striker, is fast but cross-eyed. My assistant assistant coach, Giacomo, an autistic thirty-year-old who knows all the matches in the history of water polo by heart, isn't much help in improving the performance of my ragtag team. Still, he manages to win the affection of one and all and he fits in perfectly in this Gang That Couldn't Shoot Straight. It's not just a metaphor, my team is actually named the Gang That Couldn't Shoot Straight. A name that says it all.

When I felt the first stab of pain to my belly, I was in the water and trying to teach Soap-on-a-Rope a play and I'd just shot the ball into the net when I felt a bolt of agony cut through me for a second. I file this passing pain away as a muscle cramp or a minor hernia and months go by before I think about it again. I've never really been sick in my life and the last thing I would think is that it could be anything truly serious.

How many times in your life have you heard words to that effect?

The fact remains that I start to feel sick more and more frequently; the sporadic stabbing pains are transformed into an almost constant minor pain; I'm no longer able to swim the way I used to. I stuff my face with analgesics and anti-inflammatory medicines, convincing myself that it's nothing more than an annoying and extended cramp of my abdominal muscles (or what's left of them). I tell Paola about it, and she insists on scheduling an abdominal sonogram, but I tell her that I've always had little lingering pains like this throughout my glorious athletic career, and that they always go away in time, as long as I rest up. To tell the truth, my affair with Signora Moroni isn't really something I could describe as resting up, but the pain is still tolerable even during sex. I often think back on the abdominal sonogram I never got as a scene from the movie *Sliding Doors*.

What would have happened if I'd taken Paola's advice?

Would I have lived for another ten, or twenty, or thirty years?

Or would I have been hit by a bus at the hospital entrance and killed instantly?

My personal sliding door slid shut right in front of me that day.

I just didn't know it at the time.

Little by little I talk myself into believing that it's not a muscular problem but rather an insidious and minuscule hernia. A simple operation would take care of everything, but I still decide to go on waiting, hoping against hope that one morning I'll wake up just healthy. In the meanwhile, the symptoms just go on proliferating: I start to feel more tired than usual; one afternoon I throw up; and another time I go for weeks with an annoying low-grade fever. And each time I manage to find a logical explanation: "I'm just under a lot of stress lately"; "I shouldn't have eaten what I ate last night"; "I must have gotten a chill in the pool yesterday, and 98.9 isn't really a fever at all." I still don't connect the warning signs to that single lethal enemy.

The months fly past and in the meanwhile, as you know, my family life collapses and I wind up sleeping in the back room of the pastry shop. One rainy night in early March, I try to do my part and help Oscar as he places a large tray of chocolate muffins in the oven, but without warning, a stronger jab of pain than usual makes me double over. I drop the tray to the floor and let out a shout. Oscar and his Sinhalese assistant both prop me up, confused, and help me to a chair. I tell them that these pains have been bothering me for eight months now, recurring frequently, and that I've been doing my best to coexist with this damned hernia. For too long.

"Go have a specialist take a look at you," Oscar suggests.

"Thanks, Oscar, but you'll see; I'll be all better in a couple of weeks."

"That wasn't a suggestion," my father-in-law explains. "It was an order: go have a specialist take a look at you. It might even be an ulcer. A customer of mine died of an ulcer—it's no laughing matter. One day he was sitting here eating a sweet roll with whipped cream and talking about A. S. Roma's latest win, the next day he was in the cemetery, six feet under."

Direct strike, ship sunk. Oscar managed to be both clear and direct, as always. The word "died" is a cold shower, and it finally persuades me to see a doctor, certain by now that it's actually an ulcer. So I go and see Umberto. A veterinarian is, after all, a doctor of sorts.

Umberto's waiting room is full.

Around me are sitting a little old cat lady, on her lap a carry crate containing a Persian; a thirteen-year-old boy with his mother and a chameleon; an austere man in his fifties with an obnoxious collie who resembles him to a T; and a pretty young tattooed woman in her early thirties with a mysterious basket on the seat next to her.

The cat lady stares at me curiously, then gives in to her overwhelming curiosity: "What kind of animal do you have?"

"I have ticks," I reply with a sunny smile.

She can't tell whether I'm joking or I mean it. In any case, she moves a seat away from me.

I'm the last one ushered into the doctor's office. I immediately ask Umberto just what was in the tattooed woman's basket.

"A python. Very fashionable these days," he answers nonchalantly. Then he asks me the reason for this surprise visit. It's the first time I've come to his clinic for professional reasons.

I explain to him about the abdominal pains I've been experiencing for almost eight months now. I haven't been to see a doctor in years and years. I've been avoiding the public health doctor whom I share with Paola to keep from alarming her excessively. The doctor is a friend of Paola's and certainly would talk to her about it. I'm practically certain, I explain to Umberto, that it must be an ulcer.

My friend tells me to lie on my back and he palpates my stomach with expertise. I feel a sharp stab of pain. I can see that he's a little worried.

"Does it hurt right here?" he asks.

The answer is clear from the grimace on my face.

As I get dressed, he explains that in his opinion this is neither a hernia nor an intercostal muscle strain, much less an ulcer.

"It's a small lump," he explains, "between the liver and the stomach; it's hard to say with such a generic examination. It might be a lipoma, which in layman's terms is an anomalous but benign clump of fat. I'd immediately order an abdominal sonogram. These days that kind of equipment can do a quick and accurate analysis."

"In fact, Paola recommended the same thing a couple of months ago."

"And she was right. As she almost always is, I should add."

He scolds me for a while, the way only doctors and high school teachers know how. He's right, I should have listened to my wife and kept that sliding door from slamming shut.

"I'd do a blood test too. You'll see, it's probably nothing," Umberto concludes. "You almost never drink, you don't smoke, and you're even a former athlete!"

I have no difficulty understanding that he's trying to keep from freaking me out.

I don't like the smile on his face one little bit.

Skipping over the boring parts, here's the report from the sonogram of my abdomen that was done two days later in a specialized medical clinic. I read the results while waiting for the doctor who's going to go over them with me, and I immediately consult Wikipedia on my smart phone. I look for the two words that appear in bold after the phrase "the patient was found to present a . . . ." Those two words are *hepatocellular carcinoma*.

Wikipedia is efficient as always.

A carcinoma is a malignant tumor.

Tumor. Malignant.

Two words, are each unpleasant enough taken alone.

Hepatocellular, on the other hand, means that the organ affected is the liver.

The liver.

Outstanding.

Even newborn babies know that a tumor to the liver is the most dangerous kind.

Two lines down is the size of the intruder.

It's six centimeters long.

In my cozy tummy I've been hosting a hepatocellular carcinoma

6.0 centimeters in length, with a diameter of 0.7 centimeters, as my guest.

More or less the size of a French fry.

Even newborn babies know that French fries aren't good for you.

I have a six-centimeter tumor in my liver. My blood tests also confirm the excessively elevated values of the tumor markers that show the undesired presence in my organism. There's no chance it's a mistake.

I don't even wait for the doctor who is scheduled to come break the news to me. I head out onto the street.

I have a six-centimeter tumor in my liver.

I wander aimlessly.

I have a six-centimeter tumor in my liver.

I repeat the words over and over aloud, like an obsessive mantra.

I have a six-centimeter tumor in my liver.

I can't seem to stop.

I have a six-centimeter tumor in my liver. . . . I have a six-centimeter tumor in my liver. . . . I have a six-centimeter tumor in my liver. . . . I have a six-centimeter tumor in my liver. . . . I have a six-centimeter tumor in my liver. . . . I have a six-centimeter tumor in my liver. . . .

I take a few seconds off from my impersonation of Jack Nicholson in *The Shining* and I finally have a glimmer of intelligence. I wonder to myself: "So is six centimeters very big for a tumor in the liver?"

According to the oncologist, who frowns as he studies my sonogram, that really is a very respectable size for a tumor. A handsome flourishing robust tumor. The first thing he prescribes, in fact, the first thing he orders me to do is to get an immediate and complete CAT scan of my upper body.

I schedule one, and in the meanwhile, I spend the night surfing the Web. I go back to doing something I've always hated. I study. I don't feel like doing anything else—eating, drinking, or sleeping. All

I want to do is spend hour after hour Googling the words *tumor, liver, cure,* and so on.

In the course of the next few hours I become the world's greatest living expert on carcinomas. I even discover that the first operations to remove tumor masses were done by the Egyptian scientist and polymath Imhotep, a sort of Nilotic Leonardo da Vinci, capable of designing the immortal pyramids and founding Western medical science, and ultimately actually venerated as the god of medicine. At the time, nearly all his patients, operated upon without anesthesia, either died during the procedure or else bled to death immediately afterward. I skip four thousand years of medical history and focus on more recent studies of my buddy Fritz.

I read a Web page on the subject: "Hepatocellular carcinomas are the most common type of primary liver tumors."

I've come down with an illness that isn't even particularly original.

"It develops in the liver cells and damages the other healthy cells."

Great.

"The uninterrupted growth of the tumor cells can result in a malignant form of tumor."

Outstanding.

"At first, this kind of tumor doesn't cause any particular disturbance and is very difficult to identify."

What an asshole.

"Once the tumor has reached a certain size, various symptoms may manifest, such as abdominal pains, bloating, weight loss, nausea, vomiting, exhaustion, and a yellowish tinge to the complexion and the eyes."

I've got every one of them.

"Men are more likely to develop this type of tumor. Depending on the nature and stage of the tumor, a different array of treatments can be utilized. Surgery or liver transplant are viable alternatives only if the tumor is small and contained within the liver. If however the tumor has spread and expanded, chemotherapy or radiation therapy can extend survival times, but will not cure the pathology."

They will not cure the pathology.

The words echo like one of Pavarotti's high Cs in the back of the pastry shop. I sit there staring at my laptop, locked into a freeze frame.

They will not cure the pathology.

They ... will ... not ... cure ... the ... pathology.

The findings from this search are unequivocal.

Nothing has changed since Imhotep's day.

I'm going to die.

Up till now, that's a verb in the future tense that we've all known since we were kids. We're all going to die. It's just that I'm going to die a little sooner than expected.

A little sooner than I would have liked.

A little sooner than seems strictly fair.

I'm going to die a little sooner. Period.

I still haven't said anything to Paola. Partly out of shame, partly because she never answers my phone calls, but chiefly because I still don't really believe it. I don't want to believe it, and really, I can't.

At breakfast, I tell the news to the other two musketeers: Umberto and Corrado. I meet them in a little café we've frequented since we were in high school, where neither the furnishings nor the pastries have changed since then. I even recognize a stale but optimistic brioche that's resided behind the glass display case on the counter ever since 1979.

It's a very complicated breakfast. Super complicated.

Someone ought to urgently publish a guidebook titled: *How Should You Act at Breakfast When One of Your Best Friends Tells You He Has Liver Cancer?* It's the most difficult conversation you can have, out of all the billions of possible conversations. The main problem is nailing the correct tone for the dialogue.

DIALOGUE WITH GAFFE

"Friends, I've got liver cancer . . ."

"Really? My uncle had the same thing last year . . ."

"So how is he now?"

"Oh, he's dead!"

ABSURD DIALOGUE

"Friends, I've got liver cancer . . ."

"Ah, what a relief, I was expecting something worse!"

"Worse? Like what is there that would have been worse?"

"Well, for instance . . . now let me see . . . ah yes, being a paraplegic is worse, I think."

"Thanks. Now I feel so much better."

EMBARRASSING DIALOGUE

"Friends, I've got liver cancer . . ."

"Oh my God! You were always my favorite musketeer!"

"Why are you using the past tense?"

ENCOURAGING DIALOGUE

"Friends, I've got liver cancer . . ."

"Don't worry, you're strong, you'll beat this!"

"And what if I don't?"

"Don't even take that possibility into consideration."

At this point in the encouraging dialogue the tears start to flow and we all sob wholeheartedly together for half an hour or so.

I decide to break the tension myself and discuss my own disease with irony. That's when I come up with a nickname for the amiable little

French fry that lives in my liver. I dub it "my buddy Fritz," a phrase we use in Italian to describe hypocritical friends you don't want to name outright. From that moment forward, the word *cancer* is stricken from my dictionary.

I tell Athos and Aramis that, in the afternoon, I'm scheduled for a CAT scan and that there are people who had the same cancer I have who've gone on to live for four and even five more years. By now, I know everything about hepatocellular carcinomas. I'm an expert on the subject.

They're both overwhelmed; neither one seems capable of getting out a complete logical sentence. Not that I can, for that matter. We wind up playing foosball, me in a duo with the barista's pockmarked fourteen-year-old son, and we say nothing more about it. Still, the thing is right there beside us, watching us play, never once taking its eyes off me. My team wins 6 to 4—the kid is a phenomenal goalie.

That afternoon I go to take the too-long-delayed computerized axial tomography. Three very complicated words to say that a bundle of rays analyze my torso slice by slice, separating it like a package of individually wrapped Kraft American cheese.

The result is the ugliest word in the world after *war*.

It's practically a synonym for death.

Metastasis.

My lungs are riddled with metastasizing cancer.

I read it somewhere: the first metastasis of liver cancer usually develops in the lungs.

I'm a textbook case.

HOW LONG?

The main question is: how long?

How much more time do I have?

But even as I ponder this one, there is another, which seems even more pressing. How will I tell Paola? What do I say? I can't even ponder this one. It feels strange, not part of our story. I close my eyes, imagining her face when I tell her, her expression, her eyes. I can't wrap my head around it, so I leave it alone, something to worry about later.

Then come the other questions.

Among those, the one that matters most to me is: how?

How will I die?

Will I know what's happening?

Will I suffer?

Will it be agonizing?

It is only in that instant that it dawns on me that the word *agony* is even more unpleasant than the much-maligned word *death*.

I don't know why this whole nightmare is happening to me, but I do know that I need to know how long I have.

I make another appointment to see the oncologist, for whom by now I feel a childish hatred, as if he'd popped the beach ball I was playing with in the waves. At the same time I decide not to wait to know how long. I can no longer keep this to myself. I must talk with Paola.

"Meet me near the school," I tell her, keeping my voice casual, cool. "I have something to tell you."

She parks her car. She has not seen me yet. I watch her as she picks up her bag, presses the automatic lock. She is wearing a light blue dress, which brings out the blond highlights in her hair, the green flecks in her eyes. I see, as if for the first time, her long determined stride as she begin walking toward me. I go to her. She is vivid and beautiful, and I feel a sharp pang of pain. How will I tell her? What words will best express it? In the end, I decide to keep it very simple, no gilding of the lily required. We stand by her Renault Twingo, which is parked by a broken streetlight. It flickers intermittently as I find the courage to speak the words.

"I have liver cancer," I say, "and it's metastasized to my lungs."

At first she narrows her eyes and just looks at me. I don't know how to interpret her look. It's as if she thinks I'm joking, or trying to get her to forgive me sooner than she's ready to. She stares at me as I steadily gaze back at her. I'm no actor, she knows that. If anyone has that gift in our family, it's her. Finally, she lets out a long sigh. She has decided to believe me. "That fortune-teller you took me to all those years ago, remember? She didn't really know her stuff, did she, when she promised us a long and happy married life?"

I grimace. How the past has a way of coming back to haunt you when you're least expecting it.

"When did you find out?"

I tell her what I know in short, terse sentences. "Ten days ago. I've done every possible exam and analysis. Unfortunately, there is no margin for error."

The warrior woman I married decides to take an active role in my affairs. She decides to bury the hatchet then and there and go with me to see the oncologist. Even though it's quite clear that her gesture is neither an attempt at rekindling our love nor an act of forgiveness, I feel wildly optimistic. I wonder whether it's pity, or horror, or some other such ultimately negative emotion that's inspiring her actions. She has a look of sympathy on her face, which is confirmed when she asks me to come back home to sleep. I hesitate. This isn't the way I wanted to be welcomed back to the family. Paola guesses what I'm thinking and makes it clear that she definitely hasn't forgotten what happened. "Don't start getting any ideas," she says. Love, as I thought, is a long way away. With those few words, she lets me know that the only reason she's letting me come back home is that I'm sick. There's no forgiveness either, for the moment. A truce of sorts is the best way to look at it, where I am home but not reinstated. I must earn back her love. Once I have that, forgiveness will come.

I vow to learn, to understand. She will need to be healthy for us all now, especially for our children.

Paola holds my hand while the obnoxious oncologist leaves no room for optimism. He studies my CAT scan and the results of my blood test and decrees: "Signor Battistini, your neoplasm is one of the most aggressive types and, unfortunately, we caught it only at a very advanced stage. The tumor markers in your blood are at very high levels. This is the value here: the choriogonadotropin."

This is where I feel Paola's "I told you so" glare stabbing me like a thousand daggers.

"Your CAT scan shows numerous widespread metastases in your lungs."

I start to get annoyed: "Yes, I know that . . . would you get to the point."

"If the circumstances were different, I would have suggested attempting the surgical removal of the primary neoplasia from your liver, but in your condition it would really be little more than an extremely dangerous palliative. As would a liver transplant. The percentages for a successful transplant are very low; the waiting list is very long; and in your case, the metastases have already thoroughly compromised the situation. Forgive me for speaking frankly, but I think it's important to be clear on this: there is no therapy that can really help you."

Silence. I look at Paola, who lacks the strength to lift her eyes. I've had the question locked and loaded for ten minutes and I let it fly:

"How long?"

"That's a hard answer to come up with, Signor Battistini . . ."

The bastard hesitates. Goddamn it, live up to your responsibilities! I need you to tell me how long it will be before they turn out the lights around the field.

"How long?"

"We'd need to see how your—"

"How long?!"

"Four or five months," he specifies. "It depends on the resilience of your liver. And the treatment you decide to undergo."

Silence.

"Cases range widely, though," he explains; "there are some who have lived as long as five years."

" 'There are some . . .'; like how many?"

"Let us say . . . very, very few."

Very, very few. A very, very encouraging percentage.

I ask my second question.

"How long will I be healthy?"

"What do you mean by 'healthy'? You're already a sick man."

"You know exactly what I'm asking. How long will I be able to live a normal life?"

"Here too it all depends on—"

"More or less!" I drill in, aggressively.

"A little over three months. Then the dose of painkillers you'll have to take will render you insensible and the final phase will begin."

A little over three months to live. To live a real life, I mean to say. More or less.

"A hundred days," I say under my breath.

"I beg your pardon?" asks the doctor.

"I've got a hundred days left."

"I told you that it could be longer, if . . ."

I pay no attention to him. A hundred days. The number echoes through my mind.

Paola breaks in.

"Is there anything we can do to prolong the time? Anything at all?"

"Chemotherapy, Signora, can be an excellent aid in blocking the proliferation of pathogenic cells," he explains. "But it has countless side effects that make everyday life quite complicated."

I tune back in to the medical consultation still under way.

"What kind of side effects are we talking about?"

I know perfectly well that chemo makes your hair fall out, gives you nausea, makes you vomit, and leaves you exhausted. Everyone knows it—we've all seen it in lots of documentaries and movies. And nearly everyone has had some secondhand experience of it from watching the slow demise of a grandparent or an uncle or aunt. But the truth is very different and much worse.

"Chemotherapy, Signor Battistini, isn't a very sharp tool. It kills healthy cells as well. In effect, it is a poison we inject into the body in order to kill the main enemy, but on the way to its objective, it causes a bloodbath. There are many more side effects than you may know about. There are cases of anemia, digestive problems, loss of appetite and alteration of taste perceptions, fever, coughing, sore throat, head-aches, muscle pains, jangled nerves, hearing loss, loss of sexual appe-tite, and problems with fertility."

Is that all?

If I do nothing, I'll die in a few months, with the assistance of kindly medicines to keep me from suffering in my last few days. If I subject myself to the best known type of cancer treatment, I'll die all the same, though probably later; however, in the meanwhile I'll be transformed: I'll no longer be Lucio Battistini but a 220-pound ghost, stunned and languishing on a sofa, confined to endless hours of channel surfing.

The oncologist asks me if I want to start the first round of chemotherapy. I say nothing. Very simply, I don't know.

At the door, I hug Paola good-bye and head off toward the pastry shop to get my few possessions. I'll catch up with her later at home to eat dinner with the kids.

Lorenzo and Eva.

The mere sound of their names is enough to make me want to cry.

I try not to think about it. Not now.

My father-in-law says nothing as he sits listening to my report on the appointment. I summarize: I have a hundred days left to live. A few days more, a few days less. Then what the oncologist calls the final phase will set in, and I don't even want to imagine what that will be like.

The question that Oscar asks me is horrifying but legitimate: "So how do you want to spend these hundred days?"

Another question I have no answer to.

A hundred days.

That's a very long time for a vacation.

There are only a very lucky few who've taken a vacation that lasted a hundred days.

Too bad we're not talking about a vacation.

A hundred days.

I've never thought about it.

No one's ever thought about it.

What would you do if you had only a hundred days left to live?

Long pause.

Let me repeat the question.

What would you do if you had only a hundred days left to live?

Let me offer some suggestions.

Would you get up and go to work or to school tomorrow morning?

Would you spend every minute of your day having sex with the one you love?

Would you sell everything you own and move to a tropical island?

Would you pray to the God you worship?

Would you pray to a God you've never believed in?

Would you scream as long as there was a breath left in your body?

Would you lie there staring endlessly at the ceiling, hoping for it to collapse and crush you?

I'm going to leave a couple of pages blank, for you to jot down your notes. Scribble in it, be my guest, I won't be offended.

My biological clock wakes me up at four in the morning.

Paola's asleep. She's let me back into the big bed, but no physical contact.

A hundred days.

It's the first thing to come into my head.

A hundred days.

A couple days more, a couple days less. A statistical detail.

That's quite a few days. It's 2,400 hours, and I'm going to waste about 800 of those hours sleeping.

It's 8,640,000 seconds. Eight million. If you put it in seconds, it seems like a long, long time.

But a hundred days sounds a lot more cheerful. Sounds sort of easygoing and adolescent.

"A hundred days until your final exams at high school."

What a great time that was. I went around town dressed up for Carnevale (it goes without saying that I was always dressed as one of the three musketeers) carrying a shoe box with a slot cut into it, begging for spare change. Then the whole class would enjoy a pizza buffet, paid for by generous passersby moved to pity by their memories of the old days when the tables were turned.

Back then, it was a hundred days until the beginning of my future.

A hundred days.

I go to my desk, I dig all the way to the back of a drawer, and I find an old lined school notebook. On the cover is Dino Zoff, captain of the Italian national soccer team, lifting the World Cup trophy above his head. A crude color drawing—not even a photograph. I got that notebook in 1982—I traded it for an album of soccer cards, almost complete with all the players. I think I made a not-very-smart bargain. I was nine years old. I never had the nerve to write in it. It always seemed to me like a collectible that, with the passing years, would become rare and invaluable.

I open the cover and number the pages by hand.

From a hundred to zero.

I can't remember the last time I wrote with a pen. I realize that the only thing I know how to write by now is my own signature. Nobody jots down numbers anymore, they punch them into their phones. I've regressed to the point of becoming an illiterate once again. I try to write phrases chosen at random, picked out of a newspaper lying on the desk. My handwriting is embarrassing, resembling the cuneiform-like chicken scratches of a doctor.

Maybe I'll keep a diary.

Or maybe I won't.

What good does it do to keep a diary?

Aside from Anne Frank and Bridget Jones, I can't think of a single memorable diary. Who knows how many literary masterpieces lie concealed in the notebooks and Lisa Frank desk diaries filled with ink by fifteen-year-old girls who, statistically speaking, are the most "diaryish" demographic category. Women are more interested in diaries than men. I have no idea why.

I've never kept a diary.

I put the tip of my pen down on the paper.

I stop and think.

All right—the things I'd like to do in the hundred days remaining to me.

Suddenly, I can't write.

A classic case of writer's block, or blank-page syndrome.

I look at the ballpoint pen in my hand. A dark blue Bic. One of the new model pens, with a grip.

I can't resist.

So I Google it.

"Who invented the ballpoint pen?"

The ballpoint pen, also known in many countries as a Biro, is named after its inventor, the Hungarian editor and journalist László Bíró, who came up with the idea in 1938. The story has it that he first saw how it might work while watching a crowd of kids playing boccie ball in a street dotted with puddles. The balls left wet trails as they rolled along the dry sections of road surface. In just a few years, given the reliability of the product, simplicity of use, and affordability, the Biro, or ballpoint pen, replaced fountain pens. Today it's safe to say that it's the most widespread invention of all time, after the wheel. There's at least one in every home around the world. Too bad that poor Bíró, who was penurious at best, decided to sell the patent to the American Parker company, which as you know definitely spent that money wisely.

But who *really* invented the ballpoint pen?

Who was the first person to design one, nearly five hundred years before Bíró's flash of invention?

The answer is obvious. Unsurprising. Taken for granted.

Leonardo da Vinci.

Do you think for a second that the Gyro Gearloose of Renaissance Tuscany would miss out on one of the most important inventions of all time? Please.

It was definitely the egghead born in Vinci who created the first design for a ballpoint pen. The plan, found in one of his codices, consisted of a simple tube that narrowed toward the tip with a series of grooves that allowed the ink to flow to the ball that closed off the end of the little pipe, making it possible to write.

I'm sorry to tell you, Bíró, my good man, but you came in second.

*　　*　　*

I figure out the first thing I want to do in the next hundred days.

I want to ignore my buddy Fritz.

I get dressed and head for the gym as if this were any ordinary day. I don't even wait for Paola to wake up. I wouldn't know what to say to her. I hate seeing that disoriented, slightly frightened look on her face. I pass by my father-in-law's pastry shop. I'm a couple of hours ahead of schedule. My morning doughnut is still warm. I sit down at the café table and watch the shops opening for business. I've never been here this early. Life at six o'clock in the morning is a different one from eight o'clock. Aside from my friend the sparrow, who lands next to my plate. He looks at me. If the bird could speak Italian, he'd ask me: "What are you doing here so early? Everything okay?"

And I'd answer, though I'd be lying: "Everything's fine. How about you?"

"I have some trouble at home, my girlfriend lost her job and we have four little mouths to feed still in the nest. Do you mind if I take a piece of doughnut?"

"Be my guest."

With his beak, the bird breaks off a slightly darker chunk and swallows it.

"What kind of work did your girlfriend do?" I ask, my curiosity piqued.

"She kept a retired widowed dentist company, in Prati. They had a standing date on the banks of the Tiber, where the guy used to go for a walk every morning. They'd share breakfast, more or less like you and me."

"And then what happened?"

"The old man got himself a nineteen-year-old Ukrainian girl-friend, and now they eat breakfast at home. My wife was out of work, from one day to the next."

"I'm sorry to hear that—"

"That's life. Can I have another piece? I'll take it to the little ones."

"Go right ahead."

The bird breaks off a bigger piece than usual, gives me a grateful look, and flies off, flitting elegantly around the corner.

I finish the doughnut. I lick the sugar off my lips. I shout a farewell to Oscar, who's busy at his work, and I head off to the gym.

In my pocket is my Dino Zoff notebook.

It's still blank.

I 've already wasted one day.

I don't know why but having a precise countdown helps to keep me from slipping into complete apathy. Actually, it's only a statistical sentence and today I can't quite picture what will happen after day zero. No one can ever imagine his or her own death. In fact, we refuse even to accept the possibility of it. We're all positive that an exception will be made for us.

I go out and get into my station wagon. I don't like my car.

Your cars tend to match the seasons of your life in a fairly symbolic way: first you use your father's car to learn to drive in (in my case, Grandpa's Renault 4, the most wonderful automobile ever made); then you buy a slightly sporty used car, if possible with all-wheel drive; then you get a girlfriend and you buy a comfortable compact car with a slightly bigger trunk for romantic weekend trips; then when you get married and have children, you switch to a station wagon, the absolute bottom of the barrel in terms of automotive morale. I've reached that phase, but I'm afraid I won't live to see the last two: when you're in your fifties and you buy a used Porsche to fool yourself into thinking you're a pampered twenty-year-old playboy, and then, when you're in your late sixties, you buy the same car you learned to drive in, only now it's a costly vintage model, so you get behind the wheel with your heart in your throat, and you discover that it lacks power steering, that it accelerates like a cow running a mountain Grand Prix, that it has no car radio, no GPS, no air-conditioning, no power windows, that it gets the mileage of a semi-trailer, that smoke pours out the tailpipe like a steam locomotive, and that the springs in the seats do their best to shatter your spinal cord with every pothole you hit. You take it for a spin and then you garage it for good. Luckily, I'm going to avoid this automotive disaster. I realize that I can't seem to think about anything but the past and the future. It's as if the present has lost all meaning to me. But actually it's the past and the future that don't exist, and the present really is the only thing I have left. Still, there's nothing I can do about it—my neurons go back and forth in time, navigating memories and imagination like silver balls in an out-of-control pinball machine. I let them have their way, without trying to shake or jolt the machine too much: if my brain gets a "tilt" warning, it's all over for me. I let my thoughts bob in the swimming pool of my life, free to drift where they will. I'm not especially lucid these days. I don't have brain cancer, but my mind is crashing like an old computer. If you look closely, you can actually see the old blinking bomb symbol: SYSTEM ERROR.

Every day I think I'm going to wake up and discover that this has all been nothing but a long, well-made, and very detailed nightmare caused by green peppers (which is why it is a very dangerous food to eat at dinner), but once again, that's not what happens.

I park my station wagon with care. They've already written me three parking tickets here in Trastevere; I think the traffic cop must have it in for me. I make my usual stopover in the pastry shop; I chat for a while with my father-in-law, though I make no mention of my buddy Fritz; I eat my beloved doughnut; my friend the sparrow is in a particularly good mood today; and then I proceed along the familiar route to the gym.

I know every crack and pothole in the sidewalk and every flower-bed along the way. I already know where a dog will bark at me and through which open windows I'll hear shouting voices. I try to think of the things I want to do in the next ninety-nine days. There's only one that comes to mind, but it's a very important one: make peace with Paola.

I take out my Zoff notebook. It's blank. I open it, smooth the page. Then I write my first words: Make peace with Paola.

Make peace with Paola.

Then I cross it out and rewrite it:

Get Paola to forgive me.

That's more accurate.

I get to the gym and am greeted by the sight of my morning "class," six fatching women in their early forties. That's not a typo, they truly are fat-ching, and I think I've conveyed the idea. They are a half-dozen office workers, prosperous physically if not financially, poured into hot-pink workout garb, and before they start their working day they come by the gym for my renowned legs-abs-ass class. They've long since resigned themselves to the fact that they can't have a personal trainer like the ones they see on TV, and have to settle for a chubby but amiable ex-athlete. I think they even find me sort of sexy. I admire them for the determination they show in fighting their own personal war against the passage of time. They sweat and they never give up. The results are never astounding, but their commitment is praiseworthy. Some of them even make it clear that, if I were interested . . . , but I think I've caused enough trouble with that. I focus with Michelangelo-esque concentration on sculpting their butts. This morning it dawns on me, practically in the blink of an eye, that the work I do is perhaps even less attractive than my station wagon. The only gratification I get from my work is the 1,600 euros I earn each month, but aside from that, I shove sweaty backs as they struggle against the rust in their joints and the general force of gravity; I fill out exercise plans that will never be implemented; I talk and talk about carb-free diets and inside gymnasium gossip. A classic variety of socially useful productive work.

I go to the office of the gym's manager, Ernesto Berruti, a sunlamped, steroid-pumped former bodybuilder who does nothing but uselessly take up space and oxygen here on earth, and I tell him that, at the end of the month, I'm going to end my working relationship with the glorious Rainbow Gym. He does his best to persuade me to change my mind, offering me a raise of thirty-eight euros a month (before taxes). He's a fine observer of psychological subtleties. I look at the faux-Maori tattoos on his biceps, his long gray hair (I would suggest a law prohibiting long hair if you're over forty and you have a devastating bald spot), and the tight-fitting Iron Maiden T-shirt that was already out of fashion twenty years ago. I've always detested him. Now I see him clearly. Two hundred and thirty pounds of classic Roman thug. He sells soft drugs in the neighborhood; he's the two-bit boss of a square of urban territory that runs from Porta Portese to the banks of the Tiber. Until today I've pretended to see no evil, hear no evil, speak no evil. But today I can't hold it in.

"So do you like working in this cellar office?"

He doesn't understand.

"What I mean is, when you were a little boy, did you write class compositions that read, in part: 'When I grow up I want to be the tawdry manager of a dingy gym in Monteverde?'"

He starts to suspect I might be trying to insult him. I redouble my efforts.

"Don't you see you're a stock character straight out of a small-time Roman version of the commedia dell'arte?"

At this point, I've lost him; I've overdone it with the learned references. So I lower my sights.

"You always wear the same T-shirts a size too small; you wear a ponytail, which is forbidden by EU regulations as an assault on the common sense of aesthetics; you speak an Italian that we might charitably call creative, riddled as it is with grammatical errors that defy imagination; you stuff yourself with pharmaceuticals that are bound to make you impotent in the course of a few years; and when someone asks you a question, you take so long to reply that people usually have to ask you twice!"

"What are you saying, that I'm impotent?" my employer blurts out. "What the hell are you thinking?"

The only word he understood was "impotent." I overestimated his capacity to appreciate insults.

"No," I say, "I just wanted to let you know that I've changed my mind. I'm not going to wait for the end of the month. So long, best to everyone, and thanks very much."

I head for my locker with the stride of someone who's knocked out his opponent in the last round, just when he was about to lose on points.

He shouts after me: "You loser! Get your things, get out of here, and go fuck yourself!"

An elegantly refined way of telling me that I'm fired. It's a question of how you look at it: as far as I'm concerned, I'm the one who quit. I just can't take this odor of sweat, chlorine, and Lysol anymore.

Sometimes real troubles give you a strength you never had before. When I walk out with my gym bag thrown over my shoulder, the receptionist looks at me with something like respect for the very first time. Today I'm her personal hero. I get to leave, and she has to stay behind bars. Sooner or later, I hope she'll find a way to break out.

I go back to get my car. She's surprised to see me back so soon. I smile at her and take her to the car wash. She, too, should get some enjoyment out of the day. As I wait for the rotating brushes to do their work, I reread the phrase I wrote in my notebook.

Get Paola to forgive me.

don't believe in God.

Any God, of any religion.

I hate religions. They're useless; in fact, they're counterproductive. No evolved society can allow itself to be held in slavery to ancient superstitions.

I've been baptized, I've received both communion and confirmation, but out of convention, certainly not conviction. A few years ago, I even looked into having myself unbaptized. I found out it was simple enough: all you need to do is have a notation of your decision put on the register of the parish church where your first Catholic sacrament was officiated. And once you've been unbaptized, you automatically nullify all the subsequent sacraments. But I never did get around to it, out of laziness.

Religion never counted for much in my life. At least until now. Right now any faith of any kind, even some secondary religion, however subordinate and ramshackle it might be, would certainly come in handy. Faith really helps to keep a person company. In that way, it's even better than a Labrador retriever. But fate didn't give me that gift. I'm not a believer. But I'm not an atheist either: I'm an agnostic, and as the dictionary tells us, that means I don't ask questions that I know cannot be answered in any reasonable way. It would be like trying to solve an equation with too many unknown factors. My old friend Leonardo da Vinci was an agnostic too, but back then the terminology ran more toward words like *misbeliever* or *heretic*. He mostly kept his opinions to himself to avoid winding up tied to one of those uncomfortable stakes surrounded by roaring flames and an angry mob, or seeing all his commissions for sacred art vanish, which would leave him without a livelihood. Throughout his writings, he had little good to say about the Catholic Church, priests, or religions in general. I'm in excellent company.

Lorenzo and Eva are still going to school every day—it's still a month and a half until summer vacation. Paola is likewise very busy with her classes, the way she always is at the end of April, which marks the start of that finals rush, which will culminate in being either held back or promoted to the next year's class.

I still haven't told her that I quit my job. We don't talk much. This is a bad time—there's no point in trying to pretend otherwise. Sleeping with us in our big bed is a complicated mixture of regret, resentment, affection, irritation, and awkwardness. We're never together alone. I really don't know what I can do to achieve my first and, for now, sole objective.

There's nothing special about losing a game against the top-ranked team. Nothing special and nothing surprising. But there are times when you can even celebrate a loss. Today my Gang That Couldn't Shoot Straight was beaten 8 to 6 by the best team in the league, the terrifying Real Tufello, a sort of underwater death squad. Right up until two minutes before the final whistle, we were holding steady at 6-all, going head to head with the unquestioned dominating team of the championship games. Just seven days from the final, the opposition remains undefeated as they sail smoothly toward their automatic promotion to the next series up. In contrast, we're just fighting to make it into the postseason playoffs, games that will take a few teams into the quarterfinals. Right now we're ranked twelfth, so there's still a whisper of hope in the air. We need to keep playing the way we did today and fight like there's no tomorrow.

Fight like there's no tomorrow. That's what my first coach, an ex–center defender who resembled the actor Bud Spencer but without a beard and an endearing Lucanian accent, always used to say.

"Remember, guys, it's not over till it's over."

Simple but true. God how I hate it when you are five goals behind just a minute from the end and it would take a miracle to turn the tables. Still, miracles do happen in sports. But they don't in real life. In spite of all the promotional efforts of the Catholic Church and the unbridled proliferation of blessed saints, there has never been a single scientifically recognized miracle. I'm going to be the exception that proves the rule. And they'll have to reference me in all the textbooks on medicine, religion, and magic: "Miracles don't happen, with the sole exception of a certain Lucio Battistini, who actually recovered from a hepatocellular carcinoma with extensive advanced-stage pulmonary metastasis."

In the Dino Zoff notebook, I scratch out "Get Paola to forgive me." I'm still going to do that. But I'll do it later. Right now, there's something more important I need to do.

The most important thing a person in my situation needs to do.

I write:

Don't give up.

The only doctor I'm comfortable talking to is Umberto. The location is our favorite little café. The prevailing mood is black. The subject of conversation is chemotherapy. I've read extensively on the controversial topic and I can't seem to come to an opinion that would allow me to make an informed choice.

"By now it's pretty much accepted wisdom," Umberto begins, "that the benefits of chemo are insufficient to outweigh the contraindications. Chemo is devastating and debilitating in physical terms and to the immune system of the organism being treated, in my opinion. It's as if, in order to remove a hangnail from your big toe, we decided to blast it with a shotgun. The hangnail would be gone. But so would the whole foot. I never advise my patients, or I guess I should say their owners, to undertake chemo. The only sure thing is that the animal they know and love, whether it's a dog, a cat, or a rabbit, will never be the same, it'll just lie there listless on the sofa, uninterested in eating or running around. Alive, but already dead."

"But I feel all right, I can take it. The rest of my body is healthy," I retort with a decisiveness that's not like me.

"You think you feel all right, my friend, but the truth is that your blood tests are all over the place. The cancer is progressing vigorously."

"Tomorrow afternoon I've got another CAT scan scheduled."

"But you just got one two weeks ago!"

"Maybe it was wrong."

"You can't just go on getting CAT scans, those are X-rays. They're not particularly good for you."

I refuse to listen to advice. My stubborn, overconfident brain is hoping to show that it's all been a mistake, a spectacular oversight. "Signor Battistini, we hope you'll accept my apologies and those of the lab. For the past two months we've repeatedly gotten your tests completely wrong. You're actually healthy as a horse. Please accept this briefcase which contains one million euros in cash as our way of saying how sorry we are."

Umberto keeps after me: "Do you want to start the chemo, or try some other form of treatment—what do you want to do?"

"I don't know . . . ," I reply, sounding like a boxer who's just been stunned by a sudden right hook.

The first side effect of cancer, as I understand it, is a dimming of the brain function. I want to react but I can't seem to organize a logical defense.

"What would you do?" I ask Umberto, hopefully.

"I'm a friend of yours, and a doctor shouldn't be his patient's friend."

"I understand, and that's fine, but what would you do?" I insist. I need someone else to decide for me.

"Let's wait for the results of the new CAT scan, then let's check in with an oncologist."

"I hate oncologists."

"I'll bet you do, but all I can do is offer my advice; I can't be your primary consulting physician. Remember, I'm a veterinarian and I specialize in exotic animals."

"What are you doing tonight?" I ask, ignoring every point he's trying to make.

"I'm going out with a woman dentist from Prati. Second date."

"Have you taken her to bed yet?"

"No. I was hoping that might happen tonight."

"Cancel. Dentists are boring in bed. Let's go get a pizza with Corrado."

When I fire off these dictatorial commands, Umberto invariably folds.

"Sorry to disappoint you, but tonight Corrado is in Tokyo; he'll be back the day after tomorrow. If you can do without him, we could go, just the two of us."

I've already changed my mind. We terminally ill patients can afford to be unpredictable.

"Oh well, that doesn't matter, enjoy your dentist, I'm going to the movies to see the latest from Woody Allen."

"It hasn't come out yet."

I'm batting zero today.

"Then I'll go home instead."

"Speaking of which, how are things with Paola?"

"Not well. She speaks to me in monosyllables."

"Well, in a way, that's what you deserve."

"No, please, no lectures tonight. Come on, thanks for seeing me. What do I owe you, Doctor?"

"The usual fee for large animals is a hundred euros."

"Idiot."

"Speak for yourself."

When we argue, we regress to elementary school in a flash.

I slap him on the back and say good-bye, then head for the door. He stops me to ask a question, and I know that it's been on the tip of his tongue for the past few minutes: "Why did you say that dentists are boring in bed? Have you slept with one? Maybe it was just her; maybe dentists aren't all boring."

"I've never taken a dentist to bed. It's just a figure of speech. You must have heard it: 'as boring as a dentist in bed.' People say it all the time."

"Who says it? Which people? I've never heard anyone say it."

"All the people who've ever taken a dentist to bed! They all say it."

I leave the café, abandoning him to his doubts and sticking him with the check.

I go back home and play with the kids for a couple of hours, under the watchful gaze of Shepherd. It's the only therapy that really does me any good.

"I quit my job."

I can't see Paola's face because she's in the shower, but I can imagine it perfectly.

I lie on the bed in silence for three minutes. Then my wife, wrapped in a bathrobe, appears in the bathroom door. With the light behind her, I can't see the look on her face. But I can imagine it, too perfectly.

"Which job?"

"The only one that gives me a paycheck, if that's the subtext," I reply.

"That is, you're going to go on coaching for free, but you decided to give up your salary from the gym?"

"Precisely."

"If you don't mind my asking, why would you do that when you know perfectly well that we barely make it to the end of each month?"

I could deliver a lecture on "the invalid's psychology," but I know I'd bore even myself to tears.

"I've decided that for the next little while I'm only going to do what I feel like doing. It strikes me as the only decision that has any meaning."

"That has any meaning for you."

"Are you looking for a fight? Let me warn you that I come pre-irritated, so I'd recommend against trying to set me off."

"Who's trying to set you off? You just told me how it was. Period."

"It wasn't done intentionally. It just came out that way."

"Okay, okay, don't get angry. . . . How do you feel today?"

"Thank you for asking. Aside from the fact that there's a constant pain in my gut, that I'm having a hard time breathing, and that I'm in a lousy mood, I'd say pretty good."

"Shall we go get a second opinion, see another oncologist?"

I knew she'd say it sooner or later. It's called the medical spiral, that is, consulting a series of doctors, each of whom gives you diametrically opposing diagnoses and treatments. It's a spiral you can't escape, like one of those M. C. Escher staircases.

Almost every family on earth has dealt with the pointlessness and humiliation of the medical spiral. It's a round robin of treatments that puts money in the pockets of private clinics and leads the patient by the hand into the afterlife, but only after emptying his pockets. I'm not falling for that. I promise.

"This afternoon I'm having another CAT scan. Then we can decide," I say, in the plural to make it clear to her that the importance of acting as a couple is still fundamental to me. Paola says nothing. I don't know how to make her feel better when I'm feeling so miserable myself. So I say nothing.

I take out the Dino Zoff notebook and I write in red ink:

Get Paola to forgive me.

I'm going to have two chief objectives. If I manage to beat the cancer but Paola won't forgive me, I'm a dead man anyway.

I've just received the results from the new CAT scan.

I don't have the nerve to open them.

I go out.

I decide to go see my friend Roberto, a bookseller. Well, maybe friend is too strong a word. Acquaintance. A close acquaintance. I haven't been to see him in months, because I've been too busy with the countless troubles you've been hearing about.

Roberto, looking good at age fifty-five, has a little shop selling books and graphic novels in a small street around the corner from Campo de' Fiori. A hole in the wall, a dusty picture window where you can see the latest bestsellers on display, from Giorgio Faletti to Dan Brown, side by side with classics in dated, yellowed versions. Over the years, with his help, I've managed to complete my collection of Diabolik comic books, my favorite. He sells everything at cover price. Even if the books were printed fifty years ago, and the cover price is 150 lire, Roberto converts the price to euros—say, 25 cents—and gives you exact change, down to the last penny. Best of all, in a corner there's a shelf with a few very special books. These are novels that Roberto has written over the past thirty years, between one customer and the next. There are dozens of them. Every one of them spiral-bound, each individually typewritten. Every book is a unique copy. Fixed price: 20 euros. If he sells one, the contents are gone forever. The first time he told me, I was positive he was just kidding me.

"Wait, really? You write novels and give them away without even photocopying them?"

"Why on earth should I copy them?"

"Well, I don't know . . . so you don't lose them for good? To make a little more money on them?"

"Who cares! I was happy while I wrote them. I was elsewhere. The twenty euros is just to cover costs, to pay for paper and type-writer ribbon."

It struck me as an incredibly poetic folly. Writing for the pleasure of writing, without dreams of glory, hopes of bestsellers or literary prizes.

Today I leaf through one with a blue cover, an adventure story in the style of Jules Verne. Then I look at another one, a bodice ripper set against the background of the First World War, like something the Italian romance novelist Liala might have written. In his career, Roberto has worked in every style, depending on his mood and his whims. Books that no one's every heard of, books that will never become classics. They've only been perused by a select group of his personal customers who've been lucky enough to buy them. I bought a few, over the years, about a dozen, and I always enjoyed them enormously. They're nothing special—let's be clear about it—but they're enjoyable reads, and in any case, the magic of reading (and owning) the only copy of a novel is priceless.

I sit there listening to the clickety-clack of his Olivetti typewriter for several minutes, as enchanted as if I were watching Chopin performing live. Then I preorder his next bestseller. The entire print run sells out in less than a second, a spectacular success.

After the walk I go back home and finally open the results of my test, out of Paola's sight.

*   *   *

Bad news.

Very bad news.

The cancer is metastasizing giddily, slowly consuming me. I look at the little black dots inside me and an inappropriate smile appears on my face. It strikes me that my lungs resemble a connect-the-dots game. Perhaps the disease is affecting my sense of humor, making it even unfunnier than it already is.

"I was thinking about whether or not to do chemo. Just one round, to see. What do you think?" I ask Paola point-blank, as she's draining the spaghetti.

"What made you change your mind?"

"I don't know. I can't just do nothing."

"Do you remember Gigi's father?"

Gigi, short for Gianluigi, is a close friend of Paola's, a well-known enologist, whose father died of colon cancer a couple of years ago. Gigi's dad was a renowned television anchorman, though toward the end he was reduced to doing shows for a local home shopping network. An energetic man with a sense of humor, a tornado of enthusiasm. We watched him flicker and dwindle before our eyes, as if the chemo were sucking the power out of his batteries. When he died, he looked nothing like the smiling television personality who won over the housewives of Italy in the seventies.

"That's not the right example," I argue with determination, "Gigi's dad was over seventy, he was a drinker, a smoker, and his body was already sorely tested by years of bad living. I'm an athlete. Or close to it. Crap, that's completely different, isn't it?"

"Don't swear when the kids are home."

"They know more curse words than I do. Lorenzo could teach a master class on profanity."

"Of course, he learned them all from you," she accuses me.

"Darling, he hears them everywhere, even on television; trying to avoid curse words is like trying to dodge raindrops during a thunderstorm. Come on, give me a break."

"You always have an excuse for everything."

Our arguments have no real objective. Suddenly the topic of discussion focuses on a marginal detail and the fire blazes out of control, unstoppable.

Luckily, Paola has also invented the antidote that blocks the sequence of angry retorts. She suddenly places both hands on her head, as if they were ears, and says: "I'm a cat, I don't speak your language." It always makes me laugh. A brilliant technique that undercuts all and any bellicose feelings. Too bad that, ever since she found out about what happened with Signora Moroni, she's stopped using it. Our disagreements have regularly turned into outright quarrels and even shouting matches; a couple of times there was even the crash of breaking plates. We're setting a fine example for the kids. Each of us, lately, has had his or her own reasons to be tense, and the outcome has been inevitable.

This time, I'm the one to break off the argument. I go outside and call my oncologist.

"I've made up my mind. I'll start the chemo."

My own dog doesn't like me. At all.

I don't how such a thing could be, but Shepherd has never been able to stand me. When Paola, Lorenzo, and Eva come home, he's just one big ball of wagging tail and wriggling, prancing joy. When I get home from work, he doesn't even look up from the sofa where he's sleeping. And to think that I was the one who saved him from the pound; I'm the one who always walks him for the least appealing bathroom runs, the ones in the early morning and late at night. Even when I fill his dog bowl (with, among other things, superchic, free-range chicken with vegetables purchased from a trusted local farmer), he ignores me; he never gratifies me with a raised paw, a happy bark, a wet nose. Nothing. For Shepherd I'm a perfect stranger who lives in his home and performs services for him. A butler, no, really a human slave. If you ask me, he also believes that if you go down to city hall, you'll find him registered as the legitimate owner of this apartment. The master of the house, Paola's official husband, and the biological father of the two children. I'm nothing but a miserable servant, tolerated because I'm useful, but held at arm's length.

But ever since I've fallen sick, Shepherd has a changed attitude toward me. Every so often he comes over and cuddles next to me on the couch, rubbing against me like a cat, waking me up in bed with a well placed slap of the tongue. It's as if a doggy sixth sense told him that my "slavery" was about to come to an end. And only then did he realize how fundamental I am to his day-to-day existence. This morning he looked up at me, his eyes fixed straight at me. He looked me in the eye as if he were trying to communicate.

"I understand that you're about to leave, and after all is said and done, I'm kind of sorry about that. You're not the best slave in the world—you tend to yank on the leash too much when I'm trying to hook up with those cute Fifis in the park; you put too much oil in the rice; you don't wash my blanket often enough; and you never buy me those squeaky rubber balls that I love so much—but still, you're not all that bad. You make me laugh, especially when you pretend that you're the alpha dog in our home—that would actually be me—and when you play with my little ones or try to come on to my woman, Paola. In the five years we've lived together, I've thought more than once about abandoning you by the highway, but then I realized that Lorenzo and Eva would miss you, so I decided they could keep you. Now I can see that you're sick. Do you want me to have you put down, the way a guy I know once did with his horse?"

The telepathic phrase hits me like a fist to the face.

"Do you want me to have you put down?"

"Put down" is a nice euphemism. We seem to feel shy about saying "Mario killed his sick horse," and prefer something like "He had to have the horse put down."

I look at Shepherd, who never takes his eyes off me, and I smile at him. He ignores me and walks off, as if to say: "Now don't start overstepping your bounds, human slave!"

His discreet affection and his thoughts have both done me a world of good.

If I were a horse, they'd already have had me put down.

That's what I call seeing the glass half full.

I went to the airport to give Corrado a ride home. He showed up with a spectacular flight attendant who must have spent the nights in Japan with him. He returns from every trip with a different victim. But he's not happy. I can see it in his eyes.

We stop for seafood at the restaurant Incannucciata, in the town of Fiumicino. It's our little tradition—we have lunch there at least once a year. Just the two of us, without Umberto. I tell him about my impending appointment for the round of chemotherapy; he tells me about the moment when the seductive stewardess I saw earlier at the airport revealed the fact that she was pregnant.

"Who's the father?"

"What's that supposed to mean? I'm the father. We were having dinner at the hotel from *Lost in Translation*. Do you remember it?"

"Sure, the world's most boring movie, but a great ending. Go on."

"The best sushi I've ever eaten in my life. And forget about the tempura: it melts in your mouth."

"Enough gratuitous description, get to the point."

"We were almost done eating when she says to me, without any particular emphasis: 'I'm pregnant.'"

"What did you do?"

"I choked on the tempura and took a good ten years off my life expectancy. Then I asked her the same question you asked me: 'Who's the father?' And she said: 'What's that supposed to mean? You're the father!' At that point, my heart goes into fibrillation and I ask for the check, which was expensive enough to give me another heart attack."

"So, you're about to become a father?"

"Let me finish. So we talk for two hours about where to have the baby, where we're going to live, the idea of her asking to be transferred to ground duty so she won't have to travel. I say practically nothing the whole time, I'm practically in a coma from the news."

"But do you like this stewardess, yes or no?"

"You've seen her yourself. She's Miss Mondo Alitalia, the dream of every Alitalia pilot, and she's smart as a whip. The only problem is she's out of her mind."

"So you're kindred spirits."

"I'm going to pretend I didn't hear that. The next morning, at breakfast, she tells me it was all just a joke and she wanted to see how I'd react to the possibility of becoming a father."

"Funny girl."

"Sort of. Luckily I didn't call my mother and tell her she was going to be a grandmother. When I told her it was a false alarm, she would have thrown herself off the balcony. Let's order a double *fritto misto*. The sky's the limit today."

"And you want to know the funny thing?" he goes on. "I was stunned by the news, true, but not sorry about it. Just a year ago I would have hightailed it to the airport and caught the first flight for Australia."

"That strikes me as very good news. It means that Aramis is growing up."

He smiles.

"Don't let word get out," he whispers, "or you'll ruin my reputation. You want to know something I've never told you before? I don't envy you at all, except for Lorenzo and Eva. When I see you with them, I always think that you were smarter than me."

I smile back.

"Soon you'll find a Paola for you too."

One of my fondest wishes is to see my friends settle down. No, settle down is an old-fashioned, inaccurate term. The words I want are *at peace*. That's right, I've never seen them at peace. Umberto is always the victim of his introverted and sometimes excessively polite personality, while Corrado is always hurrying off in pursuit of his next amorous conquest. So different and yet so similar in their disquiet. I realize that right here, right now, our friendship has just been given an upgrade. Corrado let the mask slip a little. He let me in. We're no longer just friends. We're brothers.

I hate needles. Not all needles, I like pine needles just fine, but I hate needles when someone sticks them into me. Vaccinations, that's what Grandma used to call them. I have never enjoyed having blood drawn, or getting shots, or even the minor intramuscular injections with antibiotics.

The chemotherapy prescribed for me by my odious oncologist is administered through an IV. Ten minutes, no more, sitting in a small room, hooked up to a bottle and a tube. A cocktail of chemical substances that bursts into my veins and lays waste to all forms of life, wanted and unwanted. I imagine what's happening to me like that old movie by Joe Dante, *Innerspace,* in which a miniaturized undersea vehicle is injected into Martin Short by mistake. The vehicle navigating through my veins makes no noise and doesn't communicate with the outside world. I lay my head back on the armchair in the little room and close my eyes.

Ten minutes with a needle in your vein is an endless amount of time. Thoughts tend to wander. I disconnect from the real world. And I wind up in a dream world that I know very well.

"Who did it?"

Stromboli's voice thundered throughout the wagon, echoing off the dozens of puppets that dangled, silent and motionless, from hooks along both walls.

Stromboli strode forward, bumping against them as he went, knocking Harlequin against the wall. The big man planted himself arrogantly at the center of his puppet kingdom.

"Come on, who was it?" he said, rolling his glinting fiery eyes around the wagon.

Harlequin slowly swung to a halt and held his breath. All the other puppets exchanged quizzical glances, doing their best not to attract attention.

Stromboli angrily waved one hand in the air, clutching an enormous leg of roast mutton.

"Who took a bite of this? If the guilty party willingly confesses . . . I won't do nothing to 'im . . ."

"Sure, sure . . . ," Pulcinella thought silently, "as if we didn't know you better than that . . ."

"Ain't you figured out that your thoughts are my thoughts, after all I made you . . . you're just sticks of wood fitted together . . . you ain't got thoughts of your own . . . you get it, Pulcinella?"

With those words he leaned down toward Harlequin's face until his beard brushed it, while with his left hand he wiped away an oily, greasy stain from the corner of the painted mouth.

"I hadn't even tasted that leg of mutton yet!" he said, staring the puppet right in its brown painted eyes.

"I was hungry . . . ," murmured the brightly colored marionette, in a faint voice with a thick Venetian accent.

The other puppets exchanged stares of astonishment: Harlequin was speaking!

"I knew it . . . ," said Stromboli, taking the marionette down and laying it on a steamer trunk. . . . "I knew it was you . . . what'd you think, that I didn't notice that when I was out you liked to go for a stroll?"

Harlequin hung motionless, folded up and tangled in his strings.

"And now what are you doing? Cat got your tongue? My friends . . .

maybe the time for puppets is over and just maybe . . . the time for puppeteers is over too. You, Harlequin, you're just the first . . . I've already figured it out . . . one by one you're all going to leave me . . . *ah-ah-chooo* . . . damned cold . . . ever since I first sneezed with that Pinocchio I haven't stopped sneezing . . . am I getting old? What do you think, oh Harlequin my friend?"

Harlequin shook his head no.

"When I saw that bite taken out of the leg of mutton I already understood it was all over . . . maybe I should put the blame on that Blue Fairy Pinocchio talked to me about . . . the fact remains that you're all about to turn into little boys and girls . . . my beloved puppets. You've all been infected."

Pulcinella thought he'd glimpsed a tiny tear quivering on Stromboli's cheek, but still mistrustful, decided he must have been mistaken.

"You're right, too, Pulcinella . . . ," the big man murmured as he ran his hand over his face, "you never thought you'd see me cry too . . . but I'm not doing it on purpose . . . they just pour out on their own . . . *atchoo . . .*"

Harlequin handed him a piece of colorful cloth to dry his tears. Stromboli took it, and as he did, he brushed the puppet's hand: it was warm.

He raised his eyes and saw before him, amidst the strings and fabrics, a handsome young boy with a mischievous face.

"I knew it . . . ," he said, wiping away the tears, "there's been a sort of epidemic of humanity . . . another few days of this and my Grand Puppet Theater will no longer exist . . . and I'll be gone with it . . . no one has ever seen a puppeteer without puppets . . . that's like a wagon without wheels . . . it won't run."

Stromboli stood up and carefully began to gather his puppets.

"People paid for their tickets again tonight and we can't disappoint them . . . as long as we can put on a show, they won't notice . . ."

Stromboli, holding all his puppets in his arms, headed toward the door. He was about to walk down the steps of the wagon when he turned back around and looked at Harlequin, who was sitting on the trunk.

"I left you a plate of mutton in the other room . . . take as much as you want, I'll just roast some more later . . . don't wander away from the wagon . . . I'll be back in an hour or so . . . if you get sleepy you can lie down over there . . . but remember to cover up with a blanket, because you're not made out of wood anymore, and you can catch your death."

With these words, and without waiting for an answer, the big man stepped out of the wagon, making the steps creak, and vanished into the fog that shrouded the hovels all around.

Harlequin sat there a little longer.

He didn't know whether to eat a little mutton or go to sleep.

It wasn't a particularly difficult decision.

He just wasn't used to making decisions at all.

"Signor Battistini?

For a moment I'm afraid it's Stromboli.

"Signor Battistini? Wake up!"

It's not Stromboli. But she resembles him closely. It's the talkative nurse who greeted me at the front entrance. She's already slipped the needle out of my vein. I had a dream. A child's dream.

I haven't had a childhood dream in years.

"Just stay seated for a few minutes . . . ," she tells me. "You might experience some dizziness."

I nod my head and obey.

I go on fantasizing with my eyes wide open.

Pinocchio is my favorite story. It might have been the first book I ever read, outranked in my heart only by *Treasure Island* with its pirates. Who can say why it would come into my mind now, of all times. And who knows if Collodi would approve my dream sequel to his story.

I've always loved Collodi, the king of one-hit wonders, writers famous for just one book. Maybe they've written dozens, but one is so much more famous and successful than the others that it wipes out the rest of his production.

Dante? *The Divine Comedy.*
Swift? *Gulliver's Travels.*
Defoe? *Robinson Crusoe.*
Manzoni? *I promessi sposi.*
Antoine de Saint-Exupéry? *The Little Prince.*
Collodi? Obviously *Pinocchio.*

The last in the list has the most memorable beginning of any book ever written. A masterpiece of synthesis, fun, and metaliterature.

Once upon a time there was . . .
"A king!" my little readers will say at once.
No, children, you're wrong. Once upon a time there was a
piece of wood.

"Midway along the journey of our life" or "That branch of the Lake of Como, which turns toward the south"—these are amateurish first sentences in comparison, the work of Sunday poets.

Collodi beats Dante and Manzoni one-nothing. Move the pen to the center of the field.

An unexpected consequence of chemo: my mind tends to channel surf.

I think about useless nonsense, I dream up lost chapters of *Pin-*

occhio, I team up great geniuses of literature as if they were formations in fantasy soccer. Not bad, for the first day of treatment.

I leave the clinic and start walking. I don't feel better, I don't feel worse. I just wish I could wake up again and discover that this, too, is just a dream.

wait for the side effects from the chemotherapy to show up like a guest late for dinner. A relatively unwelcome guest. The dinner table is set, the risotto's cooking on the stove, the candles are all lit, but the expected guest never shows up; he doesn't even answer his cell phone. You start to think he'll never get there. And instead, once the risotto is overcooked, the candles have all burned down to stubs, you've spilled wine on your white shirt, and you figure out that the milk you used for cooking is a week past its sell-by date, there it is: the criminal doorbell.

"Sorry I'm late, my friend, I know it's unforgivable, but you can never find a parking place in this neighborhood!"

Try to put up with me, I'm rambling more than usual, so . . . we were talking about side effects. I know them by heart, like a poem you learned in elementary school.

"Exhaustion, digestive problems, vomiting, loss of appetite and alteration of taste perceptions, fever, coughing, sore throat, headaches, muscle pains, jangled nerves, weakening of the hair follicles, and loss of sexual appetite."

Little by little, straggling in, nearly all of them show up.

Loss of appetite.

Only now does it occur to me that I haven't eaten anything since yesterday at lunch. I've never skipped an appointment with a meal in my life.

Got it!

Alteration of taste perceptions.

I force myself to eat an apple. It tastes a little sour. But it's just my mouth decoding it wrong.

Got it!

Coughing.

Not fair, I had a cough even before. Still, got it!

Digestive problems.

I can already taste the apple coming back up.

Got it!

Sore throat.

You know that little itch that tells you tomorrow morning you're going to be hoarse?

Got it!

Headaches.

Ibuprofen, six hundred milligrams, and my headache's gone. But it'll be back.

Got it!

Loss of sexual appetite.

In effect, I no longer seem to be obsessing over sex. I used to think about it a thousand times a day, like all males.

Got it!

Muscle pains.

Only now that I'm doing this inventory, I realize that my sciatica has come back. The sciatica is terrible, like a front door buzzer making contact at three in the morning.

Got it!

Jangled nerves.

I'm a volcano ready to erupt.

Got it!

Nausea.

Got it!

Vomiting. The apple.

Got it!

Exhaustion.

I don't feel all that different from yesterday.

I'd say I don't have that.

Weakening of the hair follicles.

I have a luxuriant head of hair, not a single white hair.

Not that one either.

The collection of side effects is still incomplete. I spend the day sitting on our little terrace. I can't even imagine going to our water polo team practice. I even lie to Oscar.

"How's it going, big Lucio?"

"Fine, so far everything's fine. I drank my chemo for breakfast."

"Outstanding. You'll see, you're going to beat this."

"You'll see, you're going to beat this." A phrase that reeks from afar of pity and commiseration. It sounds like an encouragement, but it's actually an epitaph.

We finish the phone call with some idle chitchat. Then I try to do some exercise. I'm sure of it: I'm going to feel better tomorrow.

Tomorrow is today.

I do an inventory of my side effects.

I can't even get out of bed. I'm a man in such poor shape that I flop around on my back, lacking the fine-motor skills to get up. It shouldn't be hard, left leg on the floor, pop your torso upright, right leg on the floor, push with both arms, and *alley-oop*! You're on your feet. But I look like a robot whose batteries are running down.

Exhaustion.

Got it.

I walk unsteadily down the hall, and I rinse my face.

I notice a few hairs scattered in the sink. I run my hand over my head, and a lock of hair magically detaches.

Weakening of the hair follicles.

Got it.

The complete assortment.

Now I can't tell you for sure how many of these symptoms are real and how many of them are the product of autosuggestion.

The fact is I don't feel a bit well.

Paola notices it, and for the first time since I've been allowed to return home, she behaves affectionately toward me. She helps me to get comfortable on the couch and turns the channel to a rerun of the legendary Wimbledon finals from 1980. She makes a vegetable couscous and serves it to me on a tray. Then she sits down next to me and watches the fifth set, when the hammering Borg finally defeated the brilliant and elusive McEnroe. She finds tennis boring, and I understand that sitting there with me is her way of telling me that she loves me. I've just finished my couscous when the referee exclaims: "Game, set, and match to Borg." I realize that Paola has fallen asleep against me. I feel her weight against me and I'm suddenly missing her. The fact that she's there, leaning against me, fills me with wonder. I don't have her back yet, but the old, familiar lapse into our comfort with each other makes me hopeful that she's closer to forgiveness now. I wonder whether this is what it will be like from now on—missing everyone I'm going to be leaving even before I have to leave them. Despairing, I get up and go see what's going on in Lorenzo and Eva's room—it's too quiet for my taste.

I stop at the threshold. They haven't noticed me, so I stand quietly and watch them both. Lorenzo has dismantled a fan and is trying to put it back together with his little sister's help. I stay out of sight and watch them work. Lorenzo tries to connect parts—he says he needs glue. Eva says, "Wait! I have some." She rummages in a plastic bucket near her bed and comes back with a tube in her hand. "Here," she says, handing it to him. I know what Lorenzo is going to say before he says it. "That's kiddie glue. You can't put a fan together with that."

It's a lost cause. They don't have the tools to put it back together again. But Lorenzo—my Leonardo—won't give up. I choke back tears when Eva says: "Hurry, before Papà notices!"

I know how to put that fan together again. After all, I originally assembled it. I am having such a good time watching them, I almost want to prolong their agony. But it's time. I make a little noise to announce my presence and the two coconspirators realize they've been caught red-handed. "Papà!" Lorenzo gives me a guilty look. Eva's already shaping her lips to form a strong defense of her brother. "It just fell apart when he touched it. I saw. He didn't do anything," she says.

The first phrase out of Lorenzo's mouth is brilliant: "Papà, I swear I'll buy you a new one!"

"With what money?" I ask, my curiosity piqued and my annoyance subsiding.

"With my allowance!" he replies, seriously.

"Five euros a week—it'll cost fifty or so; it might take you all summer."

"I'll help him," Eva breaks in.

I love it when they pool their resources. The most moving thing that a father can see is his children teaming up together.

To their surprise, I don't begin telling Lorenzo off. Instead, I say, "Watch me while I put it together. In case it happens again." Lorenzo's mouth falls open. He was not expecting this reaction from me. They both watch intently as I click the parts together. It's a fiddly fan—bits and pieces that need to be carefully interlocked to stay in place. Lorenzo nods slightly as each bit locks into the other. "I've got it, Papà," he says. "Let me finish." I let him. Eva is smiling. She knows her brother's a mechanical genius. We all look up as Paola comes into the room. "Look," Eva says, pointing to the now intact fan. "Lorenzo did it."

We all laugh, including Paola, who normally would have been giving Lorenzo a piece of her mind. I am grateful for this small slice of family harmony. We haven't been together like this for a while. It makes me sad. Everything, even good things, makes me sad.

I wonder how my children picture me. I've always thought that I played the good cop in our parenting dynamic, but maybe that's not how they see it.

Just seconds later, I discover that Lorenzo not only dismantled the fan, he also took apart the turntable of my old record player.

I count to ten, take a deep breath, and go back to the living room. I don't want to leave them with memories of a dictatorial father who punished them for their creative efforts. But I really cared about that record player. It was a present from Grandpa for my seventeenth birthday, and by some miracle it still worked, even though it was now starting to scratch the vinyl a little bit. I don't know why but a distant memory resurfaces, one of Giovanni Verga's novellas, which nobody reads anymore past age thirteen: *Property*. Stop reading this book and go read the Verga instead, as adults. You can find it on the Internet easily. The Sicilian author tells the story of a farmer, Mazzarò, filthy rich and so in love with his property that, on his deathbed, he's more upset at the thought that his possessions won't be able to follow him into the tomb than at the idea that he's about to die. A simple and surprising life lesson, wrapped up in a few pages that alone are as good as anything in the rest of Verga's *The House by the Medlar Tree*.

I've been Mazzarò for years and years of my life: I've purchased useless things of all kinds; I've collected comic books and records, T-shirts, and swimsuits. Perhaps I'm still a little bit like Mazzarò—I'm sorry to leave behind my own personal property. But I have a sense that a progressive release is taking place, a slow falling out of love with my possessions. I realize it when I read a comic book and I fold back the cover, wrinkling it, without the sacred respect I would have accorded it until just a few months ago. I suddenly understand that human beings aren't divided into good and bad, southerners and northerners, the intelligent and the stupid, or any of the other thousands of distinctions that we invent to liven up our existence. They're divided into "book benders" and "non–book benders." The former are happier.

I dream about my parents. Ever since I started taking industrial doses of ibuprofen to cut the pain, I've been sleeping more profoundly. I often have dreams and I always remember what happened in my mind while my body was on standby. All my dreams are of me as a child.

This time we're aboard a small red sailboat, off the coast of Ladispoli. I'm two years old, my Papà's sixty, and my Mamma's sixteen. A chronological and oneiric chaos—I never knew either of them at those ages.

At a certain point a great white shark shoots past us like a speedboat, barely a yard away, and the wake from its passage almost tosses us overboard. Even if it's a dream, a monstrous white shark 150 feet off the beach of Ladispoli remains highly unlikely. And it's not alone—there is a pack of them. They surround us, a good twenty of them, then they attack. They bare their teeth, like giant meatgrinders, an enormous razor-sharp cavern ready to take us in, chop us up, and digest us. Papà fights heroically, beating them back with his oar, and he's the first to be swallowed up, oar and all. Mamma abandons me without a second thought, diving in and trying to swim off and make her escape. A shark gulps her down like a human aspirin tablet before she has a chance to swim ten strokes. I'm left alone, it's like an Italian remake of *Life of Pi*.

I hadn't dreamed about my parents for years. I really miss them. And I really hate them. I told you that I'd only talk about them when

I was ready. Well, today I'm ready. This way, you'll have a chance to hate them almost as much as I do.

After the unwanted pregnancy, for a couple of years Mamma and Papà lived with my grandparents, whom you've already met. Then my father found a job as a disc jockey (though back then in Italy that's not what it was called) in a dance hall in Lido di Ostia and even managed to get a salary high enough to afford to rent an apartment and live there with Mamma. And so it was that at the tender age of just two, I went to live with two wretched young people in their twenties in a one-room apartment in Ostia, which makes sense in the summer, but certainly doesn't in the winter. Mamma rounded out Papà's salary by cleaning beach houses during the tourist season. At night she was so exhausted that she'd almost always fall asleep next to me, just as Papà was leaving for work at the dance hall.

I was more or less three years old when I suddenly discovered the most terrible thing a child can discover: Papà and Mamma didn't love each other. The only reason they were together at all was my arrival, and they had nothing in common, no mutual respect. The spark of love between them had never even flickered into life. The law permitting abortion in Italy dates from 1978, so they'd had no choice but to accept my unwanted presence. To understand that you were "unwanted" at the tender age of three is no fun, let me tell you. I was the cause of every fight, the scapegoat whenever anything went wrong. If I'd been fifteen, I would have run away from home, but I wouldn't be fifteen for twelve more years, and even then, I wasn't exactly lionhearted for my age.

One day, Papà announced that he'd found work on a cruise ship. A six-month stint in the Caribbean as an activities leader. We didn't even go with him to the airport. Our hasty farewells took place in the kitchen. I saw him get into a taxi from our second-story window. He never came back. Mamma cried for six months. We went back to live with her parents, and that made me happy. My grandparents were the only stable point of reference in my life. The next summer, my mother—who in the meantime was becoming an increasingly depressed hippie freak—left for India with a girlfriend to find herself. I don't know if she ever did, but I do know that we never saw her again. Motherly love was definitely not her strong suit. From that day forward, for all intents and purposes, my grandparents became my immediate family. They were everything for me. Now do you understand why I'm never really interested in talking about my loving parents?

On Sundays, Oscar's pastry shop is closed all day; it opens again at two in the morning to start making the treats for the next day. My father-in-law is bored on Sunday. Since he was widowed, or since he's become a whiplash single, as he likes to say, he only comes home to sleep. When his wife was still alive, they'd often come to our house to eat or else we'd go over to their place. Now he hangs out in Trastevere, sitting in a bar to watch the A. S. Roma game, striking up conversations with anyone capable of helping him spend a cheery fifteen minutes.

"So you know what I did last Sunday?" he asks me with uncommon cockiness.

"No, what?" I reply, following the script.

"While I was out on my walk, I saw a huge crowd of tourists emerge from the Ottaviano Metro station: a couple of classes of Scandinavian students on a field trip, a horde of Japanese photographers of all ages, and a swarm of German retirees wearing shorts. And you know what I wound up doing?"

"No, what did you wind up doing?" I hate it when he asks questions just to make sure he has the attention of his audience, which in this case is just me.

"I trooped in with the Germans. The tour includes the Colosseum, the Dome of Saint Peter's, and the Vatican Museums. The tour guide, a certain Martina, is Italian but talks to them in German so I don't understand a word. So you know what I come up with then?"

"No, what do you come up with then?" I ask in a resigned voice.

"I pretend I'm mute! Which makes everyone like me."

I smile at the thought of him munching sauerkraut sandwiches offered by coquettish Bavarian eighty-year-olds, laughing at jokes he doesn't understand, making his way up the stairs inside the big Dome of Saint Peter's, and worming his way into crowded souvenir pictures.

"And the tour guide didn't notice a thing?"

"Not a thing. But she was an interesting type. I overheard a phone call she was making in Italian, to her daughter, I think. She's a widow and works as a tour guide strictly in her spare time."

"Did you like her?"

"I didn't talk to her. I was a German mute."

"Oh, right."

"But anyway, yes, I did like her. Otherwise, I wouldn't have spent the whole day with them," he adds with a wink.

"Did you spend the whole day with them?"

"I even had dinner with them, in a restaurant over by Campo de' Fiori. I rode back to the hotel with them on the tour bus, went upstairs, and took a back exit. Then I followed Signora Martina out to the parking lot. I wanted to catch up with her and confess to my fraud. Maybe even ask her if she wanted to get a drink."

"But?"

"How do you know there's a but?"

"There's always a but. Go on."

"But a young man came to pick her up. I'd guess her grandson. They got in his car together and then she vanished into the night."

"And now you want to find her again?"

"I called the company who ran the tour, but there wasn't any Martina. And anyway they went on and on about issues of privacy."

"Maybe Martina is a nom de plume."

"For a tour guide?"

"What other clues do you have?"

"I have this."

He shows me a snapshot of him standing next to a sprightly seventy-year-old woman who looks like Miss Marple, in front of the Colosseum.

"Pretty, eh?"

I nod in response to the rhetorical question. Ever since his wife died, I haven't seen my father-in-law so interested in another woman, except for that time Catherine Deneuve came into his pastry shop to ask directions. That day is just one of a number of favorite stories that always start "When Catherine and I." So I know it's important to find this Martina or whatever her name is.

I e-mail myself a copy of the photo, pull out my Dino Zoff notebook, and jot down:

Track down Miss Marple.

How do you track down a person just from a picture of her?

I get my first suggestion from Umberto.

"I could post it on Facebook and say that it's my grandmother Martina and that she's lost. It always works for dogs."

We post the photo on my friend's cluttered time line and, after an hour, we already have dozens of sightings. Someone saw her on the Janiculum, someone else saw her on Piazza Trilussa, she was spotted in a supermarket in Prati, or on the island of Fiji, or in a karaoke bar in Tokyo. If we were going to check them all out, it would take a lifetime and the logistical resources of Interpol.

"Hello, Interpol, good morning! I'm calling from Rome. Because my father-in-law is a widower and I'd like to find him a new girlfriend, I was wondering if you could help me track down this lady whose name I don't know?"

It's an unmistakable defeat. The only thing that can help us is a piece of blind luck. I make copies of the picture and post them in the local bars, including our café. Underneath is a vague note: "Contact this number for an urgent message." We'll see how that goes.

In the meanwhile, this investigation has at least obtained an initial result: it has distracted me. Tomorrow afternoon is my second chemotherapy appointment. The side effects have subsided, but by now I've become an authority on the subject—each time they'll return with greater virulence and persistence. I decide to go meet Paola at school, forgetting that today is her day off. I wait for her like an idiot, until the last teacher emerges from the building and she recognizes me.

"Signor Battistini!"

I can't even remember her name, but I pretend to remember her perfectly.

"Teacher!"

"Today's your wife's day off, what are you doing on this side of town?"

"What am I doing here? Right around the corner there's a first-rate pastry shop, I was just going there to pick up a tray of pastries."

"Doesn't your father-in-law have a pastry shop?"

I hate nitpicking schoolteachers.

"Sure, of course he does, but he doesn't make Sicilian cannoli because his wife cheated on him with a fisherman from Caltanissetta, so, since I felt like having some cannoli today, well that's why I'm here."

"A fisherman from Caltanissetta? Caltanissetta isn't even on the water!"

Now I'm ready to strangle her with my bare hands, right there, on the street.

"True, in fact, he was out of work, and had to look for a new line of work."

She seems dubious. I try to break away, but she starts back in: "I heard you weren't well."

I hate schoolteachers who know I'm not well.

"Yes, but I'm over it already, I'm practically cured . . ." I minimize with unusual nonchalance.

"Ah, that's good, because cancer killed both my brother and my uncle, as well as a teacher here at our high school."

I also hate this conversation.

"Listen, Teacher, I'd love to stay and talk for hours, but I'm just afraid when I get there they'll be out of cannoli; they're the most popular pastry of all. Sorry to talk and run."

*   *   *

By now it's clear to me that having cancer has something in common with a funeral. Everyone comes up to you and expresses condolences. The only difference is that because the person in question isn't yet in a casket, instead of expressing condolences to the widow or the next of kin, the comforter just hands them straight to the soon-to-be dearly departed. If I ever have cancer again, I swear this time I'm going to tell everyone that it's just a bad case of tonsillitis.

As I walk, I give Paola a call.

"My love, where are you?"

"I'm at the hairdresser's."

"Do you want me to come by and pick you up?"

"I drove here; I have my car."

"Ah, great. Then should I run by and pick up the children at school?"

They attend full-time, a wonderful new invention designed to reduce the divorce rate.

"That would be great, thanks."

"Listen . . . tomorrow I'm going in for my second round of chemo."

"I'll go with you. See you later."

End of conversation. She will go with me—that's a good thing. Yet as I hear our conversation in my mind—routine and humdrum, polite, yet without affection—I feel sick. I want to win back her love, I want her to forgive me. Every day, I expect to be closer to my goal. Yet I am further away from it than ever.

econd session of chemo. In the waiting room I strike up a conversation with a talkative guy my age who confides, with a certain pride, that he's already on his third round. Twenty seconds later, he says it again. This treatment isn't helping him. From the inner room, another patient emerges, leaning on what would seem to be his wife. He's not even fifty, but he can barely walk; he's skinny as a rail, and his eyes are dull and blank.

Now it's my turn. The same nurse who looks like Stromboli comes out to call my name. Paola stays in the waiting room and I walk into the little room that I already know so well. Two minutes later, there I am again, with a needle in my vein and thousands of thoughts whirling through my head.

When I was little, there were three possible lines of work that caught my imagination.

The first, as documented by my historic essay "What I Want to Be When I Grow Up," which Grandma carefully stored in the top dresser drawer, was an amusement park ride inspector. Clever child that I was, I'd decided to mix business with pleasure. After all, there must be a man whose job it is to say, "This ride works perfectly, it's fun and it's safe, go ahead and open it to the public." I always assumed that man would have a lifetime ticket so he could come back to the amusement park whenever he liked.

The second line of work, and this takes us into the realm of criminal endeavors, was to be a cat burglar. Maybe it was because of my fascination with Diabolik, but I've often dreamed of sneaking into a jewelry shop by night and cleaning the place out. This is an ambition I've never pursued, though I confess I've stolen bathrobes from more than one hotel.

The third profession—and here I have to say that I was ahead of my time—was that of a life coach, or as I called it back then, with a naive but still very accurate term, a *recommender*. I imagine a figure who, much like Cardinal Mazarin or Richelieu for the king of France, works with his clients on the more complicated choices in life.

"Is the girl I'm dating the right one for me?"

Zap, and the recommender arrives on the scene and provides a confident answer.

"What should I do, should I take this job?"

Zap, here's the recommender ready to offer the best advice.

In the end, I didn't wind up in any of these lines of work: I neither inspect amusement parks, nor do I steal, nor do I give advice to anyone, least of all myself.

Suddenly I feel like a loser.

In the meanwhile, the needle has done its dirty work and injected me with the usual dose of poison. I no longer know whether I'm making the right decision.

"How are we doing, Signor Battistini?" the nurse inquires.

By now, I always give the same answer.

"Rotten, thanks."

I step out of the claustrophobic little room and as I walk through the waiting room, I run into the talkative patient who insists on telling me once again that he's on his third round of chemotherapy. If I were him, I wouldn't do a fourth round. I grab the arm that Paola offers me and we walk out into the fresh air. I feel like crying.

No longer going to work at the gym is a strange sensation. I stroll through Villa Borghese at an unusual time for me, eleven-thirty in the morning. I feel like a privileged soul. I think of a Latin word that we all associate with the Colosseum and its bloodthirsty games, a blend of the feral and the athletic: *moriturus*, "one who is about to die." Not bad. It's accurate and evocative, and has a nostalgic tang straight out of an elementary school textbook. Moriturus. I who am about to die: I'm a *moriturus*. I like it. It almost makes me feel like a heroic gladiator ready for the final battle in the presence of a jubilant audience. My man-eating tiger is called Fritz. A tiger with a name like that could hardly be dangerous. He's just a big harmless cat.

I feel better already.

Moriturus.

I who am about to die.

It would look pretty good on a business card: Lucio Battistini, *moriturus*.

I head down toward Piazzale Flaminio, through the pedestrian island of Piazza del Popolo with its vast encampment of tourists in shorts. I stop to look at a woman dressed as the Statue of Liberty, her face painted white and a hat with a sunburst on her head. She stands motionless at the foot of an obelisk; the paint on her face is starting to run. I sit down next to her, on the steps. I'm a perfect practitioner of the art of doing sweet FA.

Then I head off toward Piazza Venezia, zigzagging a little through the back streets. I spot a little shop I've never noticed before. The sign outside is new. I walk in, attracted by the name: Chitchat. I'm welcomed in by Massimiliano, a former policeman, now retired. Inside the shop are a fireplace with no fire, a couple of ragtag couches and an armchair facing a wide-screen TV, a fridge, a galley kitchen with a steaming teakettle, and a small table. It looks like the living room in an old-fashioned apartment, with furniture thrown together by chance. In fact, that's exactly what it is.

Massimiliano is seventy years old and looks much younger; he's never been married, he has no living relatives. He's well read and intelligent. He explains to me that after retiring, he quickly became bored; he spent his days in his ground-floor apartment, watching old movies and indulging his longtime passion for cooking. But it wasn't enough. He felt horribly lonely and his pension was too small to allow him to travel around the world. So he painted the Chitchat sign and put it out over his front door, replacing his normal door with a glass shop door. Then he waited for someone to bite.

"It's a pretty simple idea," he explains to me. "I welcome perfect strangers into my home, I make them tea with a plate of cookies, we exchange a little chitchat, as the name suggests, we watch a little TV together, that kind of thing. In other words, we keep each other company."

A chitchat shop. Simple but brilliant. Not even Leonardo da Vinci ever came up with this one. It's like a pharmacy that stocks friendship.

He adds that when the time comes to leave, his customers can pay him whatever they think is right, as a way of covering expenses (usually five euros).

"So how's business?"

"Excellent. These days, people don't lack a thing, except for someone who has the time to listen to what they have to say. I almost never have any free time for myself."

"And what kind of customers do you get?" I ask.

"It's a grab bag. Rejected lovers, retirees like me, even the occasional executive at lunchtime looking for an hour of relaxation with a 'faux grandpa,'" he says with a smile.

Massimiliano entertains all patrons with his cheerful running patter and his cookies and cakes, and now he's built up a numerous and faithful clientele in the neighborhood. It's highly therapeutic to spend a couple of hours with him; I'd recommend it to anyone—forget about shiatsu massages and antidepressants. I believe that, sooner or later, some multinational will steal his idea and open a chain of fast friends outlets, with the slogan "You deserve a friend today!"

I spend a couple of hours with him. We even watch an episode of *Happy Days* on his satellite TV and I tell him about my cancer and the treatments I've just started. Only as I'm talking to him does it dawn on me that I've already made up my mind not to go back and have another needle stuck in my vein so it can turn me slowly into a vegetable. Arrivederci, chemo. Just the thought makes me feel better.

Massimiliano explains that he's been a vegetarian for years and that his food choices help him ward off cancer. He's no expert, but he suggests I look for some alternative solutions, though he adds that I should avoid charlatans and only talk to those who use natural methods.

"I would advise you to see a naturopath."

"What does a naturopath do?"

"A naturopath will show you how to lead a healthier life. Let's say that a naturopath is a cross between a dietologist and a psychologist."

I take note of the recommendation, and then we go on talking about nothing in particular for another hour or so.

When I leave, I put ten euros down on the table.

I already feel better. I'll be back.

"There are two types of treatments for a tumor, Signor Battistini: conventional oncological treatments and those that are referred to as 'alternative' treatments, a word I don't particularly like.... Alternative to what? I prefer to call them natural treatments, because they follow the course of nature."

I listen without interrupting Dr. Zanella, a naturopath in her early fifties, practically the spitting image of Madonna.

"The first type of treatment chiefly concerns the sickness," the pop star tells me, "while the second type follows a holistic approach, which is to say, it treats the person as a whole."

I still can't say whether I'm in the presence of a charlatan, a genuine Madonna, or an enlightened guru of deeper understanding.

"The conventional approach," she continues, "attempts to restore a state of health with pharmaceuticals, pills, drugs, chemotherapy, and radiation therapy, and focuses little or not at all on the patient's lifestyle and diet. How do they think they're going to save a sick person by stuffing his body with chemicals? By continuing to poison him? The word *pharmaceutical* comes from the ancient Greek word *pharmakon*, and it's no accident that it means 'poison.'"

If I'd been listening when we studied ancient Greek at school, I never would have set foot in a pharmacy.

"A tumor almost always consists of a proliferation of cells due to a discharge of internal poisons, such as polluted air, alcohol, tobacco smoke, unhealthy foods, foods contaminated with pesticides, and other foods that are bad for the human body, such as dairy products, meat, refined sugars, and so on."

"Wait, I don't understand . . . dairy products, meat, and sugars . . . are bad for you?"

"Very bad for you, for various reasons. What do you usually eat, on an everyday basis?"

"I eat normally. Mediterranean diet . . . pasta, tomatoes, steaks, cheeses."

"That's terrible. What about breakfast?"

I hesitate.

"For breakfast I usually have a . . . a doughnut."

"Deep-fried?"

"Sure, deep-fried, the classic sugar doughnut. My father-in-law is a pastry chef."

The singer looks at me as if I'd just told her I eat roast babies every morning.

"Let me explain, Signor Battistini. A doughnut is made of super-fine baking flour that has been refined so that there are no vitamins in it, because it has been bleached and industrially processed. Super-fine baking flour—like all refined food products—causes an increase in your glycemic levels and a resulting rise in insulin, and therefore a general weakening of the organism, which thus becomes increasingly subject to disease and tumors."

I can't figure out whether she's serious or is just kidding me. She insists on dismantling all the foundations of my daily diet—from eggs, which, she informs me, come from farm-raised, antibiotic-fed hens; to milk, which has too much casein, creates inflammation, and deprives the body of calcium; to sugar, which is simply malevolent; to heated oil, which is cancerogenous.

"Can-cer-og-e-nous," She repeats the word with a perverse satis-faction. "Your morning doughnut is your worst enemy!"

I'm in shock. This may be the biggest shock of my life since my parents abandoned me and Italy was defeated in the 1994 World Cup. Doughnuts are bad for your health. I ask if I can go to the bathroom. Actually, I'm just hiding out so I can do some quick online research with my smart phone. I need to know. I'm thirsty for knowledge.

My good friend Google helps out as usual. The naturopath is perfectly right. Everything she says has a solid basis in scientific fact.

I return to Dr. Zanella's office and decide to dig a little deeper. The main question is, as always, straightforward: "Am I too late to do anything?"

"Perhaps not. A body falls ill because it's been poisoned over the course of time. With toxic foods, pharmaceuticals, drugs, alcohol, and repressed emotions."

"I don't drink, I don't smoke, and I don't take drugs, except for maybe a joint twice a year."

"But you eat doughnuts. And who knows what other crap."

I feel like an elementary school student sent to stand in the corner.

"You see, to treat cancer, you need to change the way you eat and live, and that means raw foods, vegetable drinks, plenty of sunlight, yoga breathing exercises, and the total abandonment of carcinogenic foods, medicines, and other products. If the tumor isn't too far advanced, then it's possible to limit it or even put it into remission."

"What can I do?"

"Let's start with two days of total fasting. Cancer is a parasite that lives inside you. If you don't eat, it doesn't eat either. But you have stores of energy that will let you live longer."

A question seems quite natural.

"Why doesn't everyone do it?"

"Pharmaceutical houses. Is that a sufficient answer? If people knew that the most purifying substance there is is nettle extract, what would pharmacists sell?"

"So two days of diet?" I ask, in sheer terror.

"Not diet, fasting. After the first two days of digestive rest, I'd start the diet proper. A food regimen designed to cause the tumor to regress is a partial fast on the basis of raw, organic, fresh vegetables."

She goes on drawing up a list of things that I can and cannot eat. Practically speaking, it's a vegan diet.

"At night, before going to bed, I'd recommend a plaster of cabbage leaves and spa mud, applied to the liver and the torso in correspondence to the lungs."

I interrupt her. "What are my chances of recovery?"

"I want to be straight with you. If you'd come to me a year ago, with a tumor in an embryonic state, without ever having had chemotherapy, I would have told you that the odds in your favor were ninety-nine percent. But at your present state of development of this disease, your chances are slim. Still, you do have a chance to improve the quality of life in the time remaining to you, to feel more energetic . . . and after all, you never know. The human organism is an unpredictable and complicated machine, preprogrammed to heal. It can always surprise us."

The last couple of lines seem to have been inserted just to keep me from getting depressed.

"Are you going to give it a try?" asks Madonna, finally flashing me a smile.

First day of fasting.

By noon my head is spinning and my stomach is rumbling. Luckily, the crisis passes. As soon as my organism realizes that food isn't coming, it calms down and stops emitting alarm bursts.

I head back to the Chitchat shop. I want to tell Massimiliano that I've taken his advice.

"Good, I'm glad to hear it," he replies as he makes me an herbal tea.

"Even if it's late, I want to give it a full try."

"That strikes me as the right approach."

I look ravenously at the cookies we dunked in the tea last time. I can feel my mouth salivating, just like the Big Bad Wolf when he looks at the Three Little Pigs. I ask him if he wouldn't mind hiding the cookies in the cabinet. What the eye doesn't see: that's always the best policy.

"You'll see," says Massimiliano as he locks away the precious delicacies, "eating less and better will increase the energy available to you day after day."

"I hope so. I'm already tired the minute I get up in the morning."

Just then, a new customer rings the doorbell, a tall skinny gentleman in his early fifties with a beaten-down appearance. I'd forgotten I was in a public establishment, and not at a friend's house.

"Do you mind coming back in half an hour or so?" Massimiliano asks the newcomer. "Or else, if you feel like it, you can sit and watch a little TV with us."

The thin man accepts. So there we are, all three of us, watching a rerun of *Happy Days*. The memorable episode in which Fonzie water-skis over a great white shark on a bet.

"The story is so absurd," Massimiliano explains, "that in the U.S., to 'jump the shark' is the moment when a television show has started to go downhill."

"I liked that episode," says the thin man, who it turns out is named Giannandrea. Maybe the reason he's sad is the name he was given as a baby.

"I liked it too," I agree.

"Everyone liked it. The truth is that our eyes were different than they are today."

Hunger pangs grip my belly. I say good-bye to Massimiliano and Giannandrea and head home.

The phone call from Umberto catches me by surprise.

"She wrote me on Facebook!"

"Who did?"

"What do you mean who? Martina, the tour guide. Miss Marple!"

I hurry over to his house. I can't wait to tell my father-in-law the news. But in the meanwhile, we need to answer the lady's none-too-friendly message.

"Hello, I'm the lady in the photograph. But I'm not your grand-mother and I don't know what kind of stupid game you're playing. If you don't remove my picture from your profile immediately, I'm call-ing the police."

That's what you call a downhill beginning to a love story.

I decide to tell her the truth. I write back and tell her that my fa-ther-in-law is the slightly overweight German mute from the tour two weeks ago, and that he'd like to see her again. We tried to track her down through the tour operator but they didn't know about any Mar-tina. The lady is online and she replies immediately.

"They didn't know my name because every once in a while I sub-

stitute for my granddaughter. The tour operator doesn't know anything about it. You can tell your father-in-law I knew immediately
that he wasn't mute at all, and that I'd be happy to let him take me out
to dinner. He can write me at this e-mail address. Thank you."

Two hours later, they have a date for the next evening in a little
restaurant in Trastevere. Oscar can't stop thanking me and asking me
for advice about how to dress.

As a Cupid, I really do deserve an A plus.

Soap-on-a-Rope, our unreliable goalie, comes up to me in the locker room of the swimming pool and asks me, unexpectedly:

"How are you, Coach?"

"What do you mean?"

No one on the team has ever asked me how I'm doing. If anything, I'm the one who asks them after practice or before a match.

"Well, I mean . . . I saw that you were coughing."

I was afraid that he'd found out about my illness. The team doesn't know. The only one I've told is Giacomo, my assistant coach, and he's sworn to secrecy. His partial autism helps him keep it to himself.

"I'm fine, thanks, just a touch of bronchitis."

"You must have caught a chill. Any advice for today's game?"

"Just one piece of advice: block all the balls that head toward you. Okay?"

Today we're taking on the lowest-ranked team in the league, a team we call Atletico Colabrodo—the Colander Athletics—instead of Atletico Casalpalocco. They lose by an average of fifteen goals per match. They've never even tied a game.

We drop into the water, relaxed, confident of our superiority. And sure enough, by the end of the third quarter, we're down by a goal, 8 to 7 in the Colanders' favor. I'm in a raging fury at poolside. I shout and urge my boys into the fray, calling for them to grow some balls. If we lose this match, then we can kiss our hopes of qualifying for the playoffs good-bye. Even Giacomo, usually so reserved and British in style, displays an uncustomary rage and even tosses out a few swear words.

We start the last quarter with a ferocity that is quite unlike us. We win by one goal at the very last second, but no one celebrates. I'm furious. We underestimated our opponents and ran the risk of undermining the whole season. In the locker room, I rip the team a new one, in a memorable dressing-down. Then everything goes black and I keel over.

I wake up in the tiny swimming pool infirmary. With me are Giacomo and a young female swimming instructor.

"Don't worry," she tells me. "We've called an ambulance. You just lost consciousness for a couple of minutes."

I don't want an ambulance.

"It was nothing but a bout of high pressure," I say, getting up from the cot. In reality, though, I'm afraid it's due to my fasting or the last session of chemo. Or both together.

I emerge from the infirmary and find my boys loitering in the swimming pool lobby. They look at me strangely. For a coach, for a fighting general, the worst thing is to show weakness in the eyes of his soldiers. Today my career as a coach without blemish or fear has come to an end. Or perhaps this just marks a new beginning.

As the first shadows of evening stretch over Rome, my father-in-law, Oscar, prepares for his date and I set off, like a condemned man walking to the gallows, to a meeting of the condo board.

The real question is this: Why should a man with only seventy-nine days left to live waste time at condo board meetings?

I say hello to my neighbors, already catching a glimpse of the mayhem that is about to be unleashed in their eyes. One second later I decide to spend the evening differently and walk right out of there. I call Umberto and Corrado. Immediately afterward, I call a restaurant. The very same restaurant where, just half an hour from now, Oscar has a date with Miss Marple.

When Oscar walks into the dining room, leading Martina with unaccustomed gallantry, we're seated at the table next to his. He glares at us with hatred.

"What are you doing here, damn you?" is the subtitle to his thoughts.

I give him the faintest of smiles. I certainly didn't want to miss the show.

I order a plateful of vegetables, to the disgust of my friends, who gobble down their mixed grills, and we spend the rest of the evening eavesdropping on the tall tales that Oscar is spouting to make a good impression on the lady, who is really quite nice. There are unforgettable moments when he claims to have volunteered in Africa for two years and, again, when he claims to be fat solely as a matter of public image: "A pastry chef can't afford to be skinny, otherwise what kind of cook will his customers take him for?"

By the time they're eating their entrées, I'm sure that the retired grandmother is interested and I decide that my father-in-law may well have found, in this unlikely escapade, a new companion. When he pays the check and heads for the door with Martina, we decide to leave them alone. Oscar winks at me on his way out, and I stay there with my friends, joking and laughing.

I return home and find Paola fast asleep in front of the TV; I wake her up with a kiss on the top of her head. Oscar has asked me to keep her in the dark for the moment as far as his amorous activities are concerned. I pull my notebook out of my dresser drawer and strike out the entry: "Track down Miss Marple." I take a shower. I've eaten nothing but vegetables today and, in effect, I'm feeling a little better. I feel more energetic and optimistic. But what I feel most of all is a desire to make love. It's been three months since Paola and I last had sex. A record for us. Even when she was pregnant, we were never so distant sexually. My wife comes to bed ten minutes after me, with a mug of herbal tea in her hand. I pretend I'm already asleep. Then I try to brush her with my arm. She pushes me away.

"Lucio, please."

Lucio, please.

Let me scan that sentence.

"Lucio" is a complementary vocative. The fact that she calls me neither "my love" nor "*amore*" nor "sweetheart" indicates distance and hostility. She's never called me just Lucio before.

"Please" is a functional adverb, and a highly eclectic one. We use it in many ways. But in this particular instance, it clearly denotes annoyance or impatience (Cut it out, please!) or else beseeching (Please, will you do this, or stop that). It is clear my wife is annoyed with me. If it weren't for my buddy Fritz, I'm afraid that these days we'd be spending all our time in lawyers' offices, instead of hospitals.

I turn away and dream of the day when we'll make love again.

I'll immediately add it to the list of the most important days of my life.

"Lucio, I've fallen in love."

That, of course, is Oscar talking. His audience, aside from me, is the Sinhalese sous chef who listens as he deftly assembles rows of mini tiramisus.

"That's certainly a piece of good news."

"Yes, it is, but there's also a piece of bad news to go with it."

"What's the bad news?"

"She has a boyfriend."

The word "boyfriend" used in relation to Martina/Miss Marple makes me smile.

"What do you mean 'She has a boyfriend'? Didn't you say she was a widow?"

"She's a widow with a boyfriend. He's a retired engineer who lives in Milan. They see each other once a month."

"So?"

"So last night we kissed, but then she ran away. This morning she texted me. She said that she really likes me, but she's confused."

The plot thickens. It sounds like a puppy-love story between a pair of fifteen-year-olds.

"That's a classic. What did you text back?"

"I might have been a little direct. I wrote her: 'I love you. Dump the guy from Milan.'"

"Nice, that's the way you do it—manly and decisive. Did she reply?"

"No, but it was because she'd used up the credit on her phone card, but then she called me back on her grandson's cell phone."

Oscar's ability to build up suspense in the stories he tells is well known.

"Oscar, get to the point."

"Well, so now I'm on probation. This is a runoff election with the engineer."

"A runoff election?"

"That's right, she says that she's undecided, that she doesn't know me, that she's not sure she's ready to leave a man she's been seeing for two years for what might be a flash in the pan. And that she doesn't even know if there's sexual chemistry between us."

"The lady really talk like that?" asks the Sinhalese, his interest piqued only by the spicier aspects of the conversation.

"You mind your own business and get back to work," Oscar chastises him. "She said that she'd really like to go to bed with me, but that she's not sure she's ready to cheat on the Milanese."

"I've heard the same excuse ever since I entered puberty. But after a while, if you court them a little, their objections give way."

"You think I don't know that? On Saturday night I'm taking her out to the movies. And we'll see what happens. You haven't said anything to Paola, have you?"

"Not a word."

"Let's see how things go before worrying her. I don't know how she'd react if I started seeing another woman."

"I think she'd just be happy for you."

"I certainly hope so, Lucio *mio*. How are you doing?"

"I'm surviving," I reply with a forced smile.

"Is there anything I can do for you?"

"I'm afraid not."

We stand there looking at each other for a moment.

"It's not right, Lucio. This should be happening to me. I've lived my life, done what I wanted to, I'm seventy and some change. It should be my turn to die. I swear, if I could do it, I'd take your place."

I sense that he's speaking the truth. We hug. I've never hugged my father-in-law. I sink into him. And I feel right at home.

My heart recently beat for the billionth and a half time. An important occasion given the fact that, statistically speaking, our most important organ beats three billion times before starting to sputter and die. The heart has a specific sell-by date, just like an alkaline battery, and that's why athletes often die earlier: they raise the number of heartbeats per minute and therefore consume more vital energy. My heart has already pumped along for forty years, which is to say, 14,540 days (including leap years), which is very respectable mileage.

In these past forty years I've slept 116,320 hours, watched 31,410 hours of television, eaten 4,945 pounds of bread, 9,452 bananas, and, unfortunately, 11,234 doughnuts.

I've owned four cars, six bikes, and seven mopeds.

I own 342 books, a thousand or so comic books, 58 vinyl records, and 153 CDs.

I've made roughly twenty-five thousand phone calls.

I've gotten 327 haircuts (one time I had it all shaved off).

I've watched 2,316 movies and been to see 288 plays and shows.

I've gotten drunk only four times: once was in Paris.

I've lusted after my neighbor's wife every single day of my life.

I've been to bed with 43 different women. I've made love with Paola roughly six hundred times, and she beats them all as the absolute unrivaled winner.

I've attended nine funerals of close relatives and friends, and thirty-one weddings.

Doing all these calculations cost me an entire afternoon.

Why I bothered to do them I couldn't say. I started out thinking "Now I'm going to add up the numbers of my life," then I got sucked into this childish game. And I discovered that my life, reckoned in cold data, makes me feel kind of sad.

It's seventy-seven days to the end, and all I did today was waste time. Right now, the only number that matters is seventy-seven. The diet I'm on is making me lose weight visibly and I feel like a lion. A wounded lion, but a lion nonetheless.

"Lucio! I won the race!" Oscar shouts into the phone. "Martina has decided to break up with the guy from Milan and let me court her."

"Didn't she want to see if there was sexual chemistry first?" I ask, my curiosity aroused.

"We checked it out last night. And don't worry, we've got it," my enthusiastic father-in-law replies.

I smile. I'm truly happy for him.

"Listen," he continues, "what do you say I come over for dinner with Martina tonight? At midnight we could drink a toast to Paola's birthday and then you both could meet her."

Tomorrow is my wife's birthday. I've always arranged something for her. But this time I don't know what to do.

"Very gladly. What should I tell Paola?"

"That I'm bringing a friend. Just say it's a woman I know. Keep it vague."

"Does she have any dietary requirements I should know about?"

"Thank God she's an omnivore."

"Excellent. We'll see you at nine."

I hang up and talk to Paola about it. I keep it vague but she figures it out instantly and the questions come with rapid fire.

"Just who is this Martina? What does she do? Do you like her? Do you know her?"

She seems like a mother worried about her son much more than a daughter concerned about her elderly father. The good thing is that she seems to be okay with the idea that Oscar is seeing another woman. That wasn't a given, in spite of the fact that it's been ten years since her mother died.

At nine o'clock, we're anxiously awaiting the two lovebirds. We've put out the good silver and the cloth napkins. I've cooked a chicken curry worthy of *MasterChef* and a side dish of wok-fried tender green vegetables. A light dinner to keep me feeling good and, especially, to keep my father-in-law from falling asleep over dessert. The children—who, unfortunately for them, never met their real grandmother—are excited. The new arrival has been announced to them as "grandpa's girlfriend," and without ever having met her, they've already adopted her as their own. Eva asks whether she likes animals and Lorenzo wants to know if an adopted grandmother gives Christmas presents.

When the doorbell rings, they look like a well-trained team, ready to swarm onto the field and put on an excellent show. I have to stifle my laughter as I open the door to the sight of Oscar in jacket and tie and Martina made up and wearing far too much perfume, stinking up the landing.

We have a great time at dinner. We learn that Martina is a former high school art history teacher, and, as she'd told me, she sometimes fills in for her granddaughter Claudia, who is a part-time tour guide. She has two children and four grandchildren, and she's the widow of a general in the Guardia di Finanza, Italy's financial police.

"Among other things, I found out that her husband audited me in 1991 because I wasn't giving my customers receipts. That is, most of my customers. I found the documentation, with his signature."

This coincidence makes Oscar laugh and laugh and it embarrasses Martina slightly; she is also unmistakably pained by the memory of her late husband. I change the subject and the evening sails merrily along for a couple of hours. Lorenzo and Eva show the lady their room and Eva overwhelms her with a river of words until Paola finally comes to her rescue.

"What do you think of her?" Oscar asks me the minute we're alone.

"She seems nice."

"She doesn't seem nice, she *is* nice. And you have no idea what she's like in bed. A panther."

I look down the hall at Miss Marple and have a hard time picturing her in fishnet stockings with a riding crop.

"She's already told me," my father-in-law goes on, "that we can't get married; otherwise she'll lose the benefits from her husband's pension. Which is fine with me."

I love it when he mixes topics and summarizes them.

The evening continues with a game of charades, each team captained by one of the two kids, males against females. My team loses because Lorenzo and Oscar fail to guess *Saving Private Ryan* in spite of my particularly brilliant performance as a mime.

At midnight, Paola blows out the candles on a cake filled with exotic fruit that Oscar brought. The children applaud, I film it with my iPhone. In short, we are happy. The shadow hovering over our family has left us in peace tonight.

When the two overgrown lovebirds say good night, as Paola puts our two out-of-control heirs to bed, I stay behind and clean up the kitchen. I nibble at some leftover cake, in clear violation of my restricted diet. Then I sit down. I breathe deeply. My lungs are on fire. I can't seem to choke back the tears. It was a great night. And that only makes me suffer more. This is how all my moments of sadness will be from now on: good and sad.

A little later I join Paola, who's already in bed. I slip between the sheets and smell her. I'm so in love with the scent of her. She smells like apples. I don't touch her. I know it's not time yet. Tomorrow will be the time. For her birthday I've planned a special evening. This time I won't fail.

My romantic plans have already been dashed halfway through breakfast, when Paola announces that she's made plans to go out for dinner with her best friends. The women will celebrate her birthday together. My feelings are hurt and I try to think of a way to reverse the outcome, though it's clear that I've been defeated. I come up with an idea, a gift that will astound her when she comes home tonight.

I go out and head straight for the hobbyist-novelist Roberto's bookshop.

"Do you have a copy of *The Little Prince*?"

"Of course!"

"I don't mean an ordinary copy. I want an old one, a special one. A collector's item, is what I'm trying to say."

"I have exactly what you need."

I never doubted it for a minute.

He ducks into a cubbyhole piled high with books, which exudes that particular smell of paper and glue I love so much. He reemerges a few minutes later with a copy in his hand, yellowed with age and slightly curved.

"This is the French first edition, from 1943. It came out just a few days after the English translation. But because the author was French, if you ask me, this is the first edition. It's a gift."

I insist on paying but he won't listen. He understands it's for an important occasion. And he's right, it is.

I agree to accept the gift, but only if he'll let me buy him breakfast at least once. I leave him five euros along with the twenty euros for the purchase of the new novel he's just finished. It's titled *Unchained Love* and it is the sad story of an affair between a black slave and the young daughter of the family that owns him. Once again, a plot that smacks of déjà vu, but all the same, I'm glad to buy the book.

I sit up waiting for Paola to come home. I gift-wrapped the book with a red bow and laid it on her pillow.

When she comes into the bedroom, she's dead tired and for ten minutes she doesn't even notice the gift. She only notices it when she's about to slip between the sheets.

"So what's this?"

"It's for you. Happy birthday, *amore mio*."

She doesn't blink an eye. She opens it. She looks at it.

I feel sure her heart is swelling with emotion.

I expect her to say: "Darling, what a magnificent gift! Where on earth did you find it?"

Instead, she says: "I already have this book. And my copy's in better shape. You need to return it; did you hold on to the receipt?"

Then she settles in for the night with a simple "Good night."

That's what's called a woman with personality.

After all, that's part of why I married her.

don't seem able to work up a sufficient state of sadness. I try hard to be sadder than I am.

I feel apathetic, but not sad. As if this miserable turn of events had nothing to do with me personally.

Today I went upstairs to the roof deck of the apartment building and I set up a sun bed. I turned off my cell phone. I stretched out in shorts and a T-shirt. My eyes are glued to the clouds embracing in the sky, shifting into gleaming white Rorschach blots and then dissolving.

I stayed there for a good four or five hours.

Motionless as a castaway.

I'd have stayed there forever.

I'm officially depressed.

Tonight Lorenzo and Eva are going over to their grandfather's to have dinner and sleep over; Paola's going to the movie theater with two old girlfriends of hers to see an independent film; and I'm staying home alone. It's not something that happens often.

I phone Umberto and Corrado and I organize a super spaghetti fest, just like in the old days. A kilo of carbonara between the three of us. Yes, I know, it's full of white flour, eggs, and plenty of other toxins. But we can't do without it. Pasta alla carbonara is like an old lover, and it's comforting to see it again—every now and then. It's enjoyable before, during, and after, because the complex digestion of that funky blend of flavors works to stun and blur the mind in the way a good strong joint does. We chat, stretched out on the sofas the way we used to do in high school, with a little jazz on the stereo and my coughing in the background.

"Why don't they let you use your cell phone during flight? Does it really interfere with the instruments?" Umberto asks our favorite airline pilot.

"If it really was dangerous, we certainly wouldn't rely on the common sense of the passengers to make sure they were turned off; we'd simply confiscate them during boarding," Corrado replies. "The real issue is that the speed of the plane would shift the calls from one cell tower to another and result in a series of missed calls and a jammed phone network. In the future, who knows. There are already airlines that offer wi-fi on board so you can use Skype to call people."

I say nothing, utterly indifferent to the future of the telephone industry. I cough again.

"How's the pain?" Umberto asks me.

"It's there. I've done some new tests. The condition of my lungs is deteriorating by the week. I've decided to cut out the diet. Or at least not to follow such a drastic one."

"That's the right thing to do," Corrado agrees. "From what I understand, it had become a palliative."

We've agreed to talk in unvarnished terms about my disease, without metaphors or euphemisms.

"I'm a dead man anyway. It's only a matter of time. I might as well eat whatever I like. Ah, there's one more thing you ought to know."

"What's that?" asks my personal veterinarian.

"I'm depressed. I've never been depressed in my life, but I'm pretty sure I've spotted the symptoms."

"When my mother was depressed, after my father died," Corrado tells me, "I tried to give her plenty of things to do, so she'd fill up her day. That's the only thing you can do in these cases."

"I have plenty of things to do—it's just that I don't feel like doing them."

"Can I offer a suggestion?" Umberto breaks in.

"Certainly."

"Go talk to my psychologist. Dr. Santoro—he's a genius."

"What for? So he can con me out of two hundred euros a session?"

"Aside from the fact that he charges a hundred thirty and he gives you a receipt too, so you can deduct it as a medical expense, he's a person who actually helps you. Or at least it works for me."

"Excuse me, but how many years have you been going to see him?" I ask him, skeptically.

"Almost ten years," he replies, proudly.

"Just think what shape you'd be in if you'd never gone!" Corrado says with a hint of sarcasm, beating me to the punch by a fraction of a second.

I remind Umberto that I've always considered psychologists to be people without any true calling, more or less like politicians.

"Do as you please," he retorts; "I think that it might do you good to talk to him."

Just then, Paola comes home from her night out with her girlfriends. She's kind of giddy and excited.

"Talk to whom?"

"Umberto recommended I go talk to his psychologist."

"That sounds like an excellent idea," says my wife, smiling at Umberto, who smiles back.

She tells everyone, as if I weren't there, how apathetic I've become since I found out about my cancer and stopped working.

I sit there, lost in thought. A psychologist. Huh.

Did you know that, in the seventies, there was a movement to change the name of the astrological sign Cancer to eliminate the negative association with the disease of the same name? The alternative name suggested was "Moonchild."

When you spend all your free time on the Internet searching the same few words, you wind up discovering twists befitting the puzzle magazine *Settimana Enigmistica*.

Did you know that a study done by researchers in the Department of Applied Climatology of the University of Duisburg-Essen shows that one of the most carcinogenic places on earth is a church. Churches contain high levels of toxic microparticles, which are generated by candles and incense. The concentration of these substances in churches is eight times higher than outdoors, and it remains elevated until a full day after the end of Mass.

Did you know that there are smart bras that can diagnose cancer? In clinical testing, the Breast Tissue Screening Bra attained a rate of accuracy of roughly 92 percent; it functions by monitoring temperature variations in various points of the breast. This makes it possible to identify tumors six years earlier.

*   *   *

Did you know that oral sex can cause cancer? This is the oropharyngeal tumor, whose frequency has been increasing exponentially over recent years. Use of prophylactics reduces but does not eliminate the risk of infection.

Did you know that marijuana fights cancer? In this case, we're in the presence of a paradox: the cannabidiol that marijuana contains reduces the pain and nausea and slows the growth of the tumor cells, but the fumes produced when you smoke the marijuana contain nitrogen oxides, carbon monoxide, cyanides, and nitrosamines, all of which are potentially carcinogenic. The classic serpent biting its tail.

But I never do find the news report I've been hunting for more than a month now: "Japanese scientists discover a new and infallible cure for tumors."

Still, I don't give up—somewhere out there must be a modern Leonardo da Vinci who, one fine day, will wake up and say: "Hey, guys, I just figured it out: all you need to do to cure cancer is to take two tablets of ginger, thyme, and garlic together before every meal!" Maybe the cure has always been there, right out in plain view, just like Edgar Allan Poe's purloined letter.

The closer I get to summer, the more Rome seems like what it once was. I feel the urge to walk. I wander around through the ghetto, then I walk down the steps to the banks of the Tiber. I sit down to watch this cloaca of a river flow through the city I love best.

And I happily smoke a joint.

'***ve always made fun of my friends who see psychologists. Now here
I am, sitting in an armchair across from Dr. Santoro, a little man
who looks like a Disney raccoon, and who looks at me without speaking as he jots down notes. I feel as if I've wandered into an episode of
In Treatment. Since therapy requires me to talk and him to listen, I'm
forced to chatter away, even though it's the last thing I feel like doing.

I don't know why I don't mention the cancer straight off.

*The first time I was afraid I was about to die was in 1993 and I was
twenty years old. Back then, there was no law requiring a helmet
while riding a scooter and so I gunned my Ciao moped at top speed
through the streets of Rome. I felt invincible, until the day some idiot
doored me as he got out of a parked car. The moped slammed to a stop
and I kept flying. I did a forward pike straight onto the asphalt. I don't
remember the impact, though it was reconstructed by the police accident team, but I do remember what happened ten seconds later. I
was on the ground, with ten people standing over me talking, though
their voices were muffled.*

"He's dead!"

"No, his eyes are moving."

"Call an ambulance."

"What's the point? He'll be dead in a couple of minutes."

Why were they so confident in their diagnosis? I couldn't feel any particular pain. Then a thought occurred to me and I touched my head. My hair was dripping with blood. My skull was pressed hard against the pavement, in a pool of red blood cells. I really am a goner, I decided.

It's a sensation everyone ought to have at least once in a lifetime: the thought that it's all over.

There I was, covered with my own blood, and I felt somehow lighter. Everything had regained its natural weight. I don't even remember where I was going on my moped. Maybe to practice, or else to a pub, I couldn't say.

Ten minutes later, in the ambulance, I discovered that I had a bad cut on my scalp, I'd be left with a large scar, but I was certain to survive with ease. The abundant array of blood vessels that run to the scalp had created the illusion of a much more serious injury than was actually the case. Ten days with a bandaged head and I was good as new.

Dr. Santoro has listened to the whole story with apparent attention, every so often scribbling a note. I realize that I still have a good twenty minutes before the session is over and I go on talking. But this time I just invent out of whole cloth.

The first time I killed a man, I was in third grade . . .

The raccoon doesn't blink an eye. Either he's fallen asleep with his eyes open or he's not impressed. I go on.

The victim was a custodian at my elementary school. Not one of the friendly ones, the ones who joke around with the kids. No, this was a bitter, nasty old man, a failure in life who hated young people and everything about youth . . .

I can't figure out whether the psychologist has painted-on eyes, like in a TV cartoon, or whether he's just staring at me with chilly scorn. He's stopped taking notes. He looks like a wax statue at Madame Tussauds.

I lay in ambush, waiting for him after class, and hit him in the head with a chair. He didn't die immediately, so I had go on beating him while he screamed. His screams attracted another custodian, an older woman, and I was forced to kill her as well . . .

He blinks twice. So he's alive.

At this point I decide to go on; after all, it's just a few more minutes.

The following day the school was closed while the police investigated the killings. It took a week before classes resumed, but no one ever suspected me. No one, that is, except for a classmate of mine, Umberto, who became a veterinarian. I'd told him what I planned to do, and he's still blackmailing me, all these years later . . .

He starts at the mention of his patient's name.

"So you're saying that Umberto . . . knew?"

I realize that he's been frozen solid with fear. He believes every word I've said and he's taken me for a deranged murderer for the past five minutes. A psychologist who's not much of a psychologist. A really stupid psychologist.

"Do you mind if I leave five minutes early?" I ask, laying the agreed-upon 130 euros on his desk.

"No," he replies, in a daze. He's in my hands: he doesn't even know whom he's talking to, a depressed man or a bloodthirsty killer.

I leave and buy myself an ice-cream cone, with three flavors of gelato.

Pistachio, chocolate crunch, and vanilla—together.

If you ask me, much more useful and cheaper than a psychologist.

By now the Dino Zoff notebook is full of notes, sketches, and projects. It's become my inseparable companion in my misfortunes. I check off the days as they rush past in the countdown to oblivion. A countdown that has only had a statistical meaning. Until today.

The first person to know is Massimiliano, my new friend at the Chitchat shop, and by now my preferred confidant. As he knows so little or almost nothing about me, he's often able to give me better advice than Umberto and Corrado, who are emotionally involved and therefore less objective.

The first words I say to him are pretty self-explanatory: "I've decided to kill myself."

"What are you saying?"

"Don't worry, I'm not about to jump out the window, and I'm not going to hang myself from the ceiling of your shop. I'm talking about assisted suicide, in Switzerland. I've already researched it thoroughly. I've even picked a clinic; it's in Lugano."

"Why?" he asks, with heartfelt concern.

"A thousand good reasons, but here are the main ones: I don't want to watch myself fall apart physically, but most of all, I don't want to make my wife and children witness that. I want them to remember me in tiptop shape, or something close to it. I think that's my right."

"What about the diet?"

"It's working. I'm losing weight and that's helping to alleviate the pain. But the tumor markers in my bloodstream are rising constantly,

I'm afraid. I received new test results just the other day. I discovered my buddy Fritz too late."

"Your buddy Fritz?"

"That's what I call my cancer. It takes some of the sting out of it, no?"

"It sure does. I have to say, I hope you change your mind about this."

"Not a chance. I've been trying to come to this decision for a month now. It's the only possible way out. I don't want to rot in a hospital bed."

"Have you told your wife?"

"No. We're having a pretty hard time of it lately, you know."

He pours me a glass of iced peach tea. Homemade, by him. Organic peaches and mineral water. Even Madonna would approve.

A minute later the depressed Giannandrea from last week joins us. By now he's a regular client. This time I learn that he's a tailor and his wife left him for a gas station attendant from Udine.

We play cards, an Italian rummy game called Scala Quaranta. I hadn't played Scala Quaranta in I can't remember how long. I can barely even remember the rules. It's a recurring motif of my new life, that I do things I haven't done in years or that, in some cases, I've never done at all. At last, an upside.

Corrado and I swing by to pick up Umberto at the clinic. We're going to enjoy an aperitif suitable for certified good-for-nothings in a bar in the center of town.

I haven't yet told my friends what I've decided.

I'll do it after our first Spritz.

"In sixty-nine days I'm going to Switzerland."

"That's great, are you going to take a little spin?" Corrado doesn't get it. I might not have made myself clear.

"I've made a reservation at a clinic for assisted suicide."

At the word "suicide" a surreal silence descends on the table. For a couple of minutes there's no sound except for the distant notes of a hit by Oasis. Even my cough stands shyly on the sidelines.

"Why sixty-nine days?" asks Umberto, just for something to say.

"I've run a countdown. From a hundred to zero. It's symbolic but it has a certain statistical meaning. Sometime in the days around zero, my situation is going to reach a critical point. The weeks after that are only going to be deeply humiliating for me. So I'm going to make sure day zero will be my last. I've made up my mind."

"Are you giving up?" Corrado can't wrap his head around it.

"No. It's just that I don't want to watch my body fall apart. And I don't want my children to remember a withered father who's a prisoner of a recliner chair."

"Does Paola know?" Umberto asks me.

"Not yet."

"Tell me that you're not serious!" Corrado insists, incapable of taking the idea in.

"I wish I could. Can you imagine? Friends, I don't have cancer at all; it was all just a practical joke to get a little more affection. No, it's true. And now I've decided to enjoy to the fullest the remaining two months and change that remain to me."

"That remain to us," a melancholy Corrado corrects me. "There were three musketeers, after all."

"Actually, there were four. And D'Artagnan was the most important one of all," Umberto points out.

We launch into a heated debate over Dumas' mistaken choice of a title and we fondly think back to Andrea, an old friend of ours from high school days, who was our D'Artagnan but who emigrated many years ago. With him, we made an unbeatable quartet. Then we drink another Spritz and comment on the derriere of a girl leaning against the bar in a position that lets us glimpse her thong. A conversation split into two parts, as if we were deliberately steering clear of the topic of my buddy Fritz.

"In sixty-eight days I'm going to kill myself."

Paola freezes.

"What are you saying?"

"My buddy Fritz has practically beaten me. Every day I feel a little weaker. According to the doctor, in a couple of months I'll have to live flat on my back in bed, filled to the gills with painkillers, and then the final phase will begin. That wouldn't be a pretty sight. I'll leave before that can happen. Elephants do it. I'll do it too."

She's devastated. I know it, I can see it in her face. I should have come up with a better way to tell her. I didn't think.

"I don't understand . . ."

"I made a reservation in a clinic in Lugano."

"Euthanasia?"

"Assisted suicide is the more accurate term."

"When did you decide this?"

"A week ago."

"Why didn't you say anything to me about it?"

"It's not like we've been talking much lately."

"You're out of your mind."

We remain in silence for an unbelievably long time. Then Paola grabs her purse and leaves.

I remain in the apartment.

Mourning over our lost complicity. I want it back. But I have to wait. For Paola.

I've lost so many people because of my criminal affair with Signora Moroni, and all of them live inside Paola: my wife, my best friend, my lover, my accomplice in life, my biggest fan, my everything.

My everything.

Paola is my everything. That's the correct definition.

But right now, what am I for her?

A burden, a roommate, the father of her children, a traitor.

I know that she still loves me—I can feel it.

That's the main force driving me forward.

The phrase in the Dino Zoff notebook.

Get Paola to forgive me.

I'm on the way to the pool when my car mutters something. It's having a hard time climbing the Janiculum Hill, like a cyclist with cramps on a steep incline in the Dolomites. Then it belches a cloud of black smoke and jerks to a silent halt. Great.

I back into a parking place, and then I head down the steps that lead to Trastevere. I step into a car repair place and a bored mechanic who looks about eighteen tells me that "when the boss gets back, someone'll go get your car." I entrust him with the keys and take a seat in a nearby café. This is an out-of-the-way corner of Trastevere I've never visited before. The barista, Nino, immediately wins me over. By the front door, a windowless wall overlooks the sidewalk, covered with a mural that Nino came up with. The wall, stretching about thirty feet, is divided in two: on one side, written large in red paint, is THINGS I LOVE, while on the other side, in midnight-blue paint, is THINGS I HATE. His intention was to create a collective diary of all the things we love and hate, open to anyone who felt like writing something. Next to it, Nino has written three or four little rules on compiling the wall. You're not allowed to write anything insulting or offensive, and it's forbidden to talk about soccer teams and political parties—otherwise, anything goes. I order a pineapple juice and start reading the mural. The wall is covered with colorful phrases of all sizes, both anonymous and signed by name.

The best ones?

In "things I love" I'd choose the following:

"The grated apple my grandmother used to make, Renato"

"When Fonzie hits the jukebox and starts a song, Lorenzo"

"Thunder" (anonymous)

"The happy sight of Mariasole's tits, Guido"

"The crackling of a fire, K."

"The sea in winter, Enrico"

In the section "things I hate," the winners are:

"People who drive around Rome in an SUV, Martina"

"Everyone, Gianluigi"

"The idiots who go on *Big Brother*" (anonymous)

"My hips, Loredana"

"Whoever stole my moped, Fabio"

An assortment of opinions, points of view of the world, some of them light as gossamer, others lapidary and profound. Someone really ought to photograph this wall and preserve it for posterity. A thousand years from now, Nino's wall will tell the story of this Italy to our descendants better than most history books.

I drink my pineapple juice and I write something of my own.

I love: life.
I hate: death.

Obvious but true.

I'm going to leave you two mural pages for your own personal loves and hates. When you find this book in the attic, years from now, you'll reread them with a hint of sadness, probably discovering that you still love and hate the same things.

THINGS I LOVE

THINGS I HATE

Today I'm feeling optimistic. And I do my best not to think about the end.

Of course, that doesn't work out.

I still have more than two months. Lots of time. It could have been worse. What if there were a courtesy service that alerted you only ten minutes before you died. Maybe they'd send out a handy self-deleting text message or else a courier service with messengers on mopeds would go from house to house to deliver the news.

"Hello, we just wanted to let you know that you're going to die in ten minutes!"

"Oh thanks, darn it, I'd just put some pasta on. It takes thirteen minutes to cook."

"I'm afraid you don't have enough time. Unless you want to eat it al dente."

"Too bad, I like it cooked thoroughly. Do you think I have time to use the bathroom?"

"I don't know—is it something quick?"

"Well, I did want to take a quick shower. You never know whom you're going to meet in the afterlife . . ."

"Look, sorry to burst your bubble, but there is no such thing as the afterlife; that's just an invention of organized religions. I hope you enjoy the next nine minutes of boiling pasta."

"What? I didn't steal, I didn't take the Lord's name in vain, I didn't covet my neighbor's wife . . . and now? You say there's no reward?"

"No, I'm just sorry for you, that you didn't take your chances!"

As he goes on talking, I nod off.

Like I told you, I'm feeling optimistic today.

The Dino Zoff notebook is starting to be badly wrinkled. On day sixty-five I see a stain of tomato sauce, or of something reddish. Maybe it's cherry jam.

Time flows along like this. I can't seem to figure out the right things to do or not do. I go on living, dragged along by the current of the stream. I coach my team as it continues its battle for the championship finals; I help Lorenzo and Eva do their homework; I play with Shepherd, who, by now, has accepted me into the nuclear family because he considers me a harmless rival. Paola is less upset these days, taken as she is by the routine of school and her responsibilities as a mother.

A few days ago, I commissioned Roberto to write a pirate story, a novel about corsairs, to be exact. I don't know why, but I love books set among the galleons that plied the Caribbean far more than I do those set among Malaysian praus. In other words, I prefer the Corsaro Nero to Sandokan. I hurry over enthusiastically to pick up my book. I feel like Lorenzo the Magnificent, a patron of the arts who finances unforgettable artworks from his favorite artists.

I pay my twenty euros, I grab the brand-new copy of *The Galleon of Dreams*, and I leave. I stretch out in the sun on a meadow in Villa Borghese. And I open to the first page.

The pirate galleon cut through the waves, scudding along before a lazy trade wind too weak to let it long flee the

speedier Spanish brigantines. A cannon shot rang out in the
distance, and the ball went whistling past the bridge.

That's what I call getting straight to the point. The next two hours are a succession of boarding crews taking ships, treasure hunts, cannibals, traitors, firing squads, and all the usual paraphernalia of any self-respecting adventure novel. For once, the plot isn't copied from Emilio Salgari. The main character is a haunted galleon that imprisons in its hold the dreams of its passengers. When they land, the unfortunate victims find themselves stripped of the will to live. A piratesque variant on the old tale of Pandora's box and so many other myths.

As I read the last line, I realize that, perhaps without intending to, Roberto has written a wonderful allegory of my present condition. The galleon sickness has imprisoned my energy, deleted all my dreams, and slackened my vital pace. Instead of stimulating me, it has decidedly sapped me of all vigor. The truth is, in spite of all my best intentions, I can't seem to savor the time left until the end.

But starting today, I'm turning over a new leaf.

write a very short text message: "Prank time." And I send it to Corrado and Umberto. This is our code for a call to arms. It means that it's time to roll up our sleeves and head out to play pranks, just like Count Mascetti and his best friends in the movie *Amici miei*. It has been far too long.

The prank that Corrado, our unrivaled leader in terms of messing around with other people's minds, most loves to play when he's working without accomplices, is this one: He lands at Fiumicino airport, changes out of his captain uniform, and with his suitcase in hand, blends into the crowd at International Arrivals. Then he starts scrutinizing the signs held by the waiting chauffeurs: MR. KLEBER, HELVETIA HOTEL, JAMES HELSENER, FARLES MEETING, and so on. He chooses his target—say Mr. Kleber—and walks up armed with a straight face and speaking a fractured Italian with a strong Anglo-Saxon accent. Nine times out of ten he hits a bull's-eye: the poor driver has never met "Mr. Kleber" and ushers him to the car without thinking twice. And that's where the real adventure begins for Corrado: Where is this mysterious Mr. Kleber heading? Is he expected to address a crowded conference? Or will he be housed in a fabulous suite and then ushered to a movie premiere? Or is there a table reserved for him in a charming local restaurant? Or does he have an invitation to attend an exclusive cocktail party with the high nobility of Rome? For the most part, before the switch has been uncovered (which is when Corrado is always ready to take to his heels), our hero has already eaten and drunk his fill, and generally enjoyed himself at Mr. Kleber's expense. Of course, there are times when the fraud is sussed out early, right in the airport parking lot, but it often works out wonderfully well. Once or twice, he's actually managed to spend the night in a hotel, pretending that he's lost his passport and other ID, making use of a room meant for someone else; and one time he actually enjoyed a marathon sex session with two prepaid Byelorussian girls from an escort service.

Umberto and Corrado meet me at our café. Corrado has just landed after flying in from London, while Umberto has shut down his clinic early.

Sipping our three mixed-fruit shakes, we decide our next move. Umberto is always the most cautious of the three—he always comes up with a thousand legal and ethical quibbles, but then he never shrinks from the dare.

I'm the one who suggests today's prank, and it's carried by an absolute majority.

I utter a single word.

"Vatican."

An hour later, we pile out of Corrado's Mercedes in front of a famous little restaurant near the Vatican walls: the very expensive and very exclusive Al Vicoletto. We are greeted by an excited restaurateur with an accent eloquent of his Ciociarian roots.

"Pleased to welcome you, Your Eminence."

He's addressing Corrado, who's attired in the garb of a cardinal, a rental from a theatrical costume shop owned by a friend. Umberto and I do outstanding jobs of playing his driver and his assistant. Clothes make the man, or in this case, the cardinal, despite the prelate's relatively youthful age. Corrado, with his musketeerish appearance, seems like a latter-day Richelieu, proud and dismissive. The staff welcome us into the restaurant with all the honors of the occasion. We ask to sample the specialties of the house, knowing full well that it specializes in raw bar delicacies. We start with an antipasto of oysters, the completely illegal and endangered date mussel, and a culinary triumph of extralarge mussels and clams. Corrado also orders the most expensive wine on the menu and sends it back twice, saying it's corked. No one dares to contradict His Eminence. There's not a thing we see that we don't order, what with appetizers and entrées, in defiance of any imaginable diet. We finish off with the renowned house prickly pear sorbet. A real delicacy. When the restaurateur brings us the check, for 630 euros, we don't blink an eye. I take a piece of paper and write down the phone number of my father-in-law's pastry shop. Then I hand it to the restaurateur with a half smile.

"This is the direct number to the administrative office of the Holy See. You need only give them your international bank account number and the total amount due, and they'll ask me to confirm that number over the phone before ordering the transfer. They're normally very prompt."

Corrado brilliantly slips the restaurateur a fifty-euro tip, in cash.

"For the staff."

"*Grazie*, Your Eminence, far too kind."

"The office opens in an hour or so—you can call this afternoon," I add, to enhance our credibility, which in any case has never been called into question.

"Arrivederci," says Corrado, extending a hand bearing a cheap garish ring he could have picked up anywhere, ready for the restaurateur's adoring kiss.

Two minutes later, we're in the car, laughing like idiots.

"Seventeen euros each, guys. No more than we'd pay for a pizza," said Corrado, who was spectacular in his role, a titan of the thespian's art. We're electrified with excitement and for a couple of hours I've been liberated from my sickly reality. We hurry to witness the second part of the prank, which is when the benighted restaurateur phones my father-in-law, convinced he's about to speak to the Vatican's administrative offices. Over the years, we've given Oscar's number to anyone and everyone and by now he's convinced that his line must have a faulty connection due to some poor wiring. We're sitting there in the pastry shop when the long-awaited phone call comes in. Oscar tries to explain that the man has the wrong number, and all we hear from the other end of the line are the Ciociarian-accented screams of the owner of the restaurant that we'll never go back to. He's in a blind rage and he insults Oscar freely, until my astonished father-in-law finally hangs up on him.

"These days, Rome is full of nut jobs."

Luckily, he hasn't noticed the obvious coincidence: every time the three of us are camped out at the pastry shop, some psychopath calls him on the phone demanding money.

I grow depressed for a moment, seeing a photograph of Oscar and Paola hanging on the wall. Until a few years ago, she used to come with us on our prankish excursions, and, of course, she was better than anyone else at fobbing off lies and taking on imaginary characters. Then she stopped, in part because she was too busy helping her children to grow up, and partly because she grew up herself. I only now realize that we musketeers are working hard to slow down time and remain eternally youthful.

Youthful. I haven't spoken that word in years. It's a tender word, *youthful,* so much more evocative than *children* or *kids,* or the horrendous *youngsters.* There are those who might be tempted to say that what we really are is a trio of infantile idiots in our forties. I would retort that we have won and everyone else has lost. To remain a little bit youthful is the only battle worth fighting here on earth. Even the Italian poet Giovanni Pascoli said so. Hold on there! I only just now realize that I'm starting to gain a new appreciation for all the writers and poets I always hated or, actually, held in contempt during my depressing academic career.

What does this mean?

I file it away as just one more terrible collateral effect of the disease and give it no more thought.

Three more matches until the final playoffs. We need all the points and all the extra goals we can muster to qualify.

In the locker room, I stare all my boys in the eye, one by one, doing my best to instill motivation in them. Last of all, our goal-keeper, Soap-on-a-Rope, and then Martino, our only decent striker (and that's more because of his nerve than his unerring aim). We can do this. This isn't the Olympics but we need to put our hearts into it. Today, moreover, we'll be in a direct face-off with a team we lost to in an away game. A defeat that cries out to be avenged. Lorenzo and Eva are in the bleachers with Umberto. I see them from a distance, playing something, but I can't figure out what. My friend is as good with kids as he is with animals.

This time the match runs smoothly. We immediately pull ahead by two goals and we manage to keep our lead until the final whistle. Solid, impeccable performance. If we'd always played like this, we would have won the championship. I praise the boys in the locker room and then catch up with Umberto and the kids in the parking lot.

"Good work, Papà!" Eva comes running toward me.

"You were great. Even that pussy Martino was playing like an Olympic athlete," Lorenzo points out.

I decide not to scold him for his less than gentlemanly language and I load everyone into the car. Then I feel the pain. The main tumor is pressing harder and harder against the other organs; I feel like an athlete running a long race, and the pain in my spleen and then in my liver sends me the signal that my energy is about to flag and give out. I have a harder and harder time breathing, but my cough has become less frequent; it's been replaced by a kind of asthmatic fit that squeezes my lungs, which have turned into a pair of sponges drying out in the hot sun.

We all leave together to get a *cremolato*, an Italian ice. We stop at the Café du Parc, a place near Rome's only pyramid, which makes some of the best. Once I met the director Nanni Moretti there, enjoying his *cremolato*. It must be a passion that unites all water polo players.

The children are especially excited about the fig-flavored ices, hard to find when they're handmade. Eva teases a piece of fig out of her scoop and holds it out to me. I come closer to put my lips to the upheld spoon when the fruit slips off the spoon and lands on the floor. "You weren't quick enough!" Eva says, frowning at me.

"I'm just a slow, slow person," I say. "Slower than a turtle."

"Even slower," Eva says.

I feel moved by her gesture. I see her digging deeper into the cup, looking for another piece of fruit, Disappointment fills her face and this time it's my heart, not my liver, that feels the pain.

They know knothing about the cancer. And I'm not going to tell them. I still haven't decided what to do when day zero arrives. But I know that I want to spend as much time as I can with Lorenzo and Eva, with my friends and, of course, with my wife. It seems like the only important thing.

When I get home, I make a notation in the Dino Zoff notebook, just a single word: *Cremolato*. I make a mental note to go back there with Paola.

I watch my wife on the terrace. She's watering her plants. I've seen her do it a thousand times, but now I can't tear my eyes off her. She's wearing gray tracksuit pants that used to be mine, and a faded T-shirt. Her hair is pulled back, and she's wearing gardening gloves. Every so often she puts down her watering can and plucks off a withered leaf, or she ties a bougainvillea branch to the railing, or scoops out the leaves that have piled up inside a terra-cotta vase, smothering the dirt. Skillful gestures, Zen-like in their calm. Taking care of the terrace is as good for Paola as an hour of yoga. She is so real to me, out there, doing what she loves. *She's mine,* I think fiercely, even as I know I still have to win back her love. *She's mine.*

I get out my Dino Zoff notebook, by now somewhat wrinkled and creased. I sit in an armchair from which, through the curtains on the window, I can see my wife moving around the terrace.

I title today's page: *The things I'll miss about Paola.*

On Sunday mornings, her pear, raisin, and cinnamon tart.

When she eats cherries and then rattles the pits against each other, like a castanet for gnomes.

Spying on her when she changes clothes before going out, because she never likes the way she looks.

Seeing her sleepy eyes slide shut while she's reading in bed, braced up on her pillow.

In the summer, when she gathers her hair up and makes pigtails, like a little girl.

Her calm voice from the next room as she reads the good-night fairy tale to the children, which often manages to make me go to sleep too.

Arguing about what to buy at the supermarket. I fill the shopping cart with crap and then she takes it out.

Putting up the Christmas tree together. She takes care of the ornaments, the children do the colorful festoons, and I'm in charge of the lights.

The woolen blankets on the bed, because there are never enough of them for her in the winter.

Watching her run on the beach in her one-piece, the silk, strapless swimsuit that leaves her shoulders bare.

At night, when we're on the couch watching TV, and she puts her ice-cold feet into my hands so I can massage them.

The scent of her freckly flesh, hot from the sun, after a day at the beach. It smells like something very very good, hard to explain—a wholemeal croissant with honey, fresh from the oven.

When we're having a fight—you already know this one—she'll stop everything and tell me, in all seriousness, that she's a cat, and as a cat, she can't understand the language I'm speaking, so that even a bitter fight dissolves into laugher.

Her Italian derriere.

When she wrinkles her nose because she has a decision to make.

Finding the kitchen table covered with her students' compositions, which she reads and marks with an almost sacred attention.

Her tears, real and salty, when she watches the evening news with its assortment of cruelty, injustice, violence, desperate pensioners, and poverty-stricken part-time workers.

Her teenage passion for Renato Zero.

Her silvery laughter, and the way it makes the dimples in her cheeks a little deeper.

The way she grabs my right arm like a koala, after we turn out the lights and just before we fall asleep.

Her slender, muscular legs, which she too often covers up with long skirts.

When, in the morning, before leaving for work, she says good-bye: "*Ciao amore*," reminding me that "*amore*" was just me, me and no one else, her one and only love. She hasn't done it in a while. And it's my fault, all my fault. I wonder if I'll ever hear her say it again.

I could go on. I never realized how long the list was. I know her by heart, and that doesn't make me love her any less. Like a Dante scholar who learns the entire *Divine Comedy* and then just appreciates the poem even more profoundly.

Paola is my *Divine Comedy*.

These days I'm sleeping just four or five hours a night. From four to seven in the morning, I am alone.

Books. I've drawn up a list of the novels I've bought but never read. I always seem to stop reading after the first ten pages. My maximum attention span is no longer than a Diabolik comic book.

Movies. I've been watching everything made by Hitchcock, Kubrick, and Spielberg. The rest is all superfluous fluff, made by hobbyists or paid professionals. Yesterday, I watched *Duel*. It really pulled me in. I was the one fleeing and my buddy Fritz was chasing me, at the wheel of the killer semi.

When dawn comes, I always find myself camping out on the Internet.

And I'm always Googling the same deadly words. *Death. Birth.*

This morning I discovered that every day, around the world, roughly 365,000 babies are born and about 155,000 people of every age die. In other words, every day we increase by 210,000 individuals, almost twice the population of the city of Latina. We're at an eternal subway stop, with people getting on and off. A subway car that's getting more and more packed until one day, inevitably, it's bound to explode. An obvious but effective metaphor.

I've even found a fantastic site that promises to calculate, with uncanny precision, the exact day of your death, thanks to a series of cross-referenced statistics. You have to fill out a questionnaire with your date of birth, the city where you live, your profession, the operations you've undergone, the diseases you've had, and even your allergies. Then you have to add the dates of death of all the close relatives you know and the respective causes.

I input all my details and hit Return.

I wait.

Out comes my expected date of death.

July 2, 2038.

This site is defective.

I sit there, motioness, staring at the computer screen.

I Google.

July 2, 2038.

The World Cup will be under way. The quarterfinals will just have been played. I'd miss the semifinals and the finals. It's not fair.

It's a good thing I'm going to die first.

Corrado is trying to talk me and Umberto into making a parachute jump with him. He's already done more than a hundred jumps—he has a parachute instructor's license, though he doesn't actually work as an instructor. I allow myself to be persuaded. Umberto's not going for it. He'll watch us jump from the ground and film our landing. Corrado explains that when we jump, we'll be hooked together. I realize that he's treating me like a sick child. I don't like it. I tell him and he's slightly offended.

"I was just trying to help you have a different kind of a day!"

I skate over the topic and reiterate my intention to make this leap into the void. I ask Paola if she wants to come with us, but she has class compositions to mark. She wouldn't have come anyway. Ever since the unfortunate event with Signora Moroni, she really doesn't seem to care much for Corrado.

Before heading out for the airport, I have an irresistible question: Who invented the parachute?

I should have guessed: Leonardo.

In the Atlantic Codex, my favorite inventor made a note to the effect that with a pyramidally shaped linen tent whose base was held open by rigid supports, and each of the four supports measuring twelve armlengths (circa seven meters) in length, "anyone can leap from any height without any risk."

*　　*　　*

The jump that Corrado has arranged for a beginner like me is called a tandem because, as he's already explained, he'll be jumping into the void along with me, and we'll be fastened together. We'll fly to an altitude of fourteen thousand feet aboard a Turbo Finist prop plane, and then we'll jump. A minute of free fall and then Corrado will open the parachute, roughly five thousand feet above the earth.

The description alone terrifies me.

Corrado reassures me as we climb into the tiny aircraft.

"Skydiving is like making love to the world."

"Thanks, friend, I appreciate the metaphorical finesse, but I'm still scared."

"Cut it out, we're practically there."

The little airplane takes only a quarter of an hour to reach the appropriate altitude.

As we get into the harness, someone swings the door open.

Without warning Corrado shoves me into the empty air. I swear that if I survive, I'll strangle him with my bare hands.

After a moment, though, I discover something that can't really be explained in words. "Hurtling downward" is nothing at all like "falling," in spite of what people think. It's much more like "swimming." I manage to maneuver in midair and turn in all directions just like I do underwater. I'm swimming at thirteen thousand feet and I'm drunk on the thrill and the sensations. Corrado shouts something but I can't hear a thing. For sixty seconds I'm in a trance, an air swimmer having fun doing pike dives, forcing my Siamese instructor to follow my every move. Then Corrado opens the chute, and one kind of magic ends while another begins. The world seen from high above, a landscape that we're all accustomed to seeing from an airplane, is much more exciting when viewed without the filter of a Plexiglas window. We slip downward gradually, dropping earthward under the expert guidance of my old friend, heading straight for the airport we took off from.

"Well?" he asks. "Did you like it?"

"Why haven't you ever taken me up before?" I ask him, in a state of exaltation.

"Because you're a chicken!"

He's right. I suddenly realize that I've been a scaredy cat all my life. He shows me the footage from the GoPro I had strapped to me, pointing at my face. It's the best video I've ever been in since the one of my wedding. I watch myself in the footage, I'm laughing for one minute solid. I hadn't even noticed. I'm swimming in the air and laughing like a newborn being tickled.

Paola was beautiful all the way through her pregnancies. In the hospital, she smiled widely as they brought Lorenzo, all cleaned up, into the room. He arrived quickly, a few pushes, and there he was, a glistening new arrival in the world, as if he couldn't wait to be here. He was five minutes old, the time it took to cut the umbilical cord, rinse him off, and let Paola hold him first.

I stood by her bedside, a proud father, adrenaline surging through my system, totally unsure of my role in the baby's life. Paola said, "Pick him up." I felt my hands trembling under the soft wool blanket that held him. Then they steadied. He looked up at me with milky eyes, his face as fresh as morning dew, and I just melted. I couldn't believe life had brought us this gift, that this smiling baby was ours, all ours, to take home.

Then the miracle repeated itself when Eva came into our world. She was the most alert baby I've ever seen, already poised to fight battles, to take on the world in unexpected ways. And she loved to be tickled. I held her in my arms and caressed the soft skin under her chin. She looked happy, so I kept on doing it. I seemed to live for her smiles. And I still do.

Do you know what I'm talking about when I describe one of those useless May days with a sky ready to dump waterfalls of tropical tears on the world below? Well, today.

I don't lift a finger and just sit, in my armchair, and think about death.

Giuseppe Garibaldi has his own personal commemorative stamp. And as far as that goes, I have no objections. Others who have their own stamps include Saint Catherine, Carlo Goldoni, Pietro Mennea, Federico Fellini, Emilio Salgari, Primo Levi, Ennio Flaiano, Alessandro Manzoni, Michelangelo, Massimo Troisi, the Smurfs, Enrico Caruso, Alberto Sordi, and, of course, Leonardo da Vinci. And that's not to mention a vast array of illustrious saints, poets, and navigators.

I won't have one. Philately will blithely ignore me after my death. Oh well.

I never wrote a famous song, I know that.

I never discovered a lifesaving vaccine.

I never performed a miracle.

I never took gold at the Olympics.

I never made a film masterpiece.

I never designed and built the dome of a magnificent cathedral.

I never wrote *I promessi sposi.*

I never had an enemy named Gargamel.

I have nothing to justify a marble plaque—LUCIO BATTISTINI— 1973-2013—NOTED WATER POLOIST—on the side of a building. A plaque that someone might walk by and say: "I'm going to look up this Battistini on Wikipedia and find out more about him!"

All the same, I have a wife and two children I love, a wonderful group of friends, a water polo team of boys who'd give their lives for me. I've made mistakes, and I'm bound to make others, but at least I attended the party. I was here too. Maybe in a corner. I might not have been the guest of honor, but I definitely showed up. The only regret I have is that I had to discover I was dying in order to start really living. There was an old song by Ettore Petrolini. This was the refrain: "I'm happy to die, but I'm sorry, too. I'm sorry to die, but I'm happy, too." Funny and very true.

I'm happy to die, but I'm sorry, too.

I'm sorry to die, but I'm happy, too.

From this day forth, that will be my motto.

The greatest thrill of my life was when I held Lorenzo in my arms for the first time.

Paola and I taught him to read with Mickey Mouse comics when he was three and a half, to write when he was four, to design houses with Legos when he was four and a half, to ride a bike without training wheels at five, and to cook pasta with tomatoes and basil by the time he was eight. My only abiding regret, as you already know, is that I never taught him to swim, much less kindle a passion in him for water polo. My emotions toward him are a blend of tenderness, envy, and all-encompassing protectiveness.

This morning I was watching him try to fix the leaky dishwasher. A careful five-minute examination, then he turns to look at me.

"Papà, it's just a problem with the gasket. It's a model B60, you can probably get one from the hardware store around the corner that sells spare parts. If you go get it now, I could have it working again in ten minutes."

I do as I am told and hurry out to procure the fundamental rubber ring. On the way, my head teems with all the things I'll miss most about my favorite young inventor.

When he says, "It wasn't me," but his face is smeared with chocolate.

The sly look he gets when he thinks he's outsmarted you.

The way he sleeps so hard that you actually have to shake him to wake him up.

The young adult books that he underlines in red and blue as if they were college textbooks.

His boundless love of pistachios.

His collection of photos of ugly people that he secretly takes at school and on the street.

When he tries to light a fire with a comic book from my Diabolik collection.

His letters to Santa Claus, invariably highly detailed.

His excitement when we go to the movies, just him and me, to see a superhero flick.

His openly avowed hatred for school.

When he tries to teach our hamster tricks.

His Spiderman pajamas, two sizes too small.

His English, which is better than mine.

When he forces me to watch *Harry Potter* again for the hundredth time.

The creative confusion of his little bedroom.

When he sits in the closet reading with a flashlight so no one will bother him.

When he floods the apartment while doing otherwise unexplained plumbing "experiments."

When he used to caress his little sister in her crib.

The classroom compositions in which he writes that "daddy is a failed athlete" or else that he wants to "invent a machine that does homework automatically."

When he secretly tries on my clothes.

His way of obsessively complaining when he doesn't get what he wants.

When he refuses to speak for three days because he's sulking after a punishment.

When I play tennis with Umberto and he acts as the ball boy.

*   *   *

Can you miss someone who's still around? I'm assailed by an illogical sense of apprehensive emptiness. I return home with the gasket and watch the junior plumber I brought into the world fix my dishwasher. I don't want to miss another instant of his life. I've already missed far too many.

Today we ended the game with an even score. All that's left to play now is the last game of the regular championship season. There's still a chance of moving up on points and being given the go-ahead. As a coach, I'm not bad at all. But as a sick man, I'm a mess. I just don't seem to know how to be sick. Paola scolds me every day, and I take the scolding willingly. It's a sign she cares about me. I never forget that I have only one main goal: to get her to forgive me. But it has to be for the right reasons.

This morning, as I was pouring milk into glasses for the kids, she suddenly, nonchalantly, asks me the most important question on my mind. "When will you tell the kids?" she says.

"Tell the kids what?"

"That you've got a short time with them, that you're, you know, dying?"

"Tell them that?" I am stunned that my wife thinks I should tell them. "That I'm dying?"

"Yes," she says. "They should know."

"Absolutely not," I say. "Never. Why would I do that?"

"You don't see it," she says.

"No. What is there to see?"

"That they will be here, in this world, without their father by their side. You just don't see it?"

"I don't see how it can help them," I say. "There's nothing to discuss. They don't need to know."

I ended it. I won't tell them. There's little left to me now with them. And I don't want it tainted by the fact of my dying.

The Chitchat shop has become my refuge, just like the tree house for Huey, Dewey, and Louie. I get back there every chance I have. Today I brought Corrado and Umberto with me too. This gave my old friends a chance to meet Massimiliano and Giannandrea. As a pilot, Corrado has plenty of free time when he isn't working, and I know that Umberto is taking more time off from his clinic so he can spend it with me. I really appreciate that.

The afternoon takes an unexpected turn when Massimiliano pulls a Subbuteo set out of a closet. The word *Subbuteo* alone, I feel sure, will send a thrill of excitement down the spine of any male reader over forty. While in females of any and all ages, it will instill a note of commiseration for the manifest inferiority of what is laughingly called the stronger sex.

No Italian in his forties can resist a game of Subbuteo football.

We lay the cloth out on the floor, make up a list of matches, and with five players that's no simple matter because you have to draw up a genuine Italian team chart with a complete ranking and the differentiated number of goals. Three unforgettable hours of play, crowned by a victory for me in the decisive match against Giannandrea, who turned out to be a wizard of the finger flick.

The more the days pass, the clearer it becomes to me that the small amount of money I've set aside won't do me any good in this life and will only be useful in ensuring a comfortable life for Paola and the kids. In any case, I'm happy when I play. And playing, luckily, doesn't cost anything.

Eva.

All my friends think that I called my second-born child Eva—Eve—after the first woman in human history, Adam's wife and the mother of, among others, those affectionate siblings Cain and Abel.

Wrong.

We named her after Eva Kant, Diabolik's beautiful girlfriend.

I've been in love with Eva Kant my whole life. I believe I experienced my first adolescent impulses in connection with the seductive blond cat burglar of Clerville.

I watch my little Eva as she plays in the living room. She's building an apartment with Lorenzo's Legos, with lots of interior decoration. She's a pro. Then she enamels a number of aluminum foil panels on the roof.

"Those are solar panels," she explains. "It's an ecological house."

I smile.

I sit and watch her as she finishes her fair-trade residence.

There are so many things about her that I'll miss.

Her questions, which are always specific and very difficult.

When she says good-bye by saying "Miao" instead of "Ciao."

The smell of her, so similar to her mother's. Apples.

Her upturned nose which, luckily, looks nothing like mine.

Her unstoppable patter, like what you'd expect from a radio personality.

The special organic lettuce that she grows on the terrace and which she forces us to eat every so often.

When she fights with her brother because he's neglecting to sort his recycling.

The times she makes me buy blankets and donates them to a kennel.

Her innate sense of justice.

The date book where she jots down her daily tasks and appointments.

The bizarre way she twirls her spaghetti counterclockwise.

When she calls me "Papà" in her slightly nasal voice.

Her excellent vocabulary.

Her favorite doll, Milla, who at the moment is depressed and melancholy.

Her unusual interest in the daily TV news.

When she plays on the floor with our own personal Aristocats.

Her love of wax, which we find melted in the most surprising corners of the apartment.

Her dimpled smile that greets me every time I see her.

Eva.

My little woman.

One day she asked me this question which completely knocked me out: "Papà, why don't they make cat food that tastes like mice?"

Good point, why don't they?

I didn't know how to give her a reasonable answer.

Eva.

I'd like to answer another thousand of her impertinent and inquisitive questions. And that's exactly what I'll do. Until my lights go out.

ummer 1978. Who knows why, but today my neurons have traveled back to a long-ago day in July, when my grandparents had already become my parents. I was a fat and happy boy, John Lennon was still alive, and there wasn't a hole yet in the ozone layer.

We were vacationing in Ladispoli. And for those not familiar with the place, Ladispoli is no Saint-Tropez. It's famous for its Festival of the Roman-Style Artichoke and it's a sister city with the Spanish town of Benicarló because of their shared affinity for this vegetable. The distinctive characteristic of its beaches is that the sand has a surreal pitch-black color, because of the high iron content.

One of the first loves of my life, and one of my earliest romantic memories, is Stella.

Five years old, just like me.

Freckles.

Red hair.

A charming gap-toothed smile.

A goddess.

Perhaps I still love her now.

I still remember that morning as if it were today.

Stella was playing on the sand by the water with a couple of friends her age, including yours truly. The sand castle was growing, a little lopsided, but it only had to stand for a couple of hours until the high tide came in. Mamma Franca and Papà Ugo, Stella's parents, were in the shade of a beach umbrella a short distance away. He was reading *La Gazzetta dello Sport,* she was reading a novel by Ellery Queen. My grandparents were camped out under the neighboring beach umbrella. Grandpa was catnapping on his beach recliner, while Grandma was doing crossword puzzles.

It was almost eleven when the clock struck the swimming hour: Signora Franca was obsessed with the rule of three hours after meals to digest breakfast before the kids were allowed in the water. She picked up Stella's inner tube and looked around for her daughter.

"Stella!"

But Stella was nowhere to be seen. She scanned the beach. Nothing. She called her husband and they hunted for her everywhere, increasingly alarmed, shouting her name. Her friends, me included, had seen her get up and walk away from the sand castle, but nothing more. No one had seen her for several minutes.

Panic swept over her parents.

We searched the whole beach. We had her paged over the beachfront loudspeaker system.

"A little girl named Stella Martani should come join her parents at the resort café!"

Nothing.

Stella had vanished.

Someone said they'd seen her go into the water.

Others claimed they'd seen her leave the resort facilities.

And there were a few who said they'd seen a mysterious stranger talking to her.

All of them were attention seekers who'd been out in the sun too long.

The only thing that I knew to be true was this: the one true love of my life had vanished into thin air.

An hour later her frantic parents went to report her to the police as a missing person. They searched for her, but in vain. Stella vanished from that beach between 10:58 and 11:00 that morning.

*   *   *

Today Stella would be forty years old. Ugo and Franca, now unassuming retirees, haven't heard a word from her since that day. The elderly historic bathing attendant of Ladispoli tells me that the two old people desperately, obsessively, come back every day to the same beach, now almost entirely eroded away by the unstoppable advance of the waves. They sit down on a pair of beach chairs they bring with them from home. They look out to sea and they wait. Every time they turn their gaze along the beach, they have the illusion of seeing their little girl walking along on the wet sand, running toward them with one of those gap-toothed smiles that always made them melt inside.

"Mamma, Papà, I'm back! Can we go in the water? Has it been three hours since I ate?"

They still dream of taking that swim, the three of them together. They'd give anything to make God change His mind and wind back the clock to that long-ago summer of 1978. But God doesn't change His mind, and we all know it.

When sunset comes, Ugo and Franca fold up their beach chairs and head home, hand in hand.

Today I went down to the beach and I watched them from a distance, hiding. They couldn't possibly remember me. I was five years old the last time they saw me. Ugo looked through me as if I were invisible. Franca on the other hand looked at me a moment too long, locking eyes with me. She recognized me, I'm sure of it. Women have a sixth sense. Or maybe they're just smarter. But I lacked the nerve to stop and talk with them.

I rolled up my trousers and went out onto the beach, wading in the waves. The sun had already dropped below the horizon. I only had fifteen minutes to build that sand castle I left unfinished so many years ago. My skill as an architect and builder of sand structures survives intact. I'm almost done when a rogue wave rushes in and destroys it, with indifferent viciousness.

A night out with Umberto and Corrado in the San Lorenzo district, and at the last minute Oscar decided to join us. Since he got himself a girlfriend, it's like he's one of us, even if he's thirty years older and weighs sixty pounds more. Tonight he took advantage of a chance to go out because Martina is filling in for her niece for a guided tour of Rome by night.

We've reserved a table at a romantic and pseudo-organic restaurant. The warm night allows us to sit outside, where we're surrounded by college students. Between a raw vegetable *pinzimonio* and a green lasagna, Oscar sets forth his latest scheme for improving the quality of life in Italy. His reasoning starts with the criterion applied to driver's licenses, that is, the system for a renewal every ten years. The discerning pastry chef suggests a similar renewal for anything, as a guarantee of quality for clients or consumers. The examples he offers are perfectly logical.

"For instance, would you let a doctor who finished medical school in 1962 treat you? Would you let a mechanic who learned on a Fiat 1100 fix your car? Or would you let a lawyer who passed the bar in the middle of the last century defend you?"

The answer is certainly not, and yet all three of us have to agree that it's something we do all the time.

Oscar goes on: "Guys, experience isn't enough. Medicine, science, art, and society itself have all made enormous progress. So I'm in favor of obligatory review courses and updated studies, for everyone, every ten years, otherwise cancellation of your professional licensing."

"It's true," Corrado points out, "we pilots have to do it."

"I should certainly hope so!" Oscar says indignantly; then he turns to Umberto. "What about you veterinarians?"

"We . . . well, we take refresher courses, but we don't actually have to take an exam."

"You see? I'd apply the rule to everything, even to high school final exams. Every ten years, we ought to have to retake the exams to see if we've forgotten everything or if we're still 'graduate material.'"

I'd flunk them. Every year, when I see the subjects of the high school final exams that are going to be administered over the next few weeks, I realize that I'd have no chance. I couldn't possibly sit through a Latin composition or a math test.

Oscar decides to offer an empirical demonstration of his theory. He stands up and addresses all the customers in the restaurant in a booming voice.

"Any of you who remembers why World War One broke out, raise your hand."

No one does except for a thirteen-year-old who's just taken a class in the subject.

"Because of the assassination of Archduke Franz Ferdinand and his wife, Sophie. Or at least, that was the official excuse."

"And what's a derivative? What's the future perfect tense?"

The evening ends in a collective variant of *Who Wants to Be a Millionaire?* driven by a healthy competitive impulse to show off our general knowledge. At a certain point, we become the center of attention in the place. We don't get home until two in the morning, like a group of fifteen-year-old good-for-nothings.

Madonna, my naturopath, stares at me with an inquisitorial eye.

"It's been a while since you were last in to see me . . ."

"I know," I reply, my tail already tucked between my legs. I feel as if I'm talking to a priest in a confessional.

"How is the diet going?"

"Well, so-so . . . I've definitely eaten some things I shouldn't have, but I've already lost more than ten pounds."

"Breaking the diet helps you to stick to it. I always recommend that my dieters fall off the wagon at least one day a month."

I confess that we'd be talking about more than one day a month, a lot more, and that a couple of times I went back to my father-in-law's pastry shop for some doughnuts.

Dr. Zanella asks me why I've come to see her. I try to explain that though I feel healthier and I'm sleeping a little better, I wasn't encouraged by the rapid progress of my disease.

"It's not easy to become a vegan at age forty," I sum up.

"That's true," she agrees. Then she urges me to try a little harder to stick to a fruit-based diet, at least.

"Fruitarians tend to be very long-lived. And it's no coincidence."

The word "fruitarian" makes me smile.

I explain to her that actually I've come in for another reason, which has nothing to do with me directly.

"I have two children, one's six and the other's nine. I want you to help me come up with a diet plan that's suitable for their growth. A nutritional regimen that will help them to avoid the same mistakes I made and, most important of all, to live longer than I'm going to. Unfortunately, they have my same very imperfect DNA."

The doctor gives me a warm smile. Under Fräulein Rottenmeier's icy shell beats a human heart.

We spend the next two hours chatting about diet. I take plenty of notes. Lorenzo and Eva mean my life to me. And I don't want what's happening to me to happen to them. Ever.

Midway.

It's time to celebrate.

After dinner, I persuade Paola and the kids to go out. I also invite Oscar and Martina, now a wonderful steady couple. We've done this before, and it was marvelous.

A single word, summery and appetizing. *Cremolato*. A delicious Italian ice.

No figs this time, but lemon and strawberry, and melon. The kids lap it up. I watch them swap spoons, critique with the first spoonful, retract with the second, and just enjoy it all. They aren't covetous, these two. They like what they have. They don't particularly want what the other has. That makes me happy.

Later, Paola brings it up again. By "it" I mean the one thing she and I can never agree on. "You have to tell them," she says.

"I thought we had settled that."

"You settled it. It's far from settled in my mind."

"What do you want, Paola? Misery, for my last few days on earth?"

"It's not all about you!" she says, with a flash in her eyes. "You think it's just about you."

"You're better off not knowing some things, specially when you're a kid. Trust me on that one."

"You can't judge that!" she says. "You're leaving. People who leave can't tell what's best for the people who are left behind."

Ouch. That hurts. She's hurting really badly. I look at her closely, searching her face for the forgiveness I hope to see there. But she is angry.

"You tell them then!" I say. "I can't."

Now she's furious. "*I* tell them? You're crazy, Lucio. This can never come from me."

So that's that. We face each other like rival armies across a distant battlefield.

Sunday morning.

I'm lying belly down, my face buried in my pillow.

Bells are ringing.

The Basilica Papale di San Lorenzo fuori le Mura is just a hundred yards away from my home, and it's summoning the faithful. I haven't attended Mass since the day I was married, ten years ago. I agreed to have a church wedding for Paola's sake. After confirmation, I never went back to my parish church. I'm agnostic, as I said before. And sleepy.

I open one eye, without moving. Paola, beside me, hears the rustle of my eyelids.

"You coughed all night," she tells me without turning around.

"Sorry, if you prefer I can sleep on the sofa tonight."

"No, but I'd ask you to take the doctors' advice, start doing some sports . . . it oxygenates your lungs, it forces them to breathe."

"I can't swim very well, and you know it. It hurts too much to move my arms."

"Swimming's not the only kind of sport there is. Why don't you get your bicycle out of the garage and take a ride?"

If there's one thing I hate, it's riding a bike.

A bicycle in Rome, which is all uphill and downhill, is a useless conveyance. And a very dangerous one. As a sport, on the other hand, it makes no sense at all: you can't score goals or baskets.

To me, a sport isn't a sport if it doesn't involve a ball, whatever the size. All the same, later that day I pull open the garage door. Inside is my old Bianchi bicycle. It must be twenty years old. It's hanging on the back wall, and I haven't ridden it in at least four or five years.

Who invented this machine? My research takes me to Leonardo da Vinci's Atlantic Codex, where, on folio 33, there is a noteworthy sketch of a two-wheeled vehicle that it's hard not to identify as a modern bicycle.

It turns out that the Tuscan multitasker par excellence also invented the Schwinn Cruiser.

I go back to the thankless task of unearthing my personal velocipede, buried behind years and years of junk. Stacked in front of my bike is the detritus of my life, a sort of cemetery that we call a garage, where I store all the useless things I lack the courage to dispose of. I make a sudden decision. I sort everything into the appropriate receptacle: the issues of *Quattroruote* and my schoolbooks go into paper, the chandeliers go into glass, the remote controls and the flat tire go into mixed refuse. For the rest of it, I order a large-item trash pickup. I'm emptying this place out. I want an empty garage. Garages full of objects are useless. Just like cycling.

I finally work my way back to my old Bianchi. It's still in fine condition. All it needs is a little oil on the chain, a buff and a polish, some air in the tires, and it's ready to take me around Rome. I choose a route without hills or cobblestones. The EUR district will be perfect. I'll head for the beach, down Via Cristoforo Colombo. I pop in my headphones. I carefully set up the playlist. All seventies dance tunes. I zip away to the nostalgic notes of Donna Summer.

I abandon myself to the rhythm of pedaling, as monotonous as my thoughts. I pass by a little church where four young pallbearers load a mahogany casket into a Mercedes hearse, as if putting a loaf of dough into an oven to bake. Around them stand twenty or so old people, a few with tears running down their cheeks. There's nothing on earth sadder than a funeral with a small crowd. It's like a concert by an aging rock star, attended only by nostalgic fans. If you want to avoid that dreary outcome, there's only one reliable solution: schedule your funeral early. It's always a sold-out crowd for early funerals. That's a pretty grim consolation.

I've never thought about my own funeral. And yet it's the last act, the one in which you're the guest of honor. So it's worth giving it some thought.

The first thing to do is decide what kind of ceremony to choose.

The first kind is the Italian-style funeral: held in a church with a bored priest officiating, tears and emotional phrases from our closest friends, then everyone is off to the cemetery for the burial (unless the site you had in mind has been overbooked), and finally everyone retires to the home of the closest relatives of the loved one to weep and moan until the wee hours of the night, eating cold food from a nearby roast shop.

The second kind is the American-style funeral I've seen in movies: a nondenominational ceremony in a handsome cemetery with the lawn you'd find on a golf course, with lots of music and poetry readings, then everyone troops off to the funeral party at the loved one's house, with a lavish buffet and a band playing all the loved one's favorite songs. Usually, the widow cuts loose with some acrobatic rock 'n' roll dancing with an uncle who's a professional choreographer.

You may find it blasphemous, but I would definitely opt for the second type.

I want my funeral to be a big party. Too bad I'll be attending flat on my back.

Lorenzo's birthday. The party's scheduled in a local recreation center with all his young friends, a typical blowout for the under-ten crowd. The only grown-ups present are Paola and me, accompanied by a few apprehensive mothers. It's an inferno of laughter and shouting, barely kept under control by the two young men who run the place. They're dressed as clowns and they're the butts of mockery and pranks of all kinds. They do their best to win the kids over, without success.

I stand off to one side, munching popcorn and salty snacks. I suggested some games, but they were all rejected scornfully. I understand that nine-year-olds see me as nothing more than a poor pathetic old man.

I watch Lorenzo as he roams recklessly through the big room, leading his group of friends. I gave him a giant finger-painting set and the smile he flashed me in exchange healed me completely for just a second. Only now does it dawn on me that there's something I won't be able to do myself in the future and that I absolutely have to arrange for.

"What?" Umberto asks me.

"Birthday presents. I need to buy birthday presents for Lorenzo and Eva for the coming years. There's no way I'm leaving them without birthday presents from their Papà."

"But how . . . ?"

I don't give him a chance to argue. Before I go any further, I should point out several things. One is that my wife seriously likes Umberto. She has always considered him a good friend of hers, though he's one of my best friends, and while this has sometimes made things a little prickly between Umberto and me—how much can I tell him?—I've never felt I couldn't trust him. In fact, he has proven himself to be a maestro in the difficult situation between Paola and me, continuing to be my best friend, while giving her the solace and comfort she needs from someone she considers to be a close friend of hers. Lately, when he's been over to dinner, I've seen her take him aside, enter into a conversation with him that so demands privacy, I turn up the water faucet in the kitchen and do the dishes, eager to show them both I'm not envious of their growing closeness. For it has grown. Paola leans on him now, for advice, I imagine, and for solace. How he picks his way through this difficult minefield, I do not know. But I have never felt a withdrawal from him, never a hesitation when I have asked him questions of a searching nature. He has always been available, the same good friend I have relied on all these years. So now I entrust him with the most difficult task of all—buying gifts for the children for their birthdays to come, and presenting them.

"How?" he asks again.

"Easy. I pick them out, you buy them and wrap them."

"Ah!"

"Don't try to tell me no."

"All I said was 'Ah!'"

"I'll make up a detailed list, year by year. Then, if you see that something's gone out of style or doesn't work in the meanwhile, you can choose an alternate gift. We've got to be prepared at least up to age eighteen."

"Can I tell you my opinion about this?"

I nod. All around us the buzz of voices in the café seems to fall away as if everyone else were waiting for his answer.

"It strikes me as a wonderful idea," says Umberto.

I smile at him and relax. I realize that I've been a little impetuous, but there's not much time left to me, and every so often, my enthusiasm runs away with me.

"*Grazie,*" I reply. Then I place a hand on his shoulder. Today my stomach is hurting worse than usual. I've gone back to see the oncologist and together we've gone over the latest test results. My markers just keep rising. My body, in spite of the fact that I've improved my diet and my personal habits, can't keep up, like an engine that's just been run too hard over the years. Pain, I realize, will be a constant companion from now on. I will have to bear it, with analgesics and courage.

'␣ve drawn up the list of gifts for the future birthdays of my two cubs. It took me a whole night to get it right. At breakfast, at our café, I make sure that everything's clear to Umberto. I wrote the lists out by hand, in a clearly emotional script.

"I split up the gifts by year," I explain.

He picks up the sheet of paper and reads aloud.

Lorenzo

10. A complete professional tool kit.
11. My acoustic guitar. Get new strings.
12. A workbench to be set up in the garage.
13. A mountain bike.
14. Three get-out-of-jail-free cards, guaranteeing NO SCOLD- ING for a bad grade. Must be used in a single school year.
15. Three get-out-of-jail-free cards, guaranteeing JUSTI- FIED ABSENCE for days he doesn't feel like going to school, so he won't have to pretend he has a fever the way I did. Valid until the end of high school.
16. A weekend at home without Paola and Eva, with per- mission to invite friends over. He'll appreciate it. Buy him a pack of condoms.
17. My Diabolik collection. Authorize him to sell it on eBay if he chooses. But first get him to read at least one. He might like it.

18. A used compact car, in good shape. Better if the body
    is already dinged up—that way he won't suffer the way
    I did the first time I scraped Grandpa's car against the
    garage door.

Note: Make sure Paola doesn't buy him a moped when he's fourteen. And talk her into accepting the "unconventional" gifts.

Umberto is astonished.

"I wish I'd gotten presents like this from my father," he admits.

"What did he usually give you?"

"A fifty-thousand-lire bill."

His father, who died a couple of years ago after a long, drawn-out
illness, was a man as incapable of affection as, say, Adolf Hitler. After
I'd been coming into his home on a regular basis for ten years, he still
didn't know my name. As far as he was concerned, I was "whosis, the
doorman's son."

My friend shakes off the painful memory of his father and reads
the second list of gifts:

Eva

7. A large terra-cotta vase with an evergreen shrub to
   plant and cultivate in the little garden behind her
   grandfather's house.
8. A gelato machine. And all the organic fruit she wants.
9. A weekend at the Zoomarine water park, to swim with
   dolphins.
10. A small vertical garden to install on the balcony.
11. Her choice of any rescue dog to be adopted from the
    kennel. If Shepherd is already dead, go get the dog im-
    mediately after his death. And then come up with
    something new for this slot.

12. A couple of feminine outfits. Gradually try to get her to stop wearing those factory-worker overalls.

13. Take her to the Chitchat shop if it still exists. Ten pre-paid conversations with Massimiliano. She'll need it. Thirteen is a complicated age. Explain it to Paola.

14. A novel commissioned from Roberto in which the female protagonist is called Eva and is a militant environmentalist working for Greenpeace. No one has a personalized novel.

15. Three get-out-of-jail-free cards, guaranteeing JUSTIFIED ABSENCE for days that she'll be out demonstrating. I know she'll do it. Valid until the end of high school.

16. For her too, a weekend at home with her girlfriends, also without her mother and brother to get underfoot. Remember to buy condoms for all the guests.

17. A coupon for an all-inclusive weekend, camping with whoever her boyfriend happens to be at the time.

18. A used smart car. Women, who are smarter than men in everything, mysteriously, don't seem to know how to parallel park.

He stops reading and looks up at me.

"I've never seen such a . . . a strange list of gifts."

"One last thing," I add. "When they're thirteen or fourteen years old . . . would you talk to them both about sex, and all that?"

"Me?"

"Better you than Corrado, no?"

"That's for sure. But I don't know if—"

"Also, talk Paola into sending them to the U.S. for study abroad, to improve their English."

"All right. I'll try. But you know it's no easy matter to change her mind about things."

"She'll listen to you. I'll wire money to your account for what all this will cost you. I've already purchased a couple of these gifts because they never go bad, for instance the tool kit, and I'll put an asterisk by it in the list. You'll have to get the others when the time comes, like the plant or the bike. If you have to spend more—"

"If I have to spend more, don't worry about it," he says, interrupting me.

Then I say, "And there is one other thing."

He looks up from the list. "You're determined to keep me really busy after you're gone, right?"

"Yes," I say. "Busy in the best way."

"Spill it," he says.

"I want you to step into my shoes."

He's not sure he's heard me right. "Of course I'll be there for the kids, and Paola will always have me in her life—"

I cut him short. "Marry her, Umberto. That's what I'm asking. Be a husband to her. You're already so close, she respects you and has such deep affection for you."

The expression on Umberto's face is something I've never seen before: proud, kind, caring—love, I suppose. Of the best kind. I realize with some astonishment that he is truly in love with her. In deep, as they say. He is relieved I've brought it up. Perhaps it's something that would have happened anyway, their coupling, but it means a lot to him to know I am in accord, that I give him my wholehearted approval. He nods silently. "*Grazie*, dear friend," he says finally.

I've run out of words to thank him. I'm about to hug him when he adds with a laugh: "What about Christmas?"

He brings a smile to my face.

"Santa Claus can take care of Christmas, right? What, do I have to do everything around here?"

At last I can hug him. Some great sage said you need only two or three of these in life—such friends. Sometimes I think I could settle for one. If Umberto were that one.

Today the Gang That Couldn't Shoot Straight is playing to qualify for the playoffs. If we win with at least a five-goal advantage against the second-place team, the Flaminia Warriors, then we qualify in tenth place. The last place that gets us in.

As I mentioned previously, only Giacomo, my taciturn assistant coach, is aware of my health problems. When I told him about it, he said nothing. But he grabbed me and gave me a five-minute hug. It meant a lot to me.

I've decided not to tell the team anything yet. I don't want anything to distract them. This is the first time, in our brief history, that we've had a shot at qualifying to step up to the next series.

The match is an away game, in a horrible pool on the Via Flaminia, the locker room walls covered with blistered, peeling plaster, and the tiles untended for at least a quarter century. Seated in the bleachers are the parents of our opponents, fifty or so men and women with angry expressions on their faces. We've brought six fans with us, including Corrado, who dislikes water polo and is here only because we're going out for a beer together afterward.

In the locker room I do my best to motivate the team adequately. In particular, I devote myself to the psychological recovery of our cross-eyed center defender, Martino, who screwed up two penalty shots during the last match. It's hard to mess up a penalty shot in water polo, it takes real determination and a bit of bad luck to pull it off. All you really have to do is pound the ball hard into the water and your goal is practically guaranteed. The goalie never has the reaction time to block a shot from five yards away. All the same, last Tuesday Martino sent one crashing into the crossbar and another straight into the audience. We finished even, 8 to 8, and if we'd won, we wouldn't be forced today to run up this necessary and highly unlikely string of goals.

A whistle starts the game.

The parents of the opposing team cheer deafeningly, accompanying themselves on whistles and horns. It sounds like the World Cup finals at Maracanã Stadium.

In the first quarter, we slump almost immediately, trailing by three goals. Eight minutes in which we never make a single goal attempt worth mentioning. We'll never win at this rate.

In the second quarter, we rack up 2 points to their 1 with a good offensive push. Now we're down 2 to 4.

I attack the team, heaping insults upon them. It's an old trick that almost always works.

In the third quarter, the Warriors are a little tired and distracted. We take advantage of that. Martino scores a triple and I can see the joy in the crossed eyes of my favorite striker. We score four goals and allow none in this quarter. So we're ahead, 6 to 5.

I ask the guys to make one last effort. The whole season is on the line in these next eight minutes. We need to score a goal every two minutes. In water polo that's possible.

As I've told you, I don't believe in God, I don't believe in miracles, and I don't believe we're going to make it.

But I stand corrected. After seven minutes of play, we lead, 4 to 0. At the end of the game, the total score stands in our favor, 10 to 5. A perfect result to qualify. Just thirty seconds from the end comes the dramatic twist. One of the Warriors' strikers launches a surprise counterattack. One of my players, and I'm not going to name names because that would only make him feel worse, grabs him from behind in an attempt to block him when he's within legitimate reach of the net. A very serious foul. Our player's out of the game, and the other team has an unquestioned penalty shot.

Moving up to the penalty spot is Ivan Gualazzi, a sniper who can score from any position. In the whole league, he's the third highest goal scorer. An aquatic fury.

Facing him, the bewildered eyes of Soap-on-a-Rope grow bigger. The game and our qualification for the finals both rest in his slippery hands.

His father cheers him on from the bleachers, using his real name: "Go, Alessio!"

Soap-on-a-Rope takes his position on the goal line and waits for the firing squad.

I turn away. I don't want to see this. My assistant films it all, as usual. His videos are useful for studying our mistakes and preparing for upcoming games. But if Soap-on-a-Rope fails to block this shot, there won't be any upcoming games. In fact, it occurs to me only now, this could very well be the end of my less than brilliant career as a coach.

I turn back. I decide to challenge fate and watch the most important penalty shot of my life.

Gualazzi has the ball in one hand. He's left-handed and bad tempered.

Soap-on-a-Rope kicks his feet, doing his best to stay high in the water in front of his goal.

Soap-on-a-Rope's father is standing, silent. He shoots his son a glance.

The fans of the opposing team are as silent. They know that for us this goal spells defeat.

The referee is about to whistle.

I've said it before: in water polo it's almost impossible to miss a penalty shot.

Gualazzi fires off a textbook shot: he aims straight down into the water, a cross-shot aimed with accuracy worthy of William Tell straight at the corner of the upright and the crossbar. No room for improvement, an impeccable penalty shot.

But little does the infallible striker suspect that the valiant Alessio, nicknamed Soap-on-a-Rope, has chosen that exact penalty shot to execute the finest blocking of his entire career. Like a hawk, he dives to his left and intercepts the ball just as it's about to sail into the net. An almost superhuman leap out of the water, as if a mysterious spring had just launched him into the air at precisely the right moment. The ball bounces in the opposite direction and the referee whistles an end to hostilities. We've won, 10 to 5. Soap-on-a-Rope has an overjoyed hysterical fit, swimming up and down the pool, shouting incomprehensible phrases. Everyone hugs him, cheering his name. His father in the bleachers makes rude gestures at the opposing fans, coming close to being lynched. Even Corrado, who doesn't even know the rules, screams: "Soap-on-a-Rope! Soap-on-a-Rope!"

We've qualified.

I still can't believe it.

I go a little crazy and jump into the pool fully dressed. Thereby submerging my cell phone and my wallet. Whatever.

We qualified.

My assistant coach films the whole unseemly spectacle from poolside. We celebrate in the water until one of the pool attendants comes to tell us that in just five minutes swim classes will be starting, and they still have to break down the nets.

We go on singing obscene choruses in the locker room.

I'm a happy man.

Happy as I was when I discovered I hadn't flunked out of sophomore year in high school. It's the same sensation. I can still remember it clearly. Pure happiness, practically solid to the touch, uncontaminated by any rational thought.

*   *   *

I return home and tell the news to Paola and the kids, who were too busy with the last few weeks of school to attend the game. They fail to grasp the historic significance of our qualification. My wife looks at me as if I were an idiot rejoicing over a goal scored in the courtyard downstairs. All she manages to get out is a lukewarm, murmured: "Eh, *bravi*."

The adrenaline keeps me awake until two in the morning.

It's just forty-six days till the day I die, but today I'm immensely happy.

I've taken the whole team to celebrate our qualifying to a seafood restaurant in Fregene. I love seafood, whether cooked or raw, and my pop star naturopath may hate me for that. Still, one thing I can't stand is the barbaric custom of having you personally choose the lobster that is to be boiled alive. I refuse to take part in the slaughter and I order a spaghetti with tomatoes and basil. My players, however, take turns clustering around the big lobster tank, sentencing them to death one after the other, forgetful of their shared passion for aquatics.

These days, I feel like a bit of a lobster myself. But with much less dignity. I leave the restaurant where the kids are singing in chorus as if they were in a bar and I head out to the beach. It's dark. There's no one around. I can cry in peace.

The main thing that a *moriturus* definitely shouldn't do is go out with someone who's chronically depressed. But here I am, in a grim little pizzeria with Giannandrea. By now, I like the guy, and I could hardly have turned down a dinner invitation from him. He wants to tell me the details of his unfortunate love story. I know that his wife ran away with a guy who runs a gas station in Udine, but now I find out that that's only the official version. What really happened would have thrown anyone into a state of depression.

"Marta and I worked together in a fine tailoring and alterations shop, a business I inherited from my father. We had two kids about to turn eighteen, steady hours, a normal, if somewhat unremarkable life. We had four employees. We certainly weren't rich but we weren't badly off. One day by chance I read some of Marta's e-mails and happened to discover an old chat session with her cousin in which she mentioned in passing the fact that neither of our kids is actually mine, and that they belong to two different fathers."

I don't know what to say to him. I let him talk.

"So I ask her about it and she confesses almost immediately, as if it came as a relief. The father of my older daughter is that Judas Iscariot of a younger brother of mine. In other words, it was actually my niece I had brought up as my daughter. The younger boy, on the other hand, is the son of an Austrian assistant tailor who worked with us for a season."

"Did you have a DNA test done?"

"Immediately. They're not my children."

"So what did you do?"

"I tried to murder her," he replies with seraphic tranquillity.

"You're not saying you beat her up?"

"No no, I took a knife and stabbed her. Just a scratch, to the belly, I almost missed her completely. She didn't report me to the police."

An awkward silence ensues.

"But it's been a long time. We shut down the alterations shop and three months ago the divorce became final."

"And are you doing better now?"

"No."

"No, it didn't seem like it."

"Every night, I dream of murdering my brother and declaring war on Austria."

"Try to stop thinking about it." It's banal, but I can't think of anything else to say.

Giannandrea says nothing. It's like someone switched him off. He stares into the middle distance. For the first time, I sense how deeply miserable he is, and at the same time, how dangerous.

Our dinner ends with sporadic comments on the mediocre margherita pizza we're eating and the uselessness of mosquitoes in the ecosystem.

I offer to walk Giannandrea home. "Where do you live?"

"In a bed-and-breakfast around the corner."

What he optimistically calls a bed-and-breakfast is a fleabag behind the train station with the bathroom in the hallway. I understand that the reason he lives there isn't a matter of money, because he immediately found work in Rome in a fashion house, but because he loves to wallow in his depression or, actually, feed it. I make a resolution to call him more often. He's in a worse place than I am.

When Oscar invites us over to dinner, it's always a party for the four of us. His first courses are a delight to savor, his main dishes, usually seafood, are prizewinners, and his desserts, obviously, are professional-level tours de force. But since he's become a widower, unfortunately, it hasn't been a frequent occurrence and this is the first time he's had us over since he got "reengaged." In fact, it's Miss Marple who opens the door and lets us in. She continues to wear over-sized flower-print dresses that would be unsightly even as summertime tablecloths.

"Oscar's in the kitchen. He's putting the salt-crusted sea bass into the oven."

She shows us into the dining room and we sit down around the table. When my father-in-law is creating food, he never wants to be bothered; he's like an actor in his dressing room, only ready to appear before his audience when the curtain goes up. The only sign of him is his voice booming from the kitchen.

"Do you want some chili peppers on the pasta?"

A chorus of universal approval roars back. Grandpa has even accustomed the children to strong flavors.

"Dig into the appetizers while you wait!"

We dive ravenously into a spectacular tray of mozzarella, surrounded by a magical eggplant caponata, a recipe that Oscar alone possesses. While Paola chats with Martina about how Italian schools have declined over the past decades, I look around. The living room has changed. The furniture has been rearranged into a more rational design. And it's tidier too. There are even two flowerpots on the windowsill. I wouldn't need Agatha Christie's Miss Marple to deduce that Martina is living here now. My investigation is interrupted by the arrival of the primo, the pasta dish: a baked pasta casserole *alla pugliese*, that is, with meat *ragù* and prosciutto. I've given up the health diet. I don't have much time left now.

"Ladies and gentleman, behold the specialty of the house!"

Oscar is wearing a full-length apron that emphasizes his rotundity. Ever since he got a girlfriend, his language has become more refined and courteous. That just makes me laugh, because I know his coarse and concealed Romanness all too well. As he's serving the pasta he makes an announcement.

"Family, I wanted to announce to you that a few days ago, Martina moved in with me and gave up her lease on her apartment in Prati."

Shouts of glee and a round of applause, partly for the pasta and partly for the good news. Martina is deeply moved at this official coronation, but she still manages to joke about it.

"I told him that he's still on probation. You've got to keep men on their toes."

"That's the way, Grandma," says Eva. Her spontaneous use of the term "Grandma" embarrasses everyone for a fleeting instant. Then Miss Marple finds a brilliant solution.

"Oh, why don't you just call me Martina. Like two old friends."

The suggestion strikes Eva as reasonable.

"If you say so, Martina. Do you know how to cook?"

"Yes, but Oscar's a better cook than me."

"I can confirm that, without any false modesty," Oscar declares. "But she has many other gifts."

"Like what?" asks Lorenzo, as always indiscreetly curious.

"For instance, she's the world's best hide-and-seek player."

"Really?" Eva's face lights up.

"I took gold at the hide-and-seek Olympics," Martina points out.

"There's no such thing as the hide-and-seek Olympics," Lorenzo retorts.

"Oh yes, there is," Oscar brings him up short. "The hide-and-seek Olympics were first held in 1904, and the first gold medal was awarded to an Englishman named James Ascott."

I listen to him without interrupting as he invents tall tales just to amuse my little ones, backed up by Miss Marple, who proves to be an excellent accomplice. I love my father-in-law. There are so many things about him that I'll miss.

His arrogant Roman way of acting as if he knows more about everything than you ever could.

His gigantic shadow looming up on the walls of the pastry shop.

The way he slaps me on the back, so that I always stagger a little.

His overamplified voice.

The way he philosophizes with his customers.

His secret passion for Britney Spears.

The way he pats every dog he meets in the street.

His size thirteen shoes.

The way he looks at me without speaking and I know he's already understood everything.

When he recycles a Christmas present without remembering that you gave him that same thing a couple of years ago.

His ability to fall asleep anywhere.

And, of course, his doughnuts.

I really will miss him.

orrado has an amusing habit that, at least until today, always struck me as funny: for their birthdays, he gives his friends a framed, dummied-up front page of *Il Messaggero*, with a fake obituary of the birthday boy or girl and a commemorative article. His affectionate and hilarious obituaries are devoted to office clerks, mailmen, newsstand owners, pizza chefs, pharmacists, cleaning women, and bus drivers. He's done one for me as well.

A few years ago, when he gave it to me for my birthday, I laughed all night. Today, of course, it doesn't make me laugh a bit.

The headline reads:

Farewell to Lucio Battistini, a Lifetime Devoted to Sports

(By our special correspondent Corrado Di Pasquale)

Sometime in the past few hours, heaven's water polo team recruited a new coach: Lucio Battistini. After the dismissal midway through the season of Jesus Christ, found culpable in the cheating scandal over his team's habit of walking on water, the new coach, Battistini, may perhaps succeed in turning around this badly limping paradisiacal team. In his luminous career as a player, we all recall the ninety-eight consecutive days spent on the bench (a national record) and the four goals inflicted upon him in just three minutes during his last appearance in the highest series. In the years that followed, Battistini left professional competition and continued with his successful career as a personal trainer, successfully helping Signora Dora Loriani of Rome to lose 7 kilos and Commendator Casalotti to lose 4.5 kilos. These spectacular achievements justifiably led to his appointment as the coach of the newly established water polo team at Machiavelli High School. During the first season, the coach was promptly crowned a success, and on the last day of school, the Roman team was able to celebrate its ranking—second from last—with a gala evening of music at the Circus Maximus.

We'll miss his cheerful smile, his perennially burned pot roasts, his reckless incompetence at driving motorcycles, his overabundant waistline, his enigmatic sense of humor. This morning at the funeral no fewer than twenty-three people gathered around his lovely widow, Paola, already hotly contested by her numerous suitors, and his two children. During the funeral service, the priest got his name wrong three times, once calling him Luca, another time Luciano, and finally, to the astonishment of one and all, Ferdinando. After the sermon, the water polo team burst into a spontaneous round of applause, excited at the prospect of being entrusted to a real coach. For this and for a thousand other reasons, today, in the world, we're all just a little relieved. Farewell, Ferdinando. Excuse me, Lucio.

Corrado is implacable; he manages to outline the lives of others in such a lucid and cynical manner that it proves irresistibly comic for the readers, and never overwhelmingly tragic for the subject. I've read and reread my obit. Unfortunately, my friend has once again hit a bull's-eye. He may be sarcastic but he's not lying.

Maybe I need to get busy and try to improve my impending, and all too real; obituary. In fact, strike the "maybe."

The student was seen rummaging through the supplies in the biology laboratory, where he had already taken possession of a liter of glycerine, a flask of concentrated nitric acid, and two flasks of sulfuric acid that are kept in a special locked cabinet, which the student broke into.

Beneath that text was the official, unappealable verdict: two days' suspension from school.

I can't say I'm surprised. Sooner or later, I was sure, Lorenzo would be suspended. In elementary school that's a rare thing, but I knew he'd manage to pull it off. His teacher called me immediately on my cell phone and I rushed straight over to the school—one of the advantages of being a *moriturus* with nothing to do. I'm sitting across the desk from her in the classroom, while the defendant waits for us in the hallway.

"Your son has committed a very grave infraction, Signor Battistini. He stole a number of objects that belong to the school."

"'Very grave infraction' seems to me to be overstating the case. Haven't you ever stolen a book from a library or candy from the supermarket?"

"No," she retorts sternly.

"From the list of stolen goods I'd have to guess that he had one of his usual experiments in mind."

"That's exactly what I'm afraid of: his usual experiments. Last year the classrooms were overrun with insect larvae thanks to him."

"He was just experimenting with reproduction in a damp environment, in this specific case with the pond in the school garden."

"And that strikes you as normal? What did he want to do this time? Burn down the school?"

"Excuse me for a moment. I have to reply to a message from work."

I pull out my iPhone. I lied. I Google: glycerine plus nitric acid plus sulfuric acid. Nitroglycerine. Those are the basic components of that dangerous compound. The little chemist I sired was trying to make nitroglycerine and I have no doubt that he would have succeeded. He wouldn't have burned down the school. He would have blown it up.

I downplay the seriousness of the situation in my conversation with his teacher. Clearly, she didn't do the same research I just did. I promise her I'll punish my young heir with exemplary severity.

When I walk out into the hallway, I find him sitting on a bench, eyes downcast and ears drooping like a truant who knows he's in big trouble. He silently trails after me to the car. While I drive, I try to discuss the topic.

"What were you trying to blow up?"

He's astonished that I've ferreted out his true intentions. Clearly, he underestimates me.

"I didn't want to destroy anything, I just wanted to make some fireworks for the end-of-year show."

"Don't you think these fireworks might have been a little too, shall we say, . . . powerful?"

"I wasn't going to put in much nitroglycerine."

I make him promise that he will never, ever try any further experiments with explosives, incendiary devices, or anything dangerous.

Then I consider the issue of the two-day suspension. The only thing that really scares him is his mother's reaction. I decide to tell Paola myself.

Paola shouted so loud she could be heard all the way out to the Rome beltway.

"Nitroglycerine? Your son was making nitroglycerine at recess?"

When she says "your son," that means she's well and truly pissed off.

I explain to her that the compound is very difficult to make without the appropriate equipment, and I minimize the whole incident as nothing more than a childish prank that, happily, had no bad consequences. And as a result? The one who gets the dressing-down is me. I am described as, in order of denunciation, a bad example, an irresponsible father, an underminer of education and good manners, and someone trying to poison her own children against her. When people lose their tempers, they say things they don't really mean. I hope. I try to be a cat and this time I get the result I hoped for: Paola tries to keep going but her rage sputters and dies out. A few minutes later we file away the day with a smile. We label it "the day our son tried to manufacture nitroglycerine."

But I am aware of something a lot more sinister. I might have lost him, earlier than my hundred days allowed. The thought makes me want to howl.

There's something about me you don't know. I don't usually talk about it much. My son, Lorenzo, and I are exactly the same. As a child, I was a young terror too. Ever since early elementary school, my teacher (Miranda De Pascalis, ditzier than most people on earth, and capable of explaining the multiplication tables with exactly the same words three days running, while never once remembering that she'd done it) would regularly call my grandparents to complain about my conduct. But it was never my fault alone. I had a bad influence, a fellow student who led me down the road to perdition, my own personal Candlewick. His name was Attilio Brancato, but everyone knew him as Branca; we were never in the same class together, but he attended the class next door, from elementary school to high school. An ordeal and a blight upon my record. A genuine living legend in the Rome municipal school system, a hooligan of rare quality, capable of sabotaging vending machines to provoke cascades of snacks, falsifying class attendance records, and even wrecking teachers' cars.

Grandpa hated him. One time he even decided to switch schools to get me out from under Brancato's influence.

Luckily, once Brancato managed to finish high school, he vanished. Nobody ever heard a thing from him again. I was free at last.

Many years later, the day that Grandpa passed away, I couldn't hold my terrible secret in a minute longer.

Grandpa was in bed, dressed in his pajamas, flat on his back and in appearance miles away, but I knew that he could hear me. I lean over close to the bed and whisper to him, with no need for any pre-amble: "Grandpa, Brancato never existed."

Silence.

"I just invented him. He was my scapegoat. A perfect alibi for any and all occasions. A fictitious individual."

Silence.

"Forgive me if I never told you. Brancato was me, and I was Brancato."

I think back to all the punishments, and maybe even smacks, I avoided thanks to Brancato. Then I look over at Grandpa, whose eyes are open and staring unblinking at the ceiling.

Suddenly he smiles. In fact, he laughs. He feels like laughing. Not the usual thing with someone who's about to die, a *moriturus*.

He turns to look at me with glistening eyes and reveals the truth: "Lucio *mio*, I knew it the whole time."

I smile back at him.

"Sometimes it's best for a son," he adds, "and to me you're a son, to underestimate you. It makes for a happier childhood."

He squeezes my hand. Hard. Then I feel his energy slip away, like the water dribbling out of a garden hose.

Those were his last words to me.

I had made a resolution not to think about death.

It doesn't look like I'm going to be able to keep it.

One of the worst things that can happen to you is to faint on the street when you go out to buy a newspaper with ten euros in your pocket but no wallet and no ID. It had been months since the last time I'd passed out, that afternoon at the pool. I was told later what happened. A passerby saw me drop like a sack of potatoes to the sidewalk. I banged up my arm and my head, which caused a nasty cut to the forehead and a badly scraped elbow. An ambulance rushed me to the emergency room, where a couple of hours later I came to, when my family had already tipped over into panic. Paola, after I'd been gone for two hours, started calling all the hospitals and had tracked me down there. The doctor told her that they'd given me a CAT scan and that the bang to my head hadn't caused any cerebral trauma. Then the doctor had lowered his voice and told her that he had some very bad news

"I suspect your husband may have a widespread tumor in his lungs. Let me repeat, I suspect, I'm not an oncologist. I just thought it best to warn you."

Paola's nonchalant response astonished the doctor.

"Thanks, you did the right thing. Any breaks in the elbow?"

"No."

When Paola acts out the dialogue for me, including the doctor's high-pitched voice, I laugh until my belly aches and I immediately feel a stabbing pain in my liver and surrounding areas. The clinical progression is starting to become unpleasant. I can no longer laugh.

Nicolas Chamfort, a French author, used to say that "a day without laughter is a day wasted."

How tragically true.

The doctors detain me overnight for observation. Paola stays with me until a nurse tosses her out in a fury. But before the draconian move, Paola and I stare at each other like two honeymooners. I can't believe my luck; she, bemused, sympathetic, lovely, wants to give me what I need from her. Yet she can't. I want to talk to her. But something stalls as if this is hers to work out, hers to decide. I can't force her to forgive me. That decision, like mine about telling the children, has to come from her.

I stay there in my room alongside an old man with a leg in traction who heaves a painful-sounding breath every ten seconds, a little boy who bumped his head pretty badly jumping down off a wall, and a guy in his early twenties who received multiple fractures in a traffic accident. I'm in excellent company. In fact, I feel almost healthy alongside my roommates. Tomorrow, I'll walk out of here on my own two legs and I'll go jogging. I only manage to fall asleep very late, rocked to sleep by the old man's moaning. I dream I've gone back in time, to the moment I first kissed Signora Moroni. Today I'm sure I'd be capable of resisting.

How many days of your life do you remember clearly? The special days that you could narrate in detail years and years later. And how many days are just normal ones when nothing worth mentioning happens and they slip away unnoticed? What makes a day special?

I leave the hospital with a single fixed thought. I want today to be a day I can put alongside the other three I told you about at the beginning of this story. If I had died yesterday, forty days ahead of schedule, with my skull cracked open on the sidewalk, I couldn't have forgiven myself. It was a supernatural alarm bell: "Hey, Lucio, you think you're the master of your fate, and that you have forty days left to live, but that may not actually be the case."

If I analyze the special days in my life I realize that what made them different was almost always an unexpected event, or one that couldn't have been planned: the time Lorenzo lost a baby tooth; the first time I kissed Paola; the way my grandmother hugged me goodbye when I went on my first camping trip with the Boy Scouts; that time I got a good grade on some class homework that I'd copied; the night that Corrado and Umberto and I slept in the car overnight in Florence, and the next morning when we woke up we were in the middle of a street market; the surprise party that Paola threw for me for my thirty-fifth birthday. Little things that are the concentrated essence of my life. I decide not to do anything special today and just let the day surprise me. I call Massimiliano and I tell him about my night out with Giannandrea. He tells me that he already knew all about it and he agrees that our favorite depressive needs help. Massi-miliano wants to ask Giannandrea to help him out in the shop, in his spare time, when he's not working as a tailor, doing alterations.

"If you come in and you find two friends to chat with instead of just one, all the better, no?"

I tell him it's an excellent idea.

The day continues to be nondescript until seven o'clock. Then I leave the pool and head home, open the front door, and see Eva doing her homework, sitting at the dining room table, both feet dangling inches above the floor. She turns around and, in slow motion, opens her blue eyes and looks at me. She gives me a smile.

"Miao, Papà!"

An instant flash of joy washes away all my aches and pains.

It's the magic touch that makes today a special day.

When the glass door of the Chitchat shop swings open and Giannandrea welcomes me in, I can't help but smile.

"Massimiliano will be right back," he says, "come on in."

He tells me that he started working there that morning. Massimiliano offered him half the take, after daily expenses. A very generous offer that the much-cheated-upon alterationist couldn't turn down.

"I'm happy you're working here," I tell him.

"I'm not really working—it's more like I'm helping out a friend when I get a chance. I think I'm pretty good at giving people advice."

I don't object.

"Shall we have a cup of tea?" I suggest.

Ten minutes later, there we are, sitting in our armchairs like a couple of spry little old New England ladies, sipping our Pu-Erh tea, which tastes vaguely like wet soil. This time it's my turn to confide a secret. I tell him that I'm already two thirds of the way through my final journey and that I'm actually pretty pleased with how it's been going. I've had moments of uncontrollable joy, which have alternated with other moments of profound melancholy. An emotional roller coaster.

"So it's absolutely hopeless?"

"Unfortunately, that's right," I reply in an untroubled voice. "All the tests agree that my physical state is deteriorating with dizzying speed."

I'm astonished at how I'm able to talk dispassionately about my disease. I've become accustomed to it. That's just human nature: given time you can get used to anything.

"Shall we play some Subbuteo?" I propose. "I owe you a rematch."

He accepts the challenge happily. I take Italy and he arranges the green-and-gold players of Brazil on the green felt cloth.

After a few midfield flicks of the forefinger, I'm already ahead 2 to 0. Once again, the good Giannandrea has shown that he's a careful player and an excellent technician, but I am a prize racehorse when it comes to Subbuteo, forgive the vanity, but a world-class contender. I win without any such exaggeration—5 to 2. As we're shaking hands to seal the results, Massimiliano comes home.

"You're not trying to take my job, I hope!" he says to Giannandrea with a smile, then adds: "So who won?"

"He did," the depressive replies. "I don't understand why he never played this game professionally."

We don't have time to finish commenting on the match before a new client shows up, a good-looking female executive in her early forties with the word *stress* practically stamped on her forehead. When she sees three men sitting around a Subbuteo board, she's taken aback.

"Sorry, I just came in to find out something more about the interesting name of this shop. What do you sell?"

"Chitchat, signora. Just like it says. Would you like some tea? Or an herbal tea?"

She's stumped, but she seems unable to leave.

"Yes, thanks."

We get right to work. I rinse the mugs, Giannandrea fills the electric kettle and turns it on, while Massimiliano welcomes the woman in and entertains her affably as only he knows how to do.

If I had a longer life expectancy, I'd try to start a chain of Chitchat shops. And maybe I'd save the world.

As the new arrival confides to Massimiliano that she's just lost an important contract, I smile and inquire, like a perfect English butler: "Madam, milk or lemon in your tea?"

"Milk," she replies, already relieved. "No sugar, thanks."

I shoot a glance at Massimiliano and Giannandrea: we're a perfect team.

've changed the settings on my cell phone so I have a different ring-
tone for everyone who calls. For Umberto I chose the soaring trumpet fanfares of the *Indiana Jones* theme song. It's his favorite movie.

"Are you coming to Fregene tonight? Everyone's going!"

"Everyone who?"

"All three musketeers!"

I'm already apprehensive: I can just envision the booby trap. A
mosquito-ridden discotheque on the beach, with drinks both obligatory and expensive, or wait, even worse, some Roman comedian doing a show with recycled material stapled together into a routine.

"What are we going to do there?"

"We're going to watch the sun set over the water!"

He tells me that it's a bit of a craze, a vaguely New Age trend, to
go and bid the sun farewell.

I let him talk me into it, and at eight that evening, I park by the
boardwalk and join Corrado and Umberto at the entrance to the free
beach. There are at least a thousand people lining the water, and instead of a warm westerly breeze, an unseasonably chilly north wind
is blowing.

"What time does it start?" already starts to be heard from the
audience. I hear ragged bursts of applause, and a few people start
to spread blankets on the sand. Others have picnic tablecloths,
tents, and guitars. It's a little bit of Woodstock on the Roman
coast. Dylan songs I remember from my days camping as a Scout

ring through the air, and one daring soul even tries a Joan Baez number.

We three musketeers have taken a spot to the side, sitting on a beach towel. We've taken off our shoes and Umberto even has a bandanna on his head. I don't know whether to succumb to the nostalgia or just feel like an idiot surrounded by idiots.

At a certain point a religious silence descends.

The star player has begun his show. It's a fiery orange one, and it leaves us breathless.

When the sun has left the stage (the finale, though a bit predictable, was still very effective), I find that I'm crying. Even Corrado sniffles a little bit and then, taking advantage of the darkness, huddles in the shadows with a depressed shampooist from Maccarese.

As everyone straggles away from the beach, just like at the movies when they're running the end credits, Umberto stays behind to stare at the sea. The two of us stay silent. On certain nights when I swing by and pick him up, and we go to the movies or to the theater, we can go back home practically without having exchanged a word. Only great friendships and great love affairs are comfortable with silence.

The silence is broken by Umberto.

"We're going on a trip."

"I don't understand."

"We're going on a trip."

"Who is?"

"You, me, and Corrado. I'll shut the clinic down for a week, Corrado will get someone to take one of his flights for him. And we'll go on a trip. Like in the old days."

"But I can't . . ."

"Why not? The kids have ten more days of school, and so does Paola. What's so important about wandering around Rome by yourself every morning? Is that how you want to spend your last days on earth?"

The question is straightforward and the answer is obvious: no.

"A whole week, just the three of us traveling around Europe," he continues. "We'll have fun and it'll improve your mood."

"And where would we go?"

His confident reply astonishes me: "We'll get a Eurail pass again. A discount version."

I stand there starting at him, openmouthed.

A Eurail pass.

It's a compound word that immediately conjures up memories of the penetrating smell of train tracks, steaming in the hot summer sun with freckled young Scandinavian girls, and calls home from train station phone booths. It's practically another way of saying "eighteen years old."

"At age forty we're going to go take the train with a Eurail pass?"

"Tell me one reason why we shouldn't."

"I have cancer."

"That's just one more reason to do it. Tell me another."

"I need to coach the team for the playoffs."

"You'd only miss one game."

I start to suspect that this evening's booby trap really is about to snap shut. Corrado returns from his bushy alcove. He's already done with his shampooist.

"Well, are we leaving?" he asks, with the tone of someone who knows more than he's letting on.

Obviously, this trip wasn't a spur-of-the-moment thing, but an organized plan devised by these two lunatics.

"He said yes," Umberto replies.

"I didn't say yes. We were just going over the pros and the cons."

"There are lots of pros, there are no cons. So we're leaving on Sunday," Corrado concludes.

"No, guys, I'm not coming."

They try and try to talk me into it, for a good ten minutes. But it's no good. This idea of a journey appeals to me in one way, but frightens me in another. I'm not at all well, and every so often the pain becomes too intense. I don't think that my detested oncologist would be in favor of it. Or my wife, for that matter.

I head home alone. Fifty-five miles per hour.

I call Massimiliano to talk a little, hoping to avoid driving into a bridge abutment.

He picks up after the first ring, cheerful as always.

"Ciao, Lucio! How are you?"

"Are you with a customer?"

"No."

"I'll be there in half an hour."

He has no objections. By the time I reach the Chitchat shop it's practically midnight. Rome is starting to empty out. No matter how bad the economy gets, the average Italian won't give up the luxury of fleeing the sticky heat of the city in summer, even if all he can do is travel to his in-laws' country house.

I tell Massimiliano about the suggested trip.

"Seems like a pretty good idea to me," is what he has to say.

"They suggested it out of pity."

"I don't think so. They suggested it because it's something they wanted to do. And it'll be good for them too. They're your friends, and even if they're not letting you know how hard it is, your disease is something they're dealing with too."

I'd never considered over the past few days how my sickness might have affected the people I love. Perhaps a significant portion of Paola's bad mood is a product of how hard it is to process her impending widowhood.

Paola's going to be a widow. What a horrible sentence.

I have one that's even worse.

Lorenzo and Eva are going to be orphans.

In all these months, I've only considered this sad situation from my own point of view, the one that features my inglorious death; but there's another side to the coin, a side that features the tears and sorrow of those I'll be leaving behind. She said it best of course, my Paola. Those who leave can't decide what's best for those who are left behind. Yet their sorrow eats at me now. The closer my time comes, the more I feel their pain. And yet, it gives me great satisfaction to know that I did what I had to do in order to leave. I told Umberto it was okay. Okay to want my wife. Okay to share her bed. Okay to be father to my kids.

It hurt then. It really, really hurts now. But it was the right decision. Paola shouldn't be alone. I can't bear the thought of her crying after I'm gone.

And among those who will cry longest and hardest, of course, are my longtime companions, Athos and Aramis, even though one of them will be the luckiest bugger in the world after I'm gone.

"In any case," Massimiliano goes on, "I've never told you this, but as far as I'm concerned, this countdown you're doing is actually the smartest thing you've ever done. Marcello Marchesi used to say: 'The important thing is to make sure that when death comes, it finds us still alive.'"

I wasn't familiar with this phrase. But it's wonderful. Perhaps the finest axiom of all time. Something that even Oscar Wilde would have envied.

"The important thing is to make sure that when death comes, it finds us still alive."

I look hard at Massimiliano as he prepares a pot of lemon balm herbal tea. His presence seems to have a mystical healing effect on me—he's a magical hybrid of an Indian shaman and an old wise man. I'm sorry I didn't meet him earlier. Imagine how many mistakes he could have helped me avoid.

A yawn from Massimiliano reminds me it's time to let him get some sleep. This time I put down thirty euros. He's earned them all.

I've made my decision.

On Sunday we leave.

I just have to explain it to Paola.

It won't be easy.

When I don't know how to tell Paola something, my natural adviser is the man who helped create her, and who knows her intricate and complex instruction manual by heart: Oscar.

"I don't get exactly what you're supposed to be doing on this trip."

"Oh, nothing. Don't imagine some sort of tourist's delight of erotic clubs and soft drugs."

"That's too bad, because I was thinking of coming along too," he says with a wink as he slides a pan of cat's tongue cookies into the oven. Outside the pastry shop the night is silent.

"It's just an excursion, a group of friends, a way of remembering the old days. A week's vacation. My last."

"I don't see anything wrong with that. By the way, where are you on your countdown?"

"Thirty-five," I reply: I love how he tackles complicated topics.

"Ah, thirty-five, perfect. In fact there's a codicil in the civil code: 'Anyone with thirty-five days left to live can always do just as he pleases.'"

The Sinhalese, Saman, summons Oscar back to work. They have to finish making pastries for the Monday morning opening. I stick around for a few more minutes, just long enough to eat a doughnut left over from yesterday's breakfast.

I call Paola and let her know I'm going to pick up the kids at school. I haven't been able to tell whether or not they've sensed the friction separating their parents and whether they've noticed that I'm sick. We've done everything we can to be cheerful and sunny when we're with them, but children have a sixth sense, just like animals. I wonder at what age they lose this form of extrasensory perception. For a fleeting moment, I wonder whether Paola was right about telling them. Should they hear it from their dad? Is that the best thing to do? But another voice, louder than the rest, shouts, "*No!*" That put the issue to rest. For the moment.

The fact remains that whether they're aware of it or not, they're acting as if nothing's wrong: they tell me all about their day at school, and they lunge headfirst at the pastries "Made in Grandpa" that I've brought home. Two hours later, in the living room, I broach the thorny issue with Paola. When I utter the word "Eurail" she gazes at me as if I've lost my mind.

"Are you seriously thinking of getting another Eurail pass?"

"Yes. But a discount version. A mini-Eurail."

"That's the most ridiculous thing I've ever heard in my life."

Excellent beginning.

"You're thinking of going away now?" she asks.

I know what she's saying. I've thought of it myself. Taking time away from her, from the kids, in these last few days seems like a selfish thing to do. She doesn't say it, but it's there in the expression on her face. I stay silent.

"But it strikes me as brilliant, I have to say," she finally says, with an amused smile. "A few days with your friends can only do you good."

I look at her, openmouthed. Once again, Paola has astonished me. I thought I was going to have to argue, and instead I have her blessing.

"Whose idea was it?"

"Umberto's."

She nods as if to say, "Of course."

"But please be careful not to overtire yourself. And get back in time for the kids' last day of school. We need to attend the party for the beginning of summer holiday. All the parents are going. And Lorenzo's starring in the school play."

"I wouldn't miss it."

I look her in the eye and can't keep from adding: "I love you."

"I know," she replies. And turns to go.

I let myself flop back onto the sofa.

So we're going. Corrado, Umberto, and I have been talking about taking a trip together for years.

It's now or never.

still have the old packing list I used over and over in my Boy Scout days to make sure I forgot nothing. The indispensable equipment for a vacation.

2 T-shirts
1 extra pair of pants
1 K-Way jacket
Contact lenses
2 pairs underpants
2 pairs socks
Running shoes
Sandals
Autan spray mosquito repellent
1 notebook + 1 pen
1 liquid-gas camp stove
1 spare gas canister
1 pasta pot
1 package of crackers
2 plates + 1 cup
1 spoon + 1 fork + 1 knife
1 tube toothpaste + 1 toothbrush
1 Polaroid camera + packets of film
1 box of condoms

I smile as I note a number of remarkable gaps in my planning, such as the absence of deodorant or proper shirts. I add to the list and I spend two wonderful hours choosing what to bring, including my old and still working Polaroid camera. I realize that packing for a trip might be even more exciting than the trip itself.

I sense a presence behind me.

It's Paola, watching as I select socks.

"What time are you leaving tomorrow?" she asks.

"Corrado's coming by to pick me up at six in the evening."

"Good. I hope you all have a good time."

I can't tell if there's a hint of venom or if the blessing she's just given me is genuine.

"I hope so too, my love."

She doesn't reply. She barely smiles at me and slips into the kitchen. She hasn't called me *her* love in months.

I don't know if I'll be able to enjoy myself on this trip. But I'm going to have to do my best. I'm turning into one of those little old men who never talk about anything but their aches and pains, an unpleasant person, tiresome to be around.

Umberto still has the backpack from our first trip, military surplus, beat up and none too comfortable, with a pair of straps that cut into his shoulders. Corrado and I, in contrast, have bought two ultramodern camping packs. We've decided we don't give a damn about total fidelity in our replica of the first trip.

Twenty years ago too, our train pulled out of Termini, Rome's glorious central station. Umberto, perfect Boy Scout that he is, got there early and even brought a bag with food for the first part of the trip. Corrado, who hates trains, tried repeatedly until the last minute to persuade us to take a free plane ticket on his airlines, but Umberto was having none of it: "We went by train then and we'll go by train now," he brusquely dismisses the suggestion. First stop, then and now, Munich, the obligatory destination of any Eurail pass worthy of the name. Second-class couchettes so we could feel like the youthful globetrotters we once were. We have a four-person compartment designated—probably with a twist of irony—a "C4 Comfort." The comfort in question consists of a plastic-wrapped drinking glass, an antiseptic hand wipe, a paper toilet seat cover, and—hear ye, hear ye—individually wrapped disposable slippers. While waiting for the train to pull out, we silently pray there'll be no fourth passenger. No such luck: here he is. The world's worst possible specimen of couchette mate: a nonstop talker.

I should tell you, privately, that someone about to die of cancer probably shouldn't travel by couchette sleeping car. They told me that

I coughed all night long, and I imagine that my friends considered the possibility of suffocating me in my sleep more than once. The absurd thing is that, by now, when I cough, it doesn't even wake me up anymore. That night was no exception. A night train is like a magic cradle for me. The rhythmic clacking sound resembles a lullaby sung to you by a loving nanny. I slept and slept and when I woke up, the train was pulling into the Munich train station. And that's when our trip really began to pick up.

The first contact with Germany is always slightly troubling. The German language is so different from ours that when I hear the voice come over the loudspeaker, I can't even tell the difference between advertisements and station announcements.

There's a surprise waiting for me at the end of Track 4.

A man walks toward us with a smile on his face. He's put on a few pounds, he's lost some hair, but I recognize him instantly. He's a cadet of Gascony, the fourth musketeer, the youngest of us all, the most skilled with a sword.

D'Artagnan.

Our D'Artagnan—known in civilian life as Andrea Fantastichini, last desk in the back of the classroom, on the left. I can't believe my eyes, and I practically burst into tears. I haven't seen him in twenty years. Twenty Years After, just as that great genius Dumas foretold, the three musketeers become four again. We hug trackside, first taking turns, and then in a long group hug. Seized by uncontrollable euphoria, we shout out a "one for all, and all for one!" Four Italian imbeciles making fools of themselves in the Munich central station.

A few minutes later I discover that it was Corrado who persuaded Andrea to join us on our trip. Our old friend left Denmark, where he's lived for all these years, and come to meet us. He's going to do the whole Eurail trip with us.

D'Artagnan was the best one of the four. A couple of years after finishing high school he took off for London with his guitar in search of fame and fortune. Now I can state with some certainty that he never found it. After a few years of London nightlife, he fell in love with Birgitte, a Danish fashion model who looked as if she'd stepped out of a *Playboy* centerfold, and followed her back to Copenaghen. I never heard anything more from him; only Corrado maintained sporadic contact, first by mail and later via Facebook. His carefree songs used to brighten our summer nights. These days he gives private guitar lessons in the Danish capital, while his wife, Birgitte—with whom he had two kids and who now looks like Miss Piggy—divorced him a couple of years ago. He lives in a little cottage by the sea which, from the pictures, resembles the witch's house in a fairy tale by Hans Christian Andersen. He tells me that, what with the cost of life in general and his alimony payments, he barely makes it to the end of the month. Back in high school I would have bet anything that Andrea, or Andy as everyone called him, would become a rock star. As on so many other occasions, this time I was also sadly mistaken.

I admit it: I'm happy to see him, and I'm happy I've come on this trip. But that happiness lasts only for an imperceptible instant until I notice that my friends walking a few steps ahead of me look like three old men. Three elderly musketeers hunched over beneath the burden of their backpacks and their age. Nowadays, a man who is forty and some change is hardly old. But if he pretends he's eighteen and dresses accordingly, he's old, and how.

I still haven't phoned home. I do it as we're walking toward the bed-and-breakfast where Umberto made a reservation. Eva answers: "Battistini residence!"

The formality of her telephone manners has always made me laugh.

"This is Papà. How are you? How was school today?"

"I got an A plus on my class composition."

"Good job!"

I never got an A plus in my life, except in phys ed. I've always thought that people who get A pluses in school are losers, destined to miss out in life. But my daughter is again proving me wrong.

"Let me talk to Mamma."

"She's out grocery shopping. Do you want to talk to Signora Giovanna?"

Signora Giovanna is our neighbor, a prodigious producer of marmalades and children. She is an impassioned believer in UFOs, she sees mysteries everywhere, and she is certain that the ghost of a long-ago tenant who was brutally murdered lives on in our apartment. In spite of this weird passion of hers, every once in a while we trust her with our children. As a babysitter, given her many years of motherhood, she's better than Mary Poppins.

"No, thanks. Tell Mamma that I'm in Munich and that I love her."

"I'll convey the message. Miao, Papà!"

"I'll convey the message." Her formality is no longer making me smile. I have to do something for my daughter. At age six and a half, "I'll convey the message," even when it's followed by a "Miao" that does something to mitigate it, ought to be against the law. I wonder again if she knows about Fritz, and that's why she was so cold. Perhaps she's thinking, how could he leave us and go off to have a good time now? I don't blame her. But the Papà who would have stayed would have become more and more depressed and surly. These few days away might change me, might make me a more fun person to be around. There's no reason why my little girl should know that. Her coldness was justified, even if it hurts.

There's one more thing that ought to be illegal, and which I'd gladly add to the wall in Trastevere under the section THINGS I HATE: seeing men cry. I've almost never cried in public in my life. I have an inborn shame that keeps my tears from displaying themselves in all their natural splendor.

I'd never seen Andrea cry before. He was our general, my North Star, my absolute personal myth. A man without fear, without rivals, and above all, a man who never wept.

When I saw the first tear roll down his cheek, it was like watching an absurd and supernatural event for me, like seeing the apparition of the Archangel Gabriel during a World Cup finals match.

We were left behind, alone, for half an hour in the tiny lobby of the bed-and-breakfast, waiting for Corrado and Umberto, who'd gone out to buy some souvenirs.

"I'm not a happy man, my friend," was his opening phrase.

"What's wrong?" I ask him gently.

"What's wrong is that I haven't achieved any of my childhood dreams. And life has no meaning if you never achieve them."

Andy has always been good at boiling things down to essentials.

Childhood dreams. What you write in second grade in the composition "What I Want to Be When I Grow Up." The only things that really matter in life.

I know, and I've always known, but only now does the truth of this concept explode in my face like a New Year's Eve firecracker. If you don't achieve your childhood dreams, you're a failure. My childhood dream, as you know, was to be a ride tester in an amusement park. So straight up: I'm a failure.

Andy's composition, on the other hand, was far more original than mine. From his mumblings, between one sob and the next, this is more or less how I picture it.

In the year 2000 I'll be twenty-seven years old. When you're twenty-seven you're an old man who has to work to make money for your kids. I'll urn lots of money and I'll be plenty welthy enough. I'll also be plenty handsome and tall and

*smart and inturesting. Like, the year before I'll have married
a pretty girl, like an actress, and I'll live on the beach, but I
mean right next to the beach and the café where they sell ice
cream bars. My job is going to be a very famous singer. I'll
sing at the Festival of Sanremo and I'll win four times, no
wait five times, once with another singer. My most famous
song is going to be You Who I Don't Love You No More and
it will be at the top of the charts for a whole year. I'm also
going to be very happy because all of italy loves me and
smiles at me in the streat. If they smile at you in the streat
then you're happy. If they don't smile at you in the streat
then you're sad and you jump out a window. But when I'm
thirty-seven I'll be happy. And just to be safe I'm going to live
on the grownd floor.*

I can also imagine his grade: a C minus minus, partly because of
the repetitious content, but also because of the spelling mistakes scattered liberally throughout.

"I haven't achieved anything worth mentioning in my life,"
Andy goes on, after blowing his nose. "I don't have any money for
my kids, and I hardly ever see them because that bitch can't stand
me. My songs never made it onto the charts. And nobody smiles at
me in the street," he concludes with an ironic glance that I know all
too well.

"Your songs are wonderful," I say, trying to buck him up.

"But you've never even heard them."

"Yes, I have, I remember a couple of them clearly. . . . What was
that one about the guy waiting at the station for a train that never
came?"

"'The Train Station of Life,' and it was a depressing dirge if ever
I've heard one. It might have been the worst song I've ever written."

"Well, I liked it. Andy, you're forty years old, why don't you start over? Lots of artists have been successful when they were no longer young."

"Like who?"

"Like . . . I don't know . . . Van Gogh!"

"But he was already dead!"

"Okay, it was just an example. . . . Why don't you go back to Italy? Have you ever considered that possibility?"

"Because I could never live far from my children. If they need me, I have to be there for them."

I sit in silence.

Andy has given up everything for love of his children. I've been underestimating him. He's still my hero.

We grab each other in a bear hug. This one's not like the ones at the end of some soccer game, one of those hasty, virile warrior hugs. This is a very different kind of embrace. Only now does it become clear to me that our bond has never broken in the past twenty years. Andy is still an absolute legend to me. Even if he's sobbing on my shoulder. Actually, precisely because of it.

Porthos and D'Artagnan stand there embracing for a couple of minutes, then our friends come back and the games resume. But Andy's words stay with me.

"I could never live far from my children."

The world's simplest concept.

I try to imagine what Lorenzo and Eva are doing right now. Maybe they're building a Lego Eiffel Tower, maybe they're having a Wii dance-off, or maybe I just don't know. I realize that, being so preoccupied with my disease as I am, I've sort of lost touch with them.

I can only describe the last part of our first night in Munich with this image, and the only memory I have: the four of us walking into a beer hall singing songs in Roman dialect with extremely vulgar rhymes. Alcohol has erased all the rest. The last time I got drunk I was nineteen years old, I was with my team, and we'd just won the Serie A championship. I don't even remember when, how, and in what condition we returned to the bed-and-breakfast.

M y stomach hurts, I have a hard time breathing, and there's a rock concert going on in my head. I feel like Ringo Starr is pounding with his drumsticks inside my head, to the tune of "Ticket to Ride."

I wake up before anyone else. In the twin bed next to mine, Umberto snores like a warthog with adenoids.

In the bed-and-breakfast's tiny dining room I'm greeted by a tray piled high with a pyramid of *Krapfen* and doughnuts. I taste one, but it doesn't come even remotely close to Oscar's. I leave it on my plate after the first bite. Only now do I realize that my little morning habit is one of the most treasured moments of my life.

The hyperactive Andrea has tracked down the riding stables outside of the city where we went on our first trip. A sensation of déjà vu accompanies me for the rest of the morning. And a word rattles around in my head, shoving Ringo aside: *remake.*

Actually, remakes make no sense. You might be able to go back to the same city, but to go back and do the same things is a rare and peculiar occurrence. *Demented* may be the word I'm looking for.

The riding stables are just as I remembered them. Wood, iron, and that distinctive scent you can imagine perfectly well. Leading our heroic little squadron is none other than Thomas's son, Thomas Jr., every bit as much of a Neanderthal as his father, but much less likable. He gives us thousands of tips on what to do and not to do while on horseback in the interests of our personal safety. We spot a trail and set off at a gallop to the horror of my sorely tested spinal cord, strained by the unnatural posture. After a hundred feet or so, my horse, the disquietingly named Attila, decides to throw me with a sudden halt. I go head over heels and fly straight off. My fall lasts no more than a couple of seconds, but it's enough time for me to realize what an idiotic death I'm about to die. Waiting for me as a landing pad is—not a murderously rocky crag or a picket fence—but a stinging nettle bush. It saves my life but ruins the rest of my afternoon.

The result of our outing: skin rashes all over my body, sunstroke for Andrea, lumbago for Umberto, and a sprained ankle for Corrado, whose foot got caught in the stirrups as he was dismounting. We're four slightly rusty musketeers.

All males have a shared trait: when they're twenty years old, they admire and court twenty-year-old women; and when they're forty years old, they do the same thing. It's a scientific law. But I believe that there's a nostalgic factor at work deep down. We continue to love the same movies, books, and places we loved when we were kids. The same thing applies to twenty-year-old women. Have I talked you into it?

We immediately discover that the infamous Bier und Liebe has been replaced by an aggressive little pub, the Tot oder Lebendig, which literally means "dead or alive." Inside are hundreds of German youths between the ages of eighteen and twenty-five, juggling beers, sweat, and pills of all kinds. I swear that I've never once felt so out of place. The music is too loud, preventing any form of verbal interaction, the lighting is too dim, keeping anyone with shortsightedness from reading the menu, and the air is short on oxygen, which prevents the brain from attaining adequate mental lucidity. In spite of this we do our best to enjoy ourselves. I'm immediately branded a "ball and chain" because I have no interest in getting drunk or trying to pick up a German woman young enough to be my daughter. I decide to drink a couple of fruit cocktails and allow myself to be hypnotized by the music videos that stream across a transparent wall.

Corrado takes care of livening up the evening's entertainment by getting into a fight with the boyfriend of the young woman he's chosen as the object of his desire. The guy in question is a muscleless ninety-eight-pound. weakling, but he also has lots of friends who are already several drinks in. We escape before a brawl breaks out in the beer hall and find ourselves wandering aimlessly around Munich like four classic Italian *vitelloni*. We talk until four in the morning.

I've forgotten to call home. So far away from them, I hear their voices all the time—Paola's strong, decisive one; Lorenzo's thoughtful one, with its pauses, and its "ums"; Eva's sweet girly one turning prosecutorial as she tries to convince, making me wonder what she'll sound like when the girliness goes. Hearing their voices in my head, I miss Paola and my kids so much it's killing me.

It's a sleepless night. A dreamless night.

At breakfast, Umberto describes the next leg of the trip: Vaduz, capital of Liechtenstein. Twenty years ago we won a hundred dollars or so at the casino in that picturesque little city, and we felt like wizards of the roulette wheel. I suddenly interrupt the reminiscing with a thought that's been keeping me company all night long: "What am I doing here?"

My question seems to tear into my friends like a burst of machine-gun fire.

"How do you mean?" asks Corrado.

I don't know the words to use to avoid offending them.

"I mean that I want to go home. Forgive me, but this isn't the trip I want to take. Or what I mean is, it's not the trip that I need to take."

D'Artagnan smiles at me: he's the only one who's understood.

"Your wife will never agree to it, after the mess you made," he warns.

"I'll try anyway."

"I don't understand what you two are talking about," Umberto says.

"I want to take a trip with my kids. And with Paola. I want to spend all the days that are left to me with them. Not with you."

I try to soften the blow.

"Don't get me wrong; you're my best friends in the world—we're the four musketeers. I know everything there is to know about you, your best and worst qualities, and you know the same about me. This time left to me now? That's my kids'. Right now what I need is them. And they may not know it, but what they need is me."

Silence.

"I don't have even a minute to waste."

I look them in the eyes one by one.

"Forgive me. If you want, you're welcome to finish the tour."

Corrado is the first to speak. He's always been the fastest decision maker of the group.

"There's a flight for Rome at 10:30 a.m. The pilot's a friend; he'll get all three of us on board."

Umberto checks the time: "We have ten minutes to pack our bags, guys. Let's get moving."

Andy, who really has no desire to go back to Denmark and his failure of a life, is the most obviously disappointed.

"Will I see you again?" he asks.

"Of course we'll see each other again," I reply, knowing perfectly well that it's a lie.

Then I give him a bear hug, for the very last time.

The best part of any trip is returning home. You open the door and you catch a whiff of that specific, unique scent, a mix of furniture, books, and the people you love, a fragrance unlike any other. The smell of home. There, I just thought of another one-hit wonder: Patrick Süskind, the author of *Perfume*, one of the finest novels ever written. I wish he were here right now to suggest the best words to use in proposing to my wife that we take a family trip together.

"You've just taken the shortest Eurail trip in the history of mankind," is what Paola welcomes me home with when she finds me there after coming back from work.

"My fault. I just didn't feel like it anymore."

"I told you that in your condition going on a trip was a stupid idea."

"No no, on the contrary, it did me good—I got a few good days of distraction."

"So?"

"So I want to take another trip."

"Are you sure you're okay?"

"A trip together, the four of us. You, me, Lorenzo, and Eva. We could leave right after school ends. A vacation—no, better, an adventure."

"I don't feel like taking a vacation. Much less an adventure, I assure you," Paola cuts short the discussion.

"This isn't just any ordinary vacation."

"I understand what you're saying, but I really don't feel like it. You go ahead and take a trip with the kids if you want to. Go to the beach for a week, or wherever you want."

"I was thinking of something more, you know, on the road."

"In fact, it's a classic for someone with cancer to go on the road. Listen, why don't you start taking care of yourself and stop doing things that are dangerous or pointless, or both."

"It's not pointless. I want to spend my last days on earth with my kids. And with you."

"That's what you're doing now."

"But here I never see you, and you know that perfectly well. I need to be with them."

"I've already said I have no objection to your leaving for a week. Or two weeks if you want. I'm happy right here. I'm not in the right mood—I'd only ruin the trip."

Paola, Paola, Paola. Why are you so unyielding? Massimiliano's right—the cancer has traumatized you more than it has me.

I wait for Süskind to suggest telepathically a series of intelligent supplementary arguments, but perhaps the German author is on vacation, enjoying the no doubt lavish royalties from his novel. I give up. I pull the bike out of the garage and I go for a ride.

I do a longer ride than usual, I push all the way up the coast and I take the Via Aurelia. I pedal and pedal and pedal. I pace myself like a touring cyclist. For once, I enjoy the view. I breathe in the scent of the pines, the salt air, and the exhaust from the cars that shoot past me like guided missiles. I take in the sunset from a lookout, and far below I can make out a few diehard surfers riding waves that are too lazy to carry them.

As I reach mile thirty-six, my energy begins to flag and I stop at a little beachfront restaurant. A wooden stilthouse built out over the sand that seats thiry diners at most. Working in the kitchen are a pair of old ladies, the young waiter's aunt and grandmother. The view is breathtaking. The moon is gazing vainly at its reflection in the surface of the sea. I sit at a corner table and order a mixed grilled seafood and a plate of fried anchovies. At the other tables are young couples and a very noisy Roman family. I feel very much alone. Now that I think about it, this is the first time that I've gone out to eat without company. *Chi non mangia in compagnia, o è un ladro o è una spia,* as the Italians say. Anyone who eats alone is either a thief or a spy. I've always thought that going to a restaurant alone is the saddest thing in the world. I can now confirm that.

"Well, so are you leaving or not?" asks Giannandrea. It's just like the thing with the music, the more depressed a person is, the more he tends to hang out with other depressives.

We're sitting in the Chitchat shop and Massimiliano is cooking lunch for us, a vegetable couscous that deserves a place in the Michelin guide.

"I don't want to go without Paola."

"You'll see, she'll change her mind," says Massimiliano as he chops zucchini.

"I'm afraid she won't."

"Where would you want to go?" Giannandrea asks me.

I realize I haven't considered this properly. "The only thing I know is that I don't want to do a tour of the peninsula, some sort of Giro d'Italia."

"Would you bike?" Massimiliano's curiosity is piqued.

"Yesterday I did a hundred kilometers or so on my bike and I'm practically dead today. And I was going slow, fifteen miles per hour, tops twenty, a snail on two wheels. I thought we'd go by car—there are so many places I still want to show Lorenzo and Eva, and many I want to see for the first time with them and their mother."

"It strikes me as a very nice plan," our chef comments as he tosses the vegetables onto the heat to sauté. "In ten minutes, the couscous will be ready. Can you hold out, or would you like a quick bruschetta?"

A rhetorical question. Obviously, a quick bruschetta.

"But most of all," I continue, "there are lots of things I want to tell my children and my wife. My greatest desire is for them to remember an unexpected father, funny, full of life, full of ideas."

"Where do you get all this lust for life?" Giannandrea asks, observing me with admiration in his eyes.

"When you're about to die, it'll come to you too."

"I tried to commit suicide three times."

Massimiliano had already told me this. But I want to hear it straight from the horse's mouth.

"Well, you don't seem to have been very thorough about it," I reply ironically.

"The first time was just a case of bad luck. I connected a vacuum cleaner hose to the exhaust pipe on my car, I stuck it in the car window, and I got in. I fell asleep almost immediately, but a minute later the car ran out of gas. The fuel gauge was broken and I didn't know it."

"What about the second time?"

"The second time I wound up in the hospital because I'd swallowed a bottle of sleeping pills."

"Did they pump your stomach?"

"There was no need—they weren't very strong. I slept for two days and when I woke up I felt better than before."

"And the third time?"

"I'm not going to tell you about the third time because I feel too stupid."

I smile at him.

"Come on, by now I'm curious."

"Okay, I drove my car over a cliff. But the guardrail was stronger than I expected, the air bag deployed, and I was left sitting there inside the car like an idiot. And to make things worse, I broke an arm. That was three months ago."

"Is there going to be a fourth time?"

"No, there won't be. And the credit for that goes in part to Massimiliano."

The manager of our favorite shop smiles.

"The credit for that goes above all to my couscous. Five more minutes, guys."

Massimiliano sits down across from me.

"Do you mind if I suggest a tactic for your travel plans?"

"Go right ahead."

"Get everything ready to go, as if you were just going to leave with the kids. In fact, go ahead and tell them about the trip. You'll see, Paola will change her mind. She won't let you leave without her."

"You don't know her."

"But it's as if I did, by now. Do you want to bet she'll come?"

"A dinner?"

"You've got it!"

We shake hands and Giannandrea breaks our grip to seal the agreement.

When I try to pay for the hours spent in the shop, Massimiliano refuses to take my money and smiles.

"You're not a customer anymore. You're a friend."

Giannandrea pipes up: "The same goes for me."

I have two new friends who hopped on the bus of my life near the end of the trip. I smile at them both as I put the money back into my wallet.

Lorenzo and Eva stare at me, wide-eyed.

"An adventure?" blurts out my firstborn.

"Exactly. Three weeks driving all over Italy, in search of mysterious and unknown places. Sound good?"

The answer is an enthusiastic yes from Lorenzo. Just what I expected. But Eva has some questions.

"Can I bring Shepherd?"

"No, we'll leave Shepherd with Signora Giovanna, who has to come here anyway to water the plants and feed the cats and the hamster."

"Can't I even bring Alice?"

"She'd be miserable in the car. Hamsters don't like to travel."

"No fair! Then let's at least have one day when I'm the queen of you all."

The "queen of you all" day is a reward for something major, a good grade at school or a period of good behavior at home. Invented by Paola when they were little, it's a day of total dominion over both parents, when the little queen or king can set the order of the day, choose the food, and demand anything within reasonable economic limits.

"You've got a deal," I reply to the little blackmailer. "We'll leave Saturday night, as soon as school is over."

"Saturday is the school play and the end-of-year party," Lorenzo reminds me.

"Ah, right. In that case, we'll leave Sunday."

An hour later Paola comes home, unsuspecting, having spent the afternoon preparing the final report cards with the other teachers.

The children welcome her gleefully and she immediately figures out she's fallen into a trap. They're assuming she'll come too. She takes me aside, into the kitchen.

"What is all this?"

"You said that I could take the kids on a trip, no? That's what I'm doing. We're leaving Sunday. For three weeks."

"Three weeks? Have you lost your mind?"

"You're under no obligation to come with us."

"And, in fact, I'm not coming."

"Too bad, I'm planning to end the trip in Switzerland. I'm not coming back here."

It occurs to me as I say it. I'm not coming back here. It immediately seems like the natural decision. The last journey. With the people I love.

The phrase is too violent to keep from doing damage. Paola shouts in a whisper to keep the children from hearing. Among the words she uses most are "irresponsible," "insane," and "trap."

She's right, I have been irresponsible, but I want to make up for it, I probably am insane, but that's not a defect, and there's no question, this journey is certainly a trap. A trap of love into which I hope Paoletta will fall. My chief objective of these hundred days, written in the Dino Zoff notebook, still owns pride of place:

Get Paola to forgive me.

"I'm not coming back here," I insist. "Don't make me take this trip alone. We're a family."

"We were a family. But then you destroyed it."

"I made a huge mistake. Everyone makes mistakes."

"I know that. Like marrying you, for instance."

Don't listen to her, these are the things people say in a fight, I know she doesn't really believe it.

Paola struggles for another ten minutes like a hooked tuna, then she gives up.

"What should I pack for, the beach or the mountains?"

"Everything, *amore mio*. Everything."

I've never been happier about losing a bet.

I turn on my computer and I start doing some research and making reservations.

The most fun you can have when leaving on a trip is packing your suitcase, as I've told you before. But when it's your last trip, packing a suitcase turns heartbreaking. Most of my belongings won't be coming with me.

I wander around the apartment and I scrutinize the bookshelves in particular. They're full of books I've never read and movies I've never watched. I feel like asking them all to forgive me, authors and directors, who worked so hard to provide me with hours of entertainment, and I, after leading them on by purchasing their products, have just left them to gather dust on a shelf. Perhaps they'd have remained there forever. Or else they might have had their fifteen minutes of fame during a vacation. In any case, I bid them all a fond farewell today. I bring only one novel with me, I've already put it in my suitcase, after changing my mind numerous times. The final competition was between *Pinocchio* and *Treasure Island*, and the second book won. One of these days I'll tell you why. I go on exploring the bookshelves and I gently caress my Diabolik collection. Only now does it occur to me that the most complicated thing won't be saying goodbye to my Diabolik collection, but to all the protagonists of my life.

I don't know if I'll have the strength.

I'm looking out at the Gang That Couldn't Shoot Straight. The time has come. I've summoned them all poolside an hour before the usual practice time. With them is my faithful assistant coach. I tried to jot down a couple of lines of rough text for the last speech I'll ever make to them, and after a minute I find myself forced to improvise. I know that I'm an important figure to them, and I want to leave them with a few fundamental messages. I get straight to the point.

"Guys, I have a liver tumor. It's very serious—it's metastasized to the lungs. I don't have long to live. And, unfortunately, this is the last time we'll see each other."

They aren't expecting it. They exchange glances, trying to figure out if this is a joke of some kind. But my tone of voice makes it clear that it's not. Not at all.

"A few months ago I decided to deal with my tumor with a smile. I haven't always succeeded, but I'm trying to be happy every day that I have left to live. I'm still in decent shape and I've done my best to beat the disease. But it hid inside me, and by the time I'd ferreted it out, it was too late to have any hope of defeating it. You know, at your age, I had plenty of dreams. I have to confess to you that I didn't achieve a single one of them, but I never gave up hope. Always remember that the only riches we possess are the dreams we have as children. They are the fuel of our lives, the only force that pushes us to keep on going even when things have gone all wrong. To crown the dreams of the child that lives inside you should be your chief goal in life. Don't ever forget that you'll become adults in appearance only, but that little man still lives on inside you. Dedicate yourself fully to your work, whether that work is water polo or anything else. You should try to be the best you can be in every walk of life, even if you're selling fruit in a farmers' market. Everyone should say: "What excellent fruit that guy sells." Life will present you with plenty of challenges, many of them much more important than a water polo championship playoff, and you shouldn't ever retreat in the face of those challenges. Just work, work, work, even at the risk of making mistakes. And if and when you do make mistakes, and you do hurt someone, ask for forgiveness. Asking forgiveness and admitting you've made a mistake is the hardest thing of all. But if someone else does you good, remember it always. Showing gratitude is every bit as complicated. When you happen to win something, don't mock your opponents and don't boast."

Everyone looks around in amusement: *winning* is a word they're not familiar with.

"As you know, I have two children, and knowing that I won't be able to watch them grow up is the thing that hurts me most. In a few days, I'm going to leave on a trip with them and with my wife. I won't be coming back. And I won't be able to watch the playoff games. But I'll be with you in my heart, and Giacomo will tell me everything you do. He'll be here and you can rely on him for anything you need. He's ready to coach you next year; he has the skills and the temperament to do it."

My assistant coach didn't expect this investiture and he's clearly overcome with emotion.

"I ask you only one thing: however the game turns out, fight all the way to the end. And if you can do it, win these three matches for me. It would be the best farewell gift. One day in the distant future, when you have children of your own, I hope that you'll remember your old coach and you'll take them to the pool and teach them to care about this wonderful sport we love. You've been the best team a coach could ever hope for. Even when we were losing. I'm so sorry."

I go to pieces. I'd sworn to myself I wouldn't cry, but I break that promise. I hug them all, one after the other, last of all Soap-on-a-Rope and Martino.

"I want you to listen to me, boys, make me proud of you."

Then it's Giacomo's turn.

"Have a good trip, Coach, wherever it is you're going," he whispers to me during the hug. "I won't forget you."

Oscar is alone in the pastry shop, surrounded by crunchy-good smells, when I come in late at night.

"Ciao . . ."

He turns around.

"Ciao, Lucio . . ."

"What are you doing here all alone? Did you fire your apprentice?"

"No, tonight's his night off. Usually Martina comes in to give me a hand, but tonight she's with her daughter. She's a fantastic woman, you know?"

I watch him fill beignets with cream, and note thirty years of experience guiding his hands.

"Feel like helping me out?"

"But I don't know how to . . ."

"So learn!" he says, cutting me off. The hours that follow flash by in clouds of flour and cream. I have a great time.

At dawn we fry up twenty or so doughnuts. We pull them out of the grease and wait for them to cool a little before dipping them in the sugar.

We sit in silence for a minute. Then Oscar asks a question that sums up all the others.

"Well?"

That one word is worth a thousand conversations. I say nothing. There's no need. Two minutes later, we're enjoying two doughnuts. This is the first time that he's eaten a doughnut with me. I'm biting back tears as I realize it will probably be the last.

I've arranged a special dinner just for the three musketeers. For the last time before Porthos leaves the group forever.

Umberto and Corrado. Two names that to me mean millions of things.

When they show up outside the agreed-upon restaurant, ready for an evening of sad conversation and deep emotions, my friends find a surprise. I'm waiting for them out front, but the place is closed. I welcome them with a single unequivocal word: "Prank."

It's not what they were expecting, but they enthusiastically welcome the invitation. I load them into my car and I barrel at top speed toward the Baths of Caracalla. Tonight they're performing yet another production of the immortal opera *Tosca*. I've purchased tickets for three separate seats. We enjoy the beginning with perfect behavior, and then, in the middle of the first act, while Cavaradossi gargles away in a spartan stage set meant to represent the Basilica di Sant'Andrea della Valle, Corrado stands up in the third row and shouts loudly: "Are you trying to tell us this is a tenor?" All around him pandemonium breaks loose.

"Hush! For shame! Sit down!"

Sabotaging theatrical performances is one of the stock items of our foolish repertory. Corrado keeps it up.

"This ridiculous charade is an insult to Puccini's art! Forgive them, Giacomo!"

Meanwhile, onstage poor Cavaradossi is trying to ignore us and he goes on gargling. That's when I spring into action.

"Shame on you, be seated, or else I'll show you!"

"You'll show me what? Is that a threat?"

I lunge at him, leaping over a row of seats. When we're making fools of ourselves, sickness and aches mean nothing. I'm on him with a feline agility that is long forgotten.

"Yes, it's a threat. Cut it out immediately."

"And if I don't?"

At this point, Cavaradossi, too, freezes, and the orchestra stops playing. Right now, we're the stars of the show. Mission accomplished.

This is the right moment to let the first slap fly. We land our blows skillfully, careful not to hurt each other, shoving and yanking, but the effect is stupendous. Everyone rushes to pull us apart, but we go on shouting. It's total chaos.

"Oaf!"

"The only oaf here is you! I'll report you to the police—do you understand?"

The word "report" is the signal for Umberto to make his entrance, as he pushes his way through the crowd surrounding us. He quickly flashes a pass from his tennis club.

"Police, please make way. Let's all calm down here!"

"Excellent," I say. "I'd like to file a complaint against this gentleman for assault and battery."

"No, I'm the one with a complaint to file, and I have one thousand witnesses," Corrado retorts. The second part of the prank requires a general debate over who slapped whom first. Then Corrado gets aggressive, shoves the cop, and is arrested. Usually our exit takes place with Corrado in handcuffs and me following to file a complaint. It's just that this time our clear performance enjoys an unexpected plot twist that actually should have been expected sooner or later: there's a real cop in the audience. And he can't wait to lend a hand. In thirty seconds he reveals us for the fakers we are, handcuffs all three of us, and the evening has a giddy denouement at the police station. It was bound to happen eventually. They take our fingerprints and ask a thousand questions. They don't know exactly what to charge us with, and actually they have a tremendous time going over the details of what happened. The only one who is theoretically in serious trouble is Umberto, who tried to pass himself off as an actual officer of the law. After a couple of hours, an elderly police chief who clearly wishes he was already retired decides to sweep it all under the rug and let us go. Irony of fate: our most reckless and spectacular prank is also our last.

We don't talk about anything in particular until the time comes to say good-bye. The final hug, all three of us together, is worth more than a thousand words.

All for one. And the one is me.

Peter Pan strides to center stage and shouts: "Captain Hook! Where are you?"

All around him, in a clearing in Neverland, stand the Lost Boys, Tinker Bell, Wendy with her little brothers.

Suddenly the treacherous captain appears, along with the inseparable Mr. Smee and a couple of pirates.

"Here I am!" he thunders. "And now you're done for. I'm going to feed every last one of you to Tick Tock the crocodile."

"I don't think you will!" retorts the fearless Peter.

There ensues a balletic scene of combat in which all the participants cross swords in time to the music. This is the culminating scene of Lorenzo's school play. My little actor is hidden behind Captain Hook's wicked mustachio—and I'm not just saying this because I'm his father—but he's been stealing the stage from Peter Pan for the past hour, perhaps because the Boy Who Wouldn't Grow Up is being played by a child far too obnoxious to play the hero of Neverland. Sitting next to me are Eva and Paola. We laugh and applaud alongside a hundred or so other parents and kids.

The play ends to thunderous applause. Just for the record, Captain Hook got twice the applause Peter Pan did. I take Eva's hand, link arms with Paola, and we wait for our little Laurence Olivier outside the stage door. While we wait, I notice that someone has broken the side window of our car and has stolen the GPS I carelessly left in plain view. By now, I'm a slave to the computerized voice that tells me to "turn right" and "make a U-turn." Abandoned by my portable Virgil, I'm a stranger in my own city. I've forgotten routes and one-way streets. I don't even remember how to leaf through the pages of the city map, TuttoCittà. I decide that I'm not going to buy a new GPS for the trip. I'll use folding paper road maps. I said adventure and adventure is what I meant. When Lorenzo shows up, he's greeted by mothers and teachers as the conquering hero. I'm reassured only when he promises me that he has no intention of becoming an actor.

That afternoon I have the window of my glorious station wagon replaced, then I have the car washed and I fill up the tank.

As I lay the last few items of luggage by the front door, I experience a moment of fear. The fear that comes when you've reached the point of no return. The end of the uphill climb on the roller coaster. I Google it. Point of no return: final, irreversible stage of a process or a journey.

I have just twenty-two days left, and I'm at the point of no return.

Raise your hand if you recognize the name of Edmond Haraucourt. If you don't know the name, then let me tell you that he was a French writer and that the first line of his most famous poem is something most of us take for a proverb: "To leave is to die a little."

That line has never been so true as it is for me now. The rest of the poem is pretty wonderful too. This is more or less how it runs in English:

> To leave is to die a little;
> It is to die to what one loves;
> One leaves behind a little of oneself
> At any hour, any place.
> It's a fine and final pain
> Like the last line of a poem.
> We leave as if in jest
> Before the ultimate journey
> And, in all of our farewells, we sow
> A portion of our soul.

Today we depart. As planned, we've left our German shepherd Shepherd with Signora Giovanna. Shepherd watches me load the luggage in the back of the car with a somber expression, as if he understands I won't be coming home. After all, I was his favorite slave.

The kids are beside themselves with excitement; as far as they know, this is just the beginning of a wonderful and unexpected vacation.

"Can you at least tell us where exactly we're going?" Eva asks.

"The various stops are secret," I reply. "Think of it as a treasure hunt."

The kids get comfortable in the back while Paola gathers up the last kibble and stuffs it into the station wagon's baggage compartment, already packed full.

We're ready for departure. It's five in the afternoon; we wait for the sun to slide a little way closer to the horizon to avoid the worst of the muggy June heat. I start the car, and it hacks asthmatically. Then, at last, we start off. The apartment building where we live dwindles in the rearview mirror, the last image I have of the life I once led. In a movie I can't remember the name of, the protagonist says that life is nothing but a collection of last times. Too true.

The last time you talk to your father.

The last time you see the Colosseum.

The last time you eat a fig just picked from the tree.

The last time you take a swim in the sea.

The last time you kiss the woman you love.

The list can go on forever, and every one of us has already experienced thousands of last times without even realizing it. Most of the time, in fact, you never even imagine that what you're experiencing is the last time. In fact, that's the best thing about it. Not knowing. If, instead, as in my case, you know perfectly well that these are the last times, then suddenly the rules change completely. Everything takes on a new and different weight and importance. Even drinking an ordinary *chinotto* takes on a quality of poetic melancholy.

As we drive out of Rome, I leave behind me an astonishing number of last times. So many that I finally just give up cataloging them. After so many days spent regretting the past and dreaming of a future that will no longer come, it's time to think of today.

I have the Dino Zoff notebook that I've filled with a thousand notes for this journey with me. I've made a list of things that I want to teach Lorenzo and Eva. And I have a woman to win back in the next twenty days. I don't have even a minute to waste.

I take the on-ramp and follow the highway south. I'm as excited as a little kid heading off on vacation for the first time without his parents.

I slip in a CD of television theme songs and my under-ten passengers cut loose in song. Paola stares out at the panorama, but she still isn't relaxed. I press down on the accelerator and ignore a sharper than usual stab of pain in my belly.

I'm sure that the hotel on the highway past Salerno, which deserved half a star at most, was built near a world mosquito convention of some kind. We spent the evening hemmed in by the diabolical insects, first in the trattoria and later in the room. We took a double with two trundle beds and after ten minutes it was already an encampment, partly because of the luggage and largely because of the war on the mosquitoes, which, as everyone knows, is waged by hurling various large blunt objects.

Our destination is Craco, a very special place in the region of Lucania. A ghost town.

There's only one thing that Lorenzo and Eva have in common: their fear of ghosts. They can bravely withstand zombies, ogres, witches, and vampires, but they go to pieces at the thought of ghosts. Every dark room, every curtain flapping in the wind, every door that suddenly slams, is, as far as they're concerned, an unmistakable sign of a malevolent spirit returned to earth to harm us.

I've brought them to this village, uninhabited since the sixties, to help them get over this fear. The tiny place seems forgotten by time. We walk out into the deserted main street. It's very hot and there's not a shred of shadow anywhere. Paola's wearing a flower-print dress and I wish I could wrap my arms around her, but she's walking a few steps behind us. It strikes me that this is a highly symbolic attitude.

Why is she trying not to be part of our group? I am grateful for her presence, though. I wouldn't have it any other way. As we walk, I start telling the legend of the little town's history.

"It was founded by Greek colonists in the eighth century BC and was inhabited continuously until the middle of the last century. After the last inhabitants left, it remained abandoned for a few years. Nothing but mosquitoes, wind, and the occasional dog barking in the distance."

"Why did you say for a few years? Did they come back to live here afterward?" Lorenzo was paying close attention.

"In a certain sense, yes, they did. Many noticed that the village had been abandoned, and so they moved here and took up residence."

"Many who?" is Eva's eminently legitimate doubt.

"Many ghosts."

My two heirs freeze.

"You mean this village is full of ghosts?" Lorenzo asks in astonishment.

"All the ghosts in Italy, to be exact."

"Are you crazy?" Eva exclaims.

Behind me, I can sense Paola smiling quietly.

"Let me point out first of all that ghosts never appear in broad daylight, and that it's eleven thirty in the morning. Then let me explain that because they've all come to live here, we can stop worrying about them in the rest of Italy."

"By all of them, you mean *all* of them?" asks my little daughter.

"*All* of them. They took advantage of the fact that the village was deserted, so they could have some time on their own."

"But what do they do here if they don't have anyone to scare?" Lorenzo wonders aloud.

"Look, ghosts don't enjoy frightening people. In fact," breaks in Paola, backing me up, "what ghosts like best is being left alone to mind their own business and basically do nothing. They've already done more than enough things and now they just want to get some rest."

We pull onto the little village's main piazza. The two kids look around cautiously.

"Are you sure that there are no ghosts in broad daylight?" Lorenzo asks.

"Positive."

For an hour or so, we wander through the abandoned lanes of the village. After a while, they start talking cheerfully about ghosts, wondering how many can fit into an ordinary home and whether they have a regular appointment for their appearances, the way that vampires do at sunset. When we leave the town and walk downhill to the parking area where we left our car, they even wave good-bye to the ghosts, who by now have been "normalized."

"Ciao, see you next time!"

"Miao!"

I hope that they leave all their fears behind in the lanes of this village. We stop for a bite to eat in a lovely trattoria right across the road from the ghost town. The children order their favorite— carbonara. I try to convince them that carbonara should be eaten only in Rome, where the chefs know to use proper *guanciale* and not just bacon cubes. I suggest an eggplant parmigiana, which is more typical in the south of Italy. Lorenzo seems to think about his choice.

"Do they still put real eggs in the carbonara outside of Rome?" Eva looks at me with her arms crossed.

"That is one ingredient that can't be missing, no matter where they make it."

"That's what I want, then." And Eva closes her menu, a satisfied expression on her face. Paola orders the same as me—eggplant meatballs to start with, osso buco to follow, *torta della nonna* for dessert. She says the osso buco isn't half as good as hers. I have to agree. As I sip the after-dinner drink, Ammazzacaffè, I see hundreds of faded figures crowding the street out of the little ghost village, waving at me from a distance like passengers on an ocean liner about to depart. Eva says, "Papà, you're dreaming!" I blink and they're gone. I must have overeaten.

The Salento region of Apulia. Sun. Beach umbrellas and lounge chairs for rent. Sand castles. Laughter. Salt spray. Sautéed clams and mussels.

That's how I'd imagined our second day.

Instead, thanks to my ability to read road maps, we're lost somewhere in the Apulian hinterland where I was searching for a convent that sells herb-flavored cheeses that I can still taste fifteen years after the last time I visited. Result: we neither eat dairy products nor do we go to the beach. Instead, our car gets stuck on a rutted dirt road and then gives up the ghost with a dull and definitive clunk.

"The transmission's broken," says the mechanic who's come to our aid.

"Can you fix it?" I ask hopefully.

"Certainly."

"Ah, that's good news."

"I'll have to order the parts from the manufacturer. In no more than fifteen days, it'll be good as new."

"Fifteen days? But we're traveling. We can't wait fifteen days."

"What can I tell you? Rent a real car. This one, no offense, is a rolling wreck."

It's heartbreaking to hear someone call my faithful automobile a rolling wreck. But he's right.

I have someone take me to Taranto, I rent a more high-tech station wagon, and I come back to pick up my family members in the middle of nowhere. We find a lovely little hotel with a view, and I send the kids to bed early. I have great plans for the next day.

"Like what?" Paola asks me.

"I want to rent a dinghy and go fishing."

"I can't spend the day in a dinghy. I'll get seasick after ten minutes."

I don't push. I know that she means it—it's not an excuse.

"If you prefer, we can skip it."

"No, don't worry. This is your journey. I'll wait for you here. I'm happy to read a book on the beach. I haven't done that in forever."

"This is your journey" isn't a particularly well-chosen phrase. How I wish that it could soon be changed into "This is our journey." I fall asleep and dream that I'm on Captain Ahab's boat, helping him to capture the white whale.

The thing my grandpa Michele loved best was fishing. Every August he'd lock up the concierge's booth and we'd go to the beach. Many mornings he'd wake me up before dawn and take me out onto the waters off the exotic Lido di Ostia in his wooden motorboat to fish for tattlers, which are romantic fish that choose to come into shore with the rising and setting sun. Sometimes we'd even catch a small tuna or a *palamita,* which Grandma Alfonsina would cook for dinner. Grandpa was a veritable ace when it came to lure fishing and I didn't do too bad myself.

I rent all the equipment a budding fisherman might need, two rods complete with all kinds of bait, a bottle of SPF 50, and a dinghy with a ten-horsepower outboard motor. Paola comes to wave us off from the pier. I think that having a day to herself will do her good. What with school, her children, and a sick, cheating husband, it's been an intense period for her too.

"Mamma, don't have too big a lunch because we're going to have a huge platter of grilled fish for dinner," Lorenzo boldly declares.

I back him up.

"We're going to bring back so much fish we'll be able to sell some to the hotel restaurant."

I'm pretty confident—I've never come back empty-handed from a day of fishing.

The Ionian Sea is flat as a mirror. We head out about a mile and cast our lines. The children are excited. They listen to what I have to say and pepper me with questions.

"What should we do if we catch a shark?"

"With a lure this size there's no chance of that. It's too small. Sharks are practically blind. They wouldn't see it."

"What if we catch a killer whale?"

"They're very rare in the Mediterranean. I wouldn't worry about it. This stretch of water is full of tuna."

"If we catch a dolphin, I'm throwing it back," Eva concludes.

Two hours later, the only bites we've gotten are from a stunned red mullet passing through. We don't give up, we double the bait, and we move to a new area. We pass by a buoy marking a scuba diver and we stay at a safe distance. When I see him surface, over near his support vessel, I shout, "Are there a lot of fish around here?"

"*Mamma mia*, yes, the water is teeming with fish. There are enormous schools of tuna down under. It's spectacular."

I'm reassured. We won't be coming home empty-handed tonight—it's just a matter of being patient, which is any fisherman's chief virtue.

My little helpers redouble their efforts. We're a well-oiled team. The hours fly by and the sun drops toward the horizon.

So the results of our fishing trip?

We had a lot of fun, and we caught the red mullet mentioned above, three sad little octopuses, and a plastic bottle. We've also lost one rod, which slipped through Lorenzo's fingers. In other words, a complete disaster.

"And now how are we going to tell Mamma?" Lorenzo asks.

"Don't worry. There's an incredible place where we're certain to find some fish. It's a magical place."

"Where is it?" Eva asks. "What's it called?"

"It's in town, and it's called Fresh Fish Sold Here."

"But that's cheating!" blurts my judgmental daughter.

"Exactly," I reply without hesitation.

Lorenzo is thrilled at the idea of tricking Mamma, but Eva has her doubts: she still has a well-developed sense of justice. Perhaps too well developed.

We buy an assortment of fish and two giant cuttlefish. An overflowing basket of seafood that we present triumphantly to Paola, at the very tail end of the afternoon. We proudly show her the results of our day's fishing, and she stares in astonishment.

"That's just incredible. Look at all these fish!"

"Papà is a great fisherman!" Lorenzo exclaims.

"And the water off the coast is just teeming with fish," Eva adds.

"Did Papà catch all of them?" Paola asks.

"No, the biggest fish is the one I caught and that cuttlefish is the one Lorenzo caught." Eva lies with an exceptional precision and nonchalance. A couple of certified liars. I'm proud of them both. Especially of my daughter, who's learned how to fish and how to tell lies. Not a bad result, all things considered.

We carry our loot into the hotel kitchen, and the children, overjoyed and triumphant, linger behind to play on the hotel beach. I'm left alone with Paola, and she trips me up with a single phrase.

"I didn't know that pike lived in salt water."

"What pike?"

"That one big fish you caught is a pike—you can tell from the duckbill snout."

"Ah, that's a pike?"

"Yes. And pike are freshwater fish."

"It must have gotten lost; . . . sometimes pike get disoriented. Everyone knows that," I say, climbing onto a very slippery slope.

"Eh, of course they do . . ."

Deep in Paola's gaze I glimpse a smile. Or at least the shadow of a smile.

"How much did you pay for them?"

I give up.

"Not much. The shop was about to close. It was my idea. The kids had nothing to do with it."

Now she's definitely smiling at me, as if I were an urchin caught with my hand in the cookie jar.

"That wasn't a pike. Where on earth would they find a pike around here?"

She'd laid a trap for me and I fell straight into it. Without waiting for me to answer, she catches up with the kids on the beach, slips out of her beach wrap, and waves them into the water for one last sunset swim.

Today I don't have the energy to keep up with them. The day out fishing really wore me out. I stretch out on a lounge chair and watch my little aquatic family as they chase each other around in the shallows, splashing and squealing. I wouldn't want to be anywhere else on earth.

Nighttime. Our hotel room is swathed in darkness. The windows are open. Paola's asleep. I'm not. I breathe slowly. The pain in my stomach no longer lets me have any peace. I'm coughing hard, I can't seem to stop, I'm practically emitting a death rattle. I get up, I go into the bathroom. My body contorts with every hack. I feel the urge to vomit. So I do, some goes on the floor, some in the toilet, and some on my T-shirt. Then I slump back, my shoulders against the wall, exhausted, ravaged, helpless. I can't go on like this much longer.

Paola sticks her head into the bathroom. I've woken her up.

"How are you?"

"Sick, very very sick."

My wife flushes the toilet, grabs a handful of toilet paper, cleans the floor, and comes over next to me.

"Careful, I think a whiff of my breath could kill you on the spot."

"You still feel like kidding around, so things must be okay," she says with a half smile, or possibly a little more than half.

She starts cleaning the vomit off my face and lips. Then she pulls my stained T-shirt off. She turns on the water in the bidet next to me, wets a bath sponge, and delicately cleans my neck and chest.

I let her work. I adore it when she takes care of me. I hope that she's doing it out of love and not from that odd candy-striper instinct.

She sits down on the floor and takes me in her arms. I relax into her. There's such sweetness in it. I want more. I nuzzle her neck.

"We look like Michelangelo's *Pietà*," Paola says, in an attempt to cut the drama.

I laugh. And then I start coughing again.

A few minutes later she helps me into bed and tucks me in, the way we used to tuck our children in until just a short time ago.

"We need to go home," she says, instead of giving me the expected kiss good night.

"It's just a momentary attack. I'm actually feeling much better since we got to the beach. I'm breathing much easier."

"I saw that, or rather, I heard it. Come on, Lucio, please, let's be done with this farce of a journey—it was a terrible idea. I'm not going to beat around the bush: you need medical care, especially now that the tumor is about to enter its most violent and aggressive phase."

"*Amore*, please, these are the last days of my life. I want to live them to the fullest. We still have lots of stops to make."

"I'm taking the children and going home."

"You can't do that. You can't all leave me now. If you go home, I'm not coming with you. It's just a few more days. Please."

Silent assent. She's given in. She won't regret it.

've burned a few CDs with compilations of my favorite songs. I don't want to listen to songs chosen at random by a radio network on this journey. I love the English word *compilation*, it evokes my first high school crushes and my summers at the beach all at once. My generation was the last one to be able to make compilations on tape cassettes, and to have the thrill of watching them demagnetize the first time you leave them on the car dashboard.

My compilations are completely anarchic, with no other criterion than my own personal taste. Here's what we have today:

"Romeo and Juliet"	DIRE STRAITS
"Through the Barricades"	SPANDAU BALLET
"Meraviglioso"	DOMENICO MODUGNO
"Yesterday"	THE BEATLES
"Rain and Tears"	APHRODITE'S CHILD
"Un giorno credi"	EDOARDO BENNATO
"Can't Smile Without You"	BARRY MANILOW
"In My Room"	BEACH BOYS
"Father and Son"	CAT STEVENS
"Good-bye My Lover"	JAMES BLUNT

I realize midway through listening to the playlist that they're all pretty gloomy hits. I eject the CD and tune in to a local radio station doing prank calls. We're heading for Molise, which is more or less Italy's Liechtenstein, a beautiful region that is overlooked by the tourist guidebooks. There are no famous monuments and no one famous was born there, unless you count Robert De Niro's grandparents. Just one statistic to give you an idea of how much better life is around here: there are 72 inhabitants per square kilometer here, while in Latium there are 330; in Lombardy, 412; and in Campania, 429. There's elbow room, a value we've forgotten we ever had.

The hotel we choose is a family-run place with just five rooms, only one of which looks out over the beach. I gladly give the kids that room. Paola and I take the "Gardenia Suite" with a view of the largely deserted beachfront promenade. The proprietors are a couple in their seventies, Sabino and Alba, who run the place with the assistance of their three children and a couple of grandchildren. Sabino tells us that he inherited the place from his father and he's managed to talk his descendants into coming to work and live together. A lucky man in this age when family ties and emotions are scattered to the four winds.

"If you're interested, there's a dance contest tonight in town," Sabino says, with the tone of someone offering me a ticket to the World Cup finals.

"What kind of dance?" I inquire.

"All kinds. It's an overall contest. The mayor's on the jury, and so is a guy whose name I can't remember, but he danced with Carla Fracci."

"How do you sign up?"

Paola breaks in: "I don't think that dancing is a very—"

I don't let her finish, and I repeat the question: "How do you sign up?"

"Directly in the piazza, my brother-in-law is there taking names and issuing numbers. Three euros, plus you get a beer. If the signora doesn't want to dance, there's also a market with stalls: it's the festival of the town's patron saint. My wife doesn't dance either because three months ago she slipped on a rock and broke her thigh. She's still doing physical therapy."

"Thanks, but I don't think we'll go," my spouse says brusquely, definitely sour toned today. "The trip was a long one, my husband listens to terrible music, and the children are exhausted."

"In any case, it starts at nine-thirty," says Sabino with a smile that reveals he doesn't see the dentist very often.

Two hours later, I'm with Lorenzo and Eva at the table, signing all four of us up for the contest. We voted democratically, 3 to 1, and Paola was forced to come with us. Among other things, the hotel kitchen is closed because the whole happy family that normally runs it will be competing, aside from Alba, who, now that I notice, does limp slightly. Sabino is thrilled we came.

"Which are the couples? You have to sign up by couples."

"I think I'll dance with my wife, and the kids will dance together."

"No, I'm not dancing," Paola breaks in, "I came but I won't dance. Anyway, Lorenzo doesn't seem particularly interested."

My young firstborn heir is already standing by a foosball table where the local kids are having a tournament.

I turn to Eva: "Shall we dance, just you and I?"

"But I don't know how to dance, Papà."

My sage young daughter doesn't have dance skills among her many gifts, though it would only do her good to learn of folly and lack of inhibition that's an intrinsic part of dancing.

"I'll teach you," I venture as if I were Nureyev and not Baloo the Bear.

We're the only couple with a two-foot height difference. We don't pass unobserved. I understand that in this town the contest is taken seriously. At the end of each dance, the jury casts its votes, in a brief and mysterious conclave.

At first Eva is a little cautious: we improvise a shy version of the twist. I look around and there are a few couples who look as if they came straight out of *Dirty Dancing*.

When it's time to do the mazurka I'm already sweating to an embarrassing extent. Paola wanders through the market stalls, shooting us a glance every now and then. Lorenzo cheerfully ignores us, by now completely absorbed in the challenge of a furious foosball match.

Ten minutes later Eva and I abandon the piazza entirely. Speaking metaphorically, let it be clear. My little girl and I are dancing alone on a mountaintop, and all around is nothing but snow and silence. We dance wildly, effortlessly, almost breathlessly. A state of euphoria unlike anything I've experienced in years and that I imagine my daughter's never felt before in her life. I've never seen her as happy as she was during the rock 'n' roll sequence, as I slid her through my arms, remembering the old moves from my high school dances. She's light, and that's a good thing. We go on dancing, paying no attention to the world around us. It's just the two of us. Me and my small, out-of-control princess.

Before I can have a complete cardiocirculatory collapse, a voice over a megaphone comes to my rescue.

"Stop dancing! The winners will be announced in five minutes!"

I let myself flop down onto a bench, next to my partner.

"Were we good, Papà?"

"We were outstanding."

"Do you think we'll win?"

"I don't think so—they wouldn't let an outsider win," I say, cushioning the blow, sensing in advance a less than stellar ranking.

Paola and Lorenzo catch up with us. I discover that they were cheering us on during the last few dances. My wife hands us two slices of cool watermelon. I love her for that too.

With our faces plunged into the fiery red pulp we listen as the jury proclaims the winning couple. It's the mayor himself who does the announcing, to a chorus of whistles and applause.

"The couple of Sabino and Gabriella Antinori wins with one hundred twenty-eight points."

The winner is Sabino with his daughter. Seeing that the woman's husband is one of the contest organizers, my suspicion of an Italian-style con job is more than legitimate. The two of them celebrate as if they'd just won an Oscar.

"Here's the chart with the overall rankings," concludes the mayor.

Eva immediately runs to see. I don't have the strength to go with her. She comes back thirty seconds later, all dejected.

"We came in last," she reports.

"For sure they cheated," I comment. "The next time we'll practice and it'll go better. You want another slice of watermelon?"

She replies with an enthusiastic yes, instantly forgetting the terrible contest results. I take her hand and we run to the watermelon stand, under Paola's worried gaze.

"But now you need to get some rest."

I ignore her and I order two more super megaslices of watermelon. I'm a very satisfied father. Today Eva learned to let loose and to accept losing. Two things that will come in very handy in the future. I try to decipher from her features the woman she will become. A very beautiful woman who will turn the heads of all the men lucky enough to meet her. I'm struck by the thought that I'll never see her get married. I'll never get to walk her to the altar. That was supposed to be my job.

A tear rolls down my cheek.

"Are you crying, Papà?"

"No," I assure her, "that's just sweat."

Then I hand her the super megaslice. With a smile.

did a little Internet research before we left Rome. I found one charming text that described a place with a mysterious name: Neo-sapiens Village.

This is a decidedly idiosyncratic amusement park, built to resemble an actual prehistoric village, allowing visitors to experience survival techniques of ancient times and test their skills at such activities as archery, hut building, endurance courses, and spear chucking.

I decided instantly that this would be a perfect stop on our journey. To sample for a day life in a bygone era, before the discovery of electricity or the invention of lighters or supermarkets, seems like a good idea.

When we get there, we are greeted by a good-natured guide who explains the rules: for the rest of the day, we will be forbidden to use cell phones, cigarettes, or electronic equipment of any description. He asks us to make a special effort to think and act the way primitive humans would have.

"Will there be dinosaurs too?" Lorenzo asks hopefully.

"No, there won't," the guide replies. "And let me add, luckily for us. Even with today's weapons, there's no way we could survive an attack by a *Velociraptor* or a *Tyrannosaurus rex*."

"When you say primitive, exactly what evolutionary stage would you be referring to?" Eva asks, in typical questioning mode.

"How do you mean?" blurts the astonished guide.

"Well, for instance, do we already have a shared language? Do we know how to write? Have we already invented the wheel?"

The young man gives me a puzzled look. I can see in his eyes that he's wondering if my daughter is actually a midget professor of anthropology disguised as a little girl in pigtails. Then he manages to put together a reasonable answer.

"Well . . . you have a shared language; you don't know how to write; you do use fire, but you haven't yet come up with the wheel."

"Thank you," Eva politely replies.

After an hour of striking "rock against rock" to light a fire, we give up. All around us, the other families taking part in the day of living primitively have nearly all succeeded. Lorenzo pulls a pack of matches out of his pocket and suggests we cheat. I refuse and go on clacking the rocks together, hoping to coax that long-awaited spark out of them. Paola watches me with the same sense of affection mixed with pity that is normally reserved for watching a hamster running in its wheel. After fifteen minutes, I manage to light a twig, but the flame dies out before I can get it to spread to the entire pile. I suggest we try to win back our self-respect in the next activity: archery. To shoot an arrow is a violent, instinctive act, buried deep in our DNA. An act that comes as naturally as if we'd done it every day of our lives. The best archer of us all is Paola, who seems like a latter-day Robin Hood. She hits a succession of bull's-eyes with the confidence of a multimedaled Olympic champion. I stare at her as if I were seeing her for the very first time. She looks like a Sioux woman warrior and perhaps, in a previous life, that's exactly what she was. Lorenzo and Eva work hard with their miniature bows and have more fun than I've seen them have in years.

We don't exactly excel in the javelin toss. Spear chucking requires a significant component of technique and strength that dumb luck will do nothing to help. Our spears land harmlessly just a few yards away. In the hours that follow, we watch a falconing display, I teach the kids how to read a map, we make two terra-cotta vases, and we design a sleeping hut that we don't have time to build because the park is about to close. Eva particularly wants to show off her eco-friendly construction knowledge in the building of the hut, which quickly becomes our new imagined home, and I promise her there will be room for both Oscar and Martina in the hut, should they decide to visit us. Both Lorenzo and Eva are having such fun doing these things we've never done together, I see them reappraising me, their new hands-on dad. We leave with the vases in a tote bag and a number of souvenirs, including a couple of flints. Today, for the first time since we left, I saw Paola get involved to a certain extent. Maybe she's beginning to thaw.

The next stop on our journey is the Pinocchio Park in Tuscany. This isn't a supertechnological theme park with roller coasters and 3D movies, and I have to say that's a large part of its appeal. It's a nineteenth-century kind of place where it feels as if you really can breathe the air of one of the world's most famous fairy tales. The restaurant is called the Osteria del Gambero Rosso, the original Italian name of the Red Prawn Inn, and there are lots of statues and paintings depicting scenes and characters from the story.

I feel completely at home: I know everything about Pinocchio.

"Kids, did you know that Pinocchio actually isn't a puppet at all, but a marionette? Puppets are the ones you stick your hand inside, while marionettes are the ones on strings that you move from above. The mistake comes from Collodi's own writing, and, in fact, he calls Pinocchio a puppet throughout the book."

"So was Collodi a dummy?" is Eva's impertinent question.

"No, but he does get a lot of things mixed up. For instance, he calls the monster who swallows Pinocchio a shark, but then he describes it as more of a whale. And, in fact, in the Walt Disney *Pinocchio* it's depicted as a whale."

"I don't like Pinocchio. I like Peter Pan," says Lorenzo, still filled with the excitement of his role in the school play.

"They're not really all that different," I argue. "They're both little boys who don't want to grow up. They even become friends."

"But if they're made-up storybook characters, then how could they ever become friends?" asks my little one.

"No one knows it, but the two of them met in the Land of Toys."

"There's no such place as the Land of Toys!" Lorenzo exclaims.

"There is so, and how! I've even been there. That's where I met Romeo."

"Wait, who's Romeo?" asks Paola: even she is getting involved. Little by little, I'm drawing her deep into my web.

"Romeo is Pinocchio's friend, though we all know him as Candlewick, his nickname."

"Did you meet Candlewick?" Eva asked, in astonishment.

"I didn't just meet him, we were friends."

"*The Adventures of Pinocchio* is a novel from the late nineteenth century. Just how old are you, Papà?" Lorenzo does his best to destroy all shreds of poetry with a question.

"I met him in the seventies. I was just a little boy, and he was almost a hundred."

"You were friends with an old man?" Eva asks, baffled.

"Of course! Age doesn't count among friends."

"So you were friends with a hundred-year-old donkey?" Lorenzo insists.

Oh, right, I'd forgotten that in the book Candlewick turns into a donkey.

"True, in fact, he was a donkey, then after a few years he was forgiven and changed back into a boy. I met him many years later. I wound up in the Land of Toys once when I got lost while I was out on a bike ride."

"Where is the Land of Toys?" Lorenzo asks, starting to come around.

"No one knows. The only way to get there is by accident. I immediately recognized the lit-up entrance, it looked like the way into an amusement park. Inside were thousands of children and just one little old man: Candlewick."

"So why was he still there?" Eva's curiosity is piqued by now.

"Because he didn't have any friends in the outside world. Pinocchio had moved away—no one knew where—and he'd found a job as a custodian of the Land of Toys."

"How did you become friends?" asks my little girl.

"It's a long story."

"I'll tell it to you," Paola jumps in, to my surprise.

I'm speechless. The relay-race fairy tale is a specialty of the house. Paola and I have told dozens of these call-and-response bedtime stories to our children, but today this was completely unexpected. Something on the order of a miracle.

Paola continues.

"I was on vacation with my parents in the countryside. I was about ten, I think, and I was flying a kite. It came down in the forest, and when I went in to find it I got lost. The sun was setting."

I seize the baton in this narrative relay race and go on.

"At the same time, I had just arrived in the Land of Toys and Candlewick had stopped me at the entrance because my name didn't appear on the guest list."

"Just then I show up and I pretend that Papà is my brother. And that I'm very worried about him because he has a few screws loose."

"At first, Candlewick was a little skeptical, but he finally comes around, decides he likes us, and invites us to dinner. An excellent dinner consisting of chocolate, cotton candy, and various assorted hard candies, all of them treats made by a very skillful pastry chef who worked there."

"After dinner, he takes us on a tour of the Land of Toys in his mouse-drawn carriage, purchased secondhand from the Blue Fairy. Everywhere we looked there were amusement park rides, movie houses, theaters, fun of all kinds to be had. And thousands of children just like us. An earthly paradise."

"We play all night, until the sun rises the next day, while Candlewick falls asleep on the coachman's box of the carriage. The next day he tells us that, for our own health, it might be best if we leave now. A second day in the Land of Toys is invariably fatal."

"Because you turn into donkeys?" Lorenzo asks.

"Of course," Paola replies, "that's no fairy tale, the way we thought it was. And to convince us, he shows us the stalls where they keep all the children who have been turned into little jackasses."

"That day we leave together and go back home. A few years later, Candlewick turned one hundred and retired. I grew up and never managed to find my way back to the Land of Toys."

"Too bad," Eva comments.

"Right," I say. "Luckily, though, many years later I found Mamma again."

I try to catch Paola's eye and manage to, but only for a fleeting instant. She's enjoyed the relay-race fairy tale as much as I have. But my children haven't: they're a little disappointed in a story that lacks at least a dragon, an ogre, or a mysterious horseman.

Lorenzo says, "If that's a true story, it's a miserable one. If you just came up with it now, it's not much—you can certainly do better."

At last Paola and I look at each other. We can't help laughing. I start to wrap my arms around her, but she dodges me and changes the subject.

"Let's all go get something to eat at the Red Prawn Inn. Aren't you hungry?"

The small chorus of yeses is explicit and unequivocal. We all go out to eat. I watch Paola as she steers the kids toward the restaurant, helps them order—"No, you can't start with dessert, sorry"; and "Spinach it is. You've had no greens for two days." I feel like a striker who's just scored a goal. But the emotional match still has a long time to run.

Argentario. A glittering, silvery word that has a magical significance for me and for Paola: it was here, ten years ago, that we conceived Lorenzo. I've reserved the same small hotel we stayed in ten years ago; it's under new management but it remains a deeply romantic little place. It's on the promontory between Porto Ercole and Porto Santo Stefano, in the part of Argentario least frequented by tourists. I remember it as a piece of heaven, and I can't say for the life of me why we've never gone back since.

"Did you know, Lorenzo, that Mamma and Papà conceived you here?"

"So I'm not from Rome?"

"You were born in Rome, but you were conceived here."

Eva breaks in: "What does it mean to be conceived?"

Here we go.

"That means that this is where Papà and Mamma kissed each other lots of times and decided to have a baby. Lorenzo, to be specific."

"Kisses aren't enough to make a baby," Lorenzo points out; "you have to have sex."

I take it in stride. "That's right, in fact, we had sex and nine months later Lorenzo was born. And we were right here, in this hotel."

"Was Papà already fat?" Eva asks.

Paola, who up to now has been uncomfortable, breaks into a smile.

"Yes, he was already, let's say, solidly built."

"We're here," I announce brusquely as we turn in at the hotel gate.

As we unload the luggage, I say, "Tonight Papà and Mamma are going to have dinner by themselves. I've found someone to look after you."

Paola immediately raises objections. "I have no intention of leaving my children with some teenage girl I've never met."

I savor this moment that I've been anticipating for days now.

"Actually," I begin, "it's definitely not a teenage girl, but especially it's not someone you've never met."

I point to someone behind her. Paola turns and sees Martina waving hello, at the hotel entrance. And behind Miss Marple, there's Oscar, beaming happily in a pair of sunglasses. They both look ten years younger.

"Are they acceptable babysitters?" I ask with a smile.

The children run straight at their grandparents, shouting happily.

"The pastry shop is closed today," I explain, "so I asked your father to take a trip to Argentario with Martina. I must say I didn't have to ask twice."

Paola surrenders. But it's like pulling teeth.

At sunset we entrust Lorenzo and Eva to the babysitters and I take Paola to dinner in the hotel's cozy restaurant, a romantic paradise overlooking the water. We order an antipasto of raw fish.

"Why did you bring me here?" she asks while we wait.

"Because I wanted to show Lorenzo the place where he was conceived."

"Let me repeat the question. Why did you bring *me* here?"

I give her a straight answer to a straight question.

"Because it's an important place to the two of us as a couple, and you can't imagine how badly I want to make peace with you. Forgive me, forgive me, forgive me, forgive me, a thousand times forgive me."

"You know something, Lucio?"

When she calls me Lucio and not *amore*, that's always a bad sign.

"If I'd married someone like Corrado, I'd have counted on his cheating on me; in fact, I'd have expected it on a regular basis. Let's just say that it would have been less of a letdown. But I would have sworn you weren't the type, that it wouldn't happen to us."

"I made a mistake—what can I do about it now?"

"Don't keep after me, I need more time."

"That's one thing I don't have."

She realizes what she's just said. She falls silent for a few moments, then goes on.

"I wish I could just forget everything. You don't know how much I wish that. But I closed a door emotionally when you did what you did. I know that you can't understand it, but that's how it is. That's how it is right now."

A big platter of shellfish comes to the table and cuts the tension. As we sample the prawns and shrimp, Paola continues: "Do you remember a year ago, when I went to see a new orthopedist because I had that persistent pain in my shoulder?"

"Yes," I say, suddenly suspicious at this abrupt change of topic.

"He wasn't a kind and elderly specialist, like I told you. He was forty-five years old, movie-star handsome, and incredibly fit. And he was an obvious lady-killer, a real son of a bitch. I was attracted to him."

I'm glued to my chair.

"One day, after an exam, he kissed me."

"What did you do?"

"I was surprised, and then I kissed him back and then . . ."

"And then?"

"I ran out of the room. I got a new orthopedist without telling you anything about it."

"There was just one kiss?"

"Just the one kiss. I resisted. At least, *I* did."

The first-person pronoun repeated twice draws the curtain on our conversation. I can't help the angry blur of adrenaline that fills me. Is this jealousy or just male pride? I don't know. Do I have the right to be jealous after what I did to her? I don't know where to go from here. We eat the rest of our dinner in silence, like an old and disgruntled married couple.

When we return to the lobby, we find our babysitters in the thick of a game of hide-and-seek being played not only by our children, but those of the hotel's owners as well.

"Everything okay?" Oscar asks me, when he sees the defeated look on my face.

"Everything's fine," I lie.

A little later, we say good night to him and Martina, thanking them for their lightning visit. They're staying in the same hotel, but tomorrow morning at dawn they'll head back to Rome.

"Don't get used to this door-to-door service," Oscar mutters.

"Enjoy the rest of your trip, kids," Martina calls out. Lorenzo notices I hold Oscar in a longer embrace than usual.

"Papà, you know we're going to see Grandpa again in two weeks, back in Rome!"

I break out of the hug as if I've been caught red-handed being sentimental. When the two old people move away, arm in arm, upstairs, a piece of me goes with them.

Here's the moment I've been waiting for the whole trip: the men-only day. Lorenzo and me.

We leave Paola and Eva in the hotel, both of them amply occupied, Paola for a spa day, Eva for a mini volleyball tournament, and we set off, shouldering our backpacks along the Argentario promontory. We're wearing T-shirts and bermuda shorts, we're carrying fruit and water, we have plenty of suntan cream and beach towels. We're two perfect day-trippers.

"An hour's walk from here," I explain to Lorenzo, "there's a way down to the water, carved out of the rock, that no one knows about."

"Then how come you do?"

"Your great-grandfather took me there when I was your age."

"And how did he know about it?"

"When he was in the navy, he landed one day in this area and scouted the whole coast."

I show him the little cove we're heading for on Google Maps on my iPhone. He seems convinced.

"Is the water shallow?" he asks me. His number one enemy is deep water. I reassure him.

"Yes, there's a little beach with some rocks, but you can touch bottom."

He seems satisfied. We walk at a good pace under a blazing sun. We take a trail that runs along the cliff edge. A place for mountain goats.

"Be careful, watch where you put your feet, and keep your hand on the rock face."

The path starts heading downhill, with a series of hairpin curves. The pebbly dirt is slippery and dangerous. The footing is precarious. We proceed slowly and cautiously. Every so often I cough, but I do my best to conceal my difficulties. I feel empty, drained.

My photographic memory flickers on, and suddenly I remember everything. The roles are reversed: I'm Lorenzo, and Grandpa is me. I even remember that once or twice I almost slipped and fell. Lorenzo is more surefooted, or maybe his shoes are better than the Mecap sneakers I wore thirty years ago.

"Can I ask you a question, Papà?"

"Yes, of course you can."

"Who is this buddy Fritz you talk about sometimes with Mamma? Is he a friend of yours I've never met?"

"That's right, you've never met him. He's not a very nice person and I hope you never do meet him."

"Then why do you say he's your buddy?"

"It's an ironic figure of speech. Sort of like when Eva tells you that you're the head of the class."

"So that's like making fun of somebody?"

"Not exactly. Irony is something a little more subtle. To mean one thing, you say something else that means the opposite. For example, last week, when you broke that picture frame with a soccer ball, what did I say to you?"

"You said: 'Nice work, congratulations!'"

"That's right, I was being ironic."

Lorenzo smiles. He understands.

I smile back at him. It's a shame we didn't have more of these men-only days. A real shame.

By now we're close to the water. I think we're here. I remember that there's one last section through the trees, and then we'll see the wonderful cove.

But when we get there, the cove is overrun by a horde of vacationers, conveyed there by two large boats anchored a short way off-shore, just a hundred feet or so from the beach. Beach umbrellas, noise, the scent of tanning creams, beach tennis, bikinis, water fights, tomato-and-mozzarella panini. An inlet with fifty yards of rocky beach, as crowded as a department store during a fire sale.

Lorenzo stares at me and exclaims: "This unspoiled beach is magnificent, nice work, Papà."

I see that he has a firm grip on the concept of irony. I can't keep myself from laughing.

We find a rocky corner of the cove where we leave our towels and backpacks.

"They aren't going to steal our things, are they?" Lorenzo asks.

"We'll keep an eye on them. . . . Come on, let's go in the water."

I pull off my T-shirt and gesture for him to follow. He hesitates. Then he follows.

I run into the water and then launch headlong into a dive. Lorenzo takes a few steps then stands there, water lapping at his waist. The reassuring contact with the sandy seabed is like Linus's blanket for him.

I go over to him.

"You want to try the dead man's float? I'll hold you up."

He agrees and lets me pick him up. One hand under his head, the other under his hips.

"Take a deep breath. The human body is like a piece of wood. It floats. It can't sink."

"Not even if I swallow five gallons of water?"

"What does that have to do with anything? Of course you could sink if you swallow enough water. But if you go underwater, just keep your mouth closed, and that way you won't swallow."

Lorenzo relaxes. He shuts his eyes and allows himself to be lulled by the ebb and flow of the waves. I support him easily, thanks to Archimedes' principle. Slowly, very slowly, I release him. Then I let him float free, but stay close. He doesn't even notice. His waterline is perfect, allowing him to bob easily until he opens his eyes and it dawns on him that I'm no longer holding him up. He starts to thrash and flail, trying to touch bottom, but the current has taken us out a short way and the water is too deep for him.

"Papà, I'm drowning!"

"Don't worry . . . you're not drowning," I say from six feet away, and it's enough to reassure him. "Try moving your legs the way you do when you ride a bike."

He does as he's told. But his flailing arms keep him from maintaining a proper balance.

"That's enough, Papà. Help me!"

"The more you relax the more you tend to stay on the surface. Come on, pedal your legs and sweep the surface with your arms, as if you were trying to dig a hole in the water."

Pedaling with his feet, digging with his arms . . . He's already doing better.

"Let's get back to the sand. I can't do this!"

"You *can* do it! Come on . . . pedal your legs down below, move your arms together up top, like a frog."

At last he starts to keep a regular pace. He relaxes. He's floating.

"You see, you can do it."

He smiles, amazed that he's swimming.

Legs, arms, legs, arms.

Lorenzo has just learned to swim. There'll be plenty of time for him to pick up the strokes and styles later.

I pick him up and hug him tight. He collapses, exhausted, in my arms. I carry him a few yards closer in, where he can touch bottom.

"You did great!" I exclaim.

"Are you being ironic?" he asks me as he catches his breath.

"No, I'm being perfectly serious. Here's something for later, son. Trust yourself. Even if you're really, really scared, never let on that you are."

"Why?"

"You're showing your game, you see? There's no need to let anyone have the upper hand, and by showing you're scared, you let an opponent think he's got one over you. He doesn't, but he thinks he does. And that might actually help him win."

"Um . . . what if you're so scared, you really fail? Like when you can't remember the answers to the questions the teacher asks you about history in front of the whole class? Or when you can't speak the truth because you know it'll get you in trouble?"

"Well, that can be a problem. That's true. But when you fail at something, you can actually learn from it. I failed at so many things before I learned to do them well. And some I had to give up on completely because I hurt my knee."

"Like what?"

"Well, all competitive sports were out. And in the end, I learned water polo . . ."

"Where you're a star!"

I can't help the smile that covers my face when my boy says that. "No star, Lorenzo. Good, maybe. Star, no. But I'm happy with that. See, you have to be happy."

We stretch out in the sun to dry off and eat the sandwiches we had the hotel make for us. We stay there until the boats sail away and the sun has almost sunk to the horizon. The beach is covered with trash, the remnants of the invasion of swimmers. We set out to clean it up. We make two huge piles of garbage and hope that one of the two pilots is shamed into taking it away tomorrow.

It's dark by the time we get back to our women, and we're so tired we don't even have the strength to eat dinner.

"How did it go?" Paola asks me as soon as we're alone.

"I should have spent more time with him." Sadness forms pools in my eyes.

"I know," is my wife's pained reply. "I know."

We're driving along the Via Aurelia at moderate speed, with the windows rolled down. I feel like Vittorio Gassman as Bruno Cortona in Dino Risi's masterpiece, *Il sorpasso*, the archetype of all road movies. I drive doing my best to ignore the stabbing pain in my ribs that leaves me breathless. Paola is by my side dozing off while we leave Tuscany behind and triumphantly enter Liguria. Eva's asleep too, slumped against Lorenzo, who sits alertly watching the road and the signage.

"Don't speed, Papà, they have speed cameras here."

"Thanks."

Just then we see a car coming toward us in the opposite direction. It flashes its brights.

"What did that man want?"

"He was just warning us that there's a speed trap farther on, a highway patrol squad car. You slow down because you see the speed camera, then you speed up right afterward. And the highway patrol is waiting to give you a ticket."

"But why did that guy warn you? Do you know him?"

"It's an old Italian tradition. Everyone united against the police and the Carabinieri."

"But why?"

"Good question. Because we're Italian. And we all have something to hide. Breaking the law really is the only thing we all have in common."

"Do you break the law too, Papà?"

As usual, I've wandered heedlessly into a minefield. Even if it may prove to be less than edifying, I decide to tell the truth as we sail past a checkpoint where the police ignore us.

"Sometimes. But I try not to."

"What crimes do you commit?"

"Crimes may be overstating it. Let's just say transgressions. There are all kinds of transgressions; for instance, this morning when the proprietor of the hotel asked me if I wanted an official receipt and I said no. He gave us a discount."

"But a discount is a good thing, isn't it?"

"Sure, but that means he was trying to avoid paying taxes, and I was his accomplice."

"That doesn't seem like a very serious crime."

"That's the problem with Italy, Lorenzo. Crimes that don't seem serious. For example, bootleg movies. How many of those do you download?"

"Lots. Just cartoons, though. Why, is that a crime?"

"A very serious one. It's called theft. It's as if you were shoplifting at the supermarket."

"If I shoplift at the supermarket, the alarm will go off when I try to leave. But at home no one can see me."

"Correct answer. That's why everyone downloads movies and very few people steal from the supermarket. Because no one can see you. Do you know how you can tell the difference between an honest man and a criminal? By how they act when no one can see them. Don't forget that."

I'm proud of my impromptu civics lesson. Only now do I notice that Paola is awake and heard the whole thing. She can't wait for a chance to put in a little lesson of her own.

"For example, when no one's looking, Papà sneaks into the kitchen and eats some Parmesan cheese."

"That might have happened once," I defend myself.

"And when you were little, he also used to steal your baby food."

"It was good . . ."

"And your teething biscuits."

"Delicious. Even though it wasn't technically stealing because I paid for them in the first place."

"But you bought them for me," Lorenzo points out.

"I was just tasting them to make sure they were good—I'm a protective father."

"You tasted them because you're a gluttonous piggy," says my wife.

"What are you talking about? At the very most I might have eaten one or two."

"One or two? You had a secret box all your own hidden in your sock drawer."

"You knew about that?"

"Who did you think was washing your socks? The Holy Ghost?"

I wish this conversation could go on forever. One of the finest things in life is a family argument. The kind that drips intimacy and love. The Via Aurelia continues to slide past beneath us like a conveyor belt, and I'm one happy driver.

watch Paola and the kids walking ahead of me through the narrow lanes, or *caruggi,* of Genoa. There is a special, untouchable bond linking the three of them together. It's been clear to me for years that I'm strictly on the sidelines, accepted, maybe even beloved, but excluded from that magical umbilical cord that never breaks between mother and children. By now all the tests on child psychology, widely published in summer editions of popular magazines, make it clear that during a pregnancy, a mother nourishes the fetus not only from the culinary point of view but also spiritually, creating an eternal and affectionate elective affinity. Their souls share nine months of life, their hearts synchronized to their joys and sorrows. Two human beings living together, exchanging feelings, memories, and dreams. But also, maybe I didn't try hard enough.

How can a papà who shows up after nine months of this continual imprinting hope to compete? The English word for this prenatal relationship is *bonding* and doctors urge mothers to nourish the little candidate for birth with fresh air, classical music, plenty of art, and pleasant emotions.

I go on watching the trio from a distance. Paola stops at a stall that sells focaccia from Recco, possibly the world's finest cheese focaccia, though my naturopath considers it the world's most lethal. Paola gestures to me from afar, asking if I'd like some. I nod yes. Lorenzo is saying something to Eva, who in turn laughs. Suddenly it strikes me that what I'm looking at is, quite simply, the future. I've just caught a glimpse for a few minutes of my family without me.

My family without me.

It sounds like the title of a terrible song.

I head over to the focaccia stall, doing a natural zoom on my wife's face as she offers me a piece of hot focaccia. I bite into it and savor the taste. The melted cheese drips down my chin and T-shirt. This snack gives me time to think things over and size up the situation.

Is there anything I want to do in the ten days that remain of this journey?

I don't know. The kids are having fun but I still have no idea of how I'm going to win back Paola.

Paola says something to me but I can't hear her. So she says it again.

"Everything okay?"

I reply promptly: "Of course, *amore mio*. Shall we go to the aquarium?"

Eva's shouts of joy make it clear that the decision has been made.

"Today we're going to complete the 'maritime explorer' phase of the journey and visit the cetacean sanctuary."

"What's that? A church for whales?" Eva asks, looking up at me as we walk along, hand in hand. She's still excited after our visit to the aquarium yesterday. She has a point—it's a confusing name.

"No, it's an area of the Ligurian Sea populated by dolphins, whales, and turtles."

"I want a turtle at home! Like the one we saw yesterday."

"We can't take it away from its natural habitat. It's a sea turtle."

"They've already taken it away. It's in an aquarium!"

Again, that's a solid point. We're out on a mission, to buy morning pastries—*cornetti*—for the rest of the family. They aren't as good as the ones my father-in-law makes, but they'll do. Yesterday's hotel breakfast was so depressing that today we're hunting for something yummy in the area.

Two hours later we, and thirty others, board a small vessel for a whale-watching tour.

Lorenzo is more passionately interested in the workings of the boat than in our impending encounter with the Mediterranean Sea's largest cetaceans. Paola is unusually relaxed. These days, I feel like a tour operator eager to amuse his customers with novel and original treats. Today, everyone understands, the excursion is designed to appeal to Eva's love of nature and animals.

The first ones to come and call on us are the dolphins. They pirouette in the water, chasing after our boat like performers in Cirque du Soleil who've been practicing their routine for years. It's all so beautiful that it hardly seems real.

The sun and salt air are baking me, but today I don't find it quite so tiring. I make an effort to breathe in slowly, while my daughter squeals with joy as she runs along the ship's railing. I inhale and exhale, and repeat. I listen to the ragged breath that's like a giant spray filling my damaged lungs.

I turn around and I'm greeted by a simply incredible spectacle: an enormous whale is swimming alongside the ship, spouting seawater like a geyser. I'm all alone on this side of the vessel; everyone else has hurried over to watch the highly entertaining dolphins on the far side. I feel the urge to pull my Polaroid out of my backpack, but I seem to have fallen into a trance. The huge mammal watches me. Its mastodonic eye stares at me with determination. I smile at it but it doesn't understand. It seems to want to tell me something. We study each other with care, to the background sound of chattering acrobatic dolphins. It bobs along next to the boat with no apparent effort. I can clearly hear it breathing. It's a moment of infinite peace.

For a few minutes I consider the idea of leaping into the water beside him and vanishing forever. It might be a more elegant way to go. Eva then comes running, the second passenger to spot our fellow traveler. She shouts: "A whale! Over here!"

Everyone rushes to the other side of the boat, making it roll dangerously. So long, infinite peace.

The timid cetacean promptly submerges, putting an end to the show. We encounter no other denizens of the deep for the rest of the morning. By the time we get back to port, it's long past lunchtime. Eva's happy: she's counted twelve dolphins, four seagulls, and a whale. I feel calmer, as if the giant cetacean had transmitted some of its Zen serenity to me.

Breakfast by the water. Paola is doing a crossword puzzle, I'm reading reports on an upcoming soccer championship season I'll never live to see, while Eva and Lorenzo have undertaken the construction of an outsized, overambitious sand castle that is unlikely to be there when the sun comes up tomorrow. We could be taken for any ordinary vacationing family. All we lack is an inflatable dinghy or a rubber mattress in the shape of a crocodile. Today is my birthday. We've decided to celebrate it with lunch at the best restaurant in the area. I never expected my fortieth birthday to be like this. I stand up from my beach chair and drop the newspaper.

"Lorenzo! Eva! Shall we play a game together?"

I don't have to ask twice.

A marble race.

First we build the track. Eva sits on the ground and Lorenzo and I drag her by the legs to shape the sand, making a track of parabolic curves, tunnels, ditches, and booby traps.

"Let me explain the rules to you. There are three qualification laps in which we count how many times you have to flick the marble to get around the course. The one with the fewest finger flicks wins the privilege of starting. Then we do five race laps, one flick per turn."

I pull out a bag of marbles. I've guarded them jealously over the years, the same ones I've always had, scratched and worn. I'm a champion at this game, as I am at all games requiring a precise finger flick, but I reel myself in to give the kids a chance to compete. In the end,

Lorenzo wins, Eva comes in second, and I'm third. When we go eat in a seaside trattoria, we're sweaty and excited. I ask for a rematch soon, and my kids agree.

At the end of the meal a cake is brought to the table with two candles in the shape of numbers on top: a 4 and a 0. I hurry to blow them out and I pretend to be delighted while the rest of the family applauds and sings a chorus of "Happy Birthday to You."

When we get back to the room, while Paola's taking a shower, I rummage through her suitcase in search of a phone charger because mine seems to have disappeared.

Under a pile of blouses and a pair of high heels in a carry bag, what I find isn't the phone charger. What I find is a letter. A yellowed piece of paper with a few moisture spots, torn out of a lined notebook. A letter I wrote to Paola. Twelve years ago. Possibly the last letter I wrote before getting sucked into the arid and obscene dictatorship of e-mail.

I step out onto the balcony and reread it. I can barely remember what I wrote.

Caro amore mio,

Well, the day is almost upon us. Tomorrow we're getting married. Don't be late—I'm always sorry for those husbands-to-be who have to wait outside the church and have to put up with the unfailing razzing of their so-so-funny friends: "If you ask me, she's changed her mind!" I'm sure to be emotional, possibly tired, and I won't be able to tell you everything I'd like to, so I'm going to write it to you instead. To know you and (I hope) marry you is the greatest gift that life has given me. The other day a very likable gentleman called me from the office of Fate and filled me in on a few fragments of our future life together: we're going to have four children (I know, I told him that was a lot, but Fate does as it pleases); every year we're going to spend fifteen days in Fregene with your father and mother (I bargained for a week, tops); someday our oldest daughter will tell us that she's pregnant by the man she loves and we'll all weep tears of joy; when we're sixty years old and our children have left home, we'll sell everything and go live on a sailboat, to finally sail around the world as we'd always said we would but never got around to; then we'll retire and live in a house on the beach, which everybody talks about, but we'll actually do it; and we'll grow old side by side, contemplating the sun as it sets over the sea and our lives together (that's not original, I copied it, but I can't remember from whom); then one day we'll fall asleep arm in arm and never wake up again. I've always loved you, I love you, and I'll love you always.

Yours, Lucio

I fold the letter up. I'm crying.

It's funny . . . almost all my predictions were wrong. None of what I hoped for is going to come true.

Only now do I realize that Paola is standing behind me. She's crying too.

"Did you remember it?" she asks me with a half smile.

"Yes, of course . . . ," I say, even if it isn't true. Like all men, I forget fundamental things.

Paola comes over to me. She wraps her arms around me.

I nuzzle her neck. Her appley scent envelops me. She smells like home.

An endless embrace. If that's not forgiveness, it's close enough.

Two hours later, I phone Umberto. While I was nuzzling Paola, I had an idea that strikes me as hard to implement but absolutely wonderful.

"Hey, friend. Happy birthday! I texted you."

"Thanks, I read it."

"How's everything?"

"It's all good, we're at the beach . . ."

"How's the weather? Is it sunny?"

"What do you care? Shut up for a minute, I have a big favor to ask you . . . I swear it'll be the last."

I entrust him with a practically impossible mission and he has less than a week's time to accomplish it. But I know my old Athos well. I know he'll pull it off.

The Ligurian Sea at dawn is always in the mood for a chat. I look down on it from the window of our two-star little hotel at Arma di Taggia and I listen to its stories while Paola and the kids, behind me, are still fully immersed in high-quality REM sleep.

The wind tosses my head of graying spaghetti and whispers in my ear the unbelievable tales of the adventures of an Ottoman corsair who actually lived, a certain Turgut Reis, known in this part of the world as Dragut. I remember his story very well; my grandpa told me all about him when I was Lorenzo's age. I even remember what Grandpa was wearing that night, where I was sitting, what Grandma was cooking. I remember everything, suddenly. It was a Sunday. My favorite concierges had given me, for no reason or special occasion, a deluxe copy of *Treasure Island*. I still remember the emerald-green cover, with a drawing of Jim Hawkins hiding from the cruel Long John Silver behind a barrel in the inn. It was a hardcover book, with heavy pages, full of color illustrations, and I read it that afternoon at a single sitting. It's the only book I've brought with me on this journey. Even though I know already that I won't read it. Ever since that Sunday afternoon so many years ago, stories about pirates, corsairs, and buccaneers have become my preferred form of reading. If I could be reincarnated, I'd come back as a pirate, one even more mendacious and pitiless than the valiant Dragut my grandpa told me about all those years ago.

I turn around. Paola is still in bed. The kids are camped out on a little trundle bed and didn't hear the cannon fire.

It seems like a vacation. And maybe it is.

I curl up next to my wife. I wrap my arms around her and nuzzle her. I need to fill up on this.

The day begins a few hours later, with a visit to the lookout towers of Civezza, built by the townsfolk half a millennium ago to warn of the arrival of the pirate Dragut, so I take advantage of the fact to start my story. Lorenzo and Eva, the former strangely well behaved, the latter strangely interested in a war story, sit between pairs of battlements of the fortress and listen to me with bated breath. Paola is a short distance away, taking pictures and perhaps listening to me in the background.

"The corsair Dragut was the most terrifying freebooter that ever infested Italian seas."

"What kind of a name is Dragut?" Lorenzo interrupts immediately.

"An Ottoman name. Which means Turkish. He came to Italy in search of cities and ships to loot."

"And did he find them?" asks Eva with her usual precision.

"Yes. The cities and the islands that he put to the sword and the torch still stand: Olbia, Portoferraio, Rapallo, Vieste, as well as the isle of Elba. Dragut was a big fan of the Italian seas, Italian food, and even Italian women. In fact, he had a dozen wives."

"And how did he support them?" Eva asks.

"He worked as a pirate, so he was very rich."

I put on a serious, sober voice to try to rivet their attention and keep them from interrupting me again. I decide to insert a series of imaginary variants on the true story of the Ottoman pirate.

"You should know that my great-grandfather's great-grandfather's great-grandfather's great-grandfather, et cetera, et cetera, a certain Igor "One Eye" Battistini, a fat man who was exceedingly handy with the sword and the saber, was actually Dragut's lieutenant."

"I don't believe it," Eva says immediately.

"But it's true."

"Are you trying to tell me that we have a great-great-great-great-great-great-great-great-great-grandfather who was a pirate?" asks Lorenzo, piling on.

"Well, he wasn't actually a pirate; at first he ran a tavern, but then one day a giant crow plucked out his eye and flapped off toward the sea. Igor took ship on the first passing vessel, in pursuit of the crow. That first ship was Dragut's. Little by little, he came to be the perfidious Ottoman's right-hand man. But he never did find the crow, or his eye."

"Now you're just making things up," says Eva brusquely.

"Go on," Lorenzo says, conceding his interest.

They don't actually believe it, but still the story has caught their fancy and now they want to know how it ends. My self-respect as a narrator swells.

Paola smiles from a distance. And I continue enthusiastically.

"His bitterest enemy (every pirate has an official enemy) was Andrea Doria, a name we normally assign to an ocean liner that sank. Actually, though, Andrea Doria was a valiant admiral who was born just a few miles away from here, in Oneglia. The two rivals battled fiercely for years."

"So Andrea Doria was as cruel as Lord Brooke, Sandokan's sworn enemy?" Lorenzo asks.

"No, technically Admiral Doria was the good guy and Dragut was the bad guy."

"I'm rooting for Dragut," Lorenzo decrees.

"So am I," I explain. "Sometimes we root for the bad guys. One morning in late autumn, after a pursuit that crisscrossed a thousand seas, Dragut is captured by none other than Doria and taken prisoner after a sea battle that lasted ten days."

"Anyway, he probably escapes," my firstborn speculates.

"Dragut is sent to row as a galley slave in the admiral's fleet. But a pirate of his stature certainly couldn't end his brilliant career like that."

"So he escapes," Lorenzo insists.

"No. A few years later Barbarossa—"

"Frederick Barbarossa?" asks Paola, who's finally taken interest.

"Not Frederick, but a fellow Barbary corsair named Barbarossa—or Redbeard—for the color of his beard. In any case, this pirate Barbarossa pays Andrea Doria a huge ransom for Dragut's release."

Murmurs of disappointment. My minuscule audience would clearly have preferred a daring and ingenious escape.

"By no means repentant, the unsinkable Dragut goes back to his old maritime pursuits. He attacks numerous Italian towns and ships, and finally works his way to here, in 1564, close to Arma di Taggia, in a mountain hamlet still called Civezza. Which is where we are now. The bold corsair in fact loved to roam widely, and he never limited his raids to galleons or ports. He was a creative practitioner of the art of piracy. But in this case, he hadn't taken into account the heroic resistance of the people of Civezza."

"Do they kill him?" Lorenzo asks with a note of concern in his voice.

"No. In spite of his repeated looting and sacking, the people of the little town defend themselves. They build this fortress and they oblige the corsair to suffer great losses. At the end of this raid, the Ottoman pirate decides that Italy has become a dangerous place for evildoers and he moves to Malta, which strikes him as less perilous. In 1565, along with the Turkish fleet, he takes part in the siege of Fort St. Elmo."

"What kind of name is Elmo? They all have terrible names in this story."

"It's an ancient name. Anyway, Elmo is just the name of the saint they named the fort after. In mid-June, just when Dragut is getting ready to enjoy a well-deserved summer vacation, he's wounded in the head by a piece of flying rock, shattered by a large iron musket ball fired by an enemy sniper."

"And does he die?" This time, the question is asked by both children in unison.

"Hold on. Our favorite corsair doesn't retreat, he courageously continues to lead his men to the attack, but he's bleeding badly from both ears and his mouth. So they carry him back from the front lines and put him to bed in a tent, where he dies two days later."

"And is he reborn, like Jesus?" Lorenzo asks hopefully.

"He is not reborn. His body is taken to Tripoli, and there he is buried with full military honors in a mosque. Legend has it that his archenemy Andrea Doria felt such respect for him that he named his own cat Dragut, after learning of the death of the Ottoman corsair."

"What about One Eye?" Eva wonders.

Maybe, just a little, she believes me. I pile on and season the finale with an array of wholly invented details.

"One Eye moved to Malaysia, where he met Sandokan and Yanez and formed an alliance with the two of them. He also changed his nom de guerre: in fact, in Salgari's novels, he's called Tremal-Naik."

"Tremal-Naik had both eyes and was Indian," Lorenzo points out, catching me red-handed.

I've put my foot in it. I try to find my way out of this narrative maze by explaining that in reality there were two Tremal-Naiks, but I get more and more tangled up in the knots of my second-rate creativity. I'm saved by a zealous watchman who announces that the fortress will be closing soon for the lunchtime break.

There's no question about one thing: my grandpa was a much better storyteller than I am.

That afternoon, after a massive snack made up of a bowl heaped high with *trofie al pesto*, we're struck and sent to the bottom by a classic seaside enemy, a summer thunderstorm. It catches us while we're still half a mile from the car, just the right amount of time to drench us to the bone. Once we're finally in the car, we all giggle helplessly. We can't seem to stop laughing for a good solid ten minutes. Paola looks over at me, and for the first time on this journey, gives me her real smile.

And so the ramshackle pensione Gina, where we take shelter that night, seems like a deluxe Four Seasons hotel.

chose to stay off the highway so we could keep the windows open and enjoy the countryside. We're having an on-the-road morning, to the tunes of one of my favorite Italian pop compilations: singer-songwriters from the seventies. We reach our destination before lunch.

"Well, here we are."

"Where's the hotel?" asks Paola.

"There's no hotel here. We're camping!"

The overjoyed cries of the kids drown out Paola's "No-o-o!" She closes her eyes with resignation. I went on camping trips for years in Boy Scouts and with my other musketeers. I only stopped when I met Paola. If there's one thing she hates, it's camping. When we got engaged, she promised me that one day she'd go tent camping with me. That was a wild card that I could have played at any moment. So I decide to play it today.

Our station wagon rolls triumphantly into the campgrounds.

I reserved a camping site right on the lakeshore. We park the car and start assembling the supertent that I bought at the Via Sannio street market. I'm a whiz when it comes to pitching tents, a born prodigy. There are people who play tennis, or paint, or play the piano, or cook: well, what I know how to do is pitch tents, of all and any kind. The one we have is a giant pop-up super Igloo that basically pitches itself when you throw it into the air. I show my young assistants how to dig a trench around the tent to keep it from flooding in case of sudden showers, how to drive the stakes without slamming the mallet down on their thumbs, how to blow up the air mattresses. I've secretly brought everything we're going to need.

Paola allows herself to be sucked into the fun and assembles a very efficient camp kitchen.

"Shall we try lighting it with a couple of rocks again?" asks Lorenzo, with the irony that he's by now mastered far too well.

"No. I bought a fire starter. You're hungry, aren't you?"

We canvas the grounds for branches and twigs, and in just five minutes, we have our campfire crackling merrily, safely corralled in a circle of stones. We bake potatoes wrapped in aluminum foil, we roast sausages, and we make a bean-and-egg stew. Even Roy Rogers and his friends would have been staggered by the sheer mass of food. But we eat greedily, accompanying it with bread. Just a few days from the end, I've cast aside all of my naturopath's advice. I apply one single criterion: I eat everything I feel like eating. We're almost done when the sky starts to drizzle. For the past few years, the climate in Italy has been turning tropical, but no one dares to make it official: it rains in the summer.

A minute later, the downpour is raging, accompanied by flashes of lightning and claps of thunder. We barely have time to break down our improvised camp kitchen and take shelter in the Igloo.

To be safe and dry inside a tent when it's raining is always magical. The power of the elements comes pounding down to within an inch of you, but you're protected by a bubble that really does seem like the work of some passing wizard.

The noise is deafening but all four of us lie there listening to it as if it were a concert of symphonic music. When the downpour ends, we emerge to evaluate the aftermath: the tent remains untouched, thanks to the drainage gutters that I dug with the kids, and even the camp kitchen, covered by a waterproof tarp, has emerged intact.

"That was an adventure!" Eva exclaims.

I turn and smile at her. I ask all three of them to pose in front of the tent, and I set up my Polaroid for a self-timed shot. Then I hurry over to stand beside them and force a smile onto my face.

Click!

Just then, although I didn't know it, we were taking our last group picture.

My favorite attraction at Gardaland is called Space Vertigo. It's a tower that stands 130 feet high, and your car plummets down from the top at supersonic velocity, coming to a halt just before it hits the ground. Each side seats just four people. Us.

We stand in line surrounded by a large group of young Austrians, vacationing on the lake. I get into an argument with the ticket taker because Eva isn't tall enough, and so, for safety considerations, she's not allowed to board the ride. We entrust her to Parsley, the dragon who's the park's mascot—a dragon containing a young man with a strong Calabrian accent.

Lorenzo, Paola, and I wind up sharing a seat with a high school–age girl from Bergamo who's so terrified that her reasons for boarding this ride are hard to imagine. She sobs and protests the whole way up while the three of us laugh euphorically. Up, up, up, up . . . Instead of looking down, I look up. The sky, and heaven, seem to be coming closer. Who knows why the paradise of the afterlife has always been identified with the sky. In fact, in Italian it's the same word: *cielo*. I'd actually prefer to spend my eternity by the beach.

Suddenly the ride plunges downward, my heart pops into my throat, and I feel an electric charge go surging up my spine. A four-second drop that seems to last a month. When we reach the ground we're all laughing like lunatics, caught up in the typical fun-park frenzy. The girl beside us is still crying. We wave to Parsley, who's playing with Eva, and we immediately get back into line for another ride. We have to do it again. As we ride up, this time accompanied by a taciturn young Japanese guy, I cough the whole way. Maybe they should have put a sign at the entrance saying: prohibited to children under forty-eight inches, people with heart problems, and *morituri*. My stomach hurts. I feel a pressure on my chest as if I'd been working out on a weights machine and the bar had dropped and pinned me. A sense of nausea comes over me and my heart beats like an out-of-control metronome. The descent is a pure liberation. I get out, I walk away from Paola and the kids, saying that something I ate must have disagreed with me. I signal to my wife not to worry as I lie down in a little park area, on my back on the grass. And I breathe slowly, trying to slow my heartbeat like you do in yoga.

Only an idiot would take a trip to Gardaland four days before the end. But I love amusement parks. In fact, if I had to choose my own personal idea of paradise, I wouldn't ask for the sky, and actually I wouldn't want the beach either. I'd want Gardaland, I'd want the Land of Toys.

I go back to Paola fifteen minutes later. The three of them are sitting in a restaurant chomping on cheeseburgers and French fries.

"How are you feeling?" my wife asks me, with concern in her voice.

"Better. Practically okay." I smile at the kids.

I always have to remember to smile. I imagine they find it reassuring.

Eva offers me a chewed-over piece of sandwich. I thank her and say no. I'm not hungry. But I'm terribly thirsty and I gulp down a bottle of water. I know it's a bad sign when hunger vanishes from the appointments calendar of your ordinary day.

I get up from the table and I persuade everyone to go on the pirate ship ride. I even start singing the old chantey from *Treasure Island*: "Fifteen men, fifteen men on a dead man's chest!"

We haven't even reached the pirate ship when I realize that I'm having a hard time breathing, that my head is spinning, that I'm about to fall down on the ground. I sit on a bench and tell Paola to go ahead with the kids.

"I've already seen the pirate ship a thousand times . . ."

I sit there, surrounded by a thousand childish voices, the smell of cotton candy, the sounds of happy ditties and distant screams of joyous fear. I half close my eyes. No one is paying the slightest attention to me. An old man, forty years old, sprawled on a bench in the Land of Toys, without so much as a pigeon to keep him company.

We pull into Imbersago, on the banks of the river Adda, while the sun is already straight overhead. We're just four roasted chestnuts steaming in a cast-iron pot that happens to be shaped like a car. Even the air-conditioning is powerless to do much good.

We get out and stroll down the pier.

We pay for our tickets and board the ferryboat that links Imbersago to Villa d'Adda. It's the only working hand-operated ferryboat in the world. There's a steel cable connecting both banks, and the boat is hooked to the cable. It only takes one man to push it from one shore to the other. Brilliant.

In this case, there's no doubt about the name of the inventor: this intriguing means of transportation is called the Traghetto di Leonardo.. Even though it's been modernized many times over the years, it still maintains an old-fashioned appearance that the kids love. I jump at the chance to tell them the story of this particular invention.

"Leonardo was in love with a princess named Isabella. She lived in a castle not far from the building where the young inventor lived. The two young people had met only once, but it had been love at first sight. Isabella's father, however, had already promised her hand in marriage to the son of another king he was friends with. Poor Leonardo had therefore never had a chance to so much as see her again. But he cleverly devised a way of staying in touch with her. He stealthily strung a thin dark cord from the roof of his apartment building to the little window of the princess's bedroom. Because the cord was thin and dark, it was perfectly invisible from below. He used that cord to send the princess love letters and drawings in the still of the night, in hopes of winning her heart. One unlucky day, however, her father the king discovered the cord and went to call on his daughter's courageous wooer. He threatened Leonardo with death, and the young inventor was forced to desist—this love story didn't end happily. But a few years later, he remembered how he had used the cord and applied the same idea to the engineering of a ferryboat."

"But why didn't they build a bridge?" demands the ever-skeptical Eva.

"Maybe it cost too much, or else maybe the two shores weren't solid enough for the foundations of the bridgeheads."

"You mean, you don't know," concludes my little one.

"But you haven't heard the whole story. Many years later, Leonardo, in honor of his beloved Isabella, painted his most famous painting: the *Mona Isa*."

This time, the objection comes from Lorenzo: "It's not called the *Mona Isa*; it's called the *Mona Lisa*."

"But only because of a typo in the first art history book to mention that painting."

They're dubious about that explanation but they pretend to believe me. I hurry along to the next point, to keep from giving them time to reflect.

"Do you know who invented printing?"

"Gutenberg!" cries Lorenzo like a quiz contestant hitting his buzzer.

"That's right, but who was the first person to invent a printing press equipped with an automatic paper feed just like a modern-day printer? Leonardo da Vinci."

"I'm not sure I like this Leonardo very much," Eva decrees. "He invents too many things."

We go for lunch in a little osteria that's actually called Da Leonardo. The menu features seafood and in particular a heavenly but murderous *fritto di paranza*—a fresh-catch fry. I wish this journey could go on forever. It's slowly turned into exactly the kind of real vacation I had hoped for.

It's nightfall. The banks of Lake Garda are lit up by a regular succession of torches. There's a great hustle and bustle in the campground's big meadow, which runs down to the water's edge. Dozens of people, young and old, families with little kids, are all getting settled and taking small white objects out of their backpacks. Every year, at the beginning of July, the festival of the local patron saint is held, culminating in a special ceremony. Our little campground has made sure it takes part.

Eva and Lorenzo are at my side, curiously observing the scene. Paola is slightly up ahead, taking pictures of us. She's rediscovered her old love of photography during this journey.

"What are those?" Eva asks.

"Chinese lanterns. When you light the wick, the lantern flies up into the sky and sails away."

"Like a hot-air balloon!" says Lorenzo, getting the point instantly.

"That's right, it's the same principle—heat rises and the lantern with it."

"I want one," says my firstborn, immediately followed by his little sister.

I open my backpack and pull out four.

"That's why we're here."

I hand them out. Paola comes over and grabs hers. I pull a lighter out of my pocket.

In the meanwhile, the evening's program proceeds, and a speaker invites all those present to get ready for the "launch." A very evocative piece of music starts playing.

Eva has a legitimate question: "But what are they for, Papà?"

"You make a wish, and the lanterns grant it. As soon as the lanterns start their journey into the sky, we all make our deepest wishes . . . you have to ask for what you want most, and then the lanterns will carry your message up to the stars."

I turn to look at Paola.

"Are you ready, *amore mio*?"

I see that Paola's eyes are glistening.

"Ready."

The music swells. The announcer shouts "Go!"

I light the lanterns, one after another.

Lorenzo's takes off . . .

"Remember to make a wish!"

Then Eva's . . .

"But don't tell anyone what it is, or it won't come true!"

Then Paola's . . .

"Good work, Mamma!"

As she releases her wish-laden lantern, Paola stares at me, intently. I don't know if I'll be able to grant your wish, *amore mio*, if it's what I think it is.

Last of all is mine.

My wish is simple. I wish for Eva, Lorenzo, and Paola to be happy. Long, untroubled lives. I have nothing more than that to ask of the stars.

My lantern joins the other three, and together they merge with the hundred tiny flames released by those around us. Our torch-lit parade continues climbing into the sky. A milky way climbing skyward like a swarm of fireflies.

We stand there, heads tilted back, watching as they shrink into the distance. All four of us hug. Maybe Paola and I haven't become a couple again, but at least we're a family. My family.

Lake Garda goes whizzing past to the right of our car. It's almost noon. We overslept. As I drive, I do my best to conceal the stabbing pains to my abdomen and the increasingly insistent hacking cough.

"The air-conditioning must have been bad for me," I explain to the children with a convincing tone.

Paola shoots me a conspiratorial glance, while Eva spouts out a lengthy dissertation on why we shouldn't use air-conditioning, which is bad for the environment.

I smile at my petulant daughter.

"Do you know who invented air-conditioning?" I ask her.

She shakes her head.

"An engineer from New York, a certain Willis Haviland Carrier, in 1902. Unlike so many other unfortunate inventors, however, the clever Willis started a company that's still around today, and he became a millionaire in the process. But who actually came up with the first design for an air conditioner?"

"Leonardo," Lorenzo replies.

That was an easy one.

The inexhaustible Tuscan came up with a machine to compress air and, after chilling, forcing it through a conduit to ventilate the rooms of a building. In other words, modern air-conditioning.

At this point, let me unveil my own personal theory about Leonardo. When you study his work, one thing becomes clear: there was only one thing he really knew how to do better than anyone else:

draw. All the rest is an accumulation of hypotheses, inventions, plans for machines and buildings, only the simplest projects actually built, most of them only sketched and dreamed because they were too challenging to complete with the technology of the time. So who was Leonardo, really? A brilliant inventor or something more?

Here's the answer: Leonardo was a first-class illustrator from the present day who somehow went back in time for some mysterious reason. He knew everything about our era: helicopters, airplanes, mechanical and electronic devices of every sort, but all he knew how to do was sketch them. He couldn't actually make them. Like any of us, for that matter. Who would be capable of building out of whole cloth even such a simple piece of equipment as a bicycle with the resources of the fifteenth century? Not me. Nor would most of you reading, for that matter. But I could definitely draw one, with a certain degree of accuracy. In short, good old Leonardo is the greatest faker of all times. A simple, logical solution to the mystery. And as Lieutenant Columbo tells us, the simplest and most logical solution is always the right one.

I can't seem to focus on the road.

Why didn't we take this journey last year?

Or two years ago?

Every year of our lives as a family?

Why didn't we spend more time together?

Why did I ever miss even a few days of Lorenzo's and Eva's growing up?

These are questions that don't have answers.

"We're almost there . . . ," I tell everyone.

"Where?" asks Paola.

Then she looks around, and her sleep-numbed synapses suddenly recognize the surrounding countryside. She's figured out where I'm taking her. Actually, where I'm taking her back to.

"San Rocco?"

"Flogged and Martyred," I confirm.

The little Gothic church where we were married more than ten years ago. We haven't been back once since then. It's a fundamental stage of our journey.

Paola says nothing. I can't tell if she's happy about this surprise visit.

By the time we get there, it's almost noon. We follow a road curving around a number of hills to reach our destination, and at last San Rocco appears before us in all its minuscule majesty. It looks like a small model of Paris's Notre-Dame. A bonsai version of its better-known French counterpart. But nobody's ever heard of San Rocco. It's just a small church outside of town, surrounded by greenery, the most classic kind of cathedral in the desert.

I park the car in the unpaved area in front of the entrance. All around us an unreal silence reigns, broken only by the sound of a few tireless cicadas. We get out of the car. I remember every detail of that day. Where I stood while I was nervously waiting for Paola to get there, which cars were parked out here, the face, sharp as a pencil tip, of Don Walter, the Calabrian priest who performed our wedding ceremony.

"This church, kids, is where Papà and Mamma got married," I say, but my two young heirs don't seem especially interested in the tour.

"It's small," is Lorenzo's laconic comment.

"It's a copy of that other one in Paris," is Eva's astute observation.

"Would you care to see the inside?" I ask. I don't get much of a response.

"Maybe Don Walter's still here . . . ," I add.

We head for the portal.

We're about to go in when Eva calls her mother.

"Mamma, my shoelace is untied, can you help me?"

Good old Eva, she's following my plan to the letter.

Paola falls behind for a few seconds to tie her daughter's shoelace. I stride on and go in, followed by Lorenzo. I push aside the heavy red curtain and step inside.

The little church is exactly the way I remember it, stark but charming. I have only a few seconds left to take up my position. I hurry while Lorenzo takes a seat on a bench on the left.

A few seconds later Paola and Eva come in. My wife freezes in place at the door, while the church organ plays a thunderous rendition of the wedding march.

The church is packed with people, all our friends. They clap and beam happily at the bride, all of them dressed to the nines. Umberto really has done an outstanding job. I never doubted he would. No one is missing—they're all here: Corrado standing next to Umberto himself, my two best men (and of course, exactly where they were twelve years ago); Paola's colleagues from work, including the teacher who asks too many questions; a few older couples and family friends; the unfailingly boring Gigi; Massimiliano from the Chitchat shop and the no longer depressed Giannandrea; Roberto, my fantastic bookseller; Oscar and Martina; and a number of our neighbors from home. To my surprise, even D'Artagnan is there, smiling at me. The only one absent is my assistant coach, Giacomo, and he hardly needs a doctor's note because this afternoon the Gang That Couldn't Shoot Straight is playing in the semifinals.

Standing by the entrance is Oscar, smiling at his daughter, squeezed into his navy blue three-piece suit, still reeking of mothballs.

Eva was outstanding in the way she intentionally unlaced her shoe following my explanation that we were going to play a funny trick on Mamma. Lorenzo, on the other hand, had been warned in advance, to keep him from exclaiming in astonishment when he walked in and somehow ruining the surprise. Umberto had brought everyone out there with a couple of buses from town. The logistics were seamlessly executed, worthy of a military campaign. Everything went perfectly. I'm at the altar, standing across from the wiry thin Don Walter, who looks exactly the way I remember him.

Everything's ready for my second wedding. The only thing missing is the bride's consent.

Oscar extends his arm, ready to walk her once again to the altar. "Shall we go, sweetheart?"

Paola hesitates, blinded by emotion. She never suspected a thing.

I smile down at Paola from the altar.

"Don't leave me standing here like an idiot," I think to myself. For an instant, I feel a surge of terror that she's about to turn on her heel and leave. But everyone here is rooting for me. My friends all go on clapping and cheering. The organ goes on playing the wedding march at full volume. My heart is racing at two hundred beats a minute. It hardly matters because my heart has plenty of energy stored up—I'll be turning it in still fully charged.

Paola stands motionless.

The seconds tick past endlessly.

I know, I know, I didn't play fair, but I needed the help of all the people I love best to win her back. After all, it was the one truly important thing I absolutely had to achieve in these hundred days.

When Paola extends her arm to her father so he can walk her to the altar, the applause turns into a standing ovation. And my heart is transformed into a Roman candle.

It's called a renewal-of-vows ceremony, and it's the best ceremony that's been invented yet. Marriage is a gift box full of hope, and renewing those vows means that you opened that gift box and you liked what you got.

*   *   *

"Do you, Paola De Nardis, once again take as your lawfully wedded husband this man, Lucio Battistini?"

She smiles at me. She hasn't stopped weeping once throughout the ceremony.

"Yes, of course I do."

"And do you, Lucio Battistini, once again take as your lawfully wedded bride this woman, Paola De Nardis?"

Paola is beautiful. Even in a simple yellow shift with a coral scarf, which, however elegant it looks on her, is no substitute for a white wedding dress, she's still the same excited young girl she was twelve years ago.

"I do."

Don Walter smiles.

"Then I hereby declare you, once again, man and wife!"

A burst of applause starts up unlike anything I've ever heard before. I kiss Paola like I've never kissed her before. A kiss I wish would never end.

We leave the church in a hail of rice, laughter, and applause. We have the kids in our arms. We get caught up tossing handfuls of basmati rice at Aramis, who has already hooked up with Paola's cutest colleague. Everything's perfect. We set Lorenzo and Eva down and start the most demanding part of the day: saying good-bye and kissing everyone.

The longest hug is with Umberto. Everything I have is wrapped up in that hug. What an extraordinary friend.

I slip an envelope into his pocket.

"Read it afterward . . ."

"After what?" he asks, and I have to say, he's never been the sharpest tool in the shed.

"Afterward."

A half smile appears on his face.

"Ah, got it . . ."

When he opens it, there won't be much to read. Just a few words. I hope he understands them.

> *Go right ahead, and don't think twice, old friend. I don't mind a bit.*

I've always known that he's in love with Paola, and that he's bottled it up, out of loyalty and friendship. I know it from the way he looks at her, the way he smiles at her. Feelings don't need words. I just know it, and that's enough. And I also know that he'll stand by her in any kind of trouble, that he'll never abandon her. I hope that he also finds a way of making her fall in love with him, and that he can become a substitute father for my children. If there's a right man, he's the one. After all, it's nothing more than a promotion, from uncle to Papà. I couldn't wish for anything better.

I'm then swept up by Oscar in an affectionate embrace. This time, he's the one with something for me.

"Keep this. It's for tomorrow."

He hands me a paper sack. I don't need to open it to know what's inside. There's a smudge of grease at the bottom.

The afternoon passes by happily. Umberto organized the reception in the agritourism bed-and-breakfast nearby, where there's also a pool. I swim with Lorenzo, who, now that he's comfortable in water, can't seem to stop doing cannonballs. We look like any happy group of friends on vacation.

We dance to old sixties hits on a jerry-rigged dance floor by the pool: Oscar and Martina have gone wild—they look like overweight versions of John Travolta and Uma Thurman in *Pulp Fiction*. When the first slow dance finally starts, I grab my dance partner and squeeze her close. Who knows why slow dances have gone out of fashion? If you haven't ever experienced a slow dance, you don't know what you're missing. I hope my daughter never forgets these four minutes spent in her father's arms, a foot and a half above the floor, under the smiling eyes of her mother, who's dancing with Lorenzo just a short distance away.

At six o'clock, just before the triumphant arrival of the aperitifs, my cell phone rings—it's my assistant coach, Giacomo.

"Lucio . . . we won the semifinals! 9 to 8! Their goalie fumbled at the last minute."

I rejoice like a young boy. Now, this is definitely a perfect day.

An almost perfect day.

Absolute perfection is attained a few hours later. Everyone's left the bed-and-breakfast; Umberto reserved rooms for the rest of the guests at a hotel in town. For us, instead, two magnificent stone-lined suites, with a communicating door and a view of the mountains. A perfect vacation spot.

Once the children are asleep, I watch Paola undressing for bed. It was a wonderful day, full of excitement and feelings, though it was a tiring one. But the adrenaline still works for me. If they were ever to do a drug test on me, I'd be disqualified for life.

I draw her close. I brush her naked shoulder with my fingers. She lets me.

We haven't made love in almost five months.

I'll leave the rest to your imagination. But just to help you fill in the blanks, I'll give you these hints: we did it three times (something that hadn't happened in eight years); we laughed like a couple of idiots; I bruised one of her hips against a bed knob; I banged my knee against a corner of the nightstand; and luckily we didn't wake the children.

We fell asleep, arms wrapped around each other, at four-thirty in the morning.

Now I can say that it's been an absolutely perfect day.

ast night, we forgot to close the shutters securely and the sun strides rudely into our room. I half open my sleep-dusty eyes. Paola's still asleep, and even the children, in the next room with the communicating door, are unusually quiet. I get out of bed with some effort; an intermittent stab of pain is torturing my hip. If I stop breathing, I feel practically okay. Aside from a tingling sensation spreading over my whole body. It's like an annoying internal itch that I can't scratch, as if I'd swallowed a beehive and now the bees were all trying to get out at once.

I drag myself into the bathroom. I put in my contact lenses with some difficulty, and I take a longer shower than usual. Hot, cold, I try all the settings to put a stop to this intolerable prickly itch. But there's nothing the water can do to help. I take three ibuprofen tablets, and they give me a few hours of illusory peace.

When I return to the room in my bathrobe, Paola's already woken up the kids. We go downstairs for breakfast and I play a game with Lorenzo and Eva we decide to call Mister Muffin—we make a fat chocolate plumcake argue with a smaller blueberry muffin, which we've decided is his wife. They can't make up their minds whether to vacation at the beach or in the mountains this year. Before they can agree on where to go for their summer holidays, we merrily scarf them down.

Paola is the only one who can't seem to smile today. I've done pretty well over the past few weeks. All through the journey, I've managed to conceal my pain and anxiety from the kids—I want them to remember a smiling father, funny and in good shape.

After lunch, we get going. I'm driving. I turn on the air-conditioning because the temperature today is close to a hundred. The vents immediately spew out a delightful cool breeze that keeps us alive.

I turn onto the highway. Heading north.

I turn on the car radio, with no idea of who invented it, and slip in my cubs' favorite CD. We sing along at the top of our lungs, off-key, and laughing as we sing.

"There were two chameleons and a parakeet, two little iguanas, and a pink flamingo, the cat, the mouse, and the rhinoceros, were already lined up. The only ones missing were the two green dragons!"

We're almost at the Swiss border when the kids' choir in the backseat drops off to sleep. I take advantage of the opportunity to put on something else.

Elvis.

"Always on My Mind."

Our song.

Paola recognizes it after the first chord.

Elvis's velvety voice cuts in after seven unmistakable seconds.

Paola clutches my hand and squeezes hard, unable to look me in the eye. The car seems to understand the moment—it switches over to cruise control and autopilot and continues along the highway. We look at the landscape sliding past and we listen. When Elvis recorded this song, the singer had just broken up with Priscilla, and his regret is interpreted to perfection.

When the song ends, just like in the movies, the sign appears, as if by magic: SWISS BORDER, 1 KM. We're here.

It's almost lunchtime. We stop to eat something in a little family-run restaurant. I pick at a bowl of pasta with a lackluster appetite. Real hunger vanished long ago. I watch my children, trying to memorize every moment of that lunch. We don't talk much, as if it were an ordinary lunch on any given Saturday.

The final good-bye takes place at a bus stop, where a long-distance coach is waiting that will take me to Lugano. I load my small light suitcase into the luggage receptacle in the belly of the bus, then kiss the kids and hug Paola. An embrace that never seems to end. We told the children that Papà has to travel for work. A very long job. I'm going to work in a gym in Switzerland, a place where everyone needs to lose weight, on account of all the chocolate. Someday I know that Paola will find the courage to tell them the truth. But today is not that day.

The time has come to give Paola a very special gift.

"This is for you."

I hand her a gift-wrapped package. She looks at me.

"It's not her birthday!" Eva objects.

"I know, but for her last birthday I got her present all wrong. So I got her a new one."

Paola tears open the wrapping paper. Inside is an oversized school notebook, the kind you have in junior high school. It looks used. She doesn't understand.

She opens to the first page and her breath catches in her throat.

Inside, I've copied out by hand all of *The Little Prince*, without skipping a single word and doing my best to make my handwriting legible. I worked on it in secret for most of a month.

"This is an edition you don't have. There's only one copy."

Paola bursts into tears and throws her arms around me. This time, I outdid myself.

To tell the truth, it wasn't my idea. Roberto suggested it. He was disappointed when I brought back the original first edition of *Le petit prince*.

This hug with Paola seems to go on forever. When she pulls away, her face is streaked with tears. They're tears of joy. I haven't made her weep with joy in I don't know how long.

It's time to go, but I don't seem capable of boarding the bus. A kiss, another kiss, yet another kiss. It's hard to decide which kiss will be the last. I'm stalling here. I say stupid things, just to make the kids laugh. I'm so good at saying stupid things. I hug Lorenzo, then Eva. But I can't overdo it. They can't guess that this is anything but so long, see you again soon. Arrivederci.

"Do you want us to drive you there?" Paola insists.

"No, really, thanks."

Elephants take their last journey alone. She has many hours of driving ahead of her. I'd give anything to go back with them. But I have nothing to offer in exchange.

I give Paola one last sweet kiss, and a horn blares. The bus driver has run out of patience. I break away and head for the door. Only then do I hear the phrase that I've been hoping for for almost the past hundred days.

"Ciao, *amore mio*."

My heart kindles with flames of joy. I smile at Paola and board the bus.

All I remember of the next minute is a steady stream of tears and a bus slowly pulling out.

My face is glued to the window as I watch the little trio of my heart dwindling into the distance. I send a telepathic "I love you" to Paola. She waves good-bye from far away. She must have received it, loud and clear.

Then she stands there, on the scorching hot asphalt, holding a child's hand in each of hers, until the bus becomes a dot in the blazing sun.

I imagine her regaining her composure, smiling at the kids, and getting back in the car. She's always been a great actress.

Seen from outside, the clinic I've chosen might just as easily be a seaside hotel in Rimini.

I'm greeted by a physician, Dr. Patrick Zurbriggen, with whom I've exchanged a few e-mails. He speaks Italian with a highly comical German accent and has an over-vigorous handshake.

He explains the various phases of what is going to be a very short stay with them. He never mentions the words *assisted suicide*. But that's what we're talking about. It won't be a doctor who takes my life. I'll do that myself. Swiss law allows that, but it requires that the person who wishes to take advantage of the "service" (I love the fact that they refer to it as a service) must be fully informed of the alternatives and capable of making a rational decision.

My new home.

Single room.

I have a reservation for just one night. Like in a motel.

And, in fact, my room looks a lot like the Bates Motel.

A Swiss Bates Motel.

Two hundred square feet. At least it's spacious.

The walls are an anxious celery green.

A wooden dresser.

A metal bed with white sheets.

A framed picture on the wall, with a reproduction of a watercolor of Lake Lugano. Or maybe some other lake.

Gauzy white curtains, fluttering in the breeze, straight out of a horror flick.

A pair of French doors leading out onto the tiny balcony, six feet by three.

All around are the grounds. No horizon line. Just the greenery of nature and blue sky. A natural prison.

Also, a large, immaculate bathroom, the kind you can enter even in a wheelchair.

A clean little motel that costs as much as a five-star hotel. Actually, as much as a week's stay in a five-star hotel.

Anyway, no one's going to complain afterward.

Here, the word *afterward* doesn't exist.

A male nurse sticks his head in the door. He's a dead ringer for Ralph Malph from *Happy Days*, and he asks me in a workable Italian if everything's okay.

I lie and tell him yes.

He informs me that he'll be back around seven for dinner. I ask him what's on the menu. A rhetorical question, really. All I expect is standard hospital fare, a grilled chicken breast, instant mashed potatoes, and a discount-chain fruit salad.

Instead, the answer is surprising: rigatoni with *ragù*, chicken breasts with roast potatoes, and a slice of Sacher torte with whipped cream. Maybe they're planning to kill me with a hyperglycemic collapse.

Ralph Malph leaves after flashing me a big smile.

My executioner is very likable. Well, that's something.

I move my chair out onto the balcony. I sit down. I take a deep breath.

I remove my disposable contact lenses, and the world goes blurry and out of focus. The trees and the sky are no longer distinct.

Those are my last pair of contact lenses. I don't have a pair for tomorrow. That doesn't matter.

I grab the paper sack that Oscar gave me. It's very greasy by now, and the contents are perfectly familiar. A doughnut.

Oscar is special. He isn't a father-in-law.

I look at my sugary new friend.

Sweet smelling. Inviting. Almost sexy.

None of those bad things they say about her are true. Or if they are, I don't care.

The first bite is a pure orgasm.

I chew patiently. Slowly, without haste, savoring every instant.

I sense the sugar granules dissolving on my tongue.

It's almost two days old, but to me it tastes like the nectar of the gods.

Another bite.

I don't think about a thing.

It's just me and my doughnut.

I close my eyes.

I can even hear the sea, like when you put a shell up to your ear.

A rustle of air distracts me.

I turn.

I open my eyes.

On the railing to my right a little bird has just landed.

At least I think it's a little bird. I no longer have my contact lenses.

I bring my face closer to see it better.

It's a sparrow.

It eyes me, inquisitive and impertinent.

I look at it carefully, narrowing my eyes to focus better. Would you believe that . . . no. This isn't my usual breakfast companion. This is another bird, similar but definitely glossier and in better shape. A cocky little native sparrow.

I crumble up a bit of doughnut. I extend my hand, palm up, and the sparrow lands on my thumb. It pecks hungrily away at the fragments of fried dough.

Then it stops, stiff and erect, as if to demand: "Is that all, friend?"

I don't let him chip away at my emotions.

The rest of this doughnut belongs to me, my good Swiss sparrow.

My new fellow diner understands instantly that I'm a tough customer and flies off without so much as a thank-you. I watch as he glides over the trees at the edge of the grounds and vanishes from sight. I wish I could follow him: I'd take to my wings and depart the Lilliputian launch pad on which I'm sitting.

I stand up and look down.

From a second-floor balcony it's not even attempted suicide. It's just pure idiocy.

I stand there, leaning against the railing, and finish my doughnut.

Then I lick the sugar off my lips. And I'm in heaven for one brief, delicious instant.

I return to the room and stretch out on the bed. I pull out of my pocket the last Polaroid I took. The four of us, happy together.

I set it down, pick up my phone, and select "Home."

Could they be back by now?

I don't call them.

I call Umberto.

"Ciao, Lucione!" he answers, with a completely put-on cheeriness. "I just talked to them. They're home and they're fine. How are you?"

The very question I hoped he wouldn't ask.

I tell him to try another question. I'm not going to answer that last one.

"How's the weather in Lugano?" he asks.

That one's no good either. I demand a third question.

At last he comes up with something original.

"I opened the letter. I couldn't resist. Can you forgive me?"

I knew it.

I answer with a cracking voice: "Sí." I can forgive him. Then neither of us says anything for a couple of minutes. It's a deafening silence that contains all the words we've ever failed to say to each other. A silence game for grown-ups. He loses.

"Don't worry about a thing . . . I'll look after them, old friend."

That's something else I knew. All I manage to get out is a murmured "*Grazie*."

Then, before the phone call can get too complicated, I ask him one last thing: "Give my love to Aramis . . ."

And I hang up. I stand there with the cell phone in my hand.

I know that Umberto is doing the same thing.

At seven o'clock that evening, I push away the dinner that had promised to be so delicious: the pasta is overcooked, the chicken is dry, the potatoes are rubbery. But I happily accept a savory injection of painkiller. I ask for a double dose of morphine. I want to sleep through the night, have plenty of dreams, and wake up in top form.

Tomorrow is July 14. An important day.

brought a formal suit with me. Dead people are always well dressed, even if they went through their lives as total slobs wearing ragged T-shirts and beach sandals.

When I pull the suit out of my suitcase, it immediately strikes me as a terrible idea. I can't possibly die in a jacket and tie.

Instead, I put on my water polo team tracksuit. That's more like me.

I put it on and I avoid the mirror. This morning my cough just won't give me peace and my cheeks are hollower than usual. Since I said good-bye to Paola it's as if my body has completely given up fighting; I feel like a marathon runner who collapses three feet past the finish line and falls to his knees. I have a hard time breathing and the pain in my belly is like repeated stabs by a poisoned arrow.

I open the window. Outside, the grounds are silent. There's even a timid shaft of sunlight, come to bid me farewell.

Ralph Malph appears from behind me with the breakfast tray. Two slices of melba toast, a little plastic container of jelly, a cup of coffee, and a plastic cup of discount-chain orange juice. After all, why waste good food on someone who's already slumped in a heap on the ground after the race is over.

"Thanks, I'd prefer not to eat."

"All right. The appointment is for noon," the dutiful male nurse informs me.

"I'll be on time."

"Do you want me to come back to get you, or shall we just arrange to meet on the fourth floor?"

"I'll come on my own, thanks. Can I go for a walk in the grounds?"

"Certainly. If you need anything, just let me know."

He walks out of the room, leaving me alone with my thoughts. By now Paola must be alone in the kitchen, making breakfast for the kids. A very different kind of breakfast.

A strange, desolate feeling overcomes me as I sit there, wondering what to do with myself until it's time to go. It's not unlike the feeling I experienced as a child of four when my mother went off to India with her girlfriend, and I remained with my grandparents. I didn't know my mother well, but I knew I'd been abandoned. Is there any child in the world, however little, who doesn't know that? And then it hits me, like a tidal wave. My children will think, surely, that I abandoned them, that I simply walked away. Aware of how little time is left to me now, I sit there in a cold panic. It's the reverse of what I want. I want them to know how loved they are, how leaving them is the most painful thing I've ever experienced.

Then I decide what to do, to solve the dangling issue which had been nagging at both Paola and me, and which I resolutely decided not to tend to. Namely, the issue of telling the kids. Sitting here in this sterile room, with nothing familiar around me, with only my memories to accompany me, I experience the deepest urge in the world to tell my kids I'm leaving them. I suppose the white pad of paper with its sleek matte-steel pen lying on the dresser is for just this purpose. Unfinished business like mine.

"I remember everything," I write,

> *every single thing, about you both, my kids, as I sit here and wait for death to come for me. The day you were born, Lorenzo, was the happiest day of my life—you were so angelic. If I had known you were going to morph into a mechanical*

dervish, I probably wouldn't have grinned from ear to ear whenever I saw you that first year of your life. (Just kidding! Even when you destroyed my record player, I knew, in your case, it was always in the interests of a higher calling!) You do everything with enviable concentration. The way you play the piano, pounding and stroking, as the piece requires; the way you stare at something, like a cat sharpening its eyes on an unsuspecting mouse, every time something mechanically interesting comes in your path; the way you floated that time I steadied you in the water—the smile that filled your face as you knew you were actually floating on water. You know how easy it is now, son, so keep swimming. You can float. Remember that, always. In and out of water. And here's the biggest treat of all. Remember those clothes of mine you secretly used to try out? Now these are yours. Fill them well, my son. You're the man in the family now. I know you'll know exactly what that means, and also know that our family is very lucky indeed.

As for you, Eva, my darling baby girl. I promise I'll be watching every one of your debates in the future. I've requested front-row seats where I'm going. I know you'll be fighting hard for justice, and unearthing environmental disasters everywhere, not to mention those involving animal rights, and I don't want to miss a thing. You're going to keep me glued up there, I know it. Keep asking those questions, my little one. Maybe where I'm going they'll have some of those answers you want. You lit up my life when you came into it—and you still do, as I sit here, writing to you both on the last day of my life. All your smiles are precious but the one that comes to me now is the one on your face as you handed me a bit of ice cream with a piece of fig in it. It fell to the floor and disappointment filled your face as you chided me for my slowness. Stay close to Mamma—she's always had the answers I didn't. And to

Lorenzo, who'll protect you, and fight anyone who makes life difficult for you.

As for Shepherd, the pasha of our household, who's probably heaving huge sighs of relief now that I'm gone—please don't let him off that lightly. There's a bag of unwashed clothes in my closet. Every time he starts getting cocky, you hold up one of my bits of clothing to his nose. Keep him on his toes, that dog. Or he'll be telling all of you what to do to keep him happy.

The light here is fading. This means it's time to go. But however dark it is, I am lit inside with love—for all of you, the most beautiful family a man could have wished for.

Con amore, your Papà.

I put the letter in an envelope left there, and seal it. I write *Lorenzo and Eva Battistini* on it with a steady hand. I look at it, my little parcel of love, hoping they'll find it in the words.

The grounds are quite nice. Possibly the only halfway decent thing about this Swiss prison camp. My intention to go for a stroll, however, immediately runs headfirst into a wall of aches and pains. I manage to take a short walk; I get to the lawn by the lake, and I lie down on my back on the grass. The sky overhead looks as if it had been drawn with a computer program, the compact light blue of a comic book.

An ant takes a long walk around me.

I feel like Gulliver newly arrived in Lilliput.

I shut my eyes. Here I am. Game over. The end. Time to run final credits.

The sensation is the same as the one we always feel when we're on vacation: the act of unpacking and putting your clothes away in the hotel, and the reverse act of repacking, are always far too close, far closer than we expected at the outset.

I fall asleep. I dream.

I'm in a beachfront restaurant at Ladispoli, with my grandparents. I'm eight years old. My beloved concierges are joking with the waiter, whom they've clearly known for years. I'm eating a plate of fried calamari and I toss a few of the crunchy rings to a passing stray cat. I seem happy. Is this an actual event or an invention? I can no longer tell the difference. I can't remember. I finish my calamari and I order mixed fruit gelato with whipped cream. Grandpa asks the waiter to add some crushed nuts and melted chocolate. I smile at him. Let me correct what I said: I don't seem happy, I am happy.

"Signor Battistini?"

Someone's calling my name. Someone always seems to call my name when I'm dreaming.

"Signor Battistini? Wake up."

I open my eyes and see Ralph Malph's big moon face above me.

It's twenty minutes past noon. I overslept and now I've completely put my foot in it with the Swiss, confirming all their prejudices about us Italians.

I sit up, supporting myself on one arm.

"I'm ready."

I know the procedure very well. I've studied up on it. In practical terms, it's a double injection, and you have to push down both plungers yourself. The first injection consists of a powerful anesthetic. The second is a poison. It's logical, easy, and painless. You fall asleep and you never wake up. But there are countless preparatory steps. I'm hooked up to an electrocardiogram, from the gurney where I'm stretched out. They explain to me that, after the first injection, I only have a minute to push down on the second plunger before the anesthetic will take effect. If I'm going to rethink this, now is the time to do so, Dr. Zurbriggen explains to me. It's happened before. In that case, I'd wake up on the gurney, I'd pay the bill, and I'd go home. Then he tries to defuse the tension with a very Swiss sense of humor that is completely lost on me.

"Any last wishes?"

What kind of a stupid question is that? Should I laugh?

"Yes, I have one," I reply. "I wish I weren't here. Can you do that for me?"

Five minutes later, they slip the two needles into my arms.

I don't give myself time to think, I just press down on the first plunger.

It's like a penalty shot, the important thing is not to let yourself think. If you do, you'll change your mind about the shot to take, and usually you get it wrong.

My decision was the right one. It's inevitable.

The anesthetic slips into my vein and I feel a chilly sensation.

I have one minute.

Ralph Malph smiles at me and points at the second plunger.

"Are you in a hurry?" I ask. "Is this the end of your shift?"

When death approaches I seem to get argumentative. Go figure.

Fifty seconds.

For a moment, I have half an idea not to go through with it.

Just half an idea.

Forty seconds.

"What a pity . . . ," I murmur.

Ralph Malph doesn't understand.

"What did you say?"

"Nothing, just, what a pity . . . in general . . . what a pity . . ."

Thirty seconds.

I've never liked penalty shots. Too much stress. I'm a goalie, deep down. A position for a scaredy cat. If a striker misses a penalty shot, he's a loser. If a goalie lets a penalty shot through, that's just a normal day's work. I'm a natural-born goalie.

Twenty seconds.

At my side, Ralph Malph has vanished. In his place, I now see Grandma smiling down at me. I knew she'd come. She's always come when I'm in trouble. Grandma was always there. She grabs my right hand. She squeezes it.

"It was so nice of you to come . . . ," I whisper to her.

Her eyes are glistening, but she goes on smiling.

Ten seconds.

"I'm coming, Grandma . . ."

She nods her head. She knew that already. Grandmothers know everything.

She let's go of my hand for an instant. The time has come.

I place my thumb on the plunger for the second injection.

I'm no longer afraid.

I press down all the way. And my accommodating, unsuspecting vein allows itself to be invaded by a golden yellow liquid.

At that same instant, Paola, a thousand kilometers away, is cooking lunch and feels a breath of chilly wind on her neck. She looks around. The windows are closed and it's summer. The children are playing in their room, and their voices carry. For a moment, she doesn't know what to think. Then she understands.

She goes out on the terrace and looks up at the sky, unable to keep her eyes from filling with tears.

Don't cry, *amore mio*. Please, don't cry.

I'm sleepy. Very sleepy.

The last thing I hear is my grandma singing me a lullaby. She sings it very softly to keep from waking me up. She goes on singing even after I've fallen asleep. She rocks me gently, with one hand on my belly. She goes on until she's certain that I'm fast asleep. How sad it is that rarely do people die with their grandma at their side. That ought to be obligatory.

"Hushaby oh . . . Go to sleep oh . . ."

Her voice drifts away . . .

"Hushaby oh . . . Go to sleep oh . . ."

I fall asleep.

I've done everything I was supposed to do. Everything I was able to do. I might not have been the best, but I certainly did my best.

I'm perfectly serene.

I know that when I wake back up, I'll be with my grandparents and I'll be a little boy again.

A hundred days have gone by in the blink of an eye.

And now I can say it without a doubt: those were the hundred happiest days of my life.

AFTERWARD

A fterward.

By now, I know everything about afterward that there is to know, and that's the one satisfying thing about dying before your friends. It's sort of like peeking at the answers to the puzzles that they print on the last page of the *Settimana Enigmistica*.

I can't tell you much because the internal regulations here restrict what I can say. When you get here, the guards (that's right, you heard me) ask each new arrival what age he or she would like to be for the rest of eternity. It's quite a question, and usually the line gets longer and longer while people hem and haw or change their minds afterward and lodge complaints.

What was the best year of your life?

The year you'd like to relive forever.

I answer without hesitation.

"I'd like to be eight years old, thank you very much."

Eight years old forever, when my dreams were happy thoughts, colored with Crayola crayons. When you can fly out of your bedroom window, just by turning the pages of a book by Stevenson or Barrie.

When there's no such thing as the past. And the future is light-years away.

Yesterday I saw my grandparents again. They asked to be eight years old too. What a wonderful coincidence. We hugged for a long time and then we played together all day long, which around here is a week or so in your time. Grandpa is great at capture the flag but I'm unbeatable at hide-and-seek. Everything is the way I dreamed it would be: I'm reunited with my grandparents and I'm a little boy again.

My scatterbrained, self-interested parents haven't gotten up here yet. I checked the official database of the afterlife. Look out, they're still down on earth, wrecking things.

In the list of people I want to meet, aside from my close family members, there's also, of course, a certain eclectic Tuscan whose acquaintance I've always wished I could make.

Leonardo da Vinci is thirteen years old, and an obnoxious know-it-all. He's opened a little repair shop, just like Horace Horsecollar, Mickey Mouse's horse friend. I've tried to talk to him to get confirmation of my bizarre theory, but, like all thirteen-year-olds, he has no respect or consideration for an eight-year-old boy. He dismissed me, waving me away like a pesky fly. Luckily, I have all eternity ahead of me to make friends with him.

Today the Gang That Couldn't Shoot Straight is playing the most important match of its short team history: the very last game of the playoffs, which determines access to the provincial series. I'm there in my heart.

In the first quarter we hold out heroically: 2 to 2. Martino gets two points. The Santos are having a run of bad luck: they hit an upright and two crossbars, but that's just how the game goes.

In the second quarter we collapse miserably: now the overall score is 7 to 5. It's a great game to watch, lots of goals, lots of excitement, but by now our team seems tired and listless.

Come on, guys, fight!

The third quarter is when we regain our momentum. We outscore them in that quarter by 2 to 1 and bring the total to 8 to 7. We're trailing by just one goal at this point.

Please, just don't give up now.

The last quarter begins promisingly. A courageous lob by Martino slips sweetly under the opposing crossbar: 8 all!

We actually have a shot at victory.

But of course it's too good to be true. Their star player scores an incredible goal with three minutes remaining. Score: 9–8. We are heartbroken. But, when all seems lost, Martino makes us shine again. Just one minute from the end, Martino intercepts the ball, turns it around, and scores a goal, humiliating the opposing goalie. Fifty seconds from the end of the game, we realize we can still do it—we can still push this into overtime.

Fifty seconds in which we all hold our breath.

This is the final assault. We pass the ball around, hunting for a good shot. Finally Martino takes the responsibility on himself. He shoots a straight shot from fifteen feet out, directly across the surface of the pool. Unstoppable. At least by the goalie, but not by the top bar of the goal. Our fans shout a collective "No!" of disappointment, and the other fans applaud and hug as if they'd just won the World Cup.

The referee whistles "game over."

We fought and we lost. That's all right. I'm proud of the boys. They tried right up to the last second, and they never gave up.

The audience gets to its feet. Everyone heads for the exit, including Paola, arms around the kids' shoulders. Before walking out the door, she stops and turns around.

Only then does she notice an eight-year-old boy watching her, sitting in the farthest row of bleachers.

Our eyes meet for a long moment.

She recognizes me, I know it.

I smile at her.

"Ciao, *amore mio*. And thanks."

She returns the smile, uneasily. Then she shoots me one last glance and hurries to catch up with Umberto, who's calling her name. I see him take her hand and lead her out of the building.

I sit there, watching Paola's shadow as it follows her out the door, just a couple of steps behind her.

When there's no one left in the pool and the lights buzz and go out, one after the other, I strip naked and let myself slip into the water.

I'm still a champion at the butterfly stroke.

And I swim and swim and swim and swim and swim.

Finally light as a bubble.